THE FE  PL

Annie Jones

THE FERNBERRY PLAYERS

Annie Jones

Printed by Kindle Direct Publishing

ISBN:9781710253900

Imprint Independently published

Artwork and design

A.O Designs

Images courtesy of Pixabay

I dedicate this book to all those that are battling with an invisible disability every day.

Not always understood, not always recognised. You are the real heroes in a world of idealistic and unrealistic images. You are the ones shaping the world, the innovators, the brave and the wonderful.

CHAPTER ONE

When I was fourteen, I nearly died. Well - maybe not nearly died, more that I *could* have died. Whichever way you look at it, I was lucky, and I know it.

The fact is though, I hardly remember "the accident" but I do remember the recovery, because my pelvis was shattered and I cannot even begin to describe how very, very painful that was. Also, I experienced the awful trauma of coming to terms with that I would never compete seriously in sports, as that had been my dream. Not the end of the world, but as a teenager it felt about as tragic as can be.

It wasn't until I was older, maybe when I reached twenty, that I dwelled on how lucky I was and how differently things could have turned out and how life has a funny way of throwing you seemingly insignificant situations, chance meetings...whatever... and sets you on a path that could have been the smallest step away from a completely different path.

One of these things that I often wondered about was if I hadn't met my friend Teddy.

It might have *not* happened, because when I decided to move out of my parent's house – well, my mum and my stepdad's house – the original flat I had set my heart on fell through and where I ended up; a tiny flat on the outskirts of town in my hometown of Fernberry, was how I met Teddy.

Saying that, we may have hooked up eventually,

because when he shyly and awkwardly introduced himself, he told me that he recognised me from the bookstore he owns on the other side of town that I was always browsing in, which was rather embarrassing for me as I didn't recognise him at all.

In my defence, the girl with blue hair had always served me in there, I was usually in a rush, and Teddy isn't exactly the kind of guy that stands out or draws attention to himself.

That is not a derogatory statement in the slightest, Teddy is lovely. Average build, average height, light-brown hair and glasses, he's the kind of man that you could easily miss… *but,* when you do take him in, he has the cutest, friendliest smile, the most beautiful blue-green eyes and a sense of humour and quirky character that shines through. He's a good person too… a clichéd expression, but it's true.

Most people that know me, I mean that know me but not intimately, would probably be surprised of my love of books.

Actually, it kind of surprised *me*, because when I was younger I disliked reading. In fact, I disliked most things at school, apart from drama and PE.

When I was eight years old, I was diagnosed with Attention Deficit Hyperactivity Disorder. At eight years old, I guess that didn't mean a whole lot to me and I don't really remember the process of diagnosis. As I got into my teens, I didn't really think about it and I didn't think I felt or acted differently to anyone else, but I suppose I wasn't *that* well behaved. I used to laugh at my school reports that were peppered with comments like, *Roxy is a lovely girl, but lacks self-*

discipline, or *Roxy has the ability to succeed but must learn not to chatter so much.* I wasn't horrible, but I wasn't a star student either and kind of shielded myself with a persona of ditzy blonde.

I *still* get labelled with that... I know I talk way, *way,* too much and often lose the thread of conversation, and it's easier for me to giggle and be self-deprecating than say, *look, I have this thing and I find it hard to concentrate and it's really not my fault...*

I don't feel sorry for myself because of it, not at all. I mean... there's worse things than that - terrible illnesses and things that actually kill you. Like horrible car crashes.

My love of books came when I was in hospital after "the accident", and my nan, God rest her soul, brought me in a copy of *Wuthering Heights.*

Naturally I thanked her politely, but was privately thinking, *what the actual hell?*

Anybody that has been in hospital for more than a couple of days knows how mind-numbingly boring it is. This was before mobile phones done anything more interesting than allow you to call, text or play a couple of games.

I had nobody to chat to in between visits, apart from the cheerful but busy nurses on the children's ward, and all my fellow patients were under ten.

So, one rainy afternoon when I was so bored that I could have cried, I picked up my book and began to read. After the first few pages, I was hooked.

I wasn't the fastest reader and I was naturally easily distracted, so I used to ask the nurses to draw the curtains around my bed.

At first, I was self-conscious of my new love and used to hide my book from my mum and Howard - my stepdad, and any other visitors I had. But when I was finally allowed home, I had to cave in and ask my mum to go and get me some new books.

Not a fan of anything contemporary, I devoured the likes of *Little Women* and *The Handmaid's Tale,* even *Lord of the Flies*.

Like I said, recovery was painful and also dull. The only bit of drama had been when my dad, the driver in "the accident", had turned up at hospital with a giant blue elephant and a bag full of sweets, and shortly after my mum had strode in with my younger brother Jacob and yelled at him to get out.

My books probably saved me from going nuts. Always one to be full of energy and dashing here, there and everywhere, the slow progress and lack of real exercise was awful.

I had run for under fifteens county and I had also attended dance lessons. I had belonged to the local leisure centre and loved to play squash, badminton and I swam at least once a week, although eventually swimming was one of the first activities I was allowed to do, apart from walking.

Secretly, with all the self-confidence of a fourteen-year-old, I had told myself that the medical profession were talking a load of *pants,* and I would be up and running in no time at all. I was proven miserably wrong.

Eight years later, I still cannot run for any length of time. My pelvis is completely healed of course, but I've been left with terrible aches and stabs of pain if my pelvis is under too much pressure or when I'm cold.

I swim, but only when it's not too crowded as I have the ugliest scars on my back from where glass was embedded. It's stupid and vain, I know it is, but they make me so sad.

When I turned eighteen, I joined a local gym, the same gym I attend now, and used every bit of equipment that didn't put pressure on my pelvis and spend hours a week walking on the treadmill. Not running, *walking*, and I still get terrible urges to set it on the fastest it will go and run like the devil is behind me. But I can't.

Still… I *could* have died. I could have ended up in a wheelchair for the rest of my life. A hundred other things could have happened, and things could have turned out a lot worse. But they didn't.

So… my Teddy…

I had moved into my flat one gloriously sunny June, helped by my stepdad, my best friend Dana and her boyfriend Tobias.

I had been a touch disheartened as I had *really* wanted the other flat, and this one was *tiny*. However, it was freshly decorated; the walls painted white and with beige carpeting throughout that still had that weird chemical-like smell that new carpets have. The kitchenette and bathroom were both immaculately clean but despite that, I deemed the kitchen boring, with its uniform white cupboards and light oak worktops, but only because the other flat had had a brand new black and stainless-steel kitchen with a posh oven that probably would have taken me years to work out.

Most likely picking up on my negative vibes, my stepdad soon cheered me up, talking about how we could brighten up my kitchen with some tile stickers and how a few nice rugs and things would make all the difference.

By early evening we were more or less done, and my stepdad had taken the van back to whoever he had borrowed it from, followed by Dana and Tobias in his car, with Dana telling me she would be back in an hour after a shower because we were having a 'sleepover' for my first night.

I couldn't help feeling excited despite myself - my first home. I started haphazardly unpacking boxes, the windows wide open and music blaring.

I had a minute balcony that overlooked the carpark, which had just enough room for a couple of potted plants; I decided to visit the garden centre the following day to buy some herbs. To let the air flow through I had opened the balcony door and propped the front door open with a box full of cleaning things.

I had just been throwing some cushions onto my new two-seater sofa, when I glanced up in the direction of my open door and saw a young guy unlocking the door across the corridor, a rucksack slung over one shoulder.

As if sensing my gaze, he had turned slightly and smiled as if in surprise.

'Hi,' I walked over to the door.

'I take it you're my new neighbour?' he had put a hand up in greeting.

'Yeah,' I nodded. 'Sorry, I'll turn my music down, don't worry, I'm not a noisy neighbour or anything... I'm Roxy by the way.'

'Teddy,' he had awkwardly stuck out a hand and shook mine briefly. 'Actually,' he pushed his glasses up with his thumb, 'I've seen you about...well, in my shop. Fernberry Book Store? You c-come in there.'

'Oh,' I had thought hard for a moment then smiled in what I had hoped was an apologetic smile, 'sorry, I'm not sure I've seen you.'

'No worries,' he started to push his door open with his elbow. 'Well, if you need anything, sugar, Sellotape... more boxes for your collection,' he glanced behind me at my unpacked boxes and I giggled, 'just knock, or yell.'

'Sure thing,' I had said, still giggling. 'Nice to meet you.'

And exactly one week later, it was as if we had known each other forever.

CHAPTER TWO

'So, wanna go on an adventure tonight?'

We were sitting in Teddy's car outside *Fernberry Little Theatre*. I looked over at him then glanced at the clock on the dashboard.

'It's nearly ten o'clock.'

'So?'

'So, it's like, *really* late for an adventure.'

'Who says?'

'Me says.'

'Please?' he gave me a puppy-dog look and I giggled.

'OK, give me details and I'll think about it.'

We had just finished our last performance of 'Midsummer at the Grand Hotel', a parody of A Midsummers Night's Dream.

I had played Mustardseed/waitress four, Teddy had played Puck/security guard.

As usual he had stolen the show with his comic timing and endearing looks.

I had been a member of The Fernberry Players - a small amateur dramatics group, since January, six months previously.

It had taken Teddy a *lot* of persuading to get me to audition as '*a player*', making me regret telling him how much I had loved drama at school.

It wasn't because I was lacking in the confidence to

do it, it was because learning lines was a tough task for me, requiring self-discipline and making time in my busy life to knuckle down.

However, I was so thankful he had managed to talk me around; it was the most fun I had ever had. I'd had to audition in front of the group's committee, doing a small scene they had handed me, telling me that I was to play an angry customer opposite Finn Davidson, the seemingly nice and very handsome 'golden boy' of the group.

In fact, it eventually became clear that Finn was a shallow, vain, self-entitled prat that seemed blissfully unaware that nobody liked him – apart from a select few of the female members that fancied him and couldn't see past his six-pack, which he seemed to display at every opportunity, his floppy blonde hair and slitty bright-blue eyes.

Teddy and I spent a lot of time taking the piss out of him, laughing riotously when we discovered that he had listed his job as 'Actor' on his Facebook account, when he in fact worked in Sainsbury's.

That probably sounds awfully mean and bullying, but honest to God, the man was unbearable.

It had taken a good six weeks of me becoming a member for him to get the hint that I wasn't interested in him; he had been treating me like I was privileged to have attracted his attention… he had then told Destiny, nicknamed The Happy Hippy, that I was a terrible snob and frigid.

I had been given my first small part in a week-long production in February, playing a nurse, named 'Nurse Hurry' and then we had gone into rehearsals in March for 'Midsummer at the Grand Hotel', our opening night was at the beginning of June.

The group also ran fortnightly workshops for ten to fifteen-year olds on Saturdays, none of which I had yet to be involved in as my job at the local sports store required me to work most Saturdays. Our writer and director Duncan, who was a fatherly figure but a subject of derision (mainly because of his constant dyeing of his thinning hair- that particular week it had been a startling ginger), had said that I could just 'rock up' if I had a free Saturday.

My free Saturdays were like gold-dust, and I much preferred to spend them having an extra hour in bed and having a girl's day with Dana or visiting my older sister Shauna and her baby girl Emilie.

Not that I didn't take the group seriously, because I truly did and I was already excited about the yearly Halloween week production, that year entitled *The Murder of Miss Mabel,* and was eagerly waiting for the script to see what part I wanted to audition for.

'So, how long have you known him?' I asked Teddy as we drove to the neighbouring town of Chembury.

Our "adventure" turned out to be an old friend's birthday party at some art gallery, which I thought was strange.

'Ten years or so. He moved up this way while we were in six-form.'

'I see,' I was trying to repair my face in my compact mirror in the dim light without much success. 'What's he like?'

'Jaco?' he sounded thoughtful. 'A bit of a sod at

school… and after school really. We lost touch a bit. I bumped into him a couple of weeks ago. I haven't seen him in two years.'

'Right,' I gave up trying to apply my eyeliner and dabbed on some lip gloss. 'Why is it at an art gallery?'

'Oh, didn't I say?' he turned into the main part of town. 'He owns it.'

'Oh, wow,' I looked down at my denim mini-skirt and T-shirt. 'It won't be posh will it?'

'I doubt it,' he glanced at me. 'Don't worry, you look fine.'

I fluffed up my hair, thinking that at least if I were underdressed, I had Teddy looking equally if not more underdressed in navy-blue shorts that had seen better days and a crumpled checked shirt with the sleeves rolled up.

It was a beautiful and balmy night, the lit-up restaurants and shops looking seductive in the dusky evening light. I stared out the window at some people sat outside a bar, thinking I would *much* rather be sat there with Teddy drinking a cold beer, than going to some party where I didn't know a soul.

'How come you haven't seen him for two years?' I turned back to him.

'Cor, you don't half ask a lot of questions,' he smiled to himself. 'Just haven't. We, um, move in different circles, I guess.'

'Right,' I murmured.

Teddy turned into a road off of the High Street and slowed down, leaning towards me to look out of the passenger window.

'Here we are.'

15

I looked up at a building with a white sign proclaiming *Muza* in bold black letters, with *Modern Art Gallery* underneath.

There was a busy looking Greek restaurant on one side, however the gallery looked in darkness, apart from a lit-up easel in the window with an abstract painting residing on it, painted in wild blue and yellow swirls and an angular-looking figure that could have been male or female.

'You sure you've got the right night?' I asked.

'Yeah,' Teddy muttered unsurely. 'Come on.'

We got out of his car and both stood on the pavement looking up; there were some lights on in the upstairs windows.

Teddy tried the glass doors with no avail, then as we both turned towards the sound of female laughter that came from the direction of the wide, covered alleyway on the right, we looked at each other then walked towards it.

I thought that Teddy seemed unusually quiet and kind of edgy and that was making *me* edgy.

As we turned the corner, I could hear the buzz of conversation and then spotted some black iron steps leading up to whatever was above the gallery. Teddy grabbed my hand and led me up and I soon saw there was a rather bleak concrete square where three women were smoking, all clutching wine glasses, one of them perched on an empty wooden planter.

'Hi,' Teddy said amiably. 'Jac's party?'

'Yes, darlin',' one of the women answered - I was relieved to see that her and her companions were casually dressed at least. They watched us as we went towards the peeling wooden door that was slightly ajar. I couldn't hear any music, but the voices were loud, and I could hear laughter.

Teddy let go of my hand and pushed the door open, and we stepped into a stark white painted hallway with a chipped tiled floor and a huge rubber plant in one corner with a solitary beer bottle sitting next to it. A door was wide open in front of us, the room beyond full of people.

We passed a smoky kitchen and Teddy stuck his head in, 'Jac about?'

'Teddy Boy!' a dark-haired man bowled towards us, a huge grin on his face, showing unnaturally white teeth.

'Jay,' Teddy clapped him on the shoulder, breaking into a big smile. 'How the hell are you?'

'Divorced and drunk,' he shook his head wryly, then turned his grin on me. 'Hello, how ya doin'?'

'Good, thanks,' I smiled uncertainly, feeling mightily out of my comfort zone. I looked around the kitchen; it was rammed with people, mostly men I noticed. The sides were covered in bottles and plates, the sink had several bottles of champagne sitting in it. I wrinkled my nose at the smoke and edged away from the doorway.

'-and this is my friend Roxy,' Teddy was saying. 'Rox, this is an old school friend, Jay.'

I turned my attention back to them and smiled brightly.

'Well, very nice to meet you,' Jay drunkenly beamed. 'Let's go and find the birthday boy.'

As we followed him down the hall, I noticed that

Teddy seemed to have relaxed a little. We entered a large dark-red painted living room and Jay bellowed, 'Jaco!'

I looked around curiously, straight away spotting a glamorously handsome man dressed in black with dark, glossy hair falling over his forehead turn our way, a champagne glass in one sun-tanned hand.

He had been standing by the window deep in conversation with another man and a tall, thin girl, who despite the heat of the night was dressed in a hooded sweater and black leather trousers. He immediately put his glass down on the window ledge and walked over, his eyes switching between me and Teddy.

'You came,' he shook Teddy's hand, and smiled widely at me.

Close up, his eyes were a clear Prussian-blue, almost too blue to be true, his lashes dark and thick, his jawline strong and square like a super-hero. I experienced a girly flutter of admiration and wasn't sure if I was managing to smile or not.

'Sure have,' Teddy said easily. 'Happy birthday, mate.'

'Thanks,' Jaco glanced down. 'No drinks?' he turned towards where he had been standing. 'Evie, get these two a drink, sweetheart.'

The girl he had been talking to looked up and slowly walked over, slightly glassy-eyed.

'Guys,' Jaco said companionably, 'this is Evie Blackhouse, my star artist. Evie, this is my old friend Teddy and friend?' he raised an eyebrow at me, 'Roxy... Roxy is it?'

'Yes,' I attempted a smile at her, but she had an

oddly unreceptive expression on her thin face. 'Hi.'

'Hello,' she eyed us; I was surprised that her voice was gentle and had an upper-class twang.

'Go and take Teddy to find some champagne,' Jaco patted her behind, making me wonder with an unreasonable disappointment if they were a couple. 'Thanks, sweetheart,' he added without waiting for an answer.

Teddy frowned slightly and followed her, giving me a small smile as he looked back at me.

'So, Roxy,' Jaco said warmly, 'Teddy told me all about you, I hear you're a wonderful actress.'

'Oh,' I said, feeling startled. 'Well, I don't know –' I trailed off.

'Modest,' he had such an intense gaze that I suddenly felt like we were the only people in the room. 'I'm sure you are if Teddy says so. And you live in the same building?'

'Yeah,' I hated how breathless I sounded. 'I moved in a year ago.'

'He's a nice guy, Teddy.'

'Yeah, he is.'

'He speaks very highly of you,' his eyes slowly moved over my face.

'Really?' I tried not to over-blink, but my eyes were watering. 'Have you lived here long?' I asked, not knowing what else to say.

'Oh, I don't live here,' he continued to study me. 'I live near the Farm Estate. I just hang out here.'

'Oh right,' I swallowed. 'Do you... live alone?'

'Yes,' he put his head on one side and gave a ghost of a smirk, and I felt my face grow warm. 'I live all

19

alone.'

'Right,' I nodded, then thankfully spotted Teddy returning with two glasses, Evie in tow.

'Thanks,' I murmured as Teddy handed me a glass of champagne.

As Teddy and Jaco started to talk, I had a look around the room. There were maybe about thirty people in there, most of them probably in their twenties, except a large guy with a white beard sitting on a sofa, wearing a waistcoat and surrounded by giggling girls, one of them in a short skirt with her leg hooked over his.

I then discreetly studied Evie, who was staring intently at Jaco, glancing at Teddy every now and then.

She really was very thin, her hip bones visible beneath her skin-tight trousers. She had jet-black wavy hair, clipped back off her face, showing a pale forehead and angry thick eyebrows. Her eyes, as glassy and bloodshot as they were, were a strangely mystical amber, reminding me of a bird of prey, coupled with a small but slightly hooked nose.

Her eyes flickered towards mine and I gave her tentative smile. Her mouth twitched, then she focussed back on the men.

I shifted a little closer to Teddy and watched Jaco as he chatted away. His eyes were seriously the sexiest I had ever seen, almost too beautiful to belong to a man. When he wasn't speaking, his curved mouth looked like he was trying not to smile, like he had an amusing secret that nobody else knew. My eyes wandered over his body; he was very slim but muscular, not particularly tall but in perfect proportion.

20

Trying to bring my concentration back to their conversation, I saw that Evie had been observing me giving Jaco the once-over and I felt my face grow hot again. Taking a big sip of my drink, I began to cough, and Teddy put a solicitous hand on my back and asked if I was OK.

Suddenly a man came over, clutching a bottle of red wine and Jaco broke into a beam.

'Hey geezer,' the man, who seemed too drunk to be upright, boomed. 'Sorry I'm late, happy birthday.'

'Cheers,' Jaco turned towards him and gave him a one-armed hug. 'Never too late to see your ugly mug.'

'Fuck you,' he laughed and pretended to aim a punch at him. 'Alright Eve?' he kissed Evie on the cheek, then gave Teddy and I a bleary-eyed look. 'Hello.'

'Hi,' I inched away from him, he absolutely stank of booze and unwashed armpits. Teddy put a hand up in greeting then slung his arm around me.

'Hey,' Jaco directed at us. 'If there's any left from these animals, there's food over there,' he pointed towards the back of the room. 'Catch up later, yeah?' he gave me a small wink and then pulled the drunk guy away by the elbow.

'Shall we?' Teddy asked.

'I'm starving,' I admitted; I hadn't eaten since three o'clock, before I had left for the theatre and it was nearly midnight.

We navigated ourselves through the crowd, reaching a square, covered dining table that thankfully still had some food on it.

Not trusting anything that looked like meat as I didn't know how long it had been sitting out, I grabbed

21

a plate and piled on some tortilla chips and breadsticks. Teddy, obviously not having my reservations, grabbed some smoked salmon slices and covered them in lemon juice.

'You alright?' he asked, grabbing a sausage roll and shoving the whole thing in his mouth.

'Yeah,' I picked out some celery sticks from a salad bowl and looked around. 'Kinda mad here.'

'Wanna go soon?' he asked.

'Yeah,' I secretly wanted to speak to Jaco some more, but I suddenly felt exhausted and the thought of a steamy shower and snuggling down in my bed was appealing to me.

'OK honey, let's eat and go soon.'

We turned our backs to the table and watched the party revellers. I noticed that the guy on the sofa now had his hand up one of the girl's skirt.

I tried to spot Jaco, but he had disappeared. I did however see Evie sat on the window ledge talking to a good-looking black man with muscular arms bulging out of his T-shirt, his hand on her thigh.

'This is a weird party,' I muttered to myself.

'What do think of Jaco then?' Teddy asked lightly.

'He's kind of... glamourous,' I shrugged, not wanting to admit that I fancied him madly.

'Yeah,' Teddy said quietly.

'That Evie seems a bit... odd.'

'Huh,' Teddy glanced over to her. 'That might be her friend Charlie.'

'Eh?'

'She's coked up to her eyeballs, sweetie.'

'How can you tell?' I looked over towards her.

22

'Just can.'

'I need a pee,' I set my glass down on the table and looked around.

'I think the bathroom's opposite the kitchen,' Teddy pointed towards the living room door.

I weaved my way across the room, reaching the hallway and spotting two doors that I hadn't noticed when we had arrived.

I knocked cautiously on the first door, and not hearing a response, opened it. I was greeted by the sight of a man sitting on an unmade bed, trousers around his ankles, clearly getting a blowjob from a voluptuous woman kneeling on the floor in her underwear.

'Oh, I am *so* sorry,' I squawked, hastily backing out, my heart pounding.

'Hey,' a soft voice said behind me and I swung around.

'Hey,' I gazed up at Jaco, who was grinning broadly.

'Is *this* the bathroom?' I pointed at the second door.

'Uh oh,' he threw his head back and laughed, before opening the door and looking in. 'Alright Sam? There is a lock, you know.'

'Jesus Christ,' I mumbled, then began to giggle.

'Well,' Jaco said, laughter in his eyes, 'I apologise for my guests. I guess you didn't want to witness that.'

'Not ever so,' I shook my head and he grinned widely, putting a warm hand on my upper arm.

'Well, I'll let you -' he gestured at the bathroom door.

I slid in, still giggling, and when I came out, Jaco was standing there.

'I was wondering,' he paused for a second, 'if I could have your number?'

'Oh,' I said in surprise. 'Um, sure.'

'Christ, you're so pretty,' he said, his expression suddenly serious.

'Oh,' I said again, my pulse quickening as I tried to maintain eye contact. 'Thank you.'

'I was just wondering,' he said, 'if you would be my guest at a very *boring* artists exhibition next week, then I would love to take you out for dinner.'

'OK,' I nodded as he handed me his mobile phone to put my number into. 'That sounds… nice,' I inwardly cringed at my lack of sophisticated responses.

'Unless,' he dipped his head for a second before giving me his killer grin, 'I'm not treading on anyone's toes, am I?'

'What?' I held out his phone, puzzled for a moment. 'Teddy? Oh, no. We're just mates, you know… nothing like that.'

'Yeah, he said,' he studied me silently for a second. 'Just making sure.'

'Definitely not,' I assured him.

'Good,' he took his phone and looked relieved.

Back at my flat, showered and snuggled down in my bed, I couldn't help feeling excited about seeing Jaco again - although I did have *tiny* reservations.

He wasn't like anyone I knew, he seemed so… I cast around for the right word… sophisticated… but like he had a wild side… although that could have been Teddy's earlier description of him of being 'a bit of a sod'.

Teddy didn't give me any dire warnings when I told him that Jaco had asked me out, and I knew that Teddy would have if there was anything to worry about.

I also mulled over how tongue-tied he had made me, when I usually had *no* trouble speaking to men; I was a bit of a self-confessed flirt.

I peered at the time on my phone and saw that I had exactly five hours before I had to go to work. I wasn't very good at switching my brain off, even when I was tired.

Dragging my thoughts away from Jaco, I went over the evenings performance and finally drifted off around three o'clock, my last conscious thought being that I had forgotten to pick up milk and wouldn't be able to have my morning cuppa until I got into work.

CHAPTER THREE

I sat in the Starbucks next to my gym with Dana, moodily stirring my coffee. It was Wednesday and Jaco still hadn't called.

'Why don't you just call him?' Dana suggested.

'I haven't got his number.'

'Ask Teddy for it?'

'No, that makes me desperate.'

'And you're definitely not desperate,' she giggled.

'I am *not* desperate,' I glared at her from across the table. 'I just want him to call.'

At work the previous Sunday, the day after Jaco's party, I had been in tremendously high spirits, dreamily thinking about my date with him. I had felt fluttery and excited, like I used to in my teens when I had been madly in love in the way teenagers are.

By closing time, although still in high spirits, I felt a little anxious. I had been so sure he'd have called me by then, he definitely fancied me, I could tell... it kept playing on my mind whether I had put my number into his phone wrong.

By Monday afternoon I began experiencing awful sledgehammer blows of disappointment and told myself that if I could resist checking my phone for a whole hour, he would have called.

I had Tuesday afternoon off and was sorely tempted to drive into Chembury and do some window shopping, then decided that was silly. My chances of bumping into him were next to nothing, unless I was to go past his gallery, then even that was doubtful… and desperate.

Instead I went and got my nails done and bought myself a new dress and some high-heeled shoes that I had been eyeing up for a while, thinking that the power of positive thinking and buying a date outfit would be a sure way to make him call.

In the evening I went and hung out at Teddy's flat. I preferred his flat to mine, his balcony overlooked the road, but there was a small park on the other side lined with blossom trees – it was a much nicer view than the carpark.

His flat was also slightly larger than mine and he had room for extra seating. He had picked up a rattan two-seater sofa from a second-hand shop and we had spent a fun afternoon spray painting it navy-blue in my stepdad's garage, then going to The Range and buying some nice large cushions.

It now resided opposite his balcony and it was christened 'Teddy and Roxy's drinking seat'.

He had asked if I'd heard from Jaco, and I had answered with a breezy, 'Oh, not yet,' and that had been that.

By Wednesday I decided that he wasn't going to call and if he did, he couldn't really fancy me that much, else he would have rung sooner, and maybe it was just as well; boyfriends were too time-consuming anyway.

I did however need a moan at someone, so I had called Dana and asked her to meet me after my gym session.

'What's the big deal anyway?' Dana asked curiously. 'Doesn't sound like you even spoke much.'

'We didn't,' I fiddled with my ponytail. 'He's just… different. *Really* sexy, dead handsome… I dunno,' I stared unseeingly above her head. 'He's just got something about him.'

'The unobtainable?' she asked shrewdly.

'No,' I shook my head slowly. '*He* approached *me*, it ain't that.'

'Doesn't sound like your normal muscles-rather-than-brains type.'

'If you're making a dig at Peter, he was a perfectly nice bloke,' I tutted.

Peter had been my last boyfriend and maybe not the brightest, but a lot of fun.

'Touchy today, ain't ya,' she teased. 'I'm getting another coffee and some brownies,' she stood up and went to the counter, leaving me to brood some more.

Dana is lovely. I know all girls think their best friend is lovely, but she really is. Half-Caribbean on her fathers' side, she's tall and willowy with the longest legs, she has the most exotic dark, merry eyes and perfect smooth skin. She also has the funkiest afro hair; today it was pulled back in a wild ponytail and tied with a bright-red scarf.

She is the kindest and gentlest soul, beneath her sometimes brash and loud personality, like, she won't take any shit from *anyone*, but she would also be the first to help out someone who needed it.

We have been friends since secondary school and she probably knows me better than anyone – hence the teasing. She knew I knew it was *only* teasing and she'd never, ever mean me any harm.

'Here, eat this,' she put a plate in front of me with a large, moist-looking brownie on it.

'Good job I did a million squats today,' I picked it up and took a big bite.

'Good girl,' she looked pleased. 'Chocolate makes it all better.'

'I wish,' I muttered.

'So,' she put her elbows on the table. 'You sure Teddy is cool with all this?'

'Yes,' I said impatiently.

Dana had a crazy theory that Teddy was harbouring some secret desire towards me and madly in love, just hiding it very well. This was an extreme irritation to me. I mean, I would *definitely* know, being as I spent more time with him than anyone else.

When I had first told Dana about Jaco asking me out, she had raised her eyebrows and chewed her lip, like she wanted to say something, and reading her mind I had grumpily told her Teddy was OK with it, as in he hadn't broken down and sobbed and told me not to go out with him.

'You would make such a cute couple,' she sighed. 'I love Teddy.'

'Then why don't you dump Tobias and *you* go out with him?' I finished my brownie and wiped my fingers on a napkin.

'Jesus Jim,' she laughed. 'If Jaco not ringing is making you this grouchy, I'm gonna drive over there myself and hit him over the head until he does.'

I drove home in the fading sunshine, thinking I felt *slightly* better after talking to Dana, but I was still disappointed.

I trudged up the steps to the first floor, wincing as the beginnings of an ache in my pelvis and lower-back began.

Swallowing three paracetamols, I ran a hot bath and laid in it for ages, wondering what to have for tea and deciding I would find something on Netflix and spend the evening laying on the sofa, doing nothing.

Wrapped in my towel, I went and threw open the balcony door. Spotting Teddy getting out of his dusty black Hyundai, I whistled and waved, and he waved back grinning.

I pulled on some shorts and a T-shirt, made a ham sandwich and sat down with a groan. Just as I was finding a movie to watch, my mobile phone rang, showing the number but not a name.

'Hello?' I said, as cheerily and casually as I possibly could.

'Hello,' I instantly recognised Jaco's voice and almost whooped. 'Roxy? It's Jaco.'

'Hi, how are you?' I had to fight to keep my voice even, my heart was in my throat and I had to get up to pace around.

'Ah, I'm really well sweetheart, thanks for asking. How are you? Still want to let me take you out on Saturday?'

'Yeah,' I said, feeling a smile plastered on my face. 'I would like that… and I'm good, thank you,' I added.

'I'm very glad to hear that,' he had such a nice voice, kind of gentle.

'Shall I meet you?' I asked.

'No, I tell you what,' he said slowly. 'I can't pick you up because I'll be stuck at the gallery… sorry sweetheart… but I'll send someone to pick you up and drive you over, then I'll take you out to dinner. You like French?'

'Yes,' I said, not really knowing if I did or not.

'Perfect,' he said. 'Give me your address and be ready for eight? Later if you want?'

'No, eight is fine.'

'Perfect,' he said again.

I gave him my address and we said goodbye, then I squealed loudly.

'Sweetheart,' I murmured to myself, '*ah, I'm really well, sweetheart…*' then I threw myself back on the sofa, forgetting about my aches and pains and rang Dana for a gossip.

The next couple of days dragged by, work seemed endless.

I did love my job at *Sports House Inc* though, it was fun. My manager Troy, a good-looking guy in his mid-thirties, was a *little* sweet on me… without sounding boastful… which made time off and shift swaps and the such easy. I was the only female member of staff there, which initially I thought would be a drag, but they were all great guys and we spent a lot of time messing around.

It's situated on the edge of town in a small retail park, where there is my gym, Starbucks, Pizza Hut, an M&S and a Wickes. The walk into town is only five minutes or so, and Teddy's bookstore is at the beginning of the high street, so often he would pop over at lunchtime or towards the end of my shift.

On the Friday, I had walked to work in the morning, so he came in to drive me home. Both hungry, we decided to go into Pizza Hut for dinner and a beer.

'So, big date tomorrow then?' he said as we sat down.

'I'm kind of nervous,' I admitted.

'Why?' he looked genuinely puzzled.

'He's… not my usual type,' I shrugged.

'So?'

'Oh… I don't know!' I watched him as he looked absently at his menu. 'Just first date nerves.'

'Sure,' he nodded. 'Not that I can remember that feeling…'

'Still dangling poor Crystal?'

We both laughed at that – Crystal was one of the members of The Fernberry Players and she had a thumping great crush on Teddy. She was very attractive, and she was a nice lady. Unfortunately, she was also well into her fifties and Teddy was terrified of her. She had enormous breasts that seemed to heave with a life of their own, and she always managed to press them against him.

'She'll suck me in one day,' he started sliding down the seat. 'Help,' he waved his arms furiously, 'the cleavage has got me… can't… breath…'

I shrieked with laughter as he disappeared, then popped up abruptly as a waitress appeared looking bemused.

'Hi, how ya doing?' he grinned up at her. 'Large stuffed-crust Buffalo Chicken please.'

When we reached home, he invited me to his for a cup of tea before he went off to the pub with some mates.

'Two minutes,' he said as he headed for his bathroom.

As I heard the hiss of his shower, I started to make two mugs of tea, then washed-up the seven plates and three mugs in the sink.

'Ah, you're a doll,' he said as he whipped past in a towel to his bedroom.

He reappeared a few minutes later dressed in faded ripped jeans and a blue T-shirt, his fair hair damp and on end.

'Did you only invite me in to make the tea?' I asked and he laughed.

'You make it nicer than me,' he jumped up onto the worktop and watched me dry up the last plate. 'You sure you don't want to come out tonight?' He'd already asked me at Pizza Hut.

'Nah,' I picked up my tea and rested against the opposite worktop. 'I really need to try and get a proper sleep.'

'Rough few nights?'

'Yeah.'

One of the annoying things with my condition is that I don't sleep well. On one hand, I don't need a lot of sleep, but then it eventually catches up on me and I kind of crash - my concentration gets worse with terrible brain fog, and I start to feel run down. Since the weekend before, I had maybe had twenty hours sleep.

'Aw honey,' he looked serious all of a sudden. 'Have

a nice bath and try and relax.'

'I will,' I said brightly, trying not to show how much his concern touched me.

'I've got a stack of paperwork I'm behind on if you want something to bore you to sleep,' he grinned crookedly.

'Nah, you're good,' I wrinkled my nose and his grin widened.

'I don't know how you survive on no sleep,' he sipped some tea. 'I'm tired before I'm tired.'

'That doesn't even make sense.'

'Nor do you.'

'What?'

'Yup.'

'Oh shush,' I laughed and gave his leg a little shove.

He took his glasses off and rubbed the lenses on his T-shirt and then gave me his sweet smile, 'So where is Jaco taking you tomorrow?'

'A French restaurant,' I played with my mug handle, feeling nervous just talking about it. 'But there's something at his gallery first, some exhibition, or something.'

'Cool.'

'Teddy?' I said hesitantly. 'Can I ask you something?'

'Sure.'

'You know you said that he was a bit of a sod... should I be worried? I mean... would you tell me if I had anything to be worried about?'

'Rox, that was like, ten years ago.'

'Yeah, I know,' I suddenly felt stupid and dropped my head.

'I haven't been in touch with him for two years, and a few years before that it was sketchy. Babe, we all grow up.'

'Yeah, but what was he like?'

'Just… a bit wild, I guess,' he frowned. 'The girls liked him, he liked a spliff and a drink, he played around… but that was a long time ago.'

'Right.'

'None of us has a whiter than white past.'

'I know.'

'Hey,' he said forcibly, and I looked back up. 'Don't overthink it, yeah? Go on your date, have fun, and if it works out…well, yay you.'

'Sorry,' I drew out a long breath. 'I have no idea why I'm so uptight.'

'You'll be fine,' he assured me.

I drank some tea and watched him absently twirling a pen around in his fingers – a nervous habit of his.

'I'm gonna push off,' I said eventually. 'Have fun tonight.'

'Thank you,' he slid off the side and followed me to the door. 'Bring my mug back.'

'Maybe,' I giggled – I had a bad habit of collecting his mugs and forgetting to bring them back.

I finished my tea and rinsed Teddy's mug out and dried it, then put it with the two others of his I had in my cupboard. Teddy was right, I decided. I was overthinking the whole thing. Jaco was just a guy…nothing to be scared of…

CHAPTER FOUR

By half-past seven on Saturday evening I was dressed and ready and nervous as hell.

I was wearing my new dress, a cute navy and white ditzy-print wrap-around dress that fell just above my knees, and initially I felt pleased with my appearance.

But after a glass of wine and a fiddle in my full-length mirror, I began to worry whether it wasn't dressy enough. Or too dressy.

Then I decided that maybe I should wear my hair up, then half-way through pinning it up, I changed my mind and brushed it out again. Cross that I had undone all my careful blow-drying and straightening, I plugged my hair-straighteners back in and re-did it, getting further flustered as I began to grow hot and noticed beads of sweat on my upper lip and I had to repair my make-up.

As I went back to my full-length mirror, I pondered again on the affect that Jaco was having on me. I *never* got so jittery before a date, I'd always found men such *easy* creatures... always felt in control, like I had the tiger by the tail.

It was five minutes after eight when there was a loud knock at my door.

I had a final spritz of my Jean Paul Gaultier and grabbed my small leather clutch bag before answering the door.

'Roxy?' a swarthy young guy in black trousers and a

white shirt stood there, smiling politely and stepping back a pace.

'Hi,' I stepped out into the corridor, feeling even more uptight.

'Alright?' he let me proceed him. 'I'm Billy, chauffeur for the evening.'

'Hi,' I said again, glancing back at him. 'You a friend of Jaco's or-'

'Well, I work for him, but yeah I'm a mate.'

He followed me down the stairs to the front doors and around to the carpark. Straight away I saw a sleek red Porsche and automatically looked around at Billy.

'Your carriage,' he chuckled.

'Oh, wow,' I gasped, feeling impressed.

He opened the door for me, and I slid in, wriggling down into the seat and gazing around the interior.

'This is a *cool* car,' I rearranged the front of my dress and watched him as he backed out of his space and swung the car around.

'Sure is,' he agreed. 'Not mine, sadly.'

'Oh,' I looked back at the flats as he put his foot down. 'Um, Jaco's?'

'Yep,' he shot me a sidelong look.

We seemed to reach the gallery in no time at all, and after relaxing a tad with our small talk, my nerves returned.

He parked around the back near the steps up to the flat above, and I followed him to the front of the gallery.

The painting in the window had been replaced with a startling one of a naked woman with big black birds with red beaks in place of her breasts. I also noticed as we went past that there was a smaller poster of Evie, looking ethereal in a white dress, her pale face angry and fierce.

'I'll tell Jaco you're here,' Billy said as we entered.

There was a smiling girl at a big, white desk with a phone on it and a pile of catalogues.

I returned her smile uncertainly and wandered over to the wall opposite where there was a display of prints, all in black and white.

I looked over to where Billy had gone through an arch; I could see a few people milling about and there was a low hubbub of voices.

As I turned to look at the prints again, I heard a familiar voice, 'Hey,' and I saw Jaco coming over, looking handsome in charcoal-grey trousers and a pale-blue shirt.

'Hello,' I felt my pulse quicken.

'You look amazing,' he reached me and shook his head. 'Beautiful... I forgot how bloody pretty you are.'

'Oh,' I dropped my eyes. 'Thank you.'

'No, thank *you*,' his curved mouth lifted, and I felt my stomach disappear.

'Am I dressed OK?' I looked around again. 'I wasn't sure -'

'You're dressed perfect,' he held out his hand. 'Come on, let me do my stuff then we can escape.'

I took his hand and followed him, looking around. The floor was dazzling white, almost painful to the eyes and my high heels were loud on it.

The walls were brick, painted a subtle dove-grey, small hooded lights above the paintings.

As we went through the arch, I noticed that the walls

were a slightly darker grey and the lights were a little brighter.

Maybe twenty people were standing around, some holding catalogues, talking in low voices – straight away I spotted Evie though, dressed in a see-through cream blouse and possibly the same leather trousers that she had been wearing at Jaco's party. Her hair was scraped up in a bun, making her face look gaunt, her cheeks hollowed out with a dusky blusher. I thought she looked a lot more attractive than my first impression of her at the party, but rather sinister.

She was stood with two men, all three of them holding wine glasses. One man was studying a painting behind her, the other one talking earnestly to her; she, however, was staring rather vacantly at him like she wasn't really listening.

'Joseph, Rollie, this is my guest, Roxy,' Jaco said as we approached.

They both turned towards me and smiled. Both middle-aged, one averagely attractive in a sombre suit, the other less attractive with yellowing teeth and a potbelly, they then looked at Evie.

'We've met,' she said shortly in her soft voice and gave a thin smile, showing very white, very small teeth, like a child's.

'We were just discussing *End of Obedience,*' Potbelly said, indicating to the painting he had been examining.

As Jaco replied, putting a hand on Evie's back, I stepped a little closer to take a look.

In my honest opinion, I thought my twelve-month old niece could have painted better by dipping a paintbrush in her nappy, but I'm no art expert.

It depicted a figure, most likely female as it had long hair, crouched on the ground… I say ground for want of a better word, as it looked like purple popcorn… at the feet of a triangular figure, large and completely black, its arms raised to what could have been the sun. Or the moon. It was round, anyway.

I kept my face blank and nodded at it slightly, not wanting to reveal my ignorance of the artworld by looking puzzled.

'Fascinating, isn't it?' Potbelly said, waving his catalogue at it.

'Hmm,' I agreed.

'It has an interesting sense of ambiguity,' he rumbled on, 'with no scale of proportion. Is this figure overly large, or is the viewer seeing him close up?'

Not sure if he was asking a direct question, I kind of shrugged, shooting Jaco a glance over my shoulder. He was biting his lip like he was trying not to laugh, then he gave me a subtle wink.

'Sweetheart, would you like a drink?' he asked, and I hastily nodded.

'Red or white?'

'White, please.'

He raised his arm and indicated towards me, then a young man in a waistcoat appeared with a tray.

'Thank you,' I murmured, taking an ice-cold glass.

'Sorry, I'll be back in a minute,' Jaco took my free hand and dropped a kiss on my palm, making me want to squirm in delight. 'Have a wander around. Evie?' he raised an eyebrow and she obediently followed him towards some newcomers.

Not wanting to get cornered by Potbelly talking about things that I knew nothing about, I started to stroll along the paintings displayed on the wall. One in particular seemed to be attracting attention, three or four men and two women, both in floral summer dresses stood there, looking deep in discussion.

I stood on my tiptoes and tilted my head, not really sure what I was looking at.

There was nothing I could even loosely call "a figure" or "the ground" or "the sun" … it just looked like a mess of acid-green blobs and black lines, broken up by the occasional red smear.

Bending slightly, I looked in the gap between the two women and read the card next to it.

It read *Nature and Murder;* I let out an accidental snort of derision, then straightened up quickly as lots of pairs of eyes turned towards me.

'Fascinating,' I smiled brightly at them, before walking away to look at the adjacent wall.

Here, there were some smaller paintings and I supposed you could have called them kind of pretty, painted in pale-blues and greens, but I still wasn't sure what they were supposed to be.

I stopped at one entitled *Charming Karma*, that *might* have had flowers in it, if flowers were hexagon-shaped with eyes on them.

'Do you like that one?' Jaco's voice came behind me and I swung around.

'Oh,' I blinked a few times. 'Yeah-'

'That one's been sold,' he grinned. 'Two-hundred and eighty quid for probably an hours' work.'

I looked at him, not sure if he was being disparaging

about it or not.

'Sorry to abandon you,' he continued. 'Evie won't talk to buyers unless I kick her bum. I'm all yours now.'

'Will all these get sold?' I asked.

'Some,' his eyes roved around my face like they had at his party, making me want to drop my gaze.

I looked over his shoulder where a woman was embracing Evie and talking loudly.

'How long have you owned this?' I waved my arm around, wishing his stare wasn't so intense.

'Nearly four years,' he said. 'Been a hard-upwards struggle, but worth it.'

'I bet,' I couldn't help feeling awestruck. 'You must meet some interesting people… like, the artists and that.'

'Some are, some are rather too enchanted with themselves. I much prefer the buyers, most of them have more money than sense.'

'Sorry, I know nothing about art,' I shrugged. 'They must be good though to sell for so much.'

'Relatively cheap compared to the big guns,' he said blandly. 'Keeps me in Porsches and champagne though.'

Not knowing what to say, I turned back to the paintings again, but I wasn't really taking them in.

I felt *so* out of control, he was not like anyone I knew and my attraction to him was ludicrous.

'Come on,' he put a warm hand on my back. 'Let me show you off to a few people, then we can ditch the party,' he chuckled. 'I ate a packet of Jaffa Cakes at about ten this morning and I'm *ravenous*. And I want to get to know you properly.'

I let him to steer me to the middle of the room to a group of people. I smiled politely and allowed my cheek to be kissed as he introduced me as his guest and then tried to look interested as the art chat ebbed and flowed about fifty miles above my head.

All the time I was aware of Evie, drifting in and out of my view, making me feel distinctly uneasy. Not just because I sensed some hostility towards me, there was just… something about her. Something not right. I couldn't put my finger on it. Maybe it was just an artist's temperament, or whatever they call it. But I didn't like being near her - it was almost like I felt in danger.

Jaco took me to *La Maison Du Lac*, a *very* expensive French restaurant that I'd never been to before.

As we drove in his Porsche, my nerves doubled at the thought of sitting across the table from him, attempting to keep my cool, make conversation *and* eat.

We didn't get there until after ten o'clock. He hadn't appeared to have booked a table, but he was greeted with a friendly, 'Good evening Mr Sokolov,' and he seemed to be treated with reverence.

After we had been seated, I had to ask, '*What's* your surname?'

'Sokolov,' he grinned. 'It's Russian.'

'So, you're Russian?'

'Half. My dad's Russian, my mum's Irish. Great combo. Means I can drink most people under the table,' his grin widened.

'I'm a light-weight,' I watched as the waiter handed him the wine menu.

'Wine or champagne?'

'Oh… I better stick with wine.'

'Champagne it is then,' he handed the menu back and then started to stare again, his head on one side. 'You really are a beautiful girl. How does Teddy keep his hands to himself?'

'We're just mates,' I said, almost defensively.

'Of course,' he studied me some more, then flashed his huge smile and took my hand. 'So, tell me things about you. I want to know everything.'

'Everything?' I tried a teasing note in my voice, wanting to have some of the control that I usually felt with men.

'Yes,' he nodded slowly. 'Everything.'

'Well, I'm not sure I can manage everything,' I had to drop my eyes for a second. 'I'm twenty-two,' I looked back up, 'I work at Sports House Inc, I have an older sister and a younger brother… well, half-brother; my mum remarried. When I'm not working, I'm at the gym or at the theatre, I live alone, I love reading and horror films… and I love cake but never buy it.'

'Hm, willpower, I like it,' he looked up as the waiter approached with a champagne bucket. 'Star sign?'

'Scorpio.'

'Middle name?'

'Louise.'

'Favourite film?'

'The Silence of the Lambs.'

'Favourite position?'

'Eh?' I was briefly confused, then laughed hesitantly,

not sure whether he was joking or not.

'Well, let's keep some things a surprise, shall we?' he suddenly looked serious, his eyes burning into mine, making my legs feel like jelly and my heart race. Then he broke into a smile and chuckled softly. 'Sorry, I couldn't resist.'

'Naughty,' I said lightly, hoping sincerely that he couldn't see how he was affecting me.

'Shall we choose food?' he picked up his menu, before shooting me his wicked grin again. 'Do you want a starter?'

'Only if you do,' I tried to concentrate on the menu but was finding his very presence was throwing my head into chaos. 'The Camembert sound nice,' I muttered.

'It is,' he assured me.

'I might have the Chicken Provençal,' I blinked a few more times at the menu, then gave up.

When the waiter returned, Jaco reeled off very quickly, 'The lady would like the Camembert with redcurrant sauce, I will have the Champignons á l'ail please, then to follow the chicken with dauphinoise potatoes, yes sweetheart?' I nodded. 'And Confit de canard, with frites not dauphinoise… and another bottle please.'

'I'm not sure I should drink anymore,' I demurred.

'I don't mind carrying you in,' he grabbed my hand again. 'Long as you don't puke in the Porsche.'

'So, what about you?' I tried to ignore the electricity of his hand on mine. 'I know nothing about you.'

'Grew up in London,' he said. 'Moved to Fernberry when I was seventeen. I've got a younger sister and I work like a dog.'

'Is that it?'

'Not much to tell,' he shrugged his shoulders indifferently. 'We can find out bits as we go along…if you want to.'

'Sure,' I nodded, and his curved mouth lifted.

'I really like you,' he said softly. 'I'm gonna make time for you… I don't have much free time, that's why I'm single. But I want to see you again.'

'Yeah,' I said stupidly, trying to think of something sophisticated to say and failing.

'Good,' he squeezed my hand and then let go to pour more champagne. 'Next Saturday my sister is throwing a party for her friends… joint birthday or something. Would you like to come?'

'Yes, thank you, I would,' I probably would have readily agreed even if he had suggested wrestling lions with my hands tied behind my back.

'It's only casual,' he said. 'But I'd really like you to come, even though I'd much rather spoil you rotten.'

'You don't have to spoil me,' I laughed and shook my head. 'I ain't no princess.'

'You should be,' he said seriously. 'And I'm going to spoil you. I don't want you looking nowhere else.'

'I wouldn't,' I assured him. 'I like you too.'

As Jaco drove me home, I felt a little nervous as he must have been over the drink/driving limit, but I felt awkward about saying anything.

Since "the accident" I was a nervous passenger and preferred to do the driving myself. He seemed perfectly fine though and drove carefully and didn't put his foot down like Billy had.

When he pulled up, I started to feel a nervous anticipation mixed with the hyperactive mood that usually descended on me late at night.

'Do you want to come up?' I asked.

'I'd love to sweetheart, but I must get back to the gallery.'

'OK,' I glanced at the time; it was nearly one in the morning, surely nobody was there? I hated how disappointed I felt. I had been certain the night would end in passion.

'I'll ring you in the week,' he reached over and undid my seatbelt. 'Come on, I'll see you in safely.'

Hand in hand, we walked to the main doors in silence.

'It's OK, I can see myself up the stairs,' I turned to him and smiled.

'Thank you for a lovely evening,' he put one hand on the side of my face. 'It's been fun.'

'Yeah,' I breathed.

He stepped closer and kissed me very softly on the lips, then withdrew, 'Until next time, beautiful... go on, up you go, get to bed.'

'Goodnight,' I smiled to hide my further disappointment that he hadn't kissed me properly, then turned to push the doors open, putting an extra wiggle on as I ascended the stairs, certain he was watching me.

When I was out of sight, I kicked off my shoes and ran up the remaining stairs and charged down the corridor to my door.

Turning on the lights, I threw myself onto the sofa

and grinned inanely at the ceiling.

'Oh, I'm gonna be worth waiting for, you big tease,' I shivered slightly at the thought, my stomach full of butterflies. Then I squealed like a schoolgirl, clutching a cushion against me tightly.

CHAPTER FIVE

I had just spent an hour on the phone discussing my date with Dana when Teddy knocked on my door.

'Good morning,' he greeted me, wandering in. 'I have a script for you.'

'Ooo, OK,' I took the sheets of paper inside a plastic cover off of him.

'How was the big date?' he asked, heading straight to my kitchen and switching the kettle on.

'Weird,' I put the script on the side-table, not feeling focussed enough to read it just yet.

'Oh?'

I settled myself on the sofa, happily ready to talk about it, even though I had just been talking about it extensively. 'He's a weird guy.'

'Weird how?'

'He's kind of intense,' I watched Teddy as he made two mugs of coffee, then brought them over.

'I guess,' Teddy sat himself next to me and twisted himself around to look at me.

'Like, some guy picked me up to take me there,' I said, 'and I didn't even get to talk to Jaco properly until we went to the restaurant, but he kind of acted like he knew me... I dunno, it was a little... *surreal.*'

'OK,' Teddy nodded, not really looking like he was following me.

'Then,' I felt myself blush a little, 'I thought he was full on, but he didn't do anything... like, even kiss me properly.'

'Really?' Teddy pushed his glasses up and looked pensive. 'Isn't that a good thing?'

'Maybe,' I sipped some coffee. 'But he seems like the sort of bloke that would… you know.'

'Maybe he's more of a gentleman than he used to be. And that's a good thing.'

'What do you mean?'

'Well… when I knew him, he was… you know…with girls.'

'Yeah,' I had a sudden swoop of jealousy and felt rattled.

'So, what next?'

'He's invited me to a party on Saturday,' I shook off the jealous feeling and tried to sound casual. 'I said I'll go. I'll just wait and see if he rings me, I guess.'

'I'm sure he will,' Teddy patted my leg. 'I really don't think you've got anything to worry about.'

'No,' as a distraction, I reached over and picked up my script. 'You read it yet?'

'Yeah, last night when I got in.'

'Any good?'

'Yeah, pretty good.'

'Got your eye on anything?'

'Gordon, the eldest son,' he picked up my TV remote control and started twirling it around. 'Wanna come over when you've had a read?'

'Sure,' I drained my coffee and stood up. 'I'm going to the gym first and having lunch at my mum's… be over later.'

'Great.'

I took my script to my mum's and had a scan through it after dinner.

As the day was so warm, Howard had lit the barbecue and we had eaten his famous lemon chicken and salad on the decking.

Afterwards I had made myself comfortable on my belly under their old and gnarled cherry blossom tree and put my fingers in my ears to read, an old habit I'd developed at school to help me concentrate.

It was very funny; Duncan was a near-genius in my opinion.

The play was set in an old mansion, owned by the Miss Mabel in the title, an eccentric old woman with a penchant for young men. Her current husband-to-be had three sons, all of whom she flirted with, but she was secretly in love with her butler, Benedict.

As I started to get engrossed, I was drawn to 'Milly', her young niece who was living with her after the death of her parents. She was *also* in love with Benedict.

Eventually Miss Mabel is found dead, and the mystery ensues… I flicked through to the end, hoping it was Milly who was the villain… but it was Benedict, knowing she had left him her fortune and not wanting her to change her will, naming her husband-to-be as beneficiary.

I decided I was going to audition for Milly but was sure I would end up with a lesser part. There was a selection of female parts: a maid, two of the sons had a wife, the cook and Miss Mabel's sister. I would just have to read and read some more and try my hardest at the auditions.

'Any good?' I looked up, startled – I had been too engrossed to hear Howard approaching.

'*Really* good,' I pushed myself up and sat cross-legged and Howard done likewise, looking like a big child.

If I could have picked a stepdad… or even a dad for that matter… I would have picked Howard a million times over.

He is just so *nice*, such a lame description, but it's a word that sums him up perfectly.

A history professor at the local college, he looks the part; greying beard, a little over-weight, a liking for corduroy trousers and checked shirts – he plays the flute, listens to Simon and Garfunkel and has an extensive wine collection in his garage, which he jokingly calls his wine cellar.

He married my mum when I was five and my sister was nine, but they had met when I was two, so I don't really remember him not being around.

My biological dad is always rather dismissive about him, probably because he has done a job that my dad has failed at.

Of course, I don't know all the gritty details of the demise of my mum's marriage to him, but I'd overheard more than once my mum calling him 'that bastard' and other such descriptions.

However, Howard is always polite to and about my dad and never makes a big deal about him being in our lives – which he isn't really, as he moved to Sunderland with his new wife when I was sixteen and hardly calls. What Howard thinks and says in private, I don't know, but I reckon that the fact he never displays any hostility towards him in front of my sister and I says a lot about his goodness as a human being.

We had a really great childhood, me and my sister, and even when my mum had my little brother when I was eight, Howard never treated us any differently at all.

Howard reached over and took the script off me and leafed through it, 'Seen anything you fancy?'

'Yeah,' I watched him as he stopped to read here and there. 'Milly.'

'You'll do good, kid,' he grinned at me, his light-blue eyes crinkling up. 'You always do.'

'Jacob!' my mum suddenly yelled from somewhere indoors and we both looked towards the house.

'Uh oh,' Howard struggled up and loped towards the house and after a second, I reluctantly followed.

We found her in the kitchen, kneeling on the floor, wiping something up with a tea towel.

'Problem?' Howard asked.

'He left the freezer open *again,*' my mum said through gritted teeth. 'I nearly broke a leg slipping on a puddle.'

My brother was a fourteen-year-old nightmare; he and my mum were constantly at loggerheads over something or other. Howard, the more laidback of the two, was the constant peacemaker.

'Help me up,' my mum snapped, extending an arm towards Howard.

I tried not to roll my eyes and kicked off my sandals to cool my feet on the tiled floor.

Most people say I look like my mum. I suppose I do, as in we are both blonde and not much over five-foot. She is much more volatile than me though, more like my sister, Shauna.

My mum was going through what I had decided was a midlife crisis. She had cut off her hair and wore it in a trendy pixie-cut and was wearing very non-mum clothes as far as I was concerned, skinny jeans and tight tops, and was getting her nails done all the time and had joined a gym; thankfully not mine.

'I'll load the dishwasher,' I gave Howard a small grin over her head and busied myself.

'You whispered?' Jacob appeared, a younger and lankier version of Howard but with mischief constantly in his eyes.

'How many times,' my mum began in a low voice, 'have I told you to close the freezer properly? I nearly broke my neck. All the ice cubes have melted, you *better* pray that none of the meat is ruined.'

'Sorry,' he muttered.

'Hmph,' she made shooing motions with her hands and he disappeared again. 'Roxy darling, you're putting the plates in the wrong way, here let me.'

'Come on,' Howard indicated to the door with his head. 'Let's get out the way and you can tell me all about your week.'

I hadn't been home long when Jaco rang.

'Hello,' I said in the most composed voice I could manage.

'Hello you,' his sexy voice said and I felt tingly all over. 'What are you up to?'

'Just been at my parents',' I told him. 'What about you?'

'Just about to drive into London,' he said, and I felt a tiny drop of discontent, I was hoping he would suggest meeting up. 'Are you free tomorrow night? I want to take you out for dinner.'

'Sure,' I said, then cursed myself for answering too quickly.

'Pick you up around seven?'

'That's fine.'

'Fantastic. See you then.'

'OK.'

'Bye sweetheart.'

'Bye.'

I smiled to myself... I *loved* this part of relationships... well, hopefully this would be a relationship... and I decided that I needed to pull out all the stops and look extra sexy.

I went out onto my tiny balcony and felt the earth around my herbs, making a mental note to water them once the hot sun had moved.

'Hey,' Teddy yelled from the carpark; he was walking towards the building with two Tesco bags.

'Hey.'

'Beer and script?'

'Yup.'

I waited for ten-minutes, then went across to Teddy's flat.

'Read it?' he asked, his head in the fridge.

'Yeah, it's so good,' I enthused. 'Duncan is so clever.'

'Shame he's such a mung bean.'

'Mung bean!' I laughed. 'You are so mean.'

'Yeah,' he straightened up and beamed.

Another reason that Duncan was the subject of piss-taking, apart from his frequent hair-dyeing, was because he had once been a contestant on some cookery show that nobody had heard of and that hadn't even made it on air, but he talked about it constantly. But I was in the leave-him-alone-he's-harmless camp.

We spent an hour going over the script, and as I became more negative about getting the part of Milly, Teddy became more encouraging, promising to read lines with me before the auditions on Saturday and Sunday.

My mind wasn't really on it though, I was mentally going through my wardrobe for the following nights date with Jaco and playing saucy little scenarios.

Upon leaving work the next day, I had a devastating blow. Jaco cancelled on me.

I had just reached my car when my phone rang.

'Sweetheart, sweetheart, I am so sorry, tonight isn't happening.'

'Oh OK,' I almost groaned but managed to sound breezy about it. 'Everything OK?'

'Yeah,' he sounded distracted. 'I just need to go somewhere… nothing for you to worry about. I really am sorry. Please tell me we are still on for Saturday… I'm not messing you about, I promise.'

'Of course,' I desperately wanted to ask where he had to go, but we weren't quite at that stage and I'd rather die before I sounded clingy or demanding.

'OK,' he sounded relieved at least. 'I really want to

see you. I keep thinking about you.'

'Well, if it can't be helped,' I said lightly - inside I was having a slight tantrum though.

'I'll ring you later.'

'OK, speak soon.'

'Sure will.'

'Bugger,' I said loudly as I ended the call.

Jaco rang me every evening, and we chatted for at least half-an-hour, which was better than nothing. It was making me crushed with yearning though, mixed with anticipation. And it wasn't helping my crazy sleeping habits, not one little bit.

I stalked him a little on Facebook, then took the plunge and friend requested him, which he accepted… then I went through all his photos like a starstruck teenager.

I also discussed him endlessly with Dana, who was *very* amused by my mounting obsession, telling me to play it cool.

I did occur to me that I still knew very little about him, but something was stopping me from bugging Teddy.

I also became horribly fascinated with Evie. Seeing that her and Jaco were friends on Facebook, I couldn't resist taking a look.

I was shocked to discover that she was only eighteen… surely she had to be older than that? I was also surprised to see she came from Chelsea *and* her mother was an actress that I recognised straight away, Valerie Black. She had been in a few TV dramas and wasn't huge, but a familiar face all the same.

I studied Evie's profile picture, having that same awful foreboding feeling about her and having no idea why.

On Friday my mood had picked up, knowing I was seeing Jaco in twenty-four hours.

In the middle of the afternoon I was just tidying up the footwear section with Albie, one of the guys, when Jaco frightened the life out of me by tapping me on the shoulder.

'Oh my God, hello!' I beamed, clutching my chest. 'You scared me.'

'Sorry, I couldn't resist,' he smiled lazily.

He looked gorgeous in tight, light-beige jeans and a casual white shirt and smelt of a musky aftershave that I recognised from our date.

Albie carried on tidying, after giving Jaco a curious look.

'What are you doing here?' I asked.

'Well,' he gave me the once over, making me glad that I was wearing my tight activewear pants rather than my looser jogging bottoms, and my Sports House Inc T-shirt rather than the thicker polo shirt, 'I was doing paperwork and got bored and thought, what will cheer me up? Then I thought, Roxy will.'

'That's nice,' I murmured, then shivered slightly as he reached over and touched my cheek.

'You look beautiful,' he looked me up and down again. 'What's this?' he extracted a pen that I'd tucked in my bun and he pocketed it. 'My new pen, it'll make me think about you when I'm elbow deep in shitty paperwork.'

'Smooth line,' I giggled, and after holding a serious look, he chuckled too.

'You aren't no fool, are you?' he glanced around the shop. 'I can't stop, I need to go and pick up something,' again, I wanted to ask, but didn't. 'I need a favour actually.'

'Oh?'

'Here,' he reached into his back pocket and pulled out some twenty-pound notes. 'I loathe shopping, can you grab a couple of presents for Eliza and Tom for tomorrow?'

'Who?'

'Oh, Sadie's friends, sorry.'

'What shall I get?' I baulked slightly as he counted out five notes and handed them to me. 'You know them better than me... I *don't* know them at all.'

'Not really,' he took my hand and curled my fingers over the money. 'I haven't seen Tom for years... Eliza's a larky girl though, likes a drink, get some champagne.'

'Sure, OK,' I stammered.

'Thank you,' he kissed me lightly, then smiled into my eyes. 'I'll come over to yours about half-six, Sadie only lives ten-minutes from yours.'

'OK,' I wondered if it was a possibility that he would end up staying at mine for the night, and I had to hold in another shiver.

'Ring you later,' he kissed me again then pushed his expensive-looking sunglasses down, covering his wonderful eyes, but making him look sexier than ever.

'New squeeze?' Albie sidled over as I dreamily watched Jaco leave.

'Oh yeah,' I murmured, smiling happily.

CHAPTER SIX

I managed to sweet-talk Troy, my manager, into letting me leave work early on Saturday.

I spent a luxurious hour soaking in the bath before dressing in my off-white jeans and a pale-pink top, that was low-cut and clung in all the right places.

If we were to be going out to a restaurant or somewhere, I would have spent forever doing my face and hair, but as it was *casual*, I put my hair up in a girlish pony-tail and put on minimal make-up, hoping that Jaco would be as admiring as he had been so far.

I had bought two bottles of champagne and had tied a pink ribbon on one and a blue ribbon on the other.

With time to spare, I poured a glass of wine and stood on my balcony to watch out for Jaco's car and enjoy the early evening sunshine.

When I spotted his car, my heart started to thump, and I leaned over the railing.

I watched him climb out and he looked up and waved.

'What number are you?' he called.

'Eight,' I called back, then rushed back in to spray more perfume on myself and around the room.

I jumped when he knocked and took a few deep breaths before I opened the door.

'Hi,' I stood back and watched him walk in, looking as sexy as ever in dark-coloured shorts and a pale-yellow polo shirt.

'Hi,' he put a hand on the back of my neck and kissed me, before smiling his dazzling smile. 'You look nice.'

'Thank you,' I suddenly felt all arms and legs and uncoordinated. 'Do you want a drink or anything?'

'No thanks,' he sat on the edge of the sofa and patted the seat next to him. 'But I do want to talk to you for a minute, come here.'

'Oh,' I said in surprise. 'Sure, OK.'

He surveyed me for a moment, his expression troubled, and I felt a wariness descend upon me, 'I want to apologise first of all,' he began. 'I said I'd make time for you and I've already stood you up. I haven't made time for you at all, have I?'

'Uh,' I blinked a few times, not sure what to say.

'And I know a girl like you,' his eyes swept over me, 'won't hang around if she ain't being treated right.'

'Well, if you've been busy, you've been busy,' I spread my arms and shrugged, trying to seem unconcerned, but I was terribly touched by that little statement. 'We've only known each other five minutes, it's cool.'

'No, it isn't,' he insisted, his face grave. 'I like you, *really* like you, Roxy. I've always put the gallery first, but I don't want to with you.'

'I understand though,' I cautiously put a hand on his leg. 'I told you, I'm no princess.'

'Yeah,' he said quietly and looked down at my hand, then smiled again. 'But I just wanted you to know that.'

'Well… OK,' I watched as he covered my hand with his, then trembled a little as he leaned over and kissed me properly.

'You are so beautiful,' he rested his forehead on mine and sighed. 'Thank you for understanding.'

'Don't be silly,' I murmured.

'Can we go? Before I start getting other ideas?' he shook his head, as if in despair. 'You are doing nice things to me.'

'OK,' I laughed and drew away. 'Let me just grab my bag.'

I went into my bedroom and reapplied my lip-gloss, then hugged myself joyfully, '*Oh my God*,' I whispered, wanting to let out a squeal.

We walked the short walk to his sister's house hand in hand, chatting about this and that, and it felt so *right*. Like boyfriend and girlfriend.

My thoughts were going at a million miles an hour, I was having difficulty concentrating on our conversation and was getting the urge to use up some energy. I felt like I wanted to run.

Her house turned out to be a modest terraced house on one of the quieter roads heading towards town.

Jaco knocked a couple of times, then stood back, drawing me closer to his side.

'Hello,' the door was wrenched open and there stood who I presumed to be Sadie, a tiny and beautiful girl that looked so much like Jaco that I liked her straight away.

Dark-haired with the same Prussian-blue eyes, heavily tattooed, she was even shorter than me, dressed in a clinging bronze dress.

'Come in, come in,' bare footed, she led us

to a large kitchen, where a leggy blonde girl in an orange sundress was leaning against a worktop, a glass in her hand.

'Happy birthday, Elzabub,' Jaco held up the champagne bottle with the pink ribbon and handed it to her.

'Thank you,' she smiled shyly, taking it and cradling it like a baby.

'Roxy, this is Eliza and my little sis, Sadie,' Jaco squeezed my hand. 'This is Roxy.'

'Hi, lovely to meet you,' Sadie beamed. 'We'll chat soon, I'm just-' she waved at the various trays and bowls of food on the sides.

'Sure,' I grinned back.

'Where's Tom?' Jaco asked.

'Out the back,' Sadie nodded towards the door. 'I'll be out in two.'

Jaco led me down a white-painted hall and through an opulently decorated living room to some double patio doors, where there was a small patio. A good-looking dark-haired man was sat at a table; he half-rose as he spotted us, a huge smile on his face.

'Jac,' he extended an arm and Jaco grabbed his hand.

'Tom?' Jaco sounded incredulous. 'Good to see you, man,' he set the other bottle of champagne down in front of him.

'Wow, thanks! How you doing?' he sat back down and smiled at us both.

'Great,' Jaco pulled out the chair next to Tom and I sat down. 'Tom, this is Roxy, Roxy, Tom.'

'Hi,' Tom said, 'nice to meet you.'

'Hi,' I glanced up at a tall man with a shock of fair

64

hair who was busy fanning a smoking barbecue.

'This is Bal, my b-boss and our chef for the evening,' Tom got up and stood by a large plastic tub full of ice and bottles. 'What are you drinking?'

'Wine's fine,' I told him, then smiled politely as Bal looked over and raised a hand in greeting.

'Hello, new people,' he boomed. 'Are you Jaco? You must be Jaco. You look like my Sadie.'

'Indeed I am Jaco,' Jaco looked amused. '*Your* Sadie?'

'Oh, well nearly,' Bal strolled over and rested a hand on the table. 'I'm wearing her down slowly until she loves me back.'

I let out a giggle then stopped abruptly, not altogether sure whether he was being serious or not. It was rather hard to take him seriously when he was wearing an apron with a six-pack torso printed on it with a huge sausage rising up from the crotch.

'Yeah, she has that reaction too,' he said cheerfully. 'Denial, of course.'

'Of course, mate,' Tom chipped in.

'You'll see,' Bal said, and wandered back to continue fanning the smoke.

'Jesus,' Jaco exclaimed in a low voice.

'He's c-cool,' Tom shook his head. 'Just a little… um, odd.'

He and Jaco started chatting. Jaco stood behind my chair, lightly caressing my neck and shoulder, making me want to kiss him again. Inevitably my concentration started to wane, and after watching Tom's face for a while – he really was terribly cute, even cuter to me when I noticed he had a slight stammer, which I found strangely endearing – I let my eyes wander around Sadie's garden, thinking Howard would have a field-day with it, tidying it up. It was a little over-grown and natural, but kind of beautiful in its own way.

Bal had wandered over again to join in the conversation and I tried to catch up on what they were talking about, thinking I didn't want to appear rude.

I was laughing at something Bal had said, when I saw Eliza coming out the patio doors, waving smoke away and coughing.

'Birthday girl,' Bal called.

'Hi,' she sat on the low wall down one side of the patio, still coughing.

'Nice dress,' I said, admiring her long legs.

'Thanks,' she smiled.

'Jaco,' I stood up and indicated to him to take my chair. He kissed my hand and carried on talking to Tom.

I went and sat next to Eliza, 'Is it your birthday today?' I asked, and she shook her head. 'I was a bit shy about coming,' I confided. 'It's only our second date. Don't you just loathe parties where you don't know a soul?'

'Shit, yeah,' she agreed.

She was very pretty, I decided, in an understated way. Her eyes were large and cornflower-blue with long sweeping lashes, like a camel. She also gave me the impression she had been given a smoking-hot body with no idea what to do with it. She had generous boobs; much bigger than mine, and kept self-consciously pulling her neckline up, and rearranging her dress on her slightly sunburnt legs.

'I hope you like champagne,' I said. 'Jaco, typical man, told me to grab two presents,' I glanced over at him. 'I was like, I don't know them, you know them better than me. He said he hasn't seen Tom for years though. He's nice, isn't he? Tom, I mean.'

'Yeah, he is,' she looked over at him, a small smile on her lips. 'How did you meet Jaco?'

'At his birthday party,' I told her. 'I went with this guy who knows him from school, and he ended up asking me out,' I realised how that sounded and added, 'I'm just mates with this guy… our flats are opposite each other, like brother/sister kind of mates, you know?'

'Yeah,' Eliza nodded. 'Bit like me and Tom, I suppose.'

'You were at school together, right?'

'Yes, since infants' school,' she glanced at him again. 'He's been in Ireland though for ten years, he's just back visiting for the summer.'

'How lovely,' I said. 'Bet you'll have fun. Sadie seems great.'

'She really is.'

'So much like Jaco,' I watched him swigging from a beer bottle and sighed happily. 'You must know him well?' I asked casually.

'Not really,' Eliza shrugged, then giggled.
'You like him a lot, then? He was just my mates' big brother. He used to tease us a bit.'

'Did he?' I sighed again. 'Yeah, I like him a lot.'

Voices sounded from inside, then a few moments later a beautiful and exotic-looking dark-skinned girl came out with an unshaven guy, a roll-up behind his ear and dressed in a crumpled T-shirt and combat shorts.

'I'm here,' he announced. 'The party can start.'

I looked at Eliza in alarm, then we both laughed.

A few other people wandered out, calling happy birthday to Eliza and Tom.

'Hey, babe,' the guy handed Eliza a wrapped gift and kissed her. Close-up he wasn't bad looking, just very untidy.

'Thanks,' Eliza grinned up at him and the girl.

'Excuse my scruff,' the girl directed at me as she sat next to me. 'I'm Bo,' she introduced herself.

'Excuse me,' Eliza got up and went indoors, clutching her gift.

'I'm Roxy, Jaco's girlfriend,' I liked how that sounded. 'You know Jaco?'

'Kinda,' Bo looked over at "her scruff". 'Grab us a beer, baby... only as Sadie's brother, met him twice, maybe.'

'Ah, right,' I sipped some wine, now wanting to re-join Jaco, but it seemed rude to get up.

After a few minutes however, Jaco suddenly looked over at me and got up and came over.

'Alright?' he sat down and kissed my shoulder, then nodded at Bo.

'Yes,' I said happily. 'Eliza's nice.'

'So are you,' he kissed me again.

'Aw,' Bo patted my leg. 'Love birds.'

Eliza reappeared with Sadie, both carrying trays of uncooked meat.

'Great, I'm starving,' Jaco muttered.

'There's my girl,' Bal boomed, making those

standing near him jump.

Sadie gave him a little bow, 'Start cooking, my good man.'

Jaco had been repeatedly topping up my glass and I felt unsteady by the time the meat was cooked, even though I'd been nibbling on some crisps.

Jaco loaded up a plate with chicken and lamb for us to share and we went and sat together on a crumbling stone bench on the lawn.

'Such a lovely evening,' I gazed up at the dying sunlight through the trees, feeling ludicrously contented.

'Sure is,' Jaco agreed, biting into a chicken leg. 'Are you enjoying yourself?'

'Yeah,' I picked up some lamb and took a tiny bite.

'You look so pretty,' he watched me. 'Here,' he handed me a napkin. 'I'm so glad you came… I'm so glad I asked you out.'

'Well, I'm glad I said yes then,' I smiled up at him, taking in his handsome face with his curved and smiling mouth and dark-blue eyes, adorably narrowed against the low sun. 'You must meet some very glamourous women in your job.'

'Glamourous yes, beautiful as you, nope,' he said, reaching out and stroking my cheek with the back of his hand. 'I bet every man here wants you.'

'Daft,' I looked down, not wanting to show how flattered I was. 'But thank you.'

'Come here,' he put our plate down and drew me close, one hand on my back, the other on the back of my neck. 'Not daft. Honest.'

69

He started to kiss me, and I melted against him, my heart racing crazily.

'Hem, hem,' a female voice said.

'Hey, sis,' Jaco rested his face against mine. 'Shit timing, piss off.'

Sadie stood there grinning at us, 'Can't you wait until you get home?'

'Spoilsport,' Jaco said lightly, then kissed my forehead before pulling away.

'Sorry,' she brandished a bottle of wine before topping up my glass. 'I just thought I'd say hello, check in, be the hostess with the mostest, et cetera.'

'Sure,' Jaco grinned affectionately at her. 'Great party.'

'I'm gonna crank up the music soon,' she said. 'Sorry, I haven't had time to interrogate you and warn you off of this arsehole yet,' she beamed at me.

'No worries,' I giggled. 'You've been busy.'

'No, it's rude,' Sadie placed the half-full wine bottle next to me. 'There's loads of food if you want more, come and find me if you want anything.'

I watched her as she walked back towards the patio, thinking how beautiful she was.

'She's lovely,' I said.

'Yeah,' Jaco agreed. 'Come on, eat up.'

As the sun began to set, some fairy lights sprang to life above the arbour over the patio, and some music was put on to some cheers.

I didn't manage to eat much and was feeling very drunk and unsteady on my feet.

I had a little swaying dance with Bal to some Blink

182 and shared some doughnuts with some guy that seemed more out of it than me. Even more drunk was Eliza, who was starting to look rather dishevelled. I watched Jaco talking to Tom and a group of lads, deciding that tonight was going to be *the* night. I simply *had* to sleep with him.   Then I started to feel sick.

'Jaco,' I tapped him on the arm. 'I'm not feeling good.'

'Oh, sweetheart,' he put an arm around my waist. 'Let's get you some water.'

He sat me on the wall and disappeared indoors, returning with a tall glass of water.

'Sorry,' I started to shiver. 'I'm not much of a drinker.'

'Small sips,' he crouched down in front of me, his face a picture of concern.

'Oh… oh crap,' I felt my stomach begin to heave and stood up quickly. The garden seemed to start spinning and I walked unsteadily away from the patio to the edge of the garden.

'Is she OK?' a voice that I recognised as Bal's said, then I retched horribly, before throwing up extensively in the flowerbed.

'Oh, baby,' Jaco said, rubbing my back.

I threw up again, nearly falling forwards - a pair of arms held my waist and I threw up yet again.

'There we go,' Bal said. 'Better to get it out.'

'Uh oh,' a female voice said. 'Get her some water.'

'On the wall,' Jaco said.

When I was sure I was done, I tried to stand up straight but almost fell backwards.

71

'Shit, I'm sorry,' I mumbled, feeling mortified despite my drunkenness.

'Anyone sober enough to drive?' Bal yelled.

'I am,' Tom wandered over, looking worried.

'I'm fine,' I shook my head, looking at him through watering eyes.

'Here, drink this,' Jaco gently put the glass of water in my hand.

'Sorry,' I mumbled again, shaking uncontrollably.

'Oh crap, take her home Jac,' Sadie appeared holding out a cardigan. 'Put this on, lovely,' she draped it around my shoulders.

'Thank you,' I felt on the verge of tears and hung my head, an embarrassing small burp escaping me.

'This way,' Jaco put an arm around my middle and led me across the patio, through the house and out the front door.

'I'm really sorry,' I croaked. 'I didn't realise how much I'd drunk... how embarrassing.'

'You poor baby,' he soothed.

I tried to focus on the path ahead, but things kept going into a blur and my head was spinning like mad.

I don't know how long it took us to get home, I just remember Jaco asking for my key and then the next thing I knew, I was laying on the sofa and he was removing my sandals.

'I'll get you a bowl,' he disappeared and I closed my eyes, willing the world to stop going around and around.

I felt something on me and opened my eyes a fraction; he had put my duvet on me.

'No, it's hot,' I tried to sit up.

'You'll get cold when you pass out,' he sounded like he was trying not to laugh.

'I'm sorry,' I rambled on. 'I was gonna seduce you,' I started to giggle.

'I'll keep,' he stroked my head. 'There's a bowl here and a glass of water on the table. I'm going to wait until you're asleep, OK?'

'OK,' I tried to focus on his face. 'Oh, I fancy you,' I slurred… then I don't remember anything else.

CHAPTER SEVEN

I woke up with a numb arm from it hanging off the sofa, and a very sore head.

I struggled out from under my duvet, my sluggish brain searching for the last hour or so before I passed out.

Halfway through peeing, I remembered telling Jaco I wanted to seduce him… *classy, Roxy…* and groaned. Then I groaned even louder when I remembered I had my audition in – I checked my watch – exactly one hour.

I made a cup of tea and took the fastest shower ever, then texted Jaco telling him I was sorry for throwing up and passing out, and I would ring him after my audition. Then I texted Teddy imploring him to drive me to the theatre because I was scared that I was still over the limit.

Getting flustered as I got dressed, I didn't bother with any make-up apart from trying to paint out the circles under my bloodshot eyes. It was another hot day and it wasn't helping my agitated mood in the slightest.

Dressing in the first pair of shorts I could find and a vest top, I was halfway out my door to Teddy's with my mug of tea when I realised that I hadn't put on a bra or deodorant, and rushed back in.

'Rough night, honey?' Teddy said, letting me in.

'Don't,' I grumbled. 'I made a right tit of myself in front of Jaco… have you got anything with sugar in please? I've got the alcohol shakes.'

'Uh oh,' he went to an overhead cupboard and peered in. 'Jaffa Cakes?'

'They'll do,' I remembered with a pang Jaco telling me before we went to the restaurant that Jaffa Cakes were all he had eaten that day. 'Thank you.'

'I had my audition yesterday,' he said.

'Oh, I'm sorry, yes I know, I forgot,' I gabbled. 'How was it?'

'It went pretty well, I reckon,' he took his glasses off and wiped the lenses on his T-shirt.

'Of course it did,' I went and hugged him around the middle, then stood on my tiptoes and messed up his fair hair. 'You are a natural star.'

'Well, gosh and blush.'

'You are. I'll be lucky today if they let me make the teas and sweep the floor.'

'You'll be fine, we practised loads last week.'

'I think alcohol has melted my brain,' I started eating a Jaffa Cake. 'I feel like crap.'

'You'll be fine,' he said again. 'Come on, let's go.'

Fernberry Little Theatre is set back from the main road leading out of town, between a large carpark and a block of offices.

Originally, Howard had told me, it had been the old courthouse, long before I was born.

Only seating two hundred and twenty-five, it's very basic. A small entrance hall with the box office to the right and a cloakroom to the left, double doors open into the auditorium, with a sloping gangway in the middle of the dark-red seats.

Backstage there are two *tiny* dressing rooms, only one toilet, a kitchen and a storeroom for props and scenery and the such.

We didn't even have a proper orchestra pit, just a small area in front of the stage with moveable barriers.

I loved it though; I loved the atmosphere, the Players... well, *most* of them... the whole process of production and the high jinks. It was a bit like being back at school.

There's an urban legend, with absolutely no proof or written word, that people were hung there back in the early nineteenth century and it's haunted.

I didn't believe a word of it, but even so, I didn't particularly fancy being there alone day *or* night.

Destiny the Happy Hippy, who was into the paranormal, was the only person who said she had "sensed" a presence, and had gone as far to say she had seen an apparition of a young man in the corridor that ran from the women's dressing room to the men's dressing room and the toilets.

Our caretaker, Wally Pilchard, an old Canadian guy that was a real grouch and would take a bite out of you if you so much as smirked at his name, said it was all *'hysterical bullshit'* and he had not seen so much as a ghost of a mouse.

The theatre was cool inside at least - this was good as I had felt decidedly queasy in Teddy's hot car on our way there.

As we went through the double doors into the auditorium, we were greeted by the sight of Duncan and the three committee members: Gloria Hands, a middle-aged, upper-class, cold and snooty woman that I was secretly scared of for no real reason, Kabir Kumar, a friendly and handsome man in his fifties that always gave the impression of being there just for a laugh, and Justin Green, the youngest of the bunch who smiled a lot but didn't say much.

I had never really had much to do with them. They had monthly meetings with Duncan and some of the members to discuss productions and theatre maintenance and I don't know what else – and were present at auditions.

As I hadn't been a member long, I wasn't as involved as some - unlike for example, Violet, who was in her seventies and had been a member since the beginning in the 'eighties. She was also our costume designer and maker, along with Lola, who was in her twenties but looked and acted older and had been a member since her teens.

And the nightmare that was Finn Davidson was always involved… in everything. He was self-appointed social media publicity "manager". He had adopted the "manager" part and made sure he was listed as that on our advertising.

I spotted Finn straight away, sat on the edge of the stage, a script in his hand and talking loudly.

Teddy had already told me that he had auditioned the day before for the part of Benedict, which I expected he would get.

Sitting a few rows behind Duncan and the committee was Meadow, who I suspected would also be auditioning for the part of Milly, Derek, whose blocked sinuses I could hear from the back, and Pontus our production and stage manager who also fancied himself as a bit of a writer and was always arguing with Duncan about the scripts.

Sitting alone on the other side was Destiny, who appeared to be meditating.

'Hello,' Duncan called out genially, twisting around in his seat.

'She's hungover, be kind,' Teddy said as we reached the front.

'Shut up,' I hissed, hitting his arm.

'Jolly good,' Kabir said cheerily, earning a frosty look from Gloria and causing Finn to sigh audibly.

'Who are you auditioning for, my dear?' Duncan consulted his clipboard.

'Milly,' I said, feeling queasy again.

'Good, good,' he settled back and watched as Meadow went and delicately ran up the steps and smoothed down her floral dress.

I breathed a sigh of relief as she read some lines for one of the maids in her slightly husky voice.

Finn was nodding pompously as she looked at him as if for approval, (she was one of his fans), and Teddy muttered *what a peanut*, which at least made me giggle.

When it was my turn, another wave of nausea hit me, making a sweat break out on my forehead.

'Act two, scene one, start at the top,' Duncan told me as I went up.

I suppressed a groan as Finn jumped up and stood opposite me, script in hand. I glanced at Teddy and he gave me a thumbs up.

'Miss Jones,' Finn said loudly, 'I know this is a time

of great distress, but I need you to tell me what you can remember about last night.'

'Well, I took a walk with Mr Graves,' I cleared my throat and glanced at my script. 'Sorry,' I muttered, ignoring Finn's slight head shake.

'Carry on, my dear,' Duncan waved a hand.

'We went back to the kitchen to beg a nightcap from Miss Jessop, and she was making Auntie Mabel's nightly cocoa.'

'I see,' Finn paused. 'Prior to this though, Miss Jones... and this is very important, did you see anyone in the grounds?'

'Only Herbert the gardener, he was raking up some leaves. He waved to us and said something about it being a chilly evening...'

I dropped my head dramatically and pressed a hand to forehead. 'Sorry, sir, I am most distraught. My beloved aunt-'

'Of course,' Finn reached over and patted my shoulder.

'Miss Jessop left a bottle of brandy on the table for us,' I looked up again and frowned above Finn's head. 'She took a tray with the cocoa and a plate of biscuits and left the kitchen... we took the brandy to the drawing room and talked for a bit. I did not see anybody else... I went to bed after a while.'

'Alone?'

'Of course, sir!'

'And Mr Graves?'

'I don't know, he spoke of reading for a while... his wife, Olivia, she was having trouble sleeping... he voiced concern that he might disturb her.'

79

'Excellent,' Duncan put his hands up, and I looked over.

'Yay, you,' Teddy clapped.

Relieved I had finished and not dried up, I hugged my script to me and trotted back down the steps.

'Well done, my gorgeous,' Destiny called out from the other side and I beamed at her.

'Can we go?' I mumbled at Teddy. 'I need to die somewhere in peace.'

'Junk food?'

'Junk food.'

We went to a small café nearby to Teddy's bookstore. While he went and got us some teas and bacon sandwiches, I tried to ring Jaco, but his phone was switched off.

'Alright?' Teddy returned with our teas.

'Hm,' I started to rearrange the sauce bottles, not wanting to start banging on about Jaco.

'What's up?' he asked. 'Worried about how your audition went? Because you done great, Rox.'

'No,' I shrugged. 'Well, a little maybe. It's just... I said I'd ring Jaco after my audition and his phone's off. He hasn't even answered my text from earlier. I hope I haven't blown it.'

'By getting drunk?' he looked at me incredulously. 'Don't be silly.'

'Not the sexiest thing to do though, is it? Blowing chunks all over his sister's garden then passing out on him.'

'Well,' he looked thoughtful, 'no, I guess not. But if he likes you it wouldn't put him off.'

'No,' I said listlessly.

A young girl in an apron came over and put our plates in front of us.

'Thank you,' Teddy smiled up at her, then looked back at me. 'He'll ring, don't worry.'

'Sure.'

'Stop it, you turnip.'

'Sorry,' I opened my sandwich and emptied some ketchup over the bacon. 'So, what did you do last night?'

'I, um, had a date actually,' he smiled crookedly.

'Oh?' I stopped with my sandwich halfway to my mouth.

'You're dripping ketchup… yeah… went to The Rose.'

'And?'

'Eh,' he shrugged.

'Come on, details please,' I took a huge bite of my sandwich and put it down again.

'Just a girl I met the other week when I was out with Russ.'

'And?' I prodded his arm.

'Nothing, really. Had a nice time.'

'You're no good at gossiping,' I grumbled.

'What?' he laughed. 'OK, nosy. Her name is Gemma, she works in Specsavers, she's twenty-six, she's very pretty and has a Pug called Waddle.'

'Are you seeing her again?'

'Maybe.'

'Why just maybe?'

'Jeez, Rox. I dunno. *She* might not want to see *me*.'

'And why not?' I tutted. 'You're funny and cute.'

'Oh yeah,' he agreed, then laughed. 'We'll see.'

My phone rang, making me start. I nearly dropped it in hopeful excitement then sighed when I saw it was my mum.

'Hi,' I said, trying to sound cheerful.

'Hello, darling, I need a favour I'm afraid.'

'What's that?' I shook my head at Teddy who had raised an eyebrow questioningly.

'Can you watch your wretched brother on Saturday night? We have a dinner and dance with some of Howard's boring college people,' she said without enthusiasm. 'He *was* supposed to be sleeping over at his little Scottish friend's house, you know, what's his name? -'

'Dale.'

'Yes, him… anyway, he is now grounded for a month, and as much as I'd like to get out of the dinner thing, I can't.'

'A month?' I said in surprise. 'What the hell has he done now?'

'Bun got into our garden again,' – Bun was next doors horrid little Chihuahua – 'and he drew eyebrows on her with a Sharpie pen-'

I let out a scream of mirth.

'Roxy,' she said sternly. 'It isn't funny. Poor Jeanie was very annoyed. She can't wash them off and now the damn dog looks permanently angry.'

'Oh, what a little shit,' I giggled. 'Sorry Mum… yes I suppose so. I'll come after work.'

'Thank you, darling. Now, how are you? Have you been sleeping properly?'

'Yeah, I'm fine. Yes, I'm sleeping fine,' I said

lightly. I hadn't been, but it was better than her worrying.

'Good. And are you eating?'

'Yes Mum! I'm eating right now. I'm having brunch with Teddy.'

'Lovely,' she said, sounding happy. 'Say hello to Teddy from me. OK, if I don't see you in the week, I'll see you on Saturday.'

I ended the call and giggled again, then told Teddy what Jacob had done.

'Ha,' he grinned. 'That's hilarious.'

'Ain't it?' I shook my head. 'Poor Howard though, having to deal with him *and* my mum's hysterics. So glad I moved out.'

Back at home, I had a little tidy up and hung some wet washing on my clothes airer in front of my balcony door to dry.

I kept checking my phone, becoming increasingly panicked and slightly annoyed.

If he rings, I thought to myself, *I won't answer it, let him worry for a bit.*

By two o'clock, I had done all my jobs and went to hang out at Teddy's. We sat on our drinking seat, eating our way through a tube of Pringles and discussed *The Murder of Miss Mabel.*

I was certain that Teddy would get the role of Gordon, the eldest son of Miss Mabel's new man, it had him written all over it.

Gordon had a beautiful and glamourous wife, but he was in fact *also* in love with Benedict, the handsome butler, which had so much comic potential.

'Well, we'll find out on Saturday,' Teddy nudged me as I started fretting that I wouldn't get the part of Milly. 'No point in worrying all week, is there?'

'No, I know,' I agreed. 'I hate waiting though!'

As he got up to make a drink, my phone rang; this time it *was* Jaco.

I made myself wait for a few seconds, then answered, fighting to keep my voice low and modulated.

'Hello?'

'Hello, sorry sweetheart,' Jaco said in a rush. 'I did see your text this morning, then I got a call from Evie,' I felt suddenly depressed, 'the silly cow pranged her car speeding in the early hours and I had to go and sort her out, she was at a station in Borehamwood. I forgot to grab my lead to charge my phone in the car and it died on me. So sorry, I've just got back. How are you? Are you OK? How was your audition?'

'It's OK,' I said brightly. 'Yeah I'm good, the audition went well.'

'Oh, that's brilliant,' he said. 'How was your head this morning?'

'Iffy. All good now,' I mouthed '*it's Jaco*' at Teddy as he came back with two glasses of orange juice.

'Poor you,' he chuckled. 'Blame me, I kept handing you drinks all night, I'll know next time, won't I?'

'Well, I didn't have to drink them, I'm such a lightweight.'

'But very beautiful,' he paused. 'What are you doing now?'

'I'm at Teddy's, just talking about the play.'

'Well, I was wondering if you would let me make it up to you – getting you drunk and not getting back to you sooner. I would like to cook you dinner, no wine,' he chuckled. 'What do you think? I could pick you up in a couple of hours and drive you home, I'm not drinking either.'

'Sure,' I tried to keep the ecstasy out of my voice, but I guess my face said it all, as Teddy looked down and shook his head, smiling. 'That would be lovely, thank you.'

'Great,' he said happily. 'I'll see you just after six. Is that OK?'

'Yes.'

'OK sweetheart.'

'Oh my God!' I squealed as I ended the call. 'I haven't been dumped.'

'So I gathered,' Teddy said dryly. 'Are you going to stop being a spam brain now?'

'Yes,' I took my glass off him and downed the contents. 'I need to find something to wear and make myself beautiful…oh my God!' I hugged him hard and jumped up.

'Go on Cinders,' he ushered me to the door. 'Have fun.'

CHAPTER EIGHT

The day was showing no sign of cooling down, so I
dressed in a little white sundress that didn't leave a
whole lot to the imagination but was also kind of girly
rather than seductive. I hoped that it was going to have
the desired effect.

Jaco pulled into the carpark at ten-past-six and I ran
down excitedly, slowing down as I reached the final
few steps.

'Wow, hello you,' he whistled as I slid into the
passenger seat.

'Hi,' I said breathlessly.

'You look incredible,' he gave me one of his once-
overs.

He himself looked dazzlingly handsome in grey
shorts and a white shirt with the sleeves rolled up. He
looked kind of preppy.

He smelt amazing too.

On the way to his house, he asked me all about my
audition and the play, and I happily chatted away,
thinking how nice it was that he was so interested.

When he pulled onto his driveway, I couldn't
help feeling impressed.

His house was on the edge of the Farm Estate on the
outskirts of Chembury. I'd driven past a few times and
had always wondered what they were like inside.

As he opened the black front door, I almost gasped, it
was *fabulous* - the hall was nearly as big as my living

room, full of plants on the grey quarry-tiled floor and there was a small marble sculpture of a dragon next to the staircase.

He took me past a cavernous kitchen that was all glossy black marble and shiny stainless steel, into his living room.

Then I did gasp. It was like a football field.

The room stretched to some open French doors, the carpet was thick and silver-grey, with a huge corner-suite in corded black, covered in white cushions.

There was a second staircase on one side with a built-in bookcase underneath, and modern paintings on the walls, all in black and white in silver frames.

'Oh wow,' I looked around in awe. 'This place is amazing.'

'Thanks,' he smiled at me, leading me over to the sofa.

'You're so lucky,' I sat down gingerly and continued gawping.

'Glad you approve,' he bent down and kissed my forehead. 'I just need to disappear to the kitchen. Do you want a drink? Juice? Water?'

'Juice is fine,' I told him. 'Can I look outside?'

'Sure, feel free to roam,' he stroked my head and went back out through the door and I jumped up to prowl around.

I went out the French doors onto a large patio that had a brick barbecue on one side, a big glass table with black wicker chairs, and a fancy clay chimenea. His garden was simply glorious. The lawn was in need of a cut, but it was filled with shrubs and pots spilling over with flowers in an exotic blaze of colour.

I gazed around for a minute, feeling like I was in some fairy-tale story, then went back inside to look at his bookcase.

There were a lot of art books, which didn't interest me, and some new-looking encyclopaedias. I bent down a little and saw he had some Elizabeth Barrett Browning poetry books and some Charles Dickens, all rather careworn.

'Anything you like?' Jaco said from behind me.

'Are these originals?' I asked faintly.

'Some are,' he came and stood next to me. 'My aunt in Ireland had a second-cousin or something that was a collector. Ended up in my parents' house, then ended up here.'

'Wow, lucky you,' I murmured, wanting to pick one up. 'They could be worth a bit.'

'I really don't know,' he placed a hand on my back. 'You surprise me. I thought when you said you like reading, you meant something a little more contemporary.'

'No,' I said vaguely, then turned towards him.

'Are you hungry?' he asked, pulling me back to the sofa where he'd put two glasses of orange juice on a low glass table.

'Yeah,' I sat down and took a sip. 'Um, that's alcohol.'

'Champagne and fresh orange juice, very much more orange juice than champagne, so don't worry,' he smiled and sat down next to me.

'Sneaky,' I smiled up at him, then as his face turned serious, I felt my smile fade.

'Come here,' he put a hand on the back of my neck

88

and kissed me gently.

It suddenly occurred to me that for the first time, we were alone – apart from the night before when I was drunk. I felt a tiny thrill of something that felt like fear.

'I'm gonna go and dish up,' he pulled away and traced a thumb across my jawline and I caught my breath, wondering if it was possible to have an erogenous zone on my jawline.

'OK.'

I watched him leave, then had a little wiggle, wanting to have one of my squeals and jump arounds.

He returned carrying a tray loaded with plates of things I did not recognise.

'You've been busy,' I leaned forward to take a look as he placed his tray on the table.

'Well,' he sat down, 'I'll confess, some were in my freezer, courtesy of my dad.'

'What are these?' I pointed at some little pies.

'Ah, these are *my* speciality, *piroshki*, beef and rice… here, try one,' he picked one up and put it in a napkin.

I took a tiny bite, 'Nice,' I nodded.

'This is Russian salad, kind of like potato salad,' he pointed to a blue bowl. 'And Russian blini, salmon and caviar.'

'Fancy,' I beamed.

'These are *pelmeni,* dumplings. My dad makes them all the time.'

'You've gone to so much trouble,' I tried one of the dumplings. 'Oh my God, why are there no Russian restaurants around here? These are delicious.'

He reached over and picked up a remote control and

some music came on low, 'Nothing is too much trouble for you,' he spooned some rice onto a plate and started to eat.

'I'm not much of a cook,' I confessed. 'I live on salad and anything I can put in the microwave.'

We finished eating and Jaco took the tray back out, returning with two more glasses of champagne and orange juice.

'Thank you, I'm so full up,' I snuggled back into the sofa.

'You are very welcome, sweetheart,' he sat down close to me and rested his head on mine. 'You know, I was so paranoid I'd blown it earlier, not replying to your text, then my phone dying on me.'

'Really?'

'Yeah,' he took my hand. 'We seem to be fighting the odds... and it's all my fault. I'm gonna try so hard with you.'

Not knowing how to respond, I looked down at his suntanned fingers caressing my hand.

'You really are very beautiful and very special,' he muttered.

'Thank you,' I whispered, feeling those frantic butterflies taking off in my stomach.

'I expect you're used to men saying that.'

'No,' I tried to pull away, but he wrapped his arm around me. 'Don't be daft.'

'You make me daft.'

Suddenly he lifted my chin and began to kiss me, more earnestly than he had before. I kissed him back, letting my free hand stray to his thigh.

'You,' he muttered. 'Sorry… can I take you to bed?'

I didn't answer but he stood up and pulled me to my feet, his hand sliding underneath my dress onto my bum.

The next thing I knew, he was leading me up the staircase and into his bedroom and undressing me, which didn't take long as I was only wearing a thong underneath my dress.

'You… are… so… beautiful,' he breathed, kissing me and stripping one-handed, rather clumsily.

I was only vaguely aware of his bed behind me and the fluffy carpet under my bare feet and our breathing.

As he pushed me gently onto the bed, I fleetingly begun to worry about the ugly scar that ran from my groin to my hip bone, then all was forgotten as he started to kiss my neck slowly down to my breasts, all the time murmuring endearments, some in Russian, which sounded so much more romantic.

When he finally entered me, I was almost begging for him, biting my lip and arching frantically towards him.

'That's my girl,' he whispered, his warm breath on my neck.

I kept my eyes open, almost more turned on by the sight of his dark-blue eyes, rapt and almost pained, his black hair falling over his forehead and his curved mouth. He looked so gorgeous, like some sort of fantasy.

When it was over, he gripped me hard, then rolled us over onto our sides so we were facing each other. For a while he didn't say a word, he just gazed at me, his hand tangled in my hair.

'You OK?' he murmured eventually.

I nodded and smiled, not having words to express how *OK* I was feeling right then.

'Good,' he smiled a little wistfully and a sigh escaped him. 'I wasn't planning that…I couldn't help it.'

'I didn't fight you off, did I now?' I whispered.

'No,' he kissed my forehead and his hand left my hair and sought my hand. 'I don't want to fuck this up.'

'Why will you?' I stretched my neck up and kissed him.

'You know, that's the first time that *you've* kissed *me*? I was worried maybe,' he sighed again, 'maybe you weren't feeling it… that I was into you more than you were into me.'

'Really?' I burst out in disbelief. 'I fancied you the moment I saw you.'

'Did you?' he smiled his usual big smile and seemed to relax. 'Here, wriggle up, let's get comfortable,' he sat up and plumped up the pillows then stretched his arm out for me to cuddle up to him. 'I like you naked,' he said playfully. 'It's even better than I imagined.'

'Well, thank you,' I giggled, stroking his chest. 'Perhaps we should just stay naked.'

'I'm fully on board with that,' he said seriously. 'Who needs to work? Let's just stay here.'

'I wish.'

'Roxy?'

'Hmm?'

'Sorry sweetheart, but what's this?' he reached down and traced my scar, his face concerned.

'I was hoping you wouldn't notice it,' I closed my

eyes, not wanting to see any repulsion in his face. 'I shattered my pelvis. It was… pretty bad. I had an operation.'

'Jesus,' he kissed my forehead again, then my lips. 'You poor baby. How?'

'In a car accident when I was fourteen,' I hesitated. 'I don't really remember it, just as well, I had to be cut out the car, that would have been terrifying.'

'Was anyone else hurt?' he stroked my hip gently.

'No - well my dad was a little. He was driving. He just had bad bruising. The other car was OK… I mean the people in it. The car was a write-off. It was the other drivers' fault, he was speeding.'

'You poor, brave baby,' he sounded genuinely upset and I opened my eyes again to look at him.

'I'm fine now,' I kissed his neck. 'I mean, it hurts sometimes, my pelvis. I can't run much – I used to run. But I'm fine. The worse thing is, my mum won't forgive my dad, even though it wasn't his fault. Makes it kind of awkward, but she doesn't really have to have much to do with him now me and my sister are older.'

'Protecting her cubs.'

'Yeah, I guess. I have pretty bad scars on my back too,' I said suddenly, wanting to get the worst out the way.

'Baby,' he murmured. 'Can I see?'

'I'd rather you not, but better now than later,' I sighed, then flipped over onto my front.

'Firstly,' he said eventually as I cringed, 'you have simply the sexiest bum I have ever seen. Secondly… sweetheart, they are not that bad. Probably not as bad as what you think they are.'

93

'They're ugly,' I muttered into the pillow, feeling my face colour with shame. 'I hate them. I haven't even looked at them for years.'

'Well, come on, let's look at them,' he stroked my back.

'What?'

'Up you get,' he tugged my arm. 'I don't want you to be sad about something so small.'

I rolled back over and stared at him in alarm as he stood up.

'Here,' he held out his hand and I reluctantly clambered off the bed.

'I know what they look like,' I said in a small voice.

He pulled me over to the full-length mirror on his closet and turned me around.

Feeling self-conscious as I was completely naked, I twisted my neck around and looked.

The largest scar, which is white and shiny, runs from more or less bang in the middle of my shoulder blades, down to the right side. Then there is a collection of smaller ones, like someone has slashed me repeatedly with a knife across my lower back.

'Ugly,' I muttered.

'Beautiful,' Jaco said firmly. 'They are *just* scars. You are beautiful.'

I looked up at him, uncertainty filling me. He pulled me back over to the bed and we sat down.

'Silly you,' he said, softly kissing my shoulder. 'I can honestly say that you are the most beautiful, sexiest, adorable girl I have ever met. Scars and all. Has anyone… a boyfriend… ever said anything mean about them?'

'No,' I hung my head. 'Nobody has seen them.'

'How is that?'

'Well,' I paused, feeling awkward. 'I've hidden them… like… oh God… sex in the dark, kept them covered up.'

'Right,' he nodded slowly. 'Shit, I hate the thought of you being with someone else,' he laughed dryly. 'Well, you don't have to hide anything from me, I promise you.'

I nodded and felt my eyes fill with tears, then felt stupid.

'I need to pee,' he said eventually. 'Don't go anywhere.'

I watched him leave, thinking what a nice body he had and admiring the large tattoo of a cross on his back, then scooted back up the bed, hugging the duvet to me.

Looking around the room, I once again felt impressed. All the furniture - the bedside tables, the big dresser and the built-in wardrobe doors, were a glossy white. The carpet was dark-grey and luxuriously thick, and the walls painted white. I gazed at the painting above his bed, depicting a naked couple, the man looking suspiciously like Jaco and the woman with flaming red hair.

I hazily began to re-live the last few hours, excitement bubbling up at the potential relationship between us. I truly had never felt so deliriously happy about *any* relationship with *any* man… and nobody I had been with was as glamorous or as rich as Jaco… *not* that money or status should come into it – but I was strangely turned on by it all.

Every man I had been with had been nice-looking with a good body - Jaco just seemed on a whole other level.

As he came back into the bedroom, I wiped the smile off my face from my thoughts and threw the duvet back.

'Hello,' he laid down next to me and gathered me up in his arms.

'Hi,' I melted against him and started to stroke his stomach, my fingers straying down to his thigh, teasingly running my nails up and down.

'Baby,' he groaned. 'Come here.'

As he started to kiss me in earnest, I let my hand wander to his penis and delighted in his shuddering sigh.

'You… are…perfect,' he groaned, biting his lip and staring up at me. 'My beautiful baby.'

It was starting to grow dark.

We had both half-dozed off together in that wonderful post-coital bliss, him spooning me. I didn't care that he could probably see the tops of my hideous scars and I didn't care that my hair was probably a mess (he was a bit of a hair-grabber; I found this a massive turn-on), I didn't care about anything right then – just his body close to mine and his slow breathing against me.

I knew I was falling in love.

'Turn around,' he suddenly commanded, his voice husky. 'I want to see your face.'

I rolled over to face him, 'Hi.'

'Hi,' he smiled sleepily.

I was becoming wide awake again and finding it hard to both lay still and remain silent.

'Where's your bathroom?'

'There's one next door.'

'You have more than one?'

'Yes, I have more than one,' he chuckled, his eyes full of affection.

'How many bedrooms have you got?'

'Three and a bit.'

'How can you have three and a bit?'

'One's so small I use it as a store cupboard more than anything... sweetheart, go and use the bathroom.'

I staggered out of his bed, my legs weak and with a dull pain deep in my pelvis that I knew was going to get worse.

His bathroom was *ginormous*, all cream-tiles and glossy marble, the sink set in a counter with a mirror stretching wall to wall. I almost squealed - it was *exactly* the sort of bathroom I would have loved to own.

I peed, wriggling to hurry it up, then washed my hands, staring at my dishevelled appearance.

I tidied my hair and rinsed out a glass that was sat on the side and drank some water.

Noticing the double cupboard underneath, I opened it cautiously to see if there were any painkillers. I crouched down to peer in; there wasn't much in there - an electric toothbrush, a few bottles of aftershave and some deodorant, weirdly, a credit card, and a couple of boxes at the back. I picked them up and examined the labels.

One was Tramadol, one was a plain white box, the

third was aspirin. Thinking aspirin was better than nothing, I popped a couple out and swallowed them.

'Your bathroom is a dream,' I told him when I returned.

'Come back,' he threw the duvet off and I scuttled over, noticing he had opened the blinds a little and opened the window up wide.

I cuddled up to him and we were silent for a while, him stroking my back lightly.

'Is that painting you?' I stretched my neck up slightly to look at the painting above his bed.

'Nope.'

'He looks a bit like you. Is it from your gallery?'

'It was a gift actually,' he said. 'From Evie, after her first exhibition.'

'Oh,' at the mention of her name, I felt a small drop in my happiness bubble. 'Are you two friends?'

'I wouldn't say *friends* precisely.'

'Only…because she was at your party, and then you had to sort her out when she was pulled over.'

'Sweetheart, are you jealous?' he pulled away and looked at me, his face full of amusement.

'Oh, no,' I shook my head slightly. 'I mean, Teddy is my friend and there's nothing going on with us -'

'Good,' he kissed my nose. 'I don't want you ever to feel jealous, I'm all yours. Evie is tricky but she makes me a lot of money, so I keep her sweet. She's a bit of a strange one, not many friends.'

'I got the feeling she doesn't like me.'

'Like I said, she's tricky.'

'OK.'

'She doesn't seem to like anyone, including me

sometimes,' he chuckled. 'It's just her way.'

I mulled it over, then dismissed it. I didn't want her to dent my new-found happiness.

'You're very brown,' I admired his chest and stomach. 'No tan lines.'

'Naked sunbathing,' he said seriously.

'Really?'

'I'll show you something,' he disentangled himself from me and got up, then pulled on his shorts. 'Follow me.'

Puzzled, I pulled my dress on, and unable to locate my thong, I followed him downstairs.

He took me outside and waved his arm around, 'Look, nobody can see us.'

I gazed around and saw that he was not overlooked at all. Both sides of the garden had tall trees and hedges, and all that was visible over the conifer trees at the bottom of his garden were more trees.

'So… you actually wander around naked?' I asked, not sure if he was pulling my leg or not.

'Well, I try and stay on the patio, or Mr and Mrs Leighton-Bailey might get a treat.'

'They sound posh.'

'Oh very,' he agreed. Then he calmly removed his shorts and sat on a chair. 'Over here, baby.'

As I straddled him, feeling the thrill again of such a man wanting me, I was absolutely sure that I wanted nothing more than to be Mrs Sokolov and have this beautiful man and this beautiful house as my very own.

CHAPTER NINE

On Monday evening, Jaco made a picnic and we drove to the countryside and made love in the long grass. On Tuesday he stayed over-night at my flat, we ordered a Chinese takeaway and ate with chopsticks and talked until the early hours, in between having heavenly sex. On Wednesday we went back to the French restaurant where he had first taken me, and I stayed at his house.

By Thursday I was not only exhausted, but I was feeling guilty for not going to the gym all week. I spent another wonderful night at his house, sharing a pizza in the garden and then showering together before having vigorous sex in his bedroom, the living room and against the American fridge in the kitchen.

I was absolutely *blinded* by love. I couldn't believe that this perfect, rich and sexy man had come into my life. Of course, I was trying to play it cool, but I felt on the edge of obsession.

More than anything, I wanted to know how he felt, but I wasn't going to push for that kind of conversation.

Go with the flow, I kept telling myself, but I knew if this was just a fling, and he decided to move on, I would be gutted to the core.

I had planned to go out with Dana on Friday and reluctantly told Jaco that I wouldn't be seeing him.

'Baby, it's fine,' he kissed my hand and smiled at me.

We were laying on his sofa, both semi-naked and half-heartedly watching a movie on Netflix.

'I'd rather be seeing you,' I confessed.

'Perhaps I need a night off,' he teased. 'You are wearing me out.'

'No stamina,' I kissed his throat and bit him playfully.

'Ow, you animal,' he lightly slapped my bum. 'Where are you going?'

'Cocos,' I told him. 'They are having an Ibiza Club Classics night.'

Cocos was a bar in town that was the epitome of kitsch, but I liked it.

'Sounds fun. What do you want to do on Saturday then?'

'Crap!' I smacked my forehead. 'I'm looking after my little brother; I can't really get out of it.'

'Crap indeed,' he stroked my hair for a moment. 'I could keep you company.'

'Really?' I pulled my head back a fraction to look at him. 'You sure? It'll be jolly boring.'

'It's better than not seeing you, *again*.'

'Well, OK,' I smiled uncertainly. 'Only if you want to.'

'I want to.'

My Friday night out with Dana was a lot of fun, despite missing Jaco like mad.

She came to mine to get ready – I always thought that half the fun of going out was the getting ready part.

She turned up in her pyjamas, her hair in a towel,

with a bottle of wine and some pick-n-mix sweets.

An hour later, we walked into town to meet some of our friends, slightly slowed down by her four-inch heels that made her tower over me even more.

She looked gorgeous and fierce in her black hot pants, making her legs seem endless and what I can only describe as a gold, tasselled bra.

I'd settled for my white denim shorts and white Nike Air Max trainers, which meant my feet would bake but at least they wouldn't hurt by the end of the evening. Plus, I knew I'd want to dance most of the evening and wearing heels would make my pelvis ache the next day.

It was nearly half-eleven and I was feeling hyper. After a couple of cocktails, I'd gone onto bottles of water, and had been dancing almost non-stop.

Our friend Freya had said she had to leave before midnight as she had work at six; she was going to share a taxi with our other friend Ali, as they lived nearby to each other. Dana, who had finally removed her killer heels, was crashing at mine and wanted to leave soon too.

Grudgingly, I went and sat down to catch my breath and finish my water.

'Hey, Rox,' Dana spoke in my ear. 'Don't look, but that guy's been staring at you for the last half an hour.'

'Not interested,' I said loftily. 'Where?' I *wasn't* interested in the slightest, just nosy.

'By the bar,' she looked around. 'Where are my shoes? For crying out loud… I thought he was watching the dance floor, but he watched you all the way back to the table. Dark bloke, white T-shirt, on his own at the end of the bar.'

I sat up straight and swiped my hair off of my face, casually looking over.

'I think I know him,' I muttered as he looked away and then stood up and walked towards the doors. I stared into space for a second then shook my head. 'Oh well... oh, here's one shoe.'

When we got outside and fought our way through the throng of people outside who were laughing, shrieking and smoking, I glanced across the road to the pub opposite and there was the man in the white T-shirt on his mobile phone; I was pretty sure it was Billy, the man who had picked me up to take me to the gallery.

I frowned to myself, not sure enough to go and say hello but wondering why *he* hadn't said hello to me.

Of course, if it was him, I thought, he might not have been sure that it was me... I stared for a minute, then he looked over and turned on his heel, pushing open the pub doors.

Shoving it out of my mind, I turned back to my friends to say our goodnights, before walking back to my flat with Dana, her complaining all the way that her feet were killing her.

In my lunch break the next day, I rang Jaco to see if he still wanted to come with me to watch Jacob, convinced that he would have changed his mind.

'Of course I do, I missed you last night. Did you have a lovely time?' he asked, sounding happy.

'I did,' I said. 'What did you do?'

'Not much, stayed late at the gallery, had a late

dinner and drink.'

'What are you up to now?'

'Well, I've just finished vacuuming,' I smiled at the thought of him doing something so domesticated, 'and then I'm going to pick up some groceries, then I'm popping into the gallery, *then* I'm all yours, sweetheart.'

We arranged for him to come over to mine later and one of us would drive us to my mums'.

Howard was dressed in his best suit and sitting on the decking with a glass of red wine when we arrived. I introduced Jaco, they shook hands and then began to discuss Jaco's gallery, Howard being his usual polite and gentlemanly self and asking all the right questions.

'Your mum's nearly ready,' he told me. 'She's having a hair crisis of some sort.'

I settled myself on a chair, contentedly watching Jaco chatting to Howard. They had now moved on to gardening after Jaco had complimented Howards pride and joy: his lawn.

When my mum finally clattered out, looking glamourous in a red knee-length dress and matching open-toed high heels, Jaco stood up and held out a hand.

'Hello,' he grinned boyishly at her.

'Hello,' she smiled, giving him an admiring look, then demurely placing a hand on her chest. 'Sorry to keep you waiting, I'm Sandra, how nice to meet you.'

'We are late, dear,' Howard shook his head and winked at me, seemingly amused by my mum's flirtatious tone.

'Yes, yes,' she said distractedly. 'Roxy darling, the beast is upstairs sulking. He hasn't eaten and we've left some cash on the side to order a takeaway. He's only allowed to play his PlayStation downstairs under supervision, and I want him in bed before midnight. If you're watching a film, nothing too violent, please.'

'Sure,' I kissed her cheek. 'You look nice, by the way.'

'You sure do,' Howard agreed, groaning slightly as he rose.

'Thank you,' she beamed at Jaco as if he had complimented her.

I giggled a little as they left, waving to them as they backed out in Howard's Volvo Estate.

'I think my mum is a little taken with you.'

'They seem nice,' Jaco said as we walked back round to the garden.

'Yeah, they're alright.'

'So… will *the beast* come down, or do we get some privacy?'

'Hm, he'll probably be a pain in the arse,' I muttered. 'Anyway, I need to feed him.'

'Shame,' he placed a hand on the back of my bare leg. 'Anything to drink around here?'

'Yup, Howard always has beer,' I led him into the kitchen. 'He never drinks it, just gets it in for visitors.'

'Nice kitchen,' Jaco looked around. 'What do they do? For a living I mean?'

'Howard teaches history at the college – Becks or Bud? – my mum's a doctor's receptionist.'

'Really? My mum teaches music there, bet they know each other, Katherine Sokolov.'

'No way!' I held out two bottles.

'Buds, sweetheart.'

'Small world, I guess. Dana's always saying us Fernberry folk are all interbred, it's so tiny,' I giggled.

'Well, we moved from London, but yeah,' he took his beer and I went to the cutlery drawer to find a bottle opener. 'Bumpkin town.'

'Hey,' I slapped his arm lightly.

'Sorry,' he grinned, looking unrepentant.

'Hmm,' I put my nose in the air. 'I'm gonna call Jacob.'

I left Jaco in the kitchen and went out to the hall, 'Knobhead,' I yelled. 'What do you want to eat?'

Jacob appeared at the top of the stairs, looking sulky, dressed in his combat shorts and Naruto T-shirt, 'Oh, I am allowed to eat, then?'

'Aw, are we Moody Mcmoody?' I smiled brightly and he stuck his middle finger up. 'Come down if you want food.'

Jaco wasn't in the kitchen. I found him in the living room looking at some family photos on the sideboard, 'You were very, very cute,' he said, smirking. 'Is this your sister?'

'Yeah, Shauna,' I walked over, feeling embarrassed.

'How old were you there?' he held out a framed photo of me in a tracksuit, a medal around my neck.

'Fourteen, that was just before the car crash.'

'Is it wrong that I think you were a little bit sexy?'

'Er, a bit.'

'Joking, joking,' he put it back and picked up another. 'Is this you?'

'No, that's Shauna's baby, Emilie.'

'Sweet,' he murmured. 'Good looking family, you lot.'

'Thanks,' I put my arms around his waist from behind.

'Alright?' Jacob had slunk in, still looking sulky.

'Jaco, meet Jacob, abuser of dogs faces, the little shit.'

'Nice work, my man,' Jaco swung around. 'I couldn't stop laughing.'

'Don't encourage him,' I sighed as Jacob seemed to thaw out a little.

'Mum went apeshit,' Jacob grinned and threw himself on the sofa. 'I want pizza, by the way,' he directed at me. 'Can I have a beer?'

'Absolutely not,' I put my hands on my hips. 'You better bloody behave tonight, or else.'

Of course, this threat didn't exactly strike fear into his heart as he was a good few inches taller than me and probably nearly thirty pounds heavier.

'Is that your Porsche outside?' he asked Jaco.

'It sure is,' Jaco nodded. 'Wanna go and have a look?'

Men, I thought as they went outside. I turned on the television and looked to see what films were on.

Five minutes later I heard an engine revving and went to the window; Jaco's Porsche was backing out the drive.

I was on my second beer when they both reappeared, Jacob gazing at Jaco looking starstruck.

'So cool,' he said in awed tones. 'I'm gonna buy one when I'm rich.'

'No hope then,' I muttered.

'Oh, be quiet, retail worker and order my pizza,' he gave me a cocky grin.

'You want to make a sandwich and piss off back to your shit tip of a bedroom?'

'Nope,' he continued to grin. 'You'll be sorry when I'm a famous scientist.'

He was, in fact, very clever but I refused to acknowledge that, 'You'll still be a loser.'

'Just because you have spaco disease,' he flapped his hands and made *squeee* noises, then stuck his tongue out.

I gave him a dirty look then got up and went to the kitchen to find a menu, my face colouring.

'He wants pepperoni,' Jaco said from behind me.

'What do you fancy?' I asked.

'*Spaco disease?*' he put a hand on my back, and I blinked miserably at the menu.

'I have ADHD,' I muttered.

'You do?' he said gently. 'You never said.'

'No,' I shrugged.

'Kind of makes sense,' he said thoughtfully.

'Eh?' I swung around.

'Sweetheart,' he kissed my forehead, 'you are a little… *squee.*'

'Excuse me?' I pulled away, feeling affronted.

'No, no, no,' he chuckled. 'You are a little… excitable… I like it. No… I *love* it.'

'I am? You do?' I started to smile, feeling my heart melt.

'Oh yes,' he kissed me lightly. 'I think you are adorable.'

'I should have told you.'

'You know, they thought Sadie had ADHD when we were kids,' he smoothed my hair away from my face. 'Turned out she was just a little shit.'

I laughed and smiled tentatively at him.

'Don't hide things from me,' he suddenly looked grave. 'I don't care about anything, I just want you as you are, OK?'

I nodded, 'OK.'

'Go on, order food, sweetheart.'

The evening would have been perfect, until a small nudge of doubt crept in.

We started to watch *American Sniper*. I only had half a mind on it, snuggled up to Jaco on the sofa, aware of his hand stroking my leg and his soft breathing.

The pizzas arrived and we sat on the floor around the coffee table, Jacob scoffing his down in record time, then wheedling around me until I said he could play his PlayStation in the dining room as long as he didn't tell my mum and Howard.

I'd already lost my concentration on the film, and kept chatting, until Jaco turned it off and gave me his full attention.

'Do you want to stay at mine or yours tonight?' he asked, his fingers tracing the neckline of my top.

'I don't mind.'

'I really did miss you last night.'

'Good,' I kissed his neck. 'What did you do?'

'Had my sad dinner with Billy,' he teased. 'Drank too many whiskies and went to bed lonely.'

'Billy?' I sat up a little straighter.

'Yeah, Billy. The guy that picked you up,

remember?'

'Yeah, I remember,' I murmured, my mind racing, not sure whether to mention that I thought I saw him the night before.

I fell into silence, disquiet trickling through me, then tried to dismiss it. Jaco had no reason to lie.

'What's up?' he asked, frowning at me.

'Nothing,' I smiled, then jumped as my phone rang. 'Hello?'

'Um, are you going to check your emails, my dear?' Teddy said.

'Oh,' I sat up abruptly. 'The play!'

'Yes, the play, dippy,' he chuckled. 'I got Gordon, by the way.'

'Of course you did,' I said warmly. 'I'll check now, ring you back.'

'Everything OK?' Jaco asked.

'Yeah,' I muttered distractedly as I opened my emails on my phone. 'I totally forgot… the parts were announced for the play today.'

I saw Duncan's email straight away in my inbox and hesitated before I opened it.

'Hello Roxy,' it read, *'I'm happy to tell you that your audition for the part of Milly was successful,'* I squealed, *'and we will be doing our read-through tomorrow at 7pm.'*

'I take it you got the part?'

'I got the part,' I crowed. 'I need to ring Teddy back.'

'Excuse me,' Jaco got up and went out the room, presumably to the toilet.

'I got it!' I almost yelled.

'Well done, honey,' Teddy sounded as pleased as can be for me. 'You working tomorrow?'

'Yes,' I said glumly.

'OK, come over to mine when you're home, I'll drive us.'

'Sure,' I said happily. 'See you tomorrow.'

I re-read my email and grinned to myself.

'Alright?' Jaco returned. 'Congratulations, sweetheart.'

'Thanks,' I watched him, suddenly feeling a little on edge. He had an odd expression on his face that I couldn't read.

'So, what happens next?'

'We do a read-through with our writer and director, then organise rehearsals.'

'How often are they?'

'Usually two evenings a week, probably a few extras the week before, and for costume fittings and stuff.'

'Right,' he settled back and held out an arm for me to get comfortable again. 'I hope you can still fit me in.'

'Don't be silly,' I wriggled closer and put a hand on his stomach - he had a real sensitive spot just below his navel that made him shiver if I stroked it.

'Sorry,' he kissed the top of my head and fell silent for a moment. 'Roxy... look at me a minute.'

I pulled away and looked at him, an unreasonable sense of dread rising, 'What?'

'OK,' he chewed his lip. 'OK... this might not be the right time to say this, but I need to say something.'

'OK,' I said, my heart beginning to pound horribly.

'OK,' he let out a breath. 'Roxy... I love you.'

'What?' I burst out, my hands flying to my face.

'Oh dear,' he gave a twisted smile and blinked a few times. 'Not the response I was hoping for.'

'No!' I said in a high-pitched voice, then threw my arms around his neck. 'Oh, I love you too.'

'You do?'

'Yes!' I yelled, then lowered my voice. 'Yes.'

'Why are you shouting?' Jacob called from the dining room - I had completely forgotten about him.

We gazed at each other, then both started laughing.

'Oh sweetheart,' Jaco kissed me hard. 'How can anybody *not* love you?'

CHAPTER TEN

Teddy and I arrived at the theatre the following evening a little early.

As there always was for a read-through or a meeting, a large and battered old table was sat on the middle of the stage with mismatched chairs around it.

Duncan was sat at one end, pages of script in front of him, a notebook and a bottle of water.

Finn was also there, *of course*, sitting back with his ankles crossed. He glanced at his watch as we came through the doors and Teddy said '*ball sack*' quite loudly and audibly.

'Hey guys,' Duncan put a hand up in greeting.

We sat down as far away as possible from Finn, and Teddy promptly got out his phone and started scrolling through Facebook.

'I've just filled up the kettle if you want a drink,' Duncan said.

'Hello lovies,' Crystal came through the doors, wearing a too-tight pink dress, her perfume hitting my nose way before she got near the stage.

'Help,' Teddy whispered.

She sat down next to Teddy, shuffling her chair very close, 'How are you, boys and Roxy?'

I tried not to laugh as she patted Teddy's leg, then leaned over him to talk to me, her huge breasts sitting comfortably on the table in front of him.

One by one, the members drifted in and slowly the

volume of voices rose. Violet had brought a tin of squashy butterfly cakes and people were soon disappearing to the kitchen to make tea.

It was nearly half-past seven when Duncan, who had been sitting looking around and cheerfully greeting people, cleared his throat loudly. Finn immediately sat up very straight and smoothed back his ridiculous floppy hair.

'Everyone finished getting drinks or need the lavatory?' he called out. 'No? OK, shall we begin?'

Everyone murmured assent.

'OK then,' he beamed and pulled his notes towards him. 'The Murder of Miss Mabel... we are set in the 1940s, after some deliberation,' he shot Pontus a small look, 'in the mansion of the lady of the title.'

Pontus folded his arms and continued to stare at Duncan.

'Uh oh,' whispered Francesca, a very beautiful and willowy girl that was the local secondary school's gym teacher, 'lovers tiff?'

'So... we have Violet as our short-lived star,' Duncan winked at her, 'as she gets bumped off pretty quick... Bob as her husband-to-be, Mr Graves. Roxy will be playing her niece, Milly, and Mr Graves three sons, Teddy, Jamie and Stuart as Gordon, James and William. The two wives are Francesca and Samantha,' he paused for a moment. 'Finn is playing the much-lusted after Benedict,' Finn smirked, 'Destiny as Sylvia, Miss Jessop the cook, Lola... Lizzy and Kate the maids are Meadow and Lily-Rose, Nathan as the gardener, Crystal as Flora White. Jeremy will be playing the doctor -' Teddy gave a fake shiver and grinned at me as I covered a giggle – Jeremy Finkle was as creepy as hell and Teddy had a theory that he was a secret serial killer – 'then finally our inspector and policeman, John and Derek.'

Pontus looked down the table, 'Opening night is October the thirty-first – Halloween – and we will be running for one week, one performance an evening. Any questions? OK, rehearsals as always will be twice a week, commencing next week. I'm aiming for Mondays and Thursdays unless there is a problem with anyone.'

'No,' said Finn, and Teddy aimed a finger at him and started making *pew-pew* noises.

'Jolly good,' Pontus nodded his large head and stretched his back groaning, before standing up. 'I'll give you the costume list Violet,' he continued. 'And Finn, chat later about advertising.'

'Right, act one, scene one people,' Duncan waved his script. 'We begin with Miss Mabel and Milly preparing for the dinner party to discuss wedding plans -'

Forty minutes later, my head was hurting from forced concentration. After a while Duncan's voice became rather monotonous and along with the warm air and sitting still, I was struggling.

I was very excited though, the only drawback being that in the last scene I had to kiss Finn, declaring my love for Benedict before he was carted off by the inspector.

'I auditioned for Milly too, you lucky girl,' Francesca sighed, gazing at Finn.

'Did you?' I asked in amazement, wondering why

she didn't get it and whether I should say sorry.

'I didn't think I'd get it,' she tore her gaze away and smiled at me. 'I don't look young enough.'

'Olivia's a great part though,' I said, thinking she *did* look young enough; she was only twenty-nine.

'Oh yeah,' she agreed. 'I love working off of Teddy, he's so funny.'

'Least you don't have to kiss me,' Teddy piped up from my right. 'Darling, I have a headache tonight,' he said in a camp voice and Francesca giggled.

'Be thankful you don't have to kiss Finn,' I muttered.

It was getting late by the time we had all tidied up and washed out our mugs. A few members decided to slope off to the pub for a quick drink, but I decided to go home and try and get some sleep.

'I'll come with you,' Teddy said, giving Crystal a wide berth as we walked out.

As soon as I got in, I had a shower and called Jaco as I said I would.

'Baby, how did it go?' he sounded in a good mood and rather hyper.

'Yeah, OK,' I switched on the kettle. 'Just went through the script and arranged rehearsals.'

'When will they be?'

'Mondays and Thursdays.'

'As in tomorrow?'

'Yeah.'

'I wanted to see you tomorrow,' he sounded irritable now, and I bit my lip.

'Why don't you come over now?' I asked trying to be placating - I would have happily given up my planned early night.

'I can't, I'm in the middle of sorting something out.'

'Oh?'

'Yeah, Evie is renting the flat above the gallery for a few weeks, me and Billy are just having a tidy up.'

'Oh, right,' at the mention of her name, I felt my mood drop. 'How come?'

'She's written her car off,' he said. 'Easier for a bit.'

'I see,' I said lightly, not really seeing at all. 'OK, well I'll be done by nine tomorrow, possibly earlier… if you want to do something?'

'I'll let you know,' he said. 'I've got to go, sweetheart. I'll call you tomorrow.'

'Yeah, OK,' I said, feeling like I'd done something wrong.

'Bye for now.'

'Bye.'

I stared at my screen for ages, trying to work out what had just happened, and whether I was being paranoid and too sensitive.

But whichever way I looked at it, the fact was that the night before he had told me he loved me for the first time. And just then, he had sounded undeniably frosty.

I finished making my tea, then went and laid on my bed, not feeling tired at all. It was no good, I had to speak to someone.

I looked at the time, it was nearly ten and I didn't want to bother Dana as she got up early in the week to commute to London to her job as a legal secretary in the City Centre.

I made sure my pyjama top wasn't too see-through,

then went and knocked cautiously on Teddy's door.

'Oh, hi,' he looked startled. 'Everything OK, honey?'

'Can I bend your ear?' I asked timidly.

'Come on, get your bum in,' he stood back, shaking his head with his sweet smile.

I got into bed around midnight, feeling decidedly better.

Teddy had told me not to be a 'bobble-hat' and that I was being way too sensitive. And *if* Jaco *was* sulking, he was a bobble-hat too and not to feed into it.

He was absolutely right, but as I couldn't really get across how intense my love was for him without sounding like a clingy girlfriend - he didn't know how shattered I would be if it went wrong.

But why would it go wrong? Because I was busy the following night? That was ludicrous.

I knew what was at the crux of my fears though... Evie. Just the mere mention of her put me on guard, and I had no idea why. As I started to think about her, I had that awful premonition of danger again... why? What was it about her?

Bobble-hat, I thought to myself, then smiled. I loved Teddy and his little random phrases and insults, he never failed to cheer me up.

Whoever ended up with him was a lucky girl for sure, *that* I was sure of.

Jaco rang me in my lunchbreak the next day and sounded his normal self, then mid-afternoon a huge bouquet of flowers turned up for me, the card reading 'Roxy, my beautiful super-star, well done getting your part', and then I couldn't concentrate for the rest of the day.

He had told me he would try and swing by later in the evening but wasn't sure if he could. I *really* wanted to see him but felt happier that there wasn't any kind of issue going on.

My light-hearted mood continued all the way until rehearsals, then Finn started getting on my nerves, constantly in Duncan's ear giving his pompous opinion on everything and turning on the charm for Francesca and Meadow, flashing his white teeth and smoothing his T-shirt over his muscular chest and torso.

Violet cheered me up no end however, she at least thought that Finn was a prat too.

I liked working closely with Violet, she was... I think 'fascinating' is a fair description. She was seventy-nine and looked seventy-nine but certainly didn't speak like what *I* expected a seventy-nine-year-old woman to speak like.

Small and grey-haired, you could see the visages of a great beauty underneath her wrinkles and wispy hair in its permanent bun.

For one thing, she could swear like a sailor, which to me was hysterical, hearing her well-placed F-bombs in her slightly upper-class and frail voice.

Also, she had a wicked sense of humour and a seemingly diverse past, but I was never sure if she was winding everybody up.

She claimed to have been a spy in the sixties for the MI6. Now... this was such a *huge* claim, that I could never decide whether it was true... like, who would even lie about that?

She also claimed that she had had an affair with Prince Phillip in the seventies; again, a huge claim.

Never married and childless, she lived in the nearby village of Barkenwell, which said to me that she had money, and told me once that she had a pet African snail called David Tennant and also that she had been kicked out of the villages women's bridge club for hiding a bottle of gin in her knickers.

All of this was told with a completely straight face. So, either she was the biggest liar and/or wind-up merchant *ever*, or she was one in a million. Whichever it was, I loved her dearly and she made the best cakes and cookies that I had ever tasted and was kind to those she liked. Which excluded Finn with brutal hilarity.

I had driven Teddy and I to the theatre, and when I pulled up at our flats in my little Fiat 500, I was delighted to spot Jaco's Porsche parked nearby.

'Cute car,' Jaco said as I climbed out, aware that a big grin was on my face. 'Alright, buddy?' he clamped Teddy on the shoulder.

'Yeah, this is Betty,' I went and kissed him.

'I missed you,' he smoothed my hair back and gave me his sexy up and down look.

'I'll catch you lovebirds later,' Teddy loped off towards the doors. 'I need to eat.'

'Have you eaten?' Jaco asked.

'Yeah, before I came out,' I told him.

'Good,' he took my hand. 'I need to fuck you.'

We went up to my flat, my stomach in excited knots at the prospect of his lovemaking.

He practically dragged me through the door and

started to undress me before we even reached the bedroom.

He seemed impatient and almost frantic, making me feel irresistible.

'My baby,' he muttered, pushing me onto the bed.

I smiled, inching myself backwards and opening my legs, feeling aroused before he had even got to work.

As he entered me, he started to bite my neck, making me squirm with pleasure. Then as he began to shudder, an indication that he was near climax, he bit me so hard, I squealed with pain and tried to sit up.

'Jaco,' I gasped, feeling tears in my eyes.

He bit even harder, then stretched upwards, groaning.

I put my hand up to my neck and was distressed to see blood on my fingers as I put them in front of my face.

'Oh, shit,' he grinned then his face fell as I didn't grin back. 'Oh, I'm so sorry, my angel,' he rolled off and gathered me in his arms.

'That really hurts,' I whispered, despite the pain, I felt silly for the tears.

'Sweetheart, I didn't realise,' he kissed my forehead. 'I got carried away… that's what you do to me,' he shook his head, then kissed me again.

'I need to look at it,' I slid off the bed and went into the bathroom, wincing as I examined the clear toothmarks on the side of my neck. It wasn't bleeding a lot, but the fact it was bleeding at all was telling me how hard he must have bitten me.

'Baby,' he held out his arms as I returned, his expression remorseful.

'It's OK,' I said numbly. 'You didn't mean to hurt

121

me.'

'Oh,' he kissed me and drew away. 'I'd *never* hurt you... Roxy, I'm so sorry.'

'It's fine,' I tried to smile back at him, but it really was hurting, and my face felt stiff. I laid my head on his chest to hide my expression.

'Sweetheart,' he stroked my back gently.

Eventually I dozed off. I woke up just before two in the morning and went to the bathroom to look at my neck again. It had started to bruise.

I crept back into bed and looked at Jaco asleep facing me, his handsome face looking younger and softer in his sleep and in the dim light.

I don't know how long I laid there watching him, but it seemed like a long time. The next thing I knew my alarm was going off and he wasn't there anymore.

I stumbled out of bed into the living room, my head fuzzy, and started in shock to see Jaco sat on the sofa with a mug in his hand.

'Good morning, beautiful,' he stood up and came and put his arms around me. 'Want a cuppa?'

'Yeah,' I hugged him back. 'I need a shower.'

I woke up a little as I stood under the cool water, my mind going back to the night before, my uneasiness full and intense.

'I need to shoot,' Jaco said as I came out wrapped in a towel. 'Your tea's on the side,' he walked over and kissed me, stroking my shoulders. 'See you later?'

'Yes,' I kissed him back.

'I love you, baby,' he said softly, his eyes roving around my face.

'I love you too,' I whispered.

When he left, I went to examine my neck again. The marks had gone but there was an oval-shaped bruise.

I dabbed on some concealer as I got ready for work, deciding it was hardly noticeable after all.

By mid-morning the temperatures were up in the high eighties and I was feeling it.

I had left my hair down, not wanting my bruised neck on display. Even though the two big overhead fans were on at work, I was sweaty and irritable.

I was also getting annoyed with myself, thinking about the night before… I knew that Jaco hadn't meant to hurt me, but when I pondered on it, I realised that he had frightened me a little, and that thought was hanging over me like a dark cloud.

As hot as I was, I decided to spend my lunch hour at the gym, as I hadn't been near there for days. I always had my bag ready in the boot of my car. As I walked to where I was parked, I decided I must be crazy - the heat was baring down oppressively.

I had a ten-minute warm up, then did twenty minutes of weights and another ten of rowing, enjoying the endorphin rush. After a speedy cold shower, I felt a lot better than I had before and was glad I had sacrificed my lunchtime, despite the fact my stomach was rumbling like mad.

With ten-minutes to spare, I went and got myself a coffee and a banana, then sat in the shade outside, stretching my legs out.

'Hey, you,' a male voice came from the direction of the gym entrance.

'Peter!' I exclaimed.

It was my ex-boyfriend of five months ago, amicably ended, but I hadn't seen him since our last goodbye.

'How are you?' he loped over, tall and muscular in his shorts and vest top, looking every inch the gym "meathead" that Dana had used to call him. He was in fact a nice guy... possibly *not* the most fascinating but we had had a good time in our three-month relationship, and he had made me laugh.

'I'm great,' I beamed up at him, genuinely pleased to see him. 'How are you? What you doing at *my* gym?' I teased – we had always had pretend fights over whose gym was better than whose.

'Just picking up a GoPro from a mate,' he patted his bag. 'Mine broke,' he slowly nodded his head. 'I am good, thanks.'

'Still running then?'

'Yup.'

'Cool,' I smiled. 'I need to get back to work... really nice to see you.'

'Yeah, and you,' he fell into step with me as I took my bag back to my car. 'You look great, really great.'

'Thanks,' I gave him a sidelong glance. 'You too.'

He stopped at my car, waiting for me to throw my bag in, then gave me a brief hug, 'See you around, babe.'

'Sure,' I put my hand up and went off towards my store, checking my phone as I went. Jaco had rung at the beginning of my break - I texted him to say I'd gone to the gym and would call him after work.

Back at home after work, I was just heating up a microwave chicken chow mien, when there was a loud knock at my door.

'It's open,' I yelled, thinking it was Teddy.

'Alright?' Jaco's voice behind me made me jump violently.

'Jesus,' I spun round. 'What are you doing here? I was going to ring you after I'd stuffed my face,' as I neared the end of my sentence, I faltered slightly; he looked rather stony. 'What's wrong?'

'As you didn't answer my call earlier, I drove to your work,' he was blinking rapidly. 'Who the hell *was* that, Roxy?'

'W-what?'

'That guy.'

'What guy?' I took a small step back, then my brain clicked. 'Oh… Peter… just a guy I haven't seen for a while… why on earth didn't you come over?'

'You looked busy,' he snapped, his eyes narrowed.

'Jaco,' I said faintly, 'you're scaring me here… I don't understand.'

'No?'

'No!'

'You were all over him,' he said in a dangerously quiet voice and suddenly I felt very fearful.

'No, I wasn't,' I shook my head emphatically. 'It was a goodbye hug, nothing… not whatever it is you are getting at.'

'Right,' he stared at me tight-lipped for a second then sighed, dropping his head.

'Jaco?'

'I'm sorry,' he raised his eyes. 'I got worried…no, I got *scared…* sorry sweetheart.'

'Well,' I said slowly, putting a hand on his chest. 'OK, but don't do that again, please.'

'No, I should have called instead of turning up.'

'Yeah, but not just that,' as I snapped out of my fright, I began to feel angry. 'I meant assume that I'm up to something and get mad about it. Don't you trust me?'

The microwave pinged and I jumped again.

'Yes, of course I do,' he came and put his arms around me, and I stiffened slightly. 'It's everyone else. Look at you.'

'And look at *you,*' I tilted my face up to look at him. 'I love you. I'm not going to do anything… you know, with another guy… you're being stupid.'

'Promise me?'

'Yes!' I exhaled, feeling the anger leaving me – somehow seeing this not so confident side to him made me love him even more.

'I'm a dope,' he kissed me and smiled at last. 'First I savage your neck, and now this.'

'Hmm,' I gave him a solemn look. 'I might have to put you on probation.'

'Yeah? Does that involve anything kinky?'

'Jaco,' I said warningly, then laughed.

'I love you so much,' he kissed me again. 'OK, whatever you've zapped in there smells like shit, get changed, I'm taking you out for dinner.'

CHAPTER ELEVEN

By Thursday nights rehearsals, I was feeling a lot happier again, although… in retrospect I was ignoring warning bells.

Never having experienced a jealous boyfriend before, in my naivety I convinced myself that Jaco's behaviour had been normal. I mean, I didn't think it had been *outrageous* or anything, it just seemed bizarre that he had seen me with Peter and not just come over instead of driving off again. And that evening, although we had gone to lovely little pub in a nearby village and had a meal and a drink and a perfectly nice evening together, underneath his charm and affection, I sensed something… off. Something different.

We had gone back to his house and made love, but then he had seemed restless and overly talkative – usually my problem – and I had just wanted to go to sleep.

I put it down to the impossible heat. Even with the windows wide open, no breeze made itself welcome to cool our naked bodies, and eventually we had got up and sat outside. He also had been complaining about his seasonal hayfever and had a nosebleed which worried me more than him.

We didn't go back upstairs until nearly midnight and he had a quick shower to wash the blood off his chest, coming back looking red-eyed and irritable.

Wednesday had been a completely different story,

however.

We had spent another evening at his, but this time he was happy and relaxed. He cooked us a meal of steak and potato salad, and we sat outside talking and laughing until it started to grow dark, then we had gone to bed and made love slowly and gently, him falling asleep almost instantly. And I had laid, sated but wide awake, watching him sleeping, once again counting my lucky stars that he was mine.

I sat daintily on the edge of a chair, my hands clasped together.

'But Aunt Mabel,' I pouted slightly, looking up at Violet, 'I don't *want* to sit next to Flora.'

'Mrs White, to you,' Violet said. 'And why ever not?'

'She smells funny and,' I consulted my script, 'she makes noises when she eats.'

'Well, that may be true, but it's my dinner party so you will be a good girl and sit where I ask you to. Ah, Benedict,' Finn strode across the stage, 'I've sent Kate and Lizzie home, would you be a darling and help me polish my best cutlery for tomorrow?' Violet stepped a little closer to him.

'My pleasure,' Finn smiled a dazzling smile.

'We can have a glass of wine in the kitchen together,' Violet fluttered her eyelashes. 'It's nice to relax on a Friday after all.'

'I can help,' I forced myself to gaze adoringly at Finn.

'No, no it's fine,' Violet waved her hand at me.

'Brilliant!' Duncan clapped his hands together.

I looked at my watch; it was way past nine o'clock, the time we were supposed to finish at.

I climbed off the stage and stuffed my script into my bag as everyone broke into conversation.

'You coming to the pub?' Teddy ambled over.

'Yeah for a quick one,' I untied my hair and scraped it back up again, a yawn escaping me. I wasn't seeing Jaco as he'd been in London and wasn't sure what time he'd be home – I was a little relieved as I felt a mess.

'Cool beans, you can protect me from Crystal.'

We walked the short distance to a pub across from the theatre, The Swan.

Duncan walked in front with Crystal, Violet and the creepy Jeremy, me and Teddy dawdled behind Samantha, Lola, Francesca and Derek, who was repeatedly blowing his nose and complaining about his sinuses.

'Do you think Mummy rubs Vics on his chest at night?' Teddy imitated his snuffling.

'Shush,' I admonished. 'I like Derek, he's harmless.'

'You think everyone's harmless,' Teddy slung his arm around me. 'The only two things he talks about are Dr Who and what his mum's cooking for tea.'

'So?'

'And he has a face like a Potato Smiley.'

Despite myself I laughed, 'You're mean.'

The pub was relatively empty, I suspected people had favoured the local pubs that had a garden to sit in as it was so hot.

'Drinks are on me,' Duncan rubbed his hands together. 'You all worked hard tonight.'

He went over to the bar with Teddy and Jeremy after

129

taking our orders.

'You did well,' Lola said, smiling as she settled herself next to me. 'I was going to audition for Milly but decided not to.'

'Thanks,' I studied her pale, unpainted face, so much older looking than her twenty-five years. 'You should have.'

'No,' she shook her head. 'It's so much *you*, she's described as 'young and pretty'.'

'And spoilt,' I wrinkled my nose.

'Oh no, I didn't mean -' she began, flushing slightly.

'I know,' I laughed. 'I just hope I don't regret it, it's the biggest part I've had and I'm terrible at learning lines.'

'You'll be great.'

I liked Lola, she was kind of *quaint*, and gave me a reassuring feeling. She dressed a little oddly, belying her twenty-five years, favouring sensible skirts and the sort of jeans I wished my mum would wear, instead of her skinny jeans, and wore her light-brown hair in a bun or held back with an Alice band. She also seemed to relate a lot better to the older female members, Violet, Crystal and Destiny, and shied away from our sometimes silliness at rehearsals.

The men returned with our drinks and I drained half of my orange juice in one gulp.

Yawning again, I watched in amusement as Teddy tried to ignore Crystal on his left and talk to Derek and Duncan, and half-listened to Samantha and Francesca discuss Finn in low voices, interspersed with giggles.

'Honestly girls,' Violet butted in, 'he really is a bit of a cock.'

'Violet!' I laughed as they both looked scandalised.

'He is though, isn't he?' she swirled around her wine glass and took a delicate sip, winking at me.

'He can't act for shit,' Jeremy piped up in his reedy voice.

'Now, now,' Duncan said good-naturedly. 'Let's not bitch.'

Jeremy looked at Duncan for a moment, rubbing his thumb and forefinger together and I shuddered.

Teddy made the high-pitched Psycho knife noise quietly in my ear and I coughed to cover up a giggle.

I started talking to Crystal across Teddy about the play and things in general, noticing that Derek was going red every time Francesca spoke to him.

'Aw, do you think he has a crush?' I murmured.

'No, he likes Meadow, doesn't he?'

'He does?' I said in surprise.

'She'd eat him alive,' Crystal laughed throatily, 'Destiny told me-'

'Oh, here we go,' I rolled my eyes – Destiny the Happy Hippy… everyone's confidante but a terrible gossip.

'Hush, this is good,' Crystal reached over and patted my hand, then left it casually on Teddy's leg, causing him to look at it in alarm, 'she only has one nipple,' she lowered her voice. 'BDSM accident, my darling.'

'Oh, come off it,' I shook my head. 'She's got to have made that up.'

'I reckon it's true, the quiet ones are the worst ones.'

'No worries about you, then,' Teddy bumped my head gently with his.

'Ha, ha,' I slapped his arm.

'But then again, perhaps Derek is a quiet sex animal,' Crystal squeezed Teddy's leg.

'I can't really see it,' I said, glancing at Derek in his sensible short-sleeved shirt and sensible brown shoes. 'What do you reckon?' I nudged Teddy.

'Well, I dunno,' rubbed his chin. 'But frankly I'm scared of Meadow now.'

Meadow was indeed a quiet girl, and the most unlikely candidate to be into anything kinky. Husky-voiced, a liking for floaty, floral-patterned clothes, she was a fierce vegan and made it known, took pottery lessons and done work for animal charities.

As we were laughing uproariously, I glanced up and spotted a dark-haired man putting his head around the door, talking on his mobile phone.

'Billy?' I knew for sure that this time it was him.

'Hey,' he said vaguely, frowning a little.

'Roxy?' I elaborated.

'Ah, shit, yeah,' he grinned, stepping in. 'Sorry, didn't recognise you,' he muttered something into his phone and shoved it in his pocket.

'How are you?' I noticed Teddy looking at me curiously. 'Oh, this is Teddy, he went to school with Jaco, Teddy, Billy works for Jaco.'

'Alright mate?' Teddy grinned.

Billy nodded at him, then looked around the pub frowning again, 'I'm just looking for someone,' he said. 'Must have missed them... never mind... see you around,' he smiled and nodded again and went back out.

'Man of many words,' said Teddy.

Back at home, bathed and laying on my bed trying to cool down, I felt troubled.

Seeing Billy had niggled me, because it had made me sure that it was him that I had seen in Coco's on my girls' night out... which meant that Jaco was lying about being with him that night. And that made me feel slightly sick.

But as I thought about it logically, I realised that Jaco could have said he was with *anyone*, a name I hadn't heard of and I would have accepted it... so why say Billy, especially if Billy frequented Fernberry and there was a chance I could see him?

It was a thin argument to convince myself that I was wrong, but I didn't want to think that Jaco was lying.

But my other unwelcomed thought was why was Billy even in Fernberry? He lived in Loughdon, a town on the other side of Chembury, at least a forty-minute drive from Fernberry.

Anyone with ADHD knows that we are prone to overthinking and obsessing to the point of convincing ourselves that we are right, when in fact we are way off the mark, so with the difficulty of swallowing a dry cracker with no water, I shoved the thought down and tried to switch off, or at least think about something else.

Jaco surprised me at work on Friday, swanning in, all smiles and looking suntanned and handsome, melting my heart and making me forget all of my doubts.

'Hello,' I greeted him, wishing I wasn't so sweaty and scruffy.

'Hi, baby,' he kissed me hard, making me glance

over at Troy my manager, who was nearby.

'I thought I wasn't seeing you until tonight,' I pulled him behind a display of women's polo shirts.

'I'm afraid I'm standing you up,' he stroked my hair and kissed the top of my head.

'Oh?' I hoped my expression didn't betray my disappointment.

'Sorry,' he pulled a face. 'I need to go and see a new artist, *but,*' he paused and pulled me closer, 'tomorrow night, we are going somewhere *very* nice.'

'We are?' I said, then swore under my breath. 'I need to work until eight tomorrow.'

'Can't you swap shifts or something?'

'Not really,' I bit my lip.

'Hm,' he frowned, then his expression cleared. 'OK, this is what we'll do… bring your stuff here, I'll pick you up and take you to the flat to get ready - we need to go there first anyway.'

'How come? Where are we going?' I asked impatiently.

'Oh and bring an over-night bag.'

'Please tell me,' I shook his arm.

'You're not working Sunday, are you?'

'Jaco,' I folded my arms and took a step back.

'OK, OK,' he laughed and pulled me back over. 'Ever been to The Westmill Hotel?'

I fought down a squeal; The Westmill Hotel is an exclusive, luxurious hotel on the outskirts of Chembury, only just visible through huge iron gates and a treelined road. Me and Dana had looked at the wedding packages once just to be nosy, and I'd nearly fainted at the prices.

'No,' I said, starting to fidget from foot to foot.

'Me neither,' he grinned. 'So it'll be a nice first for us, won't it?'

'Oh wow,' I breathed, then I *did* squeal and threw my arms around his neck.

'Aw baby,' he squeezed me, then disentangled himself. '*But*,' he continued, 'boring stuff to do first sweetheart, I've got a buyer viewing some paintings at the gallery first, then we have to have dinner with him and Evie.'

'OK,' I said, my excitement quelled somewhat by the mention of Evie. 'What should I wear?'

'Something sexy, I want you to wow him,' Jaco gave me one of his smouldering looks, his curved mouth lifting.

'I will try.'

I finished work at four and decided to go and see Teddy at his bookstore and ask if he wanted to have dinner, as I was free for the evening.

I was feeling a little guilty, I felt I was neglecting him and Dana since Jaco had come along, although neither of them seemed hacked off at me. And now it was going to be even harder dividing my time with two rehearsals a week, but at least I would be spending time with Teddy.

I made a mental note to ring Dana when I got home and promised myself at least once a week I would get up an hour earlier and go to the gym, as I was neglecting that too – eating out with Jaco so often and not exercising was taking its toll. I'd put on four pounds and I was panicking.

The red-painted wooden door to Teddy's shop was propped open with a little wooden stool, and in the shade of his second-hand book display outside were two plastic bowls filled with water for passing dogs.

It's in the oldest part of the town, cosily named Blossom Lane, a cobbled side-street with a tree-lined square in the centre with benches.

The shop fronts here all have that lovely *olde worlde* look and there's a tavern that in the summer has mismatched tables outside with chess boards and dominos on them.

Two doors up from Teddy is an old-fashioned bakery where Lola worked; Teddy was always bringing home freebies and compromising my fight against no cakes.

I walked in, pushing my sunglasses up on top of my head and smiled at Audrey, his blue-haired assistant.

'Hello, Teddy's in the back,' she greeted me, waving a tattooed arm covered in black bangles towards the back of the shop.

'Hey,' I called as I walked between shelves.

'Hey,' Teddy's head appeared from around a shelf, then Francesca appeared too, clutching some books.

'Hello,' I said in surprise.

'Hi,' Francesca greeted me, looking as hot and bothered as I did in tracksuit bottoms and a polo shirt with her school emblem on, her hair scraped back in a bun. 'Getting me some sunbathing reading,' she waved her books at me. 'I cannot wait until school breaks up next week, it's been hyperactive hell.'

'I bet,' I noticed a large open box on the floor, half unpacked.

'A new batch of second handers,' Teddy said. 'I've put one to one side for you but have a rummage before they go on sale.'

'Ooo, thanks,' I crouched down to have a look.

'OK, well I will shoot off,' Francesca directed at Teddy. 'About eight o'clock?'

'Sure,' Teddy replied.

I watched Francesca walk to the counter, tall and graceful, 'Where are you off to?'

'She asked me out for dinner,' Teddy crouched next to me. 'She's had a crappy day, apparently. I thought, why not… was planning on a lonely pizza and a Netflix binge.'

'Oh right,' I paused in my rummage. 'Exactly what I was about to ask you out for.'

'Aw honey, join us if you want, we're going to El Huerto.'

'Yum, Mexican,' I stood up and stretched my back. 'No, it's OK,' I wasn't sure *why* I was declining because I liked Francesca a lot – but I had an illogical feeling that she wouldn't want me to tag along as it was her that had asked him out.

'Come on,' he looked up at me.

'Nah,' I shook my head. 'I should probably learn some lines anyway and try and get some sleep.'

'OK,' he stood up too. 'If you change your mind, I'm leaving at half-seven. I'll get your book.'

I followed him to the counter where he reached down underneath and then handed me a battered-looking book, 'Rebecca!' I grinned. 'Thank you.'

'I didn't think you'd read it,' he turned to Audrey who was perched on a stool, eyes closed, face an inch from a desk fan. 'You alright to shut up shop?'

'Yeah,' she nodded.

'Can I cadge a lift?' Teddy ushered me out of the shop in front of him. 'You wait, the minute I'm out of sight, she'll be gone,' he muttered.

As it happened, I never did learn any lines *or* get an early night.

I rang Dana as soon as I got home and she was in a steaming bad mood after an argument with Tobias, which surprised me, and came over with a bottle of Prosecco and a Chinese takeaway.

I was glad that the argument wasn't anything particularly serious; it turned out it was a bit of a domestic about him not sharing the household chores and knowing how feisty Dana was, he possibly came out the loser.

The evening was fun, and I realised that I needed to do it more.

Jaco flitted in and out of my thoughts, but there is nothing like an evening with your best friend, being silly and screaming with laughter and putting the world to rights.

As she left, she hugged me then held me at arm's length, 'Babe, great night… you *are* OK though, aren't you?'

'Eh?' I said in surprise. 'Yeah, of course I am.'

'Good,' she smiled her beautiful smile. 'Enjoy your hotel shag tomorrow.'

CHAPTER TWELVE

I had mixed feelings the next day about my evening ahead. I kept having sneaky looks on my phone at the hotel, and the rooms looked amazing - the most expensive ones were like something out of a movie.

But... Evie. Every time I thought about her, I still had that strange inexplicable feeling of ominous dread. I didn't want to get ready at the flat she was living at, albeit her temporary home, and I didn't want to spend an evening with her.

Just grit your teeth and think about the rest of the night in your room with Jaco, I kept telling myself, and had butterflies of excitement fluttering around in my stomach every time I focussed on that.

In my lunch break I went into town and bought a very sexy, *very* revealing black nightie that would hardly cover my bum, complete with suspenders and stockings, and kept picturing Jaco's expression as I drifted out of the bathroom wearing it, ready to seduce him.

I had fifteen minutes of my shift left when Jaco appeared, looking nothing short of breath-taking in an expensive-looking suit, and smelling gorgeous.

'Hi, you ready?' he asked as he approached the counter where I had been serving.

'Not quite,' I looked at my watch, then glanced at Troy who was talking to Kyle nearby.

'Go,' Troy grinned. 'She's been checking the time all afternoon,' he added to Jaco.

'Thank you,' I went and grabbed my bag from the staffroom and hurried back out.

'Have a nice evening,' Troy said as we passed.

'He seems a bit of a cocky sod,' Jaco muttered as we walked out into the sunny carpark.

'Really?' I said, feeling puzzled. 'Nah, he's OK.'

We reached a dark-blue BMW and I looked at him in confusion.

'I'm driver tonight,' he explained. 'We are slumming it.'

'Hardly,' I handed him my bag as he opened the boot and got in the passenger seat. 'Yours?'

'It is indeed. I missed you last night,' he started the engine then leaned over and kissed me before backing out.

'Me too.'

'Good,' he grinned.

'So,' I settled back. 'Who's this guy tonight?'

'Edward Brown,' he chuckled quietly. 'A complete dick but a rich one. Knows sweet fuck all about art, modern or otherwise, but thinks it will impress his new bimbo wife... apparently, she saw some of Evie's work on Instagram and likes it.'

'I see... how comes his wife isn't coming tonight?'

'Well, I gave him a couple of dates that Evie could grace us with her presence and the first one he and bimbo were in Florida. This time bimbo is at their holiday home in Marbella recovering from a boob job and probably shagging the pool boy,' he laughed maliciously. 'She's seriously beautiful but common as

140

shit… mind you, so is he, he only made his pile of money eight years ago but thinks he's royalty.'

'Is it the usual thing for customers to meet the artist?' I asked curiously.

'No, unless there's an exhibition at the gallery. But he asked and I'm delivering, although Evie isn't happy about it. We are going to make a *lot* of money by the sounds of it, so I sweet-talked her.'

'I see,' I muttered, feeling a heavy drop of jealousy. 'How many of her paintings is he buying?'

'Not sure, at least half a dozen. I've had Billy painting the back wall in the gallery and hanging twenty-five of them for him to view… who knows?'

He put his foot down as we reached the dual carriageway and I stiffened a little.

'Sorry, sweetheart,' he slowed down a little and patted my leg; he knew I was a nervous passenger.

'I hope my dress is OK,' I began to feel nervous. 'Can I have a shower at the flat?'

'Sure you can, and I'm sure your dress is fine, you always look beautiful.'

The flat door was wide open when we got there, and loud rock music was playing from inside.

'Turn that shit down,' Jaco yelled, leading me in with one hand and carrying my bag with the other.

The hall looked as worn and bleak as I remembered it. I glanced in the kitchen as we passed; it was pretty basic without the crowds of people in there with white cupboards and beige tiles, and an unused look.

Evie appeared in the living-room doorway, cigarette in her hand, dressed in a tight black pencil skirt and a sleeveless white blouse, her curly hair swept back off her thin face, a blood-red choker around her neck – she looked like a character from a French noir film.

'Hello,' she smiled briefly and took a drag from her cigarette.

'I wish you'd do that outside,' Jaco said, irritation in his voice.

'Hi,' I said, trying to smile naturally.

The living room was larger than I recalled with two curtainless big windows. The walls were a deep red and the only furniture was two worn-looking black leather sofas opposite each other, a glass-topped coffee table covered in mugs, glasses and a full ashtray, a table against one wall and four chairs and a newer looking oak sideboard with a television on top and a wilted yucca plant.

All of this I took in secondly, what I took in first was a paint-stained sheet on the floor in front of the windows and a large easel, its back facing us. Next to it was a wooden crate on its side, a jam jar residing on it filled with paintbrushes.

'Billy downstairs?' Jaco asked.

'Yep,' Evie made a derisive noise. 'Feeding the fat pig champagne and no doubt the finest Columbian.'

I glanced in puzzlement at Jaco as he shot her a glare that looked like a caution.

'Shall I get ready?' I asked hesitantly.

'Yes baby,' Jaco handed me my bag. 'The shower's not the most reliable so make it speedy.'

'You'll have to excuse the mess in the bedroom,' Evie said, shrugging her thin shoulders.

Jaco led me to the bathroom, opening the door and

142

glancing around before letting me in, 'Sorry, she's a slob,' he kissed my shoulder. 'Look, we need to go down, just come on down when you're ready, sweetheart.'

'OK,' I looked around, the bathroom was nothing short of a mess, towels on the floor and toiletries with their lids off on the glass shelf below the mirror. 'Is there a clean towel?' I whispered.

'In the cupboard,' he bent down and opened a cupboard door and extracted a faded pink towel that was more hand towel than bath towel. 'Sorry baby, I promise your accommodation tonight will be better than this.'

He shut the door behind him, and I pulled the bolt across, then turned on the shower while I stripped off, feeling more uncomfortable than ever.

I rummaged in my bag and swore as I realised that I had forgotten to pack my shower gel. I looked up at the shower head and there was a men's Radox one hanging up; I supposed that would have to do.

After two minutes under the shower the water started to come out cold, so I stepped out and rubbed myself dry with the miniscule towel.

Unbolting the door and sticking my head out into the hall, I deduced that Jaco and Evie had gone and dashed to the bedroom next door, having an unwelcome memory of the guy receiving a blowjob in there at Jaco's party.

The room wasn't much tidier than the bathroom. The bed was unmade, and clothes littered the floor and the chair in front of an old-fashioned dressing table. The room smelt of a musky perfume that wasn't unpleasant but made me feel uneasy.

I hadn't washed my hair as I already had that morning. I brushed it out and pinned it up in what I hoped was a sophisticated bun, but it was really hard to see in the dusty mirror what I was doing. I picked up a single sock that was hanging over the mirror and wiped the dust off, then turned my back and tried to look at the back of my head holding up my tiny compact mirror. I quickly applied my make-up, light foundation and a touch of bronzer on my cheeks and over my eyelids, finishing with a raspberry pink lipstick.

Normally I would have taken a *lot* longer with my face, but I was hoping my dress would be my saving grace.

Rose-gold and classily cut an inch above my knees, tight-fitting and low-cut, it was both sexy and classy, one of my more expensive dresses, bought for a friend's wedding. I finished the look with dusky-pink high-heels and a gold choker.

Feeling nervous again, I left the flat and walked carefully down the stairs and around to the front of the gallery, taking a few deep breaths before I pushed open the door.

The reception was dim in the fading light. I could see lights and hear voices at the back and walked towards them.

I was greeted by the sight of Jaco, a champagne glass in his hand. He was standing with his back to me, his other hand on Evie's back; I faltered slightly, not liking that he was touching her. Billy stood beside her, and next to him was a large man in a shiny grey suit, his hands clasped behind his back.

'Hello,' I said hesitantly.

Everyone turned their heads, Jaco grinning broadly.

'And who do we have here?' the man, presumably Edward, smiled widely, showing very large and white teeth.

'This,' Jaco held out a hand, 'is my girlfriend, Roxy.'

I took his proffered hand and after giving Billy a brief smile, I looked up into the red face of Edward and decided he looked like someone's fat, drunk uncle at a wedding.

'Roxy,' he boomed, 'nice to meet you.'

'You too,' I murmured as Jaco squeezed my hand.

'You look amazing,' Jaco whispered in my ear. 'I cannot wait to fuck you.'

I felt my face go hot, sure that Evie had heard him. She raised an eyebrow and took a step closer to Edward.

I looked up at the wall in front of us. It had been painted a subtle gold and Evie's paintings hung impressively under the downlights. On either side of the display were potted miniature magnolia trees; I wasn't sure whether they were real or fake, but they set off the display strikingly.

'I'm spoilt for choice,' Edward stepped closer to a painting of a green cactus-looking plant with what looked like blood dripping from black spikes, a figure of a wide-eyed woman behind it with her arms outstretched.

'Ah, Motherhood,' Jaco said. 'A lot of interest in this one.'

'Yeah?' Edward glanced at him and then Evie. 'It's spectacular.'

145

'Thank you,' Evie said demurely.

Edward opened the catalogue he had rolled up in one hand and looked intently at it, 'OK, this is a maybe.'

'No hurry,' Jaco said pleasantly, his mild voice belied by the brief look of distaste on his face.

Edward wiped the sweat from his upper lip, and I caught Evie's eye. To my surprise she wrinkled her nose and smiled at me.

Half an hour later I was beyond bored and restless. Edward was a pompous windbag I decided, and really had no idea what he was talking about.

It was approaching ten o'clock when Jaco announced that we were already late for our table, and subtly indicated to Billy, who had started collecting glasses and turning off some of the lights.

'We can discuss what you like over dinner,' Jaco said mildly. 'The paintings aren't going anywhere, my friend.'

'Sure,' Edward agreed amiably.

Jaco drove to the hotel with Edward in the front, still waffling on, and me and Evie in the back. She was very quiet, sitting jammed against the door and gazing silently out of the window.

As we drove up towards the hotel through the gates, I stared eagerly up at the impressive building.

'Been here before?' Evie suddenly asked in her soft voice.

'No,' I said in surprise. 'You?'

'Once or twice,' she eyed me then turned away again.

As we walked across the gravelled carpark, I turned

to Jaco, 'My bag's in the flat,' I said, feeling unnecessarily panicked.

'It's OK sweetheart,' he put a hand on the small of my back. 'I have to take Evie back.'

'Is *he* staying here?' I nodded at Edward, who was walking in front with Evie.

'Yes,' he lowered his voice. 'And it's on me, so the big oaf better be spending what he's hinted at.'

Once inside the resplendent reception, Jaco ushered us towards the bar and we sat down while he spoke to the maître d'.

'We are *so* late,' he grumbled on his return, shooting Edward a dark look.

It was only a few minutes before we were seated, and I tried not to look too stunned at our surroundings… I mean, I'd been to some nice places, but this was another world - all shining chandeliers and polished silver and polite murmured conversation. I reminded myself to keep my voice down and no squealing.

'Madam,' a smiling man in a waistcoat pulled out my chair and then done the same for Evie.

Edward, who was not keeping his voice down at all, took charge of the wine menu and started being rude to the waiters.

'Christ,' Jaco whispered.

I was handed a menu and looked down the list of starters, feeling out of my depth, not knowing what half the things were on there.

'Please don't let me order anything that is remotely related to snails or that's raw,' I murmured to Jaco and he chuckled, briefly kissing me and looking at me, his eyes full of fondness.

147

'I love you,' he put his hand on my knee and watched me frowning down at my menu.

'I wonder how fresh the sea bass is,' Edward looked greedily at his menu.

'Very, I should imagine,' said Jaco.

'So, Miss Blackhouse,' Edward turned to Evie. 'You're very young to have reached such success, your parents must be very proud of you.'

'I'm sure they are,' she smiled thinly. 'I haven't spoken to them for two years.'

'Oh,' Edward faltered slightly. 'Well I'm sure there's big things in your future.'

'Who knows?' she closed her menu and tucked her hands under the table. 'I'm one of many new artists.'

'Young Jaco here will get your name out there, I'm certain of that.'

Her yellow eyes flickered towards Jaco, then she nodded slightly.

'Of course,' he chortled, 'being so beautiful must help, eh?'

I guessed it was supposed to be a flattering comment, but it just sounded lecherous.

'Not one bit,' she said shortly, her expression not changing but her voice full of distaste.

'Shall we order, guys?' Jaco said loudly, a small note of laughter in his voice. 'Kill me now,' he whispered in my ear.

The food was incredible. I ordered clementine and honey roast salmon for my starter and if I were at home, I would have licked the plate. Jaco and I both had duck with a port and cherry sauce for our main

148

meal, and I found it hard not to make yum noises with each mouthful.

I noticed that Evie ate very little, but Edward made up for it, eating his steak at great speed, then stealing Evie's discarded potatoes.

He really was a crude and revolting man. He was very dismissive of the smiling waiters and aggressively finger snapping, and whenever he spoke to either me or Evie it was with a leer. I caught him at least three times staring at my breasts and had to resist the urge to tug my neckline up.

A muscle kept twitching in Jaco's cheek; I could tell he was getting angry with him but of course had to be civil.

I wasn't sure however whether Evie was going to bite her tongue for much longer. Twice Edward had touched her arm, and not only did she look furious, the second time she almost snarled.

Jaco excused himself after the second course, telling me to order more wine if the waiters came in his absence.

I sat, feeling uneasy to be left with the strange and distant Evie, and Edward, who was by now slurring his words.

I studied her as she turned to listen to whatever Edward was now droning on about. She was *kind* of beautiful in a fierce and almost androgynous way, her body was rather angular and boyish, and her jawline square; I couldn't help thinking she *would* be beautiful if she wasn't so very thin.

Jaco returned, sliding onto his seat and sneezing three times in quick succession.

'Damn lilies in the gents,' he grumbled.

'That reminds me,' I said, 'I bought you some antihistamines for your hayfever,' I blushed as Evie smirked.

'Aw, how very sweet of you,' he kissed my hand.

'You should eat local honey,' Edward said pompously.

'Can't stand the stuff,' Jaco smiled blandly. 'What do you want for sweet, my sweet?' he kissed my hand again.

I shivered slightly as Evie looked at me with slightly narrowed eyes, still a mysterious smirk on her lips.

After we had finished, we went back to the bar and Jaco bought four brandies, which I didn't really like but was too embarrassed to say so. I would have much preferred a nice mug of tea, but that wasn't very sophisticated.

'I'll take you up to our room soon,' he told me quietly. 'Then I'll take madam back and bring your bag up, then I need to talk business with that lump.'

I looked at my watch and saw that it was gone midnight. I hoped that I didn't fall asleep before I had Jaco to myself.

The woman behind the bar was turning lights off and kept glancing over.

'Come on,' Jaco said eventually. 'Here,' he threw his car keys to Evie, 'I'll see Roxy up and be down in a sec.'

Edward went to get his bag while Jaco booked us in, and then we took the lift up to the third floor.

'Oh,' I whispered when he opened the door to our

room, then I squealed in delight. 'Look at it!'

'Like it?'

'I love it!' I threw myself on the bed, then knelt up and stared around.

The carpet was a sandy yellow and the walls a delicate blue, reminding me of the seaside. Heavy gold curtains held back with tasselled cord revealed French doors with a balcony outside, which Jaco went and opened up.

'How pretty,' I scrambled off the bed and went to look at the view of a walled garden with a lit-up fountain in the middle.

I gazed out for a second then looked up into Jaco's smiling face.

'We will come here again, alone, for a whole weekend soon,' he touched my cheek with the back of his hand. 'There's a spa here and a pool, how does that sound?'

'Wonderful,' I threw my arms around him and he laughed, squeezing me tight.

'I love you, baby,' he said - a lock of his dark hair had fallen on his forehead, his eyes were shining, and I caught my breath, thinking he had never looked so handsome.

'I love you too,' I whispered.

We looked into each other's eyes for a few silent seconds, and I felt a glorious rush of desire.

'I need to go and get your bag,' he said softly. 'I'll bring it up then I'll go and see Edward in his room. I won't be long, sweetheart… you go and have a soak or something.'

'OK.'

After he had left, I spent another few minutes on the balcony enjoying the gentle breeze of the night on my warm face, then went to explore the bathroom.

The bathroom was as amazing as the rest of the room. It was all black onyx and mirrors, and the sink unit had a big basket of miniature toiletries on it next to some folded up white and fluffy towels.

Finding a bottle of bubble bath called *Exotic Waterlily and Rose,* I started to fill the bath, pouring half of it in. I stripped off and watched the bubbles rising, enjoying the heady perfume smell filling the room.

I'd only just settled back and heaved a contented sigh when I heard Jaco letting himself in.

'Hello,' I called, sitting up a little so my breasts were exposed.

'Hey you,' he walked in, a broad grin on his face.

'Don't be long,' I pleaded.

'Oh, I most definitely won't be,' he crouched down next to the bath and lightly stroked a nipple. 'Leave the water in, sweetheart.'

He stood up, looking reluctant, then backed out the room, blowing me a kiss.

I laid for another few minutes, then climbed out, excited to put my new nightie on for him.

Twenty minutes later, I was laying across the bed on my side, eagerly waiting for Jaco's return.

As I heard him outside the door, I shook my hair out a little, arranging the front over one eye and smiling seductively.

'Sorry,' he said as he walked in, loosening his tie, then stopped dead in his tracks staring at me.

'Hi,' I looked at him from under my lashes.

'What the fuck are you wearing?' he almost shouted, his face livid.

'Jaco?' I sat up, feeling the blood leaving my face.

'Take it off,' he snapped.

For the second time in just a few days, I felt fearful.

'I-I got it as a surprise,' I stared up at him in dismay, feeling all the anticipation of the evening ahead trickle away.

'I don't want you dressing like a whore,' he said bluntly, wrenching off his tie and throwing it on the floor. 'Why did you have to do that?' his expression was stony as he glared at me, then he looked down, his chest rising and falling. 'Rox... sorry, baby. You made an effort, I know you did,' he looked back up. 'You don't need to do that, you're my angel, my baby. You're perfect.'

'There was no need to yell at me like that,' I brushed an angry tear away. 'Perhaps I should just go,' I looked down at myself, feeling ridiculous now in my stockings, especially as it was so hot.

'No,' Jaco strode over and gathered me up in his arms. 'Sorry, I'm sorry,' he kissed my forehead and sighed deeply. He smelt of whisky and aftershave.

'It's OK,' I whispered, feeling miserable and confused but as always melting at his touch.

'No, it's not OK, not one bit.'

'I thought you'd like it,' I mumbled against his shoulder. 'I wanted to look sexy.'

'You don't need to dress up to look sexy,' he said

153

quietly. 'Maybe your exes liked it, but I don't.'

'Why are you saying that?' I felt tears splash down my cheeks.

'Just be my baby,' he whispered. 'Don't be anything else.'

We fell into silence, then when I couldn't stand it anymore, I pulled away and stood up abruptly and started to undress, rolling down the hateful stockings until I was down to my black thong.

He watched me mutely, his eyes troubled.

'Better?' I sat down and folded my arms over my breasts.

'Much,' he gave a me a twisted smile.

'I left my water in,' I said numbly.

'Cool,' he stood up. 'I won't be long.'

I watched him go into the bathroom, then went and climbed into the huge bed, throwing the cushions across the room with unnecessary force.

Did that really just happen? I thought, my eyes filling up again.

I curled up on my side, facing away from the bathroom door, concentrating hard on not giving way to sobbing my heart out. I heard him sneezing, the spray of deodorant and then him sneezing again.

'Sweetheart?'

I rolled over to look at him; he had a towel around his hips, his dark hair damp and slicked back.

'I thought you'd gone to sleep,' he walked over and laid down next to me.

'No,' I murmured pointlessly.

'You're angry,' it was a statement, not a question.

I shrugged.

'OK,' he muttered, more to himself than to me. 'OK. Roxy, look at me... I want to tell you something... and if I've blown it, then OK... it's entirely my fault, and I'll accept that.'

'Right,' I said slowly, panic rising. I was upset and I was angry, but the possibility of our brief relationship ending was an unbearable thought.

'I meet a lot of women in my business,' he looked evenly at me. 'Some rich, some just... *ordinary*... I have money,' he paused and sighed, 'you would not believe some of the unbelievable flirting and come-ons... you really wouldn't.'

'Are you trying to make me jealous?' I asked, feeling perplexed.

'No,' he said quickly, placing a hand on my upper arm. 'I'm not playing games.'

'I don't see where this is going.'

'Roxy, when I first saw you, I was bowled over,' he smiled and shook his head. 'I couldn't stop looking at you.'

'So?' I said shortly, secretly flattered.

'You're...different to other women, you're special.'

'No,' I frowned. 'I'm just... normal.'

'Oh, baby,' he closed his eyes briefly. 'No. You are so, so special. You're my angel and I love you. You're a good person and you are beautiful inside and out.'

'Jaco,' I whispered, tears filling my eyes again.

'I got mad,' he continued, 'because what you done, how you dressed... was like something another woman would do. I just want you, as you are... no dressing up, no games... just you.'

155

'But I thought you'd like it,' I swallowed hard. 'I'm sorry you didn't, but there was no need to yell and make me feel bad.'

'I know, I know,' he let out a shuddering breath. 'I'm an idiot. I'm sorry.'

'And I'm not an angel, or a baby, or perfect... I'm not,' I looked away. 'Don't put me on a pedestal.'

'I'm sorry,' he drew me towards him. 'I just love you.'

I closed my eyes and tried to get a grip on my emotions - not an easy thing for someone like me. I wanted to stay mad, but my heart was aching, and I wanted to throw myself into his arms and tell him that it didn't matter.

'Rox?'

'Jaco,' I looked into his eyes, his beautiful and inky eyes, so full of remorse. 'I love you too... just... just please don't do that again. Don't scare me again.'

'Oh, I won't, not ever,' he kissed me gently. 'I love you, I love you so much.'

He began to kiss me in earnest, his hands tugging the duvet away gently.

Feeling like I should be resisting, I responded hesitantly, then as desire started to wash over me, I let him take over with his skilled lovemaking.

CHAPTER THIRTEEN

Not one to hold a grudge, I was surprised at how bothered I still felt the next day.

Jaco had apologised so profusely, I felt silly bringing the whole thing up again, but my mind kept playing it over and over.

We didn't fall asleep until the early hours and woke up just before nine. He seemed overly talkative and wide awake while I felt like treacle had been poured into my brain.

We went and had a buffet breakfast; I just picked at some scrambled eggs and toast while Jaco demolished eggs and bacon and black pudding, his chatty mood making up for my withdrawn one.

I wasn't doing it on purpose, and I wasn't sulking, I just couldn't forget how he had made me feel... then I felt a strange sort of shame, because we had made love lovingly and passionately. I clearly couldn't have been *that* mad at him.

He dropped me off at home, telling me he would ring me later, and I had gone up to my flat, crawled into bed and cried before falling asleep until the middle of the afternoon.

Monday night rehearsals came around and I still hadn't shaken myself out of my troubled state.

'Earth to Roxy.'

'Oh, sorry,' I looked up into the kind and lined face

of Bob, the man playing Mr Graves, Violet/Mabel's husband-to-be.

'I bet you haven't looked at your script all weekend,' Finn said in a bullyingly voice from behind me.

'Oh, piss off,' I muttered under my breath. 'Sorry Duncan,' I said and stretched, trying to re-focus.

'It's OK, dear,' he waved a hand from the edge of the stage where he was perched. Today he had turned up with rather dramatic black hair, a slight shock after his ginger colour that had been slowing fading into an odd peach.

'I don't want to run over tonight,' Finn complained. 'She's come in yawning and forgetting half her lines, maybe she should swap parts.'

'Finn!' Destiny, who was playing Sylvia, Mabel's sister, bore down on him. 'Don't be rude.'

'Just saying,' he muttered, looking a tiny bit wary. Destiny may have looked the epitome of "hippy" in her long skirts and floaty cheesecloth blouses, and spouting peace and inner serenity, but she had a wicked temper that surfaced occasionally.

'Well,' Teddy interjected mildly. 'I have a small idea. How about you *don't* just say? Just a thought.'

I giggled and tried to turn it unsuccessfully into a cough, causing Bob to chuckle too. I cleared my throat and looked around, surprised to see Francesca giving Finn a sour look; she was normally immune to Finn's nasty comments.

'Can we just get on?' Finn said crossly.

'Oh, go step on some Lego, you STD,' Teddy said quietly so only me and Bob could hear, and we both burst out laughing.

'OK,' Duncan stood up. 'Carry on, children.'

'Milly, my dear girl,' Bob continued, his eyes still watering from laughing, 'I'm sure you will look as pretty as a picture.'

'But lavender is really *not* my colour,' I put my hands on my hips.

'Ah, but it's Mabel's decision, you will have your own day, one day in the future.'

'Oh, I do hope so,' I gave a Finn a soppy look, trying to keep my dislike off of my face.

'Miss Milly,' Teddy flounced over. 'You will look fabulous in lavender, it's *so* in this year.'

'Brilliant,' Duncan called, as a few members laughed quietly. 'Francesca, you must look furiously embarrassed. Also slightly worried.'

'That's a hard expression to get down,' Francesca shook her head. 'Sorry Dunc, but wouldn't Olivia have known her husband was as camp as Julian Clary *before* she married him?'

'Hmm,' Duncan scratched his chin. 'Maybe she was carried away with his dashing handsomeness.'

'Yes,' Teddy agreed. 'I'm such a pretty flower.'

'You are,' she put a hand on his chest. 'The prettiest.'

'OK,' Duncan pointed at me. 'Carry on.'

'But I do so like pink,' I said.

'Oh, me too,' Teddy agreed.

'What do you think, Benedict?' I gave Finn a coy look.

'I think you will look a delight,' Finn said politely. 'As will Miss Mabel.'

'Oh Benedict,' Violet patted his arm and looked up at

him.

'Long that out,' Duncan called.

Violet continued gazing for a few seconds, then shook her head as if in a daze before joining Bob and holding his arm.

Teddy then took Violet's spot and stared up at Finn as she had, while Finn looked stiffly ahead, to more laughter.

'Oh, Teddy,' Francesca giggled. 'You are so funny.'

'I will check on Lizzy and Kate,' Finn took a tiny sidestep. 'Make sure they have laid the table to your standards, Miss Mabel,' he nodded curtly then walked away, but instead of leaving the stage via the side as he would in performance, he went and sat in the front row.

'I will help him,' Teddy said and hurried after him, but sat on the edge of the stage.

'That boy is very handsome,' Destiny said. 'But isn't he a little over familiar?'

'Oh. Not nearly enough,' Violet blinked at her.

'At this point, Jamie... or rather James, will be pouring more wine for the guests,' Duncan said. 'But unfortunately, he's absent tonight.'

'Great,' Finn said sarcastically. 'Shall I read for him?'

'Please,' Duncan nodded.

'His wife has just had twin boys,' Destiny tutted. 'Have some understanding, he's probably sleep-deprived.'

I had a quick scan of my script and hid another yawn behind my hand.

'I went to see them last week,' Francesca said. 'So

cute.'

'I must get a card,' I said. 'What have they called them?'

'Jaydon and Faddon,' Francesca replied. 'Spitting of Jamie, bless them.'

'I'm not sure about these modern names,' Violet pulled a face.

'I'll get a card for Thursday,' Stuart, who was young and slightly balding and playing the youngest son, William, offered. 'We can all sign it.'

'But I took one last week,' Francesca told him.

'Don't matter,' he said kindly. 'It'll be nice if all our names are in there.'

'Shall we put some money in?' I wondered out loud. 'Like, a fiver each?'

'Excuse me,' Finn said loudly. 'Can we carry on?'

'Yes, come on my dears,' Duncan said pleasantly, raising his eyes slightly at Finn's back.

We left late, being grumbled at by Wally the caretaker as we filed out.

'You OK, chicken?' Teddy asked as we walked to his car.

'Not coming for a drink?' Francesca asked from behind us.

'No, not tonight. I want to get Yawny McYawn Gob home.'

'It's fine,' I linked arms with him. 'I can walk, it's like ten-minutes.'

'Nah,' he said. 'I'm knackered too.'

We climbed into his car and he started the engine, but didn't pull out of his spot, 'So?'

'Huh?'

'Are you OK?'

'Yeah, I'm good.'

'Uh huh,' he tapped his fingers on the steering wheel. 'I asked how your night was Saturday and I get a "fine" … when *I* know you were excited as hell about it… you're not yourself tonight,' he added in a gentler tone.

'I'm just sleepy,' I played with the hem of my skirt.

'Hm,' he finally pulled out and swung out of the car park.

He drove, singing quietly to The Doors… but I knew he hadn't finished with me yet.

I scrambled out as soon as he cut the engine, planning on making a quick escape.

'Want a night-cap?' he caught up with me.

'No, I want a shower and to crash out.'

'Me too, honey. But we are having a night-cap.'

I inwardly sighed but obediently followed him into his flat.

'Tea or coffee?'

'Tea,' I went and sat on our seat. The doors had been left open, letting in a welcome breeze.

'So,' he came over with two mugs and sat next to me. 'Spill.'

'I'm not sure I can,' I bit my lip, feeling disloyal and a tiny bit embarrassed.

'OK,' he continued to look at me, until I couldn't ignore his gaze anymore.

'It's silly, really,' I started to fidget. 'I feel kind of… silly,' I ended lamely.

'Silly, eh?' Teddy took a sip of his tea then nudged

my arm. 'You're upset though.'

'Am I?' I tried to smile, wanting to make light of it all, but I felt my chin wobble like a traitor and tears filling my eyes.

'Oh, sweet,' he put an arm around me. 'I've made you sad... look, I'm sorry. If you don't want to talk about it, it's fine. I just worry about you.'

'You do?'

'Yes! You're my buddy, my drinking pal,' he said jokingly, then sighed. 'I do worry about you, course I do. But I won't push it.'

'Oh Teddy,' I blinked my tears away. 'I just... it's just... I'm really confused.'

'OK,' he stroked the back of my head and I closed my eyes fleetingly.

'Can you just not look at me while I tell you,' I pleaded, and he sat back, looking forward. 'OK, so... I bought, like, this nightie... a sexy nightie. For the hotel,' I added, feeling my colour rising. 'It was... kind of... I suppose, *tarty*, I dunno... with stockings.'

'Right,' he said softly.

'And while Jaco was gone-'

'Gone?'

'Oh, he went to get my bag, then had to talk business with this guy.'

'OK.'

'Well, I got ready, like, put it on and waited for him,' I paused, taking a deep breath. 'Well... he didn't like it.'

'What do you mean?' he asked, sounding puzzled.

'He got mad,' I heard my voice break and paused again. 'He, he said... he didn't want me dressing like a

163

whore… like, he shouted at me. Then, he got sad and apologised and said he didn't want me to dress up.'

'Christ,' he muttered.

'It probably sounds worse than it is,' I hung my head. 'I got mad back and he was sorry, really sorry. But… he frightened me.'

'Oh, Rox,' Teddy swung around and tugged my arm. 'Look at me, babe.'

'What?'

'If I was *ever* lucky enough to have a hot chick like you do that for me… well… I'd be as happy as a hamburger. Even if he is weird enough to not like… *that* kind of treat, he still should not have shouted at you, or frightened you.'

'I know,' I squeezed my eyes shut and felt an awful cloak of depression surround me. 'He *was* sorry, he was. He explained some stuff, and he was really upset and felt bad, I could tell… but I can't help thinking about it.'

'Roxy… do you love him?'

'Yeah,' I nodded and sniffed.

'Can I just say this… don't let your love cloud your judgement, honey. You deserve the best, you do. Don't let him or *anyone,* ever make you feel bad.'

'I know,' I muttered. 'Teddy, if I had said I don't love him, what would you have said?'

'Honestly?'

'Yeah.'

'Dump him.'

Teddy, and *maybe* Dana, were possibly the only two people that could have given me that advice and not have made me mad.

However, as kindly as Teddy had said it, I was still stung.

At the root of my uneasiness though was the fact that Jaco had said he couldn't see me until Wednesday, which was fine, but I couldn't help thinking that after what had happened at the hotel that he would have wanted to see me and make sure everything was OK.

But, by how he had been the following morning, he clearly didn't see it as a big deal. That just led me to my next worry: was it me? Had I over-reacted? Was I making mountains out of molehills?

Deep down I thought not, backed up by Teddy's take on it… but was he just being over-protective?

I rarely thought about my ADHD as a factor in my life and in all honesty, I found it a struggle to see it as a disability, even though it is classed as one. Like, I don't know how to feel any different to how I feel and how I see things. But right then, I was wondering if I was perceiving my situation differently to a "normal" person. I could accept that I was high-energy and excitable. I could accept that I had trouble concentrating sometimes. But I really didn't know if I was reading too much into something that didn't matter.

I was apprehensive about seeing Jaco on Wednesday and I hadn't slept well the night before. I had got up an hour earlier than usual to go to the gym, and after a vigorous work-out, my pelvis was hurting all day.

Dana had a day off work, so we met up for lunch. The fact that I didn't confide in her was also a worrying tell-tale sign that I knew that things were not well. I just couldn't bear her telling me that Jaco's behaviour had been wrong.

Jaco texted me during the afternoon asking what I fancied doing and I replied, saying that I didn't mind, then worried that I sounded off, I added half a dozen X's. He said he would come to mine around seven.

By the time I got home the skies were grey, and thunder was in the air, making me all the more uneasy.

It was dreadfully hot, the clouds seeming to trap all the days heat under their dark cover. The wind had got up, but it was doing nothing to cool the air.

I showered and pulled on a vest top and shorts, thinking I could always get changed if Jaco wanted to go out. I rarely drank in the week, but I poured a glass of white wine and soda, then went and stood on my balcony, watching the increasingly darkening clouds roll across the sky while thunder rumbled ominously in the distance.

The first fat drops of rain started to fall after a slightly louder rumble of thunder, the smell of the hot ground immediately hitting me. I shuddered slightly as a fork of lightening lit up the sky, followed by a booming crack of thunder.

Retreating inside, I curled up on the sofa and watched the rain as it became heavier and louder.

Sleepy and entranced by the sound of the storm, I lost track of time and jumped when there was a loud knock at my door.

'Hi, baby,' Jaco stood there as I opened the door, his hair soaked and his white shirt clinging to him.

'Blimey,' I stood back, my heart and stomach doing their crazy somersaults as they always did when I saw him. 'You walk here?'

'A thirty second run from the car,' he smiled ruefully, wiping his face. 'Can I borrow a towel?'

'Sure,' I went and fetched one from the cupboard in my bedroom as he took off his trainers in the hall.

'Thanks, sweetheart,' he rubbed his face, then his hair, leaving it appealingly messy.

I watched him, feeling confused and weak; weak because I knew that I was aching to fall into his arms despite my doubts, despite the persistent feelings of all not being well and of knowing I should proceed with caution... *too late Roxy.*

'Rox, you OK?'

'Yes!' I said straight away, smiling automatically.

'Come here,' he held out his arms and I wrapped my arms around his waist, resting my face on his damp chest. 'I've missed you so much this week,' he said. 'I hate it when I can't see you.'

'You're here now,' I murmured.

'I am,' he sounded happy. 'All yours. What do you fancy doing? Have you eaten? Do you wanna go out?'

'No, I haven't eaten yet,' I looked up into his face, my doubts turning misty at the sight of his curved mouth and his eyes full of warmth.

'Well,' he grinned. 'How about we order food, I get out of these wet clothes and you just get out of your clothes anyway?'

'Perfect,' I felt the last bit of my resistance slide away as he kissed me.

'Perfect,' he agreed, his hand stroking my bum.

167

We never got around to ordering food. We spent an energetic hour in bed, then I made some cheese on toast, which we ate on the sofa while watching the rain together, him laughing at the amount of ketchup I had on the side of my plate.

'That stuff is disgusting,' he said through a mouthful of toast.

'I put it on everything,' I brushed crumbs off my bare legs.

'I'm still hungry,' he got up and went into the kitchen. I heard him opening cupboards and muttering to himself. 'You have nothing unhealthy.'

'I don't buy it,' I ate the last of my toast and smiled to myself.

'Well, you should.'

'I'd just pig out,' I called back. 'If I want cake or biscuits, I go and see Teddy.'

'Right,' he appeared in the doorway. 'Come on, put clothes on, we're going to mine.'

'Really?'

'Yep.'

Arriving at Jaco's house, he put the kettle on and proceeded to pile packets of biscuits onto a tray, as I watched in amusement.

'Is this all you eat?' I asked.

'When I'm busy,' he grinned over his shoulder as he stood at his opened cupboard.

'*So* unhealthy.'

'Yeah, yeah, yeah.'

'I will need to double my gym efforts,' I sighed,

running a hand over my stomach.

'I like a bit of padding,' he gave me a slow look up and down, before closing the cupboard.

'You calling me fat?' I frowned.

'Hardly!' he started to make two mugs of tea. 'You are just right... beautiful with a little bit to grab hold of.'

I looked down at myself, now dressed in jeans and a T-shirt, wondering if he had noticed my weight gain.

'Can I put my bag upstairs?'

'Sure.'

I slid my bag off the island where he had put the tray and went upstairs.

Not having been upstairs via the hall staircase, I poked my head in each room as I went past. There was a small shower room and toilet that looked brand new and unused next a bedroom that had a double-bed and a seagrass storage box; there were no curtains at the window and the floor was bare floorboards. Across the landing was a locked door, I assumed that was his bedroom he said he used as storage, then finally another bedroom opposite his bathroom with a sofa-bed covered in cushions, a folded throw over one arm and dressing table with a laptop on it.

As I threw my bag on his bed, I wondered what it was like to live all alone in such a big house. Having always thought it would be rather fabulous, I decided it seemed a lot lonelier than my cosy little flat... of course it would be a great home for a big family and I smiled to myself thinking about lots of pretty little children with my blonde hair and Jaco's amazing dark eyes.

169

'Roxy?' Jaco called from the living room. 'You got lost up there?'

'Sorry,' I ran down the back stairs. 'I was just nosing around,' I found him sitting with a mug of tea, his bare feet up on the coffee table. 'It's like a hotel up there.'

'I used to live in that pokey flat,' he watched me as I came over to him. 'After a year of not even liking to call it my home, I decided I was going to buy the best house I could afford.'

I badly wanted to ask how much his house was worth, but that sounded shallow. I thought that he must sell an awful lot of paintings to get so rich so young.

'Come here,' he pulled me over towards him. 'Don't let me eat all these on my own.'

'Oh my gosh,' I sighed. 'Shortbread, I love shortbread.'

'So, how come Teddy buys you biscuits?' he asked suddenly.

'He doesn't,' I swallowed a mouthful of shortbread. 'He just buys junk food and I don't.'

'Right,' he looked thoughtful.

'Jaco… you're not *jealous* of Teddy, are you?'

'No,' he raised an eyebrow. 'Should I be?'

'No!' I said laughingly. 'He's like… a brother.'

'Sure,' he stroked my arm, still the thoughtful look on his face. 'He must fancy you though.'

'Nah,' I shook my head. 'We are just mates.'

'Doesn't mean he doesn't though.'

Not sure how to respond to that, I tried to gauge his mood, but his face was impassive.

'Nah,' I repeated and picked up another biscuit.

'So, he's never tried anything?'

'No!' I said in shock. 'Never.'

'I'm surprised,' he said musingly, 'Teddy being what he is.'

'Meaning?' I asked, perplexed by that statement.

'Bit of a player, isn't he?'

'A player? Teddy?' I laughed. 'Not that I have ever seen.'

'Well, I suppose you haven't known him as long as me.'

I wanted to argue that maybe not, but I was sure I knew him better – but decided it wasn't a good idea as I suspected that Jaco had slight reservations about our friendship.

Instead I shrugged and tried to look unconcerned, even though I had a disconcerting feeling of discomfort at the thought of Teddy being anything but... well, Teddy.

'The Fernberry Players... could have been us ten years ago,' Jaco chuckled. 'We used to get up to all sorts.

'I bet,' I forced a laugh, but felt slightly sick.

'I guess we all have a past.'

'I guess.'

'Even you.'

'Well,' I said lightly, 'I'm younger than you, not much past for me.'

'Hey, you calling me old?' he teased, squeezing my thigh.

'Oh, ancient,' I said, glad that the conversation had turned light-hearted.

'Cheeky,' he pulled me closer and kissed my neck.

'Let's go to bed.'

CHAPTER FOURTEEN

Rehearsals on Thursday reminded me of why I loved The Fernberry Players so much.

Despite Finn being his usual irritating self, I spent most of the evening laughing.

Meadow, the supposed BDSM fan and Lily-Rose, a quietly beautiful girl from a rich family with the politest disposition, were playing the two maids. In Duncan's notes, he had said that they both spoke in cockney accents. Meadow had got it down to a 'T', Lily-Rose however just couldn't erase her Home-Counties accent, resulting in fits of giggles from the pair of them.

I was sitting on a rickety stool opposite Violet, trying to get through a rather long dialogue without looking at my script, but it was very distracting. Lily-Rose, despite being the "posh girl" had a filthy and throaty laugh that kept setting everyone else off, even Finn.

Nathan, our "daddy" of the group, who was playing the gardener, was a rough diamond, an ex-semi-pro wrestler and all-round nice guy. He was trying to help out, but not very successfully.

The three of them sat on the edge of the stage to one side, 'Darlin'' he said, 'you need to drop some letters, that is all.'

'OK, OK,' Lily-Rose sat up straight and blew out a long breath, clearly trying to compose herself.

'Right,' he said calmly. 'Repeat after me… I 'ope

we've got ba'on and eggs for tea.'

'I 'ope… we've got bacon… oops, sorry… *bayon* and eggs for tea,' she immediately burst into peals of laughter again and stuffed her blonde plait in her mouth. 'Sorry.'

'A bit better,' Nathan said, looking up at everyone with despair on his face.

'Perhaps you should watch a video on YouTube or something?' Lola suggested shyly. 'That's what I did when I had to do a Scottish accent.'

'*Knees up Mother Brown, knees up Mother Brown, under the table you must go, ee-aye, ee-aye, ee-aye-oh,*' Teddy started to sing, dancing past them.

'Thanks, Lola,' Lily-Rose nodded, then wiped her eyes. 'Stop, Teddy.'

'Sorry guvnor,' he stopped dancing and sat down on a vacant chair.

'You'll get there,' Duncan, who had been chuckling too, looked unconcerned.

'I will, I promise,' Lily-Rose dropped her head and looked at her script.

'OK,' Duncan struggled up onto his feet. 'Roxy, how are we getting on with the scream, my dear?'

I groaned… in the scene where I discovered Mabel/Violet dead in her bed, I had to let out a scream. As somebody who is quite… *screamy*… I was finding it difficult.

'Well, I haven't really practised properly,' I said guiltily. 'Like, I've tried, but feel stupid.'

'No need,' Duncan gave a lop-sided grin. 'Just imagine finding a big spider.'

'I'm not scared of spiders.'

'Imagine finding Jeremy in your bathroom when you open your shower curtain,' Teddy whispered in my ear and I let out a squawk of mirth.

'Well, what *are* you scared of?' Duncan asked.

'Oh,' I thought for a second. 'Well, I don't like pigeons, but I'm not exactly scared of them.'

'Hmm,' he scratched his neck. 'OK, finish what you're reading, and we will practice.'

Totally losing track of the dialogue, I consulted my script, then carried on with Violet, now distracted because I was worrying about my scream.

Fifteen minutes later we had finished, and Violet beamed at me.

'I'm almost sorry that I have to die soon,' she said. 'But at least I can concentrate on the costumes. I need to go through what we've got already and see what I can do… I hope nobody's put on weight.'

'Hmph,' I thought grumpily about my weight and made a promise to myself to stick to my diet.

'Dear Lola is making the maids aprons over the weekend,' she continued. 'I need to Google what an inspector would wear.'

I glanced over at Johnny, our inspector, who was sitting in the second row deep in conversation with Destiny and Pontus. Even though he was *well* into his forties and completely bald, he was also kind of *hot*, in an experienced man-of-the-world way.

He also seemed to have brought the maternal side out in the women after coming to rehearsals the year before in floods of tears after discovering his wife of fifteen years had been sleeping with his best friend.

Since then he was constantly being invited

to people's houses for dinner, and Violet regularly brought in her homemade cakes for him to take home.

Even Samantha, who was a little cold and snooty, obsessed with her teacup Poodle Heidi, and rarely joined in social events, had been flirting with him and went out of her way to speak to him.

'Don't forget it's Johnny's birthday drinks Saturday night,' Violet reminded me.

'Oh, crap,' I put my hands over my eyes. 'I had.'

'Oh, you must come,' she frowned at me.

'I will,' I had no set plans but would rather have spent a night alone with Jaco.

'Hey, ladies,' Stuart had ambled over. 'I have a card for Jamie and Ellie for you to sign.'

'Oh, right,' I took the card off of him, examining the picture on the front of a blue elephant cradling two baby elephants. 'Lovely,' I scribbled my name underneath Francesca's curly scrawl and handed it to Violet.

'I'll collect gift money after we're done here,' Stuart said, and went over to where Teddy and Lola were standing.

'OK, children,' Duncan called loudly. 'We all seem a little distracted tonight,' he grinned. 'We've got fifteen minutes to go before Mr Pilchard comes and grumbles at us... shall we practice your scream, Roxy?'

'If I must,' I inwardly groaned, standing up and walking to the centre of the stage.

'Tuck your tummy in,' Violet came and put her hand on my midriff. 'Blow out air and then deep breath and scream.'

Ignoring all the pairs of eyes upon me, I did as she

told me and let out an impressive scream, only spoilt by starting to cough towards the end.

'Here,' to my surprise, Finn offered me his bottle of Evian.

'Thanks,' I took a tiny sip and cleared my throat.

'Try and fill your lungs, like you're going under water,' Finn said.

'Or giving a blow job,' Violet said loudly to peals of laughter from most of the group; Lola went bright red and Jeremy looked at Violet sinisterly.

'Violet!' I giggled.

'One can breathe through one's nose doing that,' Crystal said serenely, giving Teddy a smouldering look.

'Oh, my God,' I now couldn't stop my giggling and covered my face with my hands for a moment.

'You lot are incorrigible,' Duncan shook his head.

'OK, OK, I got this,' I composed myself and stared straight ahead, before taking a deep breath, then screamed before I thought about it too much, trying to do it less ferociously as to avoid another coughing fit.

'Brilliantly done,' Duncan clapped. 'We'll be rehearsing that scene on Monday, have a practice at home.'

'I'll try, but I'm very aware of my neighbours.'

'Practice at mine,' Teddy said. 'Jim below me is deaf and I don't like the couple next door anyway. Hopefully the Demon will die of fright.'

'The Demon?' Francesca asked.

'Their cat, Jethro,' I told her. 'Teddy says it's plotting his death.'

'Jethro!' Francesca laughed.

'It is,' Teddy interjected. 'Bloody great ginger thing with one eye. It sits on their balcony staring over at mine. It hissed at me the other day. I swore it said '*Teddy*'.'

'He's quite sweet, really,' I said. 'He was asleep on my mat in the corridor the other day, I gave him a little tummy tickle.'

'Probably waiting for me to get home,' said Teddy darkly.

'How did he lose his eye?' Francesca frowned.

'Fight with a Rottweiler. Jethro won.'

'You liar!' Francesca shoved his arm playfully. 'Aw, I love cats.'

Suddenly there was a boom of thunder and we all looked up to the windows that ran high-up along the auditorium seats.

'Can't believe this shit weather just as school has broken up,' Francesca said grouchily.

I left Teddy and Francesca talking and went to grab my bag from the edge of the stage.

'You OK, my beauty?' I looked up as Destiny walked over.

'Hi, yeah,' I checked my phone. 'Tired.'

'You need more vitamin B12,' she said wisely.

'Uh huh,' I smiled agreeably, used to her advice on such matters. 'Or more sleep.'

'Ah, too much bed, not enough sleep,' she smiled, tucking her red hair behind her ears. 'How's the new man?'

'Not ever so new now,' I shoved my phone back in my bag. 'Yeah, all good.'

'Lovely,' she put her head on one side. 'I love a

happy romance.'

There was another boom of thunder, followed by a low rumble.

'I hope Heidi is OK,' Samantha joined us, also checking her phone. 'My husband's looking after her.'

'Bless her,' I murmured vaguely.

'She peed on the kitchen floor the other night, she was so scared,' she pulled a hairband off of her wrist and scraped her dark curls up into a bun. 'Poor baby.'

'Oh, I had the same problem,' Teddy trotted down the steps.

'I didn't know you had a dog,' Samantha said.

'I haven't,' he grinned broadly.

Samantha narrowed her pale eyes and gave him a dirty look.

'You're such a silly sausage,' Destiny smiled and shook her head.

'Look at that rain,' I looked up at the windows.

'I'm collecting money,' Stuart came over with the baby card.

'Ooo, OK,' I dived back into my bag for my purse.

There was a crack of thunder again, then a bang of the doors in the entrance. Everyone nearby looked up; the double doors were pushed open and to my surprise, Jaco strode in.

'Hello,' I said, feeling confused as to why he was there, watching him walk up the aisle towards me.

'Hi, sweetheart,' a smile was on his face, his eyes firmly on me. 'Thought I'd come and surprise you, give you a lift home,' he reached me and kissed me lightly, then grinned at Teddy. 'Alright, buddy?'

'Jac,' Teddy nodded.

'Ah, the new man,' Destiny gazed at him.

'Indeed,' Jaco chuckled.

Aware of curious looks, I gave an embarrassed smile, 'Everyone, this is Jaco.'

'Hello,' Jaco said politely, putting a hand up.

'*Nice,*' Violet mouthed at me, giving a not-so-discreet thumbs up.

'I'm nearly done,' I said to Jaco.

'No hurry,' Jaco kissed me again, then sat on one of the front seats.

'Rox?' Stuart waved the card at me.

'Oh, yeah,' I opened my purse and pulled out a ten-pound note.

'I'll bung in a tenner,' Teddy said, pulling some money out of his pocket, shoving the change back in.

'What's this?' Jaco asked.

'New babies,' I elaborated. 'Twin boys.'

'Oh, let me,' Jaco stood up.

'Oh, no,' I protested. 'You don't even know them.'

'So?' Jaco frowned. 'You do.'

He pulled out his wallet and handed a wad of twenties to Stuart.

'Ah, mate,' Stuart smiled in delight. 'That's *stellar*, cheers, mate.'

I watched as Finn stuffed a five-pound note back into his pocket.

'Oh, what a sweetie,' Crystal descended upon us, her breasts threatening to spill out of her tight top.

Jaco gave her a self-deprecating grin and slung an arm around me.

'That's nearly three-hundred quid,' Stuart counted his collection. 'They'll be chuffed to bits.'

'When's he back for rehearsals?' Finn asked.

'Monday for sure,' Stuart carefully put the money in the envelope and sealed it.

'Pub, anyone?' Duncan said, jogging down the steps.

'Not me,' Samantha said briskly.

'Nor me,' Jeremy said. 'Donna's on a night-shift.'

'Shame,' Teddy muttered.

'I must get home too,' Violet added.

'Roxy?' Jaco squeezed my shoulders, kissing the top of my head.

'If you want to,' I secretly would have rather gone home and showered.

Wally had already shuffled in, looking grimly at the mess of chairs and various members milling around.

'We're just off,' Duncan called to him meekly.

'Did anyone turn off the kitchen lights?' Teddy whispered. 'He shouted at us last time.'

The pub across the road was practically empty, which was just as well as we took up four tables.

'Everyone keeps telling me their names,' Jaco muttered in my ear at the bar. 'I can't remember who's who.'

'Don't worry,' I giggled.

'What you drinking, Teddy?' Jaco asked over my head.

'Half, I'm driving,' Teddy shifted closer to us away from Crystal.

'She seems nice,' Jaco grinned wickedly.

'Shh,' I elbowed him.

'Ah, not my type,' Teddy said taking off his glasses and rubbing the lenses on his T-shirt.

'Oh, my love,' Crystal grabbed his face and beamed at him. 'I've never seen you without your glasses, so handsome. You should wear contacts.'

'I'll keep that in mind,' Teddy looked terrified and Jaco burst out laughing.

'Oh, but he is,' Crystal looked at Jaco, clearly mistaking the reason for his laughter.

'Absolutely,' Jaco nodded.

'*Help me,*' Teddy mouthed at me, then, 'What was that, Derek? Excuse me.'

He hurried over to the nearest table towards Derek who was looking at him in confusion.

'Go and sit down, sweetheart,' Jaco patted my bum.

'Poor Teddy,' Destiny said, inching her chair over to me. 'He worships the ground you walk on, that boy,' she added.

'I hope so,' I looked over at Jaco.

'I meant Teddy,' she said, winking.

'He's a good mate,' I said, feeling stunned by her comment.

'He's very handsome.'

'Jaco or Teddy?'

'Jaco!'

'Yeah, he is,' I smiled to myself.

'I wouldn't say Teddy is handsome... cute, yes. Handsome is so over-rated.'

'You reckon?'

'Oh, yes,' she smiled her thanks at Stuart as he put a large glass of wine in front of her. 'Like my Robin... he's not a handsome man,' I tried to keep a straight face - her husband Robin was a skinny, straggly-haired man, 'he is a gentle soul and it shines through all his...

physical faults.'

'Sure,' I nodded.

'Teddy *does* have a nice body though,' she said musingly. 'Nice bottom.'

'Yeah?' I said as evenly as I could manage.

'Francesca thinks so, I reckon,' she nodded towards the bar where Francesca had joined Teddy and Jaco. 'They'd make a nice couple.'

'Hmm,' I shrugged.

'Of course, I could be wrong,' she took a gulp of wine. 'Urgh, Robin's homemade is *so* much better... I mean,' she continued. 'We all thought you and Teddy were... well, you know.'

'Oh!' I exclaimed. 'Really? Who?'

'Me, Meadow, Lily, Jamie, Bob.'

'Yeah?' I studied her for a moment, then shook my head. 'We are just mates.'

'Nice to have good mates,' she nodded agreeably.

'There we go,' Jaco came over and put my glass of orange juice down.

'Thank you,' I hoped that Destiny was going to shut up now.

'Teddy was just telling me about your scream,' he sat down next to me. 'I can help you later,' he whispered.

It was nearly eleven o'clock by the time we got back to my flat. Jaco was in good spirits, saying everyone seemed like a terrific bunch.

Excusing myself, I went and had a shower, then threw on a T-shirt and shorts, before joining Jaco on my bed.

'You tired, sweetheart?'

'Ish,' I stretched out next to him. 'My body is more tired than my head.'

'Baby,' he stroked my tummy. 'Roll over.'

I did as I was told and he began to gently stroke my back, occasionally tracing my scars.

'That's nice,' I murmured.

'Did you have fun tonight?' he asked.

'Yeah,' I sighed.

'That Finn seems a bit of a prat,' he chuckled. 'He was telling me about his acting 'career'.'

'He's an idiot.'

'Yeah, I got that.'

'Lucky me, I've got to kiss the idiot,' I said without thinking.

'You what?' Jaco's stroking stopped abruptly.

'Last scene,' I explained quickly. 'Just a stage kiss, mouth firmly closed.'

'Right.'

He started stroking again.

'Don't be jealous or anything,' I said. 'Like, it's just in the script.'

'I don't get jealous,' he sounded derisive, and I twisted around to look at him. 'I'm not that insecure.'

I wanted to disagree after his behaviour when he saw Peter and I, but I remained silent.

'Have you and Teddy ever had to *stage kiss*?'

'No,' I said lightly.

'That would be weird for you, I guess.'

'Oh, totally,' I agreed, desperately wanting to get off the subject.

'Would you, though?'

'If it was in the script,' I started to feel uneasy. 'Do

you want a drink? I fancy a cuppa.'

'Sure.'

I slid back off the bed and went to the kitchen.

'Can I jump in the shower?' Jaco called.

'Yeah,' I called back.

Waiting for the kettle to boil, I opened up the window above the sink to let in some cool air - it had stopped raining at last and there was a light breeze.

As I listened to the hiss of the shower, I forced myself to ponder over the uneasiness that Jaco had made me feel *again*.

I knew that I couldn't keep ignoring it, but I really didn't know how to address it… or what exactly it was that I would be addressing.

Like, '*Jaco, you keep saying things I don't like,*' sounded ridiculous… '*Jaco sometimes you scare me a little,*' … I suddenly felt tears fill my eyes and fought to keep them under control. I *wasn't* scared of him, was I?

No, not scared… wary? Unsure of him? I stared unseeingly at the dark window that showed my dim reflection from the light under the cupboard. *Sometimes he seems so… unpredictable, I can feel something under the surface and sometimes he's like two different people. Is it me though? Is it my stupid one-hundred-miles-an-hour brain tricking me? I don't know… I love him though, I really love him…*

As I pulled myself out of my reverie, I jumped as I saw Jaco's reflection behind me.

'Sweetheart,' he said as I turned around, 'you were miles away, you OK there?'

'Yes,' I smiled. 'Sorry, head full of lines and stuff…

185

I'm always like this after rehearsals.'

'Baby,' he blinked down at me, his eyes tender. 'Go on, I'll make the tea, you go and get comfy in bed.'

'Thank you,' I kissed his jaw and then left him in the kitchen, my mind full of uncertainty.

CHAPTER FIFTEEN

Johnny had invited Jaco along for his birthday bash on Saturday evening. I had quickly explained to Jaco that I had totally forgotten about it. Jaco had affectionately tugged my ponytail, telling me it didn't matter and then happily accepted.

We met up at a quaint little pub on the outskirts of Fernberry called The Fat Hen which was Johnny's local.

The pub had put on a little spread for him and was playing some 'seventies and 'eighties music.

We had got a taxi with Teddy as we all wanted to have a drink, picking up Derek along the way who happily told us that his sinuses were clear now the weather had turned cooler.

'Snappy dresser,' Jaco had murmured in my ear, taking in Derek's khaki trousers and neatly ironed white short-sleeved shirt.

'Sh,' I nudged him, wriggling over in the back seat to make room for Derek.

Even though it hadn't rained since the day before, everything was still wet, and the pub garden smelt kind of *mouldy* as we made our way in.

'Happy birthday,' I spotted Johnny at the bar with Nathan and Duncan. 'For you,' I handed him a card and a wrapped bottle of whisky and kissed him on the cheek.

'Thanks, my love,' he beamed, then shook hands

with the men.

'Guys,' Francesca waved to us from a table nearby – used to seeing her dressed sportily or super-casual, I admired her in a slinky pale-gold dress, her long legs crossed showing a lot of toned thigh.

Lola was sat next to her, looking less glamourous in dark jeans and a floral blouse, her hair in a pink Alice band.

'Hi,' I waved, telling Jaco I wanted a gin and lemonade, then went over to them. 'Wish I'd put a dress on now,' I grumbled as I sat down opposite them, feeling drab in my denim mini-skirt and T-shirt.

'You look lovely,' Lola said quietly, smiling shyly.

'Your hair!' I suddenly noticed that her fair locks were a pretty shade of golden blonde. 'Wow, I love it.'

'Oh, thank you,' she patted it self-consciously. 'Went to the hairdressers today.'

'Baby,' Jaco appeared behind me, putting my drink down. 'Hi… Lola?' he frowned, and she nodded, blushing. 'How are you? And, Francesca?'

'Correct and hello,' she smiled.

'You OK for drinks, ladies? You sure? OK,' he sat next to me, draping an arm along the back of my chair. 'I stuck a ton behind the bar,' he told me.

'Oh gosh, why?' I tutted.

'Why not?' he looked around the pub. 'Nice here… he seems like a good guy, Johnny.'

'He's a sweetie,' Francesca said.

More people arrived, converging on Johnny and handing him cards and gifts.

Teddy ambled over as the bar began to fill and sat himself next to Lola. As he and Jaco started to talk across the table, I turned to wave Violet over, who had just turned up clutching a huge bunch of flowers.

'Johnny doesn't seem like a flowers kind of guy,' Francesca giggled as Violet handed them to him before coming over to our table.

'Hello, my dears,' she settled herself down and promptly took out a half-bottle of vodka from her bag.

'Oh, for goodness sake,' I glanced towards the bar. 'Vi, if they see that, they'll kick you out.'

'They shouldn't charge so much, then,' she shrugged her frail shoulders, looking indifferent.

'Well at least be discreet,' I patted her hand. 'You're so naughty.'

'Yeah,' she shrugged again and smiled serenely.

'Oh, Violet,' Lola giggled.

The evening was fun and Jaco seemed to get on with everyone, even Finn.

He didn't insist on being glued to my side either, which was surprising as he only really knew Teddy.

Initially I felt a tad uncomfortable as nobody else had brought a plus one, but he was definitely a hit, particularly with the girls.

I had been sitting with Teddy sharing a plate of sausage rolls and pizza, watching in amusement as Crystal, Destiny and Meadow cornered him, all fluttering their eyelashes and giggling at whatever he was saying to them.

'I should be offended,' Teddy said through a mouthful of food. 'It seems Crystal has transferred her affections.'

'Aw, Teddy,' I put my head on his shoulder and

made a sad face.

'If he disappears down her cleavage, I ain't rescuing him.'

Jaco glanced over and I waved, 'Well he looks happy enough.'

'Strange combo, a man-eater, a hippy and a BDSM fanatic-'

'Allegedly.'

'Allegedly… he should be very afraid.'

We watched as Finn strode over to join them.

'Do you think he's feeling left out?' I said as he started talking to Meadow.

'Probably, the doughball. I've never met anyone so enchanted with their own waffle.'

'I know, right?' I agreed, then sat up straight and winced.

'You OK, honey?'

'Pelvis,' I muttered. 'I overdid it at the gym after work.'

'You need a painkiller?'

'I think I've drunk too much, I daren't.'

'Come on, let's go and walk around, that helps, doesn't it?' he put the plate down and stood up, holding out a hand.

'Yeah,' I let him pull me up and I wiggled my hips then stretched my back.

'Who shall we go and annoy?' he looked around.

'Hey,' Jaco had come over - he was smiling, but his eyes were narrowed.

'You escaped then,' I said.

'Go on, have a wander,' Teddy patted my back and went off towards Francesca and Nathan, who were at the bar.

'What's up?' Jaco asked, frowning.

'Oh, my pelvis had a twinge, that's all,' I said.

'You OK?'

'Fine, I just need to walk around for a bit.'

'Let's go outside,' he took my hand. 'I need some fresh air, been gagging on Crystal's perfume,' he chuckled.

Relieved that he wasn't angry after all, I followed him outside, past the two or three people smoking, then walked up the path that ran through the pub's garden.

We stopped near a play area and he sat on the edge of a table.

'Rox, I've got to say, you and Teddy looked a bit *too* cosy there,' he said, catching me off-guard.

'You what?' I felt that familiar inner drop of dread and sighed. 'Jaco, don't be daft… it's just me and Teddy.'

'Yeah, yeah,' he looked up at the sky, his jaw tense. 'I know.'

'Hmm,' I tried to joke, 'for someone who doesn't get jealous, you don't 'alf get jealous.'

'No, not jealous,' his head snapped down and he looked affronted. 'I just don't appreciate you snuggling up to him like that.'

'We were just messing about,' I folded my arms, starting to get angry. 'He's my friend. You are friends with Evie, aren't you?'

'That's work,' he said in a low voice.

'Right,' I stared at him. 'But, kind of not just work.'

'So, you have a problem with her?'

'What? No!' I lied. 'Just saying.'

'Sure,' he stared back at me, his expression indecipherable.

'Jaco, please don't be like this,' I said shortly. 'We've had a nice evening and you're being silly. Teddy is my friend and I'm sorry if you don't like it, but that's how it is.'

I said all of this in an even voice, and I could hear a note of exasperation, but my heart was hammering wildly, and I felt sick to the stomach.

'Right,' he stood up and glared at me, then looked away. 'Baby, I'm sorry, I just know what he's like. And it bothers me.'

'What's he like?' I exclaimed. 'What's your problem with him? You were friends for ages and you've been perfectly nice to him all evening!'

'He's a player,' he snapped.

'No, he's not,' I wanted to laugh. 'And even if he was, we've been friends for long enough for him to have tried it on. And he ain't, so stop it!' I almost stamped my foot, before striding off.

'Rox,' he hurried after me. 'Roxy, wait,' he caught up with me.

'What?' I stopped and put my hands on my hips.

'Feisty little minx aren't you?' he smiled. 'Listen, will you?'

'Go on.'

'Look, I know he's your friend,' he put a hand on my shoulder. 'That's fine, that's cool… and I know you don't want to think he's that way, OK. I'm just uneasy because I love you. And I do love you, so much.'

'Yeah?' I exhaled and relaxed slightly. 'I love you too… but Jaco, sometimes you… sometimes I don't like how you get,' there, I'd said it... but instead of relief, I felt despondency.

'Eh?' he looked genuinely perplexed.

'Well... this... and about me having to kiss Finn-'

'What? I'm interested in your acting! Is that a crime?'

'No,' I faltered slightly.

'I think you've read me all wrong,' he bit his lip. 'D-don't you want to be with me?'

'Yes,' I said quickly, starting to doubt myself - doubt my *doubts*.

'You're frightening me,' he blinked a few times. 'Look, I'm sorry if you're thinking things that aren't there... if I come across as... whatever you're thinking.'

'I'm not... thinking anything,' I felt the final bit of fight leave me, then felt guilty, *then* felt weak.

'Good,' he bent down and kissed me softly. 'Good. I love you, Roxy.'

'I love you too.'

'Well... good,' he held out a hand. 'Let's go and get another drink.'

I followed him back in, disturbed that the last ten-minutes seemed bizarrely blurry... I went to the bar alone while Jaco went to the gents.

'Alright, Roxy?' I turned to see Jeremy standing next to me, smiling his creeper smile, showing his small teeth with their wide front gap.

'Hiya, enjoying the party?' I asked breezily, standing on my tiptoes trying to attract the attention of the barmaid.

'Yes, thanks. Nice to get out.'

'Hm.'

There were so many things about Jeremy that put me on edge. It wasn't just that he looked creepy, with his small, pale-grey eyes that would fix on you with intensity, his combed back hair, showing a strangely smooth forehead and his skinny frame, he was just so... *peculiar*.

He had two young children and a wife, that was all I knew about his personal life as they were only mentioned when he bemoaned about her working long hours with almost hateful resentment.

He was *too* quiet, never raised complaints, but would fix the person that had angered him with a dark and foreboding stare... and he seemed to get angry a *lot*. Even the jovial Duncan seemed to tick Jeremy off frequently.

That all said though, he was a good actor and slid with ease into any role he played.

He raised a finger and to my irritation, the barmaid came straight over.

'Half a bitter,' he said unsmilingly.

'*Or die a terrible death,*' I muttered to myself, then giggled, randomly wishing Teddy was stood next to me and had heard me.

I looked around for Jaco, my eyes resting on Teddy who was sitting on a low stool, animatedly talking to a few people. Francesca was sat next to him, her arm touching his and watching him, laughing every now and then. I sighed miserably - I really wished Jaco hadn't said all of those things about Teddy. I was sure they weren't true... but why would Jaco lie? He knew him from old... and I supposed in a timeframe, Teddy was a *new* friend to me.

As if sensing my stare, Teddy looked over and grinned, then spotting Jeremy he clamped his hands over his face, peeking out as if in fright.

I let out another giggle, then stopped immediately as Jeremy, now with his drink in his hand, turned his head and looked at me.

'Catch you later,' he nodded and walked away.

'Please don't,' I said quietly, then at last spotted Jaco coming towards me, followed by Meadow and Destiny.

'Not been served?' he leant over the bar and the barmaid came back over, all smiles.

'Hello, Rox,' Meadow said. 'He's lovely, your Jaco,' she lowered her voice, her pretty dark eyes round. 'He just told me that *he* tried vegetarianism once, but got too grumpy,' she laughed. 'Not sure if he was winding me up.'

I gazed at her in amazement; Meadow took her vegetarianism *very* seriously, she *never* joked about it… I thought that it said a lot for Jaco's natural charm.

'Couldn't tell you,' I shrugged.

'I told him I could convert him, but he said he likes steak too much.'

'Ha, yeah,' I eyed her, wondering if she knew how flirtatious she sounded.

'Sweetheart,' Jaco handed me another gin.

'Thank you,' I smiled and took a huge sip.

'White wine for you, Destiny,' he slid a glass along the bar. 'Grapefruit juice, you poor soul,' he gave Meadow one of his big grins.

I wondered briefly if he was trying to make me jealous. Meadow was very attractive with her long dark

195

hair and lithe figure underneath her simple beige dress... I suddenly thought about her supposedly missing nipple and started to smile, resisting the impulse to stare at her chest.

'Shall we go and socialise?' Jaco said, bringing me out of my trance.

'Sure,' I said, wondering if I should still be acting a little mad at him... then thinking I really couldn't muster it. I had had too much to drink to think straight and I was incredibly tired after a few nights of not sleeping that well.

We went over to where everyone was sitting, people in various states of inebriation.

Johnny the birthday boy was slurring his words and hugging everyone - even Jeremy, so I guessed he had drunk more than was good for him.

Teddy started chatting to me as I sat down, and I hated how wary I felt of Jaco's scrutiny.

Jaco himself seemed super-hyper, I wondered if he was trying to prove a point or something after our tiff outside... feeling woozy on too many gins and not much food, I couldn't decide what was going on at all. I felt slightly depressed and a little removed from it all, laughing and chatting in autopilot.

I thought that Teddy gave me a couple of enquiring looks, but decided it was my imagination.

All in all, I was glad when last orders were called, and I could go home.

Jaco stayed at my flat, but I over-exaggerated my drunkenness and curled up on my bed as soon as we got in and closed my eyes. I eventually fell asleep listening to the TV and whatever film Jaco was watching out in the living room.

I woke up still dressed and curled up, to the smell of bacon and noises from the kitchen.

'Jaco?' I croaked, rolling off the bed and shuffling out.

'Good morning, beautiful,' he stuck his head out of the kitchen door. 'Tea, coffee or orange juice?'

'Where did the bacon come from?' I asked in confusion.

'I've been up since seven,' he grinned. 'Had a shower, went to Asda and folded up your laundry,' he pointed to my basket full of neatly folded clothes that had been in a tangled mess for two days.

'Wow,' I smiled, then pulled a face. 'I need to brush my teeth and shower.'

'Go ahead baby, I'll turn the bacon down.'

I showered and wrapped a towel around myself, seeing a plate piled with bacon and eggs on the coffee table with my bottle of tomato ketchup next to it as I went back into the living room.

'I'll never eat all that,' I laughed and sat down.

'Yeah you will,' he called from the kitchen. 'What do you want to drink?'

'Juice, thank you.'

As I started to eat, I wondered whether this was his way of apologising for the night before. If it was, it was a lovely gesture, but I still felt there had been a lot unsaid. The feeling of unfinished business was large and uncomfortable, and as much as I wanted to put it out of my head, I knew I had to say something.

'Can you even taste anything, apart from ketchup?'

197

he came and joined me on the sofa with his plate. 'Oh, sorry… do you want any bread?'

'No, this is great, thank you. Eat yours.'

He gave me an affectionate grin and started to eat at speed, 'You got any plans today?'

'Well, I need to go to my mums', she's been nagging… which reminds me,' I swallowed some juice and tried to look apologetic, 'she keeps asking when I'm bringing you around again.'

'That's nice.'

'Yeah?' I watched him chop up an egg with the side of his fork. 'Want to come today?'

'Sure!'

'Really?'

'Yes,' he nodded. 'Why wouldn't I?'

'Well… I dunno,' I shrugged.

'Well, there we go then.'

CHAPTER SIXTEEN

I rang my mum and she ended up insisting that we had lunch there, telling me that Shauna and her husband Liam, and baby Emilie of course, would be coming too, and '*what the heck*', she would do a big family roast.

Jaco seemed chuffed to bits, and on our way there he stopped to buy a bouquet of flowers for her.

'Sucking up, eh?' I gave him a poke in his side.

'*Always* be nice to the in-laws,' he said jokingly – even so, I smiled to myself wondering if that would be true one day.

'When do I get to meet your lot?'

'You've met Sadie,' he said.

'I meant your parents.'

'Yeah, I know,' he glanced at me. 'Yeah, you will, soon.'

I had to content myself with that as we were turning into my mum's road, but I thought he seemed… reluctant.

'Hello!' my mum came out the front door as we pulled up, waving madly.

'Urgh,' I sighed and climbed out. 'Hi Mum,' I kissed her cheek.

'You look lovely,' she eyed me. 'Putting on weight at last,' I gave Jaco a glare as he chuckled.

'Hello again,' she beamed up at Jaco as he gave her the flowers.

'Hello,' he winked at me over her head. 'Thanks for the invite… I haven't had a roast for ages, my mum never cooks them.'

'Oh, you are in for a treat, then,' we followed her indoors. 'I'm cooking roast chicken *and* roast gammon… Roxy's favourite, isn't it, darling?'

'Yup,' I looked into the living room as we went past; Jacob was slumped on the sofa glued to his phone. 'Alright, loser?'

'Bimbo,' he muttered.

'Virgin,' I called over my shoulder as I went down the hall.

'Spaco!' he shouted.

'Jacob!' my mum stopped in her tracks. 'Go and get a drink in the kitchen,' she commanded as she thrust her flowers at me and then re-traced her steps. A moment later we heard the living room door close and her yelling at Jacob.

'Uh oh,' Howard was standing at the kitchen sink, peeling potatoes. 'What's he done now?' he turned slightly and peered over his glasses. 'Hello Jaco, how are you?'

'I'm very well, thank you.'

'Sorry,' I put the flowers on the table. 'Partly my fault.'

'Oh, don't apologise,' Howard chuckled, continuing his peeling. 'There's probably a few misdemeanours of his we have missed, a little telling off never hurt anyone.'

'True,' I went to the fridge. 'Can we grab a beer?'

'You sure can,' he nodded. 'Shame we can't sit outside, damn rain.'

'Never mind,' I handed Jaco a beer and we both sat on the kitchen bench.

'Roxy tells me that your mother is Kat Sokolov,' Howard said. 'Nice lady, very talented.'

'Yeah,' Jaco agreed. 'Unfortunately, my sister inherited all the musical talent.'

'Yes, she's spoken about Sadie before, says she shunned classical music though,' he threw a smile over his shoulder. 'She says she sings like an angel though.'

'She really does,' Jaco nodded. 'She should have taken it up professionally.'

'Ah, well,' Howard gave him a wise look, 'hard business to break into. I hear her tattoo parlour… parlour? Do they call it that?... I hear she is doing well.'

'Flat out, all the time.'

At that moment my mum came in, a tightness around her mouth, 'He's sulking now,' she announced. 'Roxy, please don't wind him up though, you get to go home. I'm stuck with the little beast.'

'I won't,' I assured her.

'I'll go and defrost him,' Jaco kissed my cheek and stood up.

'Oh, he's a love,' my mum watched him leave.

'Nice boy,' Howard said.

'He is,' I smiled to myself.

'When's Shauna and Liam getting here?' Howard asked.

'Soon,' my mum replied sharply, and I thought I saw Howard curbing a sigh.

I wouldn't say that she has a problem with Shauna exactly, although they clash occasionally – similar personalities and all that – and she *adores* being a grandma… but she isn't convinced that Liam is the *'right sort of husband'* for her daughter.

I like Liam a lot, he is kind and he is a hard-worker and he is a good father - but he has a bit of a bad boy past.

I didn't think it mattered one bit, it was *ages* ago, like when they met in their early twenties. I knew he had been heavily into drugs and was arrested for stealing a car, and I knew that he used to drink a lot too. But he had sorted himself out and I couldn't see what the problem was.

My mum also hadn't forgiven them for getting married in secret when she fell pregnant with Emilie. I personally didn't blame them, my mum would have tried to talk her out of it, then when that didn't work, she would have taken over the wedding preparations.

'I'm just going upstairs,' Jaco stuck his head in the door. 'He's thawed out,' he added in a whisper. 'He's showing me his new game.'

'Oh, my goodness, you are kind,' my mum's expression turned soft immediately.

'His PlayStation back upstairs, then?' I asked.

'Yes, well,' she looked defensive. 'The noise was driving me mad,' she busied herself putting her flowers in a vase. 'I confiscated that awful game… um-'

'GTA,' Howard interjected.

'Yes, that,' she frowned. 'So much swearing.'

'Well, it *is* an eighteen,' I told her.

The front door banged loudly, and I jumped up, 'I'll get it,' I rushed down the hall and opened the door, impatient to see my niece.

202

'Hi,' Shauna beamed, looking pretty in a denim pinafore, her fair hair tied back. Liam stood behind her with Emilie in his arms.

'Give!' I commanded, holding my arms out. Liam laughed and handed her to me.

'With pleasure, the little monkey,' he chuckled as they followed me in.

I simply *love* Emilie, she is so beautiful and chubby and happy, 'Hi,' I kissed her nose and she smiled, showing her four tiny teeth, top and bottom. 'I've missed you, yes I have,' I squeezed her to me gently and she giggled.

'Shall we go home?' Shauna joked. 'She's been a right grouch all weekend with her teeth.'

'Aw is my clever girl getting new toothy-pegs?' I crooned, and Emilie chanted 'Ce-Ce', her word for 'Roxy'.

Soon as I reached the kitchen, my mum descended upon us and took her off of me, 'There's Nana's little angel,' she cried. 'Hello, you two,' she added smiling at Shauna, then somewhere above Liam's head.

'Sit down, sit down,' Howard was wiping his hands on a tea towel. 'I'll get drinks, how are you, young man?' he shook Liam's hand and then bent and kissed Shauna's cheek.

'Pretty good, fella,' Liam dumped the baby bag on the table, then removed it as my mum tutted. 'I'll put this in the hall,' he got up and left the room.

'Why don't we put the youngsters in the living room?' Howard said, watching my mum. 'And we can get on with dinner?'

'Come on,' I said to Shauna, then took Emilie back.

'She doesn't miss an opportunity, does she?' she grumbled. 'Living room,' she added to Liam who was coming back up the hall. 'Get out of the dragons' way.'

'Shh,' I whispered.

'Well!' she hissed, her expression irritated.

'I know, I know,' I said placatingly.

'What have I missed?' Liam looked confused and I just shook my head.

'So where is the new man in your life?' Shauna asked once we were settled in the living room, her tone light again - I'll give Shauna her due, for a hothead she always recovers quickly.

'Been dragged upstairs by Jacob,' I said from the floor where I was holding Emilie's hands as she took wobbly steps. 'Clever girl!'

'How's it going?' Liam asked with interest.

'Pretty good,' I smiled brightly, ignoring the nudge of *all not being right*, but what else could I say?

'Cool,' he grinned, his eyes on Emilie and his expression slightly gooey.

I studied his face – I'd always thought he has really pretty eyes, a weird hazel/green that change colour, and with the *best* eyelashes. Emilie has Shauna's blue eyes, almost the same as mine but slightly lighter.

'Mum says he's better looking than Peter,' Shauna rolled her eyes. 'She always flirts around your blokes.'

'She does not,' I giggled.

'You won't have that problem with me,' Liam smiled wryly.

'Oh, I'll flirt with you,' Shauna blinked coyly and snuggled up to his side.

'Urgh, stop it,' I pretended to gag.

'Flirt is all I can do, we haven't had sex for three weeks,' Shauna said in her usual blunt way. 'Either she wakes up or we are too knackered.'

'I'll have her over-night,' I said hopefully. 'You know I will.'

'I know hun,' Shauna said gratefully. 'It's just she's so much hard work.'

'I hardly sleep anyway,' I shrugged. 'We can snuggle all night and watch Disney movies.'

'Hi,' Jaco's voice came from behind me and I twisted around as he came through the door.

'Ah, at last,' Shauna beamed.

'Jaco, this is Shauna and Liam... oh, and Emilie,' I kissed one of her chubby hands. 'Guys, this is Jaco.'

'She's beautiful,' Jaco sat down on the floor next to me and Emilie eyed him before making a grab for his hand.

'Oh my, what a flirt,' Shauna giggled. 'Hello, nice to meet you.'

I glanced up at Liam and was surprised to see his face slightly... *hostile?* ... I wasn't sure.

'Nice to meet you,' Jaco held out a hand to him and after a slight hesitation, he shook it briefly then sat back.

'Alright?' Liam said gruffly.

'I've just been introduced to the world of God of War,' Jaco rolled his eyes. 'Wants me to play after lunch, I said I'll see.'

'You don't have to,' I put a hand on his arm.

'Ah, I don't mind, he's an alright kid.'

'He's a little turd,' Shauna said, and we all laughed

205

except Liam, who got up and excused himself before leaving the room.

'Is he OK?' I whispered.

'Tired as fuck,' Shauna said. 'Teething is hell on earth… he's been doing long hours too.'

'Bless him,' I murmured.

'But you are a cutie, aren't you?' Jaco held out both hands and Emilie grabbed them and took unsteady steps to him, then grabbed his shirt front and giggled.

'Don't be fooled,' Shauna said dryly. 'She is a devil in disguise.'

'Oh no,' Jaco stood up and scooped her up with him. 'I don't believe that,' he went over to the long mirror in the hall. 'Look at you,' he said in a sing-song voice. 'Who's that pretty lady?'

'Oh my God,' Shauna whispered. 'Marry him and have ten kids, how sweet is that?'

'Yeah,' I watched him, feeling fluttery and weak with longing. 'That's sweet.'

Dinner was served in the dining room. I sat next to Shauna and opposite Jaco, who was now the hero of the hour. Somehow, he had managed to get Emilie to sleep by walking around with her and she was now in the portable cot that was kept in my mum's living room.

'You are a miracle worker,' Shauna said happily. 'We might actually get to finish a meal in peace, eh Liam?'

'Yeah,' Liam nodded, his smile rather forced I thought.

I wondered if my mum had upset him, she had made

206

a great show of bringing Jaco's flowers into the dining room and putting them on the sideboard.

Also, Jacob had only given Liam a cursory 'Hello' and was talking to Jaco and looking at him in hero-worship.

When Howard started carving the meat, Jaco jumped up and asked what wine people wanted and opened the bottles; I noticed Liam's shoulders going up a fraction when he looked at my mum's smile of pleasure, then he looked down, his jaw tense.

Shauna had noticed too, we looked at each other and she widened her eyes slightly and gave a subtle shrug.

I'm not sure if there was an atmosphere during the meal, I'm not always good at picking up on those things, but Howard seemed to be focussing most of his attention on Liam and being the genial father-in-law.

Dinner was scrumptious at least. I ate way more than I should have and immediately felt sleepy.

'That was awesome, thanks mum,' Shauna got up laboriously. 'I'm gonna check on Em.'

'Is there pudding?' Jacob asked, still scraping up gravy.

'I've made an apple pie and a cherry pie,' Howard told him. 'If you can fit it in.'

'Hollow legs,' my mum said.

'My mum used to say that about my little sister,' Jaco smiled at her. 'She still eats everything in sight.'

'Nothing wrong with a good appetite,' my mum glanced at Liam's plate - he had left a roast potato and a few carrots, but she frowned like he had left a mountain of food.

'Still sparko,' Shauna returned. 'I better not let her sleep too long, she won't go down tonight. What on earth was you singing to her?' she asked Jaco.

'Some Russian song my dad used to sing,' he grinned.

Liam suddenly looked at him briefly, his expression somewhere between fear and repulsion, and I felt a chill run down my back.

'OK, who's for pudding?' Howard asked.

Jaco dropped me off and went home, saying he had some paperwork to do and that he'd ring me the next day.

I tried to settle down to learn some lines for rehearsals, but Liam was on my mind.

Twice I went to text Shauna to ask if he was OK but stopped myself. It was probably just resentment... I didn't want Liam to feel like that though. I liked Liam but I also didn't want Jaco to be the cause of it.

Overthinker, overthinker, stop it you idiot, I thought to myself in irritation.

I gave up with my lines after half an hour and rang Dana for a gossip, then done some dusting and vacuuming, *then* got my script out again and laid on the floor next to my balcony door, on my belly, fingers in ears.

I was just squeezing my eyes shut and reading a long line aloud when my mobile rang.

'Hello,' it was Shauna.

'Hi,' I said in surprise, pushing myself up and crossing my legs.

'Are you home tomorrow night?' she sounded...

weird.

'I've got rehearsals, but I'm home around nine-thirty. Why?'

'Oh, that's kind of late.'

'Is everything OK?' I started to feel concerned.

'Yes!' she said quickly. 'Um, Tuesday night?'

'Yes, I'm free, why? Why do you need to see me?'

'I just… I just need to talk to you.'

'Can't you talk on the phone?'

'No.'

'Shauna, you're worrying me,' I got up and started pacing. 'Why not on the phone? Is it Liam?'

'Kind of.'

'OK, well, shall I come over to yours?'

'No,' she paused. 'I'll pop over on Tuesday. Half-seven OK?'

'Yes, that's fine… are you sure you're OK?'

'Yeah, I'm sure. I'll see you Tuesday, OK? I need to go… see you then.'

'See you,' I ended the call and stopped pacing. Whatever she said, I knew that she was definitely *not* OK.

Teddy and I went for a burger before rehearsals on Monday, and I told him about lunch at my mums', Liam's withdrawn behaviour and then Shauna's phone call.

'Hmm, my spidey senses tell me that something is not right,' Teddy said, raising an eyebrow.

'Right?' I pinched his gherkins that he'd removed from his burger. 'She sounded so odd! I think she's had a row with him.'

'Perhaps he's jealous of Jaco?'

'Perhaps.'

'Your mum shouldn't be like that to Liam, it's Shauna's choice, isn't it? And he's pulled himself together.'

'Oh, my mum is world grudge-holding champion.'

Teddy's phone rang, I glanced at it on the table and saw it was Francesca.

'You gonna answer that?' I asked as he carried on shovelling fries into his mouth.

'We'll see her in a minute,' he swallowed hard and drank some cola.

'Is there… anything going on with you guys?'

'Me and Francesca?' he looked startled. 'No… why?'

'Dunno,' I tried to read his expression, but he simply looked nonplussed. 'I reckon she fancies you though.'

'Really?' he frowned. 'Nah. Although, I'm pretty much useless at reading women. But… nah.'

I thought about that… if he was the player that Jaco insisted he was, he must have been lying.

'She's so pretty though,' I said.

'Yeah, I suppose. A bit tall though. Tall women scare me.'

'They do?' I giggled.

'No, scrap that. Women scare me, full stop.'

We walked into the theatre together and both spotted the new dad, Jamie, straight away.

'You're back!' I rushed over and kissed him. 'How are you?'

'Oh,' he shook his dark head ruefully, 'wondering

why people have children… I'm so sleep deprived I threw my trainers in the bin yesterday and thought I was going mad when I couldn't find them this morning.'

'Poor you,' I said as Teddy laughed. 'It doesn't last forever.'

'Yeah, I know,' he grinned. 'Little crackers they are, but two of them… man, it's hard work.'

'You should have pulled out… I mean the play!' Teddy said, then dropped his head. 'Bad choice of words, sorry mate.'

'It's a small part,' Jamie said, then yawned. 'Sorry… nice to leave the house for a bit if I'm honest.'

'Come on, come on,' Duncan called from the stage. 'Lots to do tonight, my dears.'

'I'm dead tonight,' Violet said from the front row. 'You better cry loads, Roxy.'

'I will,' I giggled and dumped my bag in the nearest seat.

I was in fact dreading it a tiny bit as I had a lot of dialogue with Jeremy, who was playing Doctor Sithole.

I walked towards a chair that was representing Violet laying dead in her bed, 'Auntie, it's gone eight o'clock,' I said softly.

'Roxy,' Duncan said from the edge of the stage, 'stop and look puzzled for a moment.'

I complied then said slightly louder, 'Auntie, wake up!' I bent down slightly.

'OK, at this point you would touch her shoulder,' Duncan said.

'Auntie Mabel?' I looked up at Duncan.

'Then you touch her face,' he consulted his script. 'Then take a quick step back.'

I took a step back, then filling my lungs, I screamed, my hands clutching my chest.

'Well done,' Duncan clapped.

'Nicely done,' Teddy gave me the thumbs up.

'Quick break,' Duncan called, 'then Bob, Jamie, Samantha and Finn come rushing in, OK folks?'

I went to fetch my bottle of water from my bag, then flopped down on a seat.

'Alright, lovie?' Destiny looked over from a few seats away.

'Yeah,' I grinned. 'A lot of lines tonight.'

'Fantastic scream.'

'Thanks.'

I checked my phone and saw that Jaco had texted me to say he would be over later. I stared unseeingly at the stage above and in front of me, not sure whether I was pleased or not.

We were now at the scene where Doctor Sithole had arrived.

'Seriously,' Teddy said, slightly hesitantly. '*Sithole*, Duncan?'

'Ah, I've been researching, dear boy,' Duncan said. 'We all like a bit of sinister, don't we?'

'Moses Sithole was a South African serial killer,' Jeremy piped up, causing everyone to turn and look at him.

'He was indeed,' Duncan cut in.

'Jesus,' Teddy muttered.

'I thought it would be a vague but fun name,'

Duncan gave Jeremy a worried look.

'He raped and killed in the nineties,' Jeremy said.

'Super fun,' Teddy said in an overly enthusiastic voice, causing a few people to laugh.

We went through the scene smoothly, Jeremy as usual was word perfect.

'Right, before you all escape,' Duncan said loudly, 'I would like you to come in on Wednesday for costume fitting and a meeting with Brad and Tilly.'

Brad was the set designer and Tilly was in charge of the stagehands, the guys that changed the scenery.

Everyone agreed in varying degrees of enthusiasm.

'Drinks on me afterwards,' Duncan added.

'Well, if you insist,' Teddy said to sounds of agreement.

CHAPTER SEVENTEEN

On Tuesday evening I felt awfully apprehensive waiting for Shauna. I hadn't mentioned it to Jaco, but I guessed I seemed distracted after rehearsals the night before because he asked a couple of times if I were OK. I brushed it off as tiredness, which wasn't a complete lie.

As I waited for her with a rare midweek glass of wine, I told myself I was being paranoid. As it turned out, I couldn't have been more wrong.

She knocked on my door just before half-past seven, and I answered it with the brightest smile I could muster.

'Hi,' I stood back as she came in.

'Hi,' she said, eyes downcast.

'Do you want a glass?' I held my glass up. 'Or tea? Do you want tea?'

'No, I'm fine,' she sat on the edge of the sofa and looked up at me, a strange glint in her eyes. 'I can't stay long.'

'OK,' I sat down too and put my glass down on the floor. 'So... what's wrong?'

'OK, OK,' she seemed to brace herself, closing her eyes briefly. 'I need to tell you something.'

'OK,' I felt my heart start to hammer and I experienced a horrible premonition of dread.

'Rox,' she stared at me for a few seconds. 'Jaco... I

don't think... I think there's something you should know.'

'Huh?' I tried to smile, but my face felt stiff.

'Shit,' she looked up and exhaled. 'Jaco... he's a... fuck. He's a drug dealer.'

There was a ringing silence as I took in her words, then I laughed hoarsely, 'I'm sorry?'

'Please listen,' she clasped her hands together on her legs. 'I know this is terrible, but... Liam, he knows him.'

'I'm confused,' I tried to untangle my thoughts... I wanted to laugh, but... she looked so grim. 'You need to explain... that's ridiculous!'

'Liam,' she whispered, her eyes filling with tears, 'when he was...you know. He recognised Jaco. They used to call him The R-Russian... he was their dealer, supplier... whatever.'

'No,' I shook my head violently. 'He's wrong... if that was true, Jaco would have recognised him! Liam's wrong.'

'No,' she looked down at her hands. 'Liam looked different, he was... thinner... he was *a mess*, you must remember.'

'Sure,' my voice sounded like it was coming from far away, my ears were filled with a buzzing. 'He didn't know what day it was. How the hell would he remember what some dealer looked like? No, sorry, he's wrong. Jaco is successful, he's *loaded*... he isn't some sleazy druggie.'

'Rox,' Shauna looked back up at me, a bleakness in her eyes, 'he's not wrong.'

I stood up abruptly, knocking my glass over in the

process, 'Shit,' I stepped away. 'Look, I understand if Liam was upset that mum likes Jaco, I know it's unfair that she's crappy to him, but he can't just say stuff that's…that's not true. He's wrong, he's lying.'

'No,' she shook her head, tears now falling freely down her cheeks. 'I can't make you believe me, but it's true,' she stood up. 'I'm going to go; let you think it over.'

'This is bullshit,' I followed her to the door, my legs weak and my mouth dry. 'You can't just come here, land *that* on me and go!'

'Rox,' she turned at the door and looked at me with pity in her eyes. 'I'm sorry, I had to tell you though. I know you love him, but he's… he's not a nice man.'

'You don't know him,' I whispered thinly.

'No, I don't,' she opened the door and walked out, then turned around and faced me squarely. 'I don't know him at all… but, do you?'

I watched her walk down the corridor, her shoulders down and audibly crying. I slammed the door and stood for what seemed like ages, my mind racing, at first unaware that I was crying silently.

'No,' I muttered, closing my eyes and clenching my fists. 'He's wrong… so wrong.'

I went back into the living room and stared down at my over-turned wine glass. Then I gave into my tears and sunk to the floor, a huge and painful sob escaping me.

How long I sat there, my knees drawn up to my chest and my arms wrapped around them, I don't know… I can't remember much, just awful bleak howls of pain and confusion… then I remember picking up my glass and hurling it across the room and hearing the tiny *plink* of broken glass against the wall... then I dragged myself up and sat on the edge of the sofa, trying to gather my thoughts and find a logical answer, a reason why Liam thought that Jaco was what he said he was... and I couldn't. I just *couldn't*.

Eventually I got up and fetched my dustpan and brush and swept up the glass, then cleaned the spilt wine with some kitchen roll and my lemon and lime kitchen cleaner spray. Then I went and swallowed three paracetamol and ran a bath, trying to keep my mind blank, because I didn't want to think about it anymore.

Three times my phone rang, and I ignored it, not knowing if it was Jaco or Shauna or somebody else; I simply couldn't talk to anyone.

The next day I got to work and slunk in quietly. I felt nothing short of rotten after hardly sleeping at all and I knew I didn't look much better.

'Morning, Roxy,' Spencer said as I passed him on my way in.

'Morning,' I mumbled, heading out the back to hang up my bag.

'You alright?' Troy was making his disgusting herbal tea and eating a muesli bar.

'Yeah,' I smiled as credibly as I was able and went to the fridge. 'Who's drunk my apple juices?' I muttered to myself. 'For crying out loud.'

'Were they labelled?' Troy asked.

'Yes,' I snapped. 'Bet it was Albie.'

'Very possibly,' he said casually. 'I'll ask him... are

you sure you're OK?'

'Yeah,' I straightened up. 'I'll go and open a till.'

I felt his eyes on me as I walked out and was immediately ashamed for being snappy and rude – he was my manager after all.

I kept myself to myself all morning and tried my hardest not to keep thinking about Jaco and what Shauna had said.

I had texted him the night before; it was him that had rang me all three times. I told him that I had fallen asleep and that I had a migraine and I would see him after the meeting at the theatre.

I had vaguely made up my mind to just tell him what had happened, but I was scared… really scared. Not so much of him being annoyed, more that he would tell me it was true, or worse, that he denied it but I would be able to tell he was lying.

As the unwelcome thoughts began to creep in, I started needlessly tidying a display of sports bottles on the till that were on special offer and collecting pens that were scattered around and checking the carrier bags underneath to see if we needed more from the box out the back, even though we had only had maybe a dozen customers all morning.

'Looks like we're gonna get a week of sunshine before the rain comes back,' Spencer said cheerfully from in front of me where he had been arranging some children's back to school PE kits, which to me didn't make sense as they'd only just broken up for the summer.

'Great,' I mumbled.

'I need to top up my tan before I go on holiday… did

218

I tell you that me and Jade are going to Turkey?'

'Yup.'

'Can't wait.'

'I bet.'

I looked up in irritation at Albie who was messing around with some kids' plastic footballs in a basket by the open doors.

'Hey, on the head!' Spencer called, and Albie threw one over. Spencer completely missed and it sailed over the counter, just missing me and it rebounded off the wall, knocking over the pot of pens that I'd just tidied away.

'Oh, for fuck sake!' I screamed. 'Can't you two just pack it in for five minutes?'

'Sorry, it was an accident,' Spencer looked at me with a startled expression.

'You're always pissing about,' I stormed, picking up the pens from the floor. 'Now look what you've done!'

'Jesus, Roxy. Calm down,' Albie came over... then I promptly burst into tears.

'Right, you,' Troy came over. 'Early lunch, you and me,' he gently took my arm and steered me away. 'You two, pick these up and stop playing silly buggers.'

We went outside and he silently led me to Starbucks, holding the door open for me and then sitting me down away from the window before disappearing to the counter.

I was feeling very silly now, mortification sprang up as I realised that my little tantrum had been *way* over the top.

Troy returned with two coffees and sat down

opposite me, 'I ordered you a chicken and bacon panini.'

'Thank you,' I muttered, looking at my hands clutching a tissue on the table.

'Talk,' he said kindly.

'I'm sorry,' I dared to look up; he was smiling a little and his dark eyes were concerned.

'That wasn't like you, Roxy. I don't think I've *ever* heard you swear before... come on, what's up?'

'Oh, nothing really... just a stupid... argument,' I honestly didn't know what else to call it.

'I see,' he nodded slowly. 'With your new fella?'

'No, my sister,' I swallowed and fought down another fresh wave of tears. 'But it was about him. It's nothing really... it's just upset me a bit. I'm fine.'

'Hmm,' he handed me a fresh tissue. 'You don't seem fine. It's OK... you don't have to tell me anything that you don't want to. I just want to make sure you're OK.'

'Thank you.'

'Do you want to go home?'

'No,' I shook my head.

'OK,' he reached over and patted the top of my arm. 'I do want you to apologise to those two clowns though. I think you frightened Spencer.'

'I will,' I promised.

A young girl came over with our food, looking at me curiously.

'Her goldfish has just died,' Troy said gravely.

I laughed feebly and gave the girl an apologetic look.

'That's better,' he grinned. 'Let's see that lovely smile of yours.'

I watched him bite into his sandwich with his perfect white teeth, his eyes still on me.

He was very handsome, and he had a great body... if we were both single I would have definitely flirted around him. I wondered what his wife was like and whether she trusted him. He was a nice guy and I don't want to sound vain, but I was certain he would take me up if I offered him anything.

I started to eat my panini, feeling temporarily shaken out of my misery.

'Troy?' I said as I swallowed the last bite. 'Can I just ask you something?'

'You sure can.'

'If somebody – somebody you trust, told you something that you were certain was a lie... or maybe a mistake... maybe... would you ignore it?'

'Well,' he frowned for a moment, 'if it was someone I trust, I would assume it wasn't a lie, I guess.'

'OK, a mistake then?'

'I would go with my gut.'

'Right,' I digested this, then laughed bitterly. 'What if your gut was the thing you didn't trust?'

'Honestly?' I nodded. 'I don't know, Roxy. Sometimes you just need some alone time to think and work things through.'

'Yeah,' I breathed, feeling unhappy and lost.

'Look,' he said, 'I don't know what's happened, but it sounds like you're confused. I think you need to give yourself breathing space and come to your own conclusion about... whatever this is.'

'What if I can't?'

'Don't under-estimate yourself. You'll get there.'

'Sure,' I tried to smile but it felt like a grimace.

Teddy drove us to the theatre that evening. I knew he could tell all was not right with me, but he didn't push it. I wanted to talk to him so badly, but I simply couldn't bring myself to repeat what Shauna had said.

'I don't even know why we all have to be there,' I grumbled.

'Because we are a team,' Teddy said in a super-eager voice in a good impersonation of Duncan.

'I s'pose,' I stared gloomily out of the window, trying not to dwell too much on seeing Jaco and confronting him later on.

Most of the members were there already when we walked in, sitting around the usual table.

'Hello,' Duncan rose slightly from his seat. 'Grab a drink, hopefully we won't be long tonight.'

I went and sat down next to Derek as Teddy went to make the teas, leaving a space for Teddy next to Jeremy.

'Alright?' I said.

'The lesser of two evils, eh?' Derek whispered.

'We are just waiting for Tilly and Brad,' Pontus said. 'Violet has brought her costume list,' he handed down a sheet of paper for me. I had a look and saw I had four costume changes altogether - some wide legged trousers and a blouse, a long dress that someone had pencilled in '*glam – maybe silky*', a nightdress and a plain A-line dress. Someone had also pencilled in '*shoes.*'

'There's so much for you and Vi to do,' I said to Lola on the other side of Derek.

'It's OK,' she smiled her shy smile. 'Violet's good at improvising. She's got most of it sorted already.'

'Mind yourself, honey,' Teddy put a mug of tea in front of me and sat down.

'Thanks,' I settled back in my chair and looked at the costume list again.

I heard voices from the foyer and twisted around. Brad and Tilly came in, Brad talking noisily as usual.

Brad Blows, our set designer, was everything a set designer should be. He was camp, flamboyant, totally stuck in the 'eighties with his bleached hair and loud shirts, and he was never separated from his large drawing pad and his pencil with a pom-pom on the end. He took his role *very* seriously – he was a hairdresser by trade, did the occasional DJ gig, and was a lot of fun.

Tilly Michaels was almost the complete opposite. In charge of scenery and the stagehands, she was gruff and humourless and also rumoured to have once been called 'Trevor.' Like most rumours it was probably not true, but I still kept checking for an Adam's apple.

'I have arrived,' Brad declared, then giggled at himself. 'Sorry we're late,' he walked towards the stage and pointed at Tilly over his shoulder with his pencil, 'her fault,' he whispered.

'Come on, come on, sit down,' Duncan beckoned, and they took the two empty chairs next to Pontus.

'I'm a man down,' Tilly said without preamble. 'Three guys, Owen can't do it.'

'Oh, how come?' Duncan queried.

'His wife died and he's selling the house,' she said bluntly.

'Oh, gosh,' Duncan frowned at her. 'How awful, poor man.'

'Yeah,' she tucked her grey, frizzy hair behind her ears. 'I reckon we'll cope without him.'

'*Jesus,*' Teddy murmured.

'Shall we crack on?' Pontus said, looking like he wanted to laugh. 'Brad? Let's see what you've got.'

'You are in for a treat, my darling,' he opened his book and turned it outwards for us all to see. 'First scene, the drawing room. I've gone for shades of plum and gold.'

'Um,' Finn raised a hand. 'Our sofa is blue, it won't match.'

'Then we buy a new sofa!' Brad waved a hand, then added as Pontus gave him an incredulous look, 'I am joking! Chuck a throw on it.'

'Did people have throws in that era?' Samantha asked the table at large.

'I'll Google it,' Stuart whipped out his phone. 'Don't think they did, mate,' he said after a minute.

'No matter,' Brad sighed to the heavens. 'We will do teal and gold… I was planning on teal for the dining room, we will just swap.'

I started to glaze over and rested my temples on my hands, hoping that I just looked like I was concentrating.

'Don't fall asleep,' Teddy joked.

I had only been home for a few minutes when Jaco arrived. He looked tired but he was in a good mood, kissing me hard as soon as I let him in and telling me that he'd missed me.

'How was the meeting?' he asked.

'Dull,' I went and fetched him a beer from the fridge.

'Thanks, baby,' he sat down and patted the sofa besides him. 'I need this, been a long, long day.'

'Has it?' I was putting off the conversation I knew we had to have.

'Mm,' his eyes wandered over me. 'A good day though. I've made a lot of money.'

'That's nice.'

'Anymore headaches?' he stroked my forehead with his forefinger. 'You look tired.'

'No, no, I'm fine.'

'Good,' he smiled before drinking more beer. 'I was worried about you.'

'Was you?'

'Yes!' he frowned, then smiled. 'How was work?'

'OK,' I shrugged.

'Sure? You don't seem yourself.'

'Jaco, I have to ask you something,' I blurted out.

'Sure,' he looked at me questioningly.

'At my mums,' I said slowly, aware my voice was shaking slightly, 'did you… did you recognise Liam?'

'Liam? No… should I have?'

'Well, I don't know,' I paused. 'Only, Shauna said he recognised you.'

'Really?' he raised his brows, looking perplexed. 'Where from? I don't think I do… I'm usually good with faces.'

'Right,' my heart was really pounding now. 'I'm just going to say it… Liam used to be a drug user… like pretty bad. He said, he said that y-you were his dealer.'

I braced myself, my stomach tight and painful. I

225

watched his expression go from interest, to puzzlement, amazement and then mirth.

'What?' he laughed, then stopped suddenly. 'Oh my God, Roxy, are you *serious?* Shit, you are, aren't you?'

'Shauna was so sure,' I whispered, feeling tears forming. 'He said he recognised you but she s-said that you p-probably wouldn't recognise him b-b-because he was thinner and looked different.'

'Bloody hell,' he grabbed my hand. 'That is crazy! Baby, look at me… that is ridiculous. Please don't think it's true! I'm as much a drug dealer as… Howard.'

I almost laughed, 'But, she was so certain,' I wiped my face with my free hand.

'Well, she is mistaken… Liam has got me muddled up with someone else. Let's face it, if he was as big a user as you say, he's not a reliable source.'

'I suppose not,' I stared at him, then remembered something else. 'He said that they called you The Russian.'

'How very James Bond,' he laughed. 'I'm sure I'm not the only Russian guy around here, plus I'm half-Irish.'

'It's a huge coincidence though,' I muttered.

'I guess,' he agreed. 'Look, sweetheart… I can only tell you the truth. I can't make you believe me though. I would tell you if I had done something like that, I would. I love you to bits, I wouldn't hide anything from you.'

'Really?' I bit my lip, wanting to believe him.

'Really,' he touched my cheek and smiled sadly. 'I'm

not perfect, but I certainly don't condone drug dealing. I'm sorry that Shauna said those things, but please don't think they're true. I love you.'

'I love you too,' I felt myself edge towards him. 'I just... she was so sure.'

'Maybe so, but she's mistaken, I swear to you, I swear on my life.'

'Oh shit,' I bowed my head, realising that he was being sincere. 'I'm sorry.'

'No, you had to ask me, didn't you?' he put his arms around me, kissing the top of my head. 'Poor baby, you should have told me straight away, I hate the thought of you being upset like this.'

'I'm sorry,' I returned his embrace, feeling like the worst person in the world.

'Don't be silly,' he whispered. 'It's all forgotten.'

That night he made love to me with so much tenderness and passion. I knew that I loved him more than anything and that I had to ignore my stupid doubts and scatter-brained thoughts.

CHAPTER EIGHTEEN

I went to work the following morning, my pelvis killing me after hours of sex but feeling loved and in love.

However, I was in for an unpleasant shock.

I wandered in, my head full of Jaco and the relief of not worrying and fretting, to be greeted by Kyle and Spencer both looking grave.

'Rox,' Kyle walked towards me from the counter. 'Have you heard about Troy?'

'What? No,' I immediately felt tense; he looked so solemn.

'He's in hospital, he was attacked last night.'

'Oh my God,' I stopped in my tracks. 'Is he OK? What happened?'

'I've only spoken to Mila, his missus,' he said. 'Apparently he went to the gym,' he indicated with his head the direction of my gym, 'and just as he got to his car, someone jumped him from behind, hit him over the head.'

'Oh, that's awful,' I shivered slightly, feeling disturbed that all this happened only a few metres away. 'Is he OK?'

'Well, he was knocked out, but he's had a scan, she said, and no head damage. He's got some broken ribs and bruises, looks like they kicked the fuck out of him while he was unconscious.'

'Poor Troy, that's horrible.'

'The police are looking at everyone's CCTV,' Spencer chipped in. 'Weird thing is his wallet was in his pocket and his phone was found smashed nearby, so not a mugging.'

'That's just scary,' I glanced out at the carpark. 'Who on earth would just do that for the hell of it?'

'I know, right?' said Kyle unhappily.

'Do you know what ward he's on?'

'No, but Mila said he's allowed home later today.'

'Perhaps I'll go and see him at home,' I slid my bag off my shoulder and started towards the staff room. 'If he feels like visitors… oh bugger! I've got rehearsals tonight.'

'He might not feel like it tonight anyway,' Kyle followed me. 'Mila's ringing me later, I'll ask if we can visit over the weekend.'

'OK,' I unseeingly hung my bag up and put my lanyard around my neck.

'Aw, come on,' Kyle put his arm around me. 'He'll be OK, he's a toughie.'

'I know,' I said, a solid nauseous feeling in my stomach. 'But it's so horrid, Troy wouldn't hurt a soul, would he? And it's so well-lit around here… and there's always people about, going in and out of Pizza Hut and the gym.'

'Yeah,' he looked troubled. 'There is some good news though.'

'What's that?'

'I'm in charge today, so chop chop!'

'Terrific,' I managed a smile and slapped his hand that was still hanging over my shoulder. 'I'll tell tales if you're rubbish.'

'Snitch.'

I would have quite happily skipped rehearsals that evening. I couldn't shake off the horrible image of Troy being beaten to a pulp, exacerbated when I left work by the sight of his dark-grey Toyota still in his usual parking spot by our building.

'Jesus, poor bloke,' Teddy said as I told him on our way to the theatre. 'Hope they catch whoever it was.'

'Mila said the CCTV footage wasn't great according to the police,' I trembled slightly. 'They appeared to have walked from across the road from the direction of the roundabout, and all that was made out was that he was average height and stocky with a dark-coloured baseball cap on. They're not even sure what he hit him with.'

'Well, at least he's OK, could have been a tragedy,' Teddy said bracingly.

'Yeah, I know,' I murmured. 'Nobody feels safe now though. I'm dreading when the clocks go back and it's dark when we leave.'

'Honey, if I have to, I will come and escort you every evening,' he glanced at me as he pulled into the carpark, 'but I'm sure you'll feel better by then.'

'Thank you,' I touched his arm before climbing out and waiting for him.

Violet descended upon us as soon as we walked in, brandishing a tape measure.

'Urgh, I've put on weight,' I muttered to Teddy.

'Teddy, my darling,' Violet beamed. 'I've found a fabulous suit for you.'

'If it's from a charity shop, please can we wash it,'

he said cagily.

'Give me some credit,' she draped her tape measure around her neck. 'Roxy, we need to discuss shoes.'

'I have like, a million pairs. I'll have something suitable.'

'Splendid,' she retreated back onto the stage.

'Rightio my loves,' Duncan said loudly. 'Tonight, we are being interrogated by Inspector Nobel and sidekick PC Trowbridge,' he smiled at Johnny and Derek. 'Guilty faces galore.'

I glanced at Teddy in helpless silent laughter; Duncan had dyed his hair again, a vibrant auburn, but his sideburns were still tinged with his previous black.

'Oh no,' Teddy looked horrified.

'Oh, please don't make me laugh,' I begged.

'But… oh no,' he shot me a mischievous grin. 'That shouldn't be allowed.'

'I'm going to ignore it,' I walked purposely up the steps to the stage, aware that Teddy was snickering quietly to himself.

Despite my anxious mood, rehearsals went well, taking my mind off of Troy's attack.

As we left the building, to my surprise Howard was sitting on the low wall by the doors.

'Hello,' I greeted him as he stood up.

'Hello,' he smiled, then nodded to Teddy. 'I wondered if you fancied a bite to eat?'

'Um,' I was suddenly filled with suspicion. 'Sure… how come?'

'Ah, well,' he scratched his neck. 'I'm sure you know why.'

Teddy gave me a baffled look.

'Teddy, I'll catch you later,' I said resignedly.

'Sure,' he frowned at me, then trotted off towards his car.

'Subtle,' I said, then sighed.

'Sorry,' Howard smiled wanly.

He drove me to a coffee shop on the other side of town that stayed open late and made the best sandwiches.

Howard ordered us a turkey and chutney roll each and two cappuccinos.

'Come on then, let's have it,' I clasped my hands between my legs. 'I take it that Shauna's been sneaking.'

'Now then,' he said slowly. 'That's harsh. She's very upset, Roxy.'

'Does Mum know?' I asked warily.

'No,' he gave a ghost of a smile. 'Just me.'

'Go on then,' I said, aware that I sounded slightly belligerent.

'Well,' he surveyed me for a moment, his eyes concerned. 'Frankly, I'm worried about you.'

'No need,' I took a sip of my cappuccino. 'I spoke to Jaco, it's all a misunderstanding.'

'I see,' he smiled somewhat sadly. 'I do need to say something though.'

'What?' I felt horribly shaky but tried to keep my expression neutral.

'I spoke to Liam too,' he said gently. 'He's not lying.'

'Wow,' I breathed. 'You're all ganging up big time. I think I'd know if *my* boyfriend is lying.'

'OK, OK,' he looked up as a young guy came over with our rolls. 'Thank you,' he smiled.

I irritably took off the cress sitting pointlessly on top of my roll, aware that Howard was watching me. 'Look,' I said eventually. 'Liam is mistaken. Jaco isn't perfect, but he absolutely does not condone drugs… he said so. And I believe him.'

'OK,' he said simply. 'Well… that's good, as long as you're sure, Roxy.'

'One hundred percent,' I said firmly.

'Roxy,' he paused. 'OK, I love you a great deal. I do not want to see you get hurt… you are a vulnerable young woman. But you are also an adult, so if you are sure, then OK.'

'Vulnerable?' I felt myself stiffen. 'So, basically, because of my… my *condition*, my ADHD, you're saying that I'm incapable of making up my own mind.'

'No,' he looked troubled. 'Not at all.'

'Then what are you saying?'

Howard finished chewing a mouthful of his roll before answering, 'I'm saying that as a parent I worry, and as a parent I will always play out the worse scenarios, because that's what we do. I also know that being in love can cloud your judgement and that we want to see the good side in the people we love.'

I felt a rush of affection towards him that took the edge off of my annoyance, 'Sure. And I'm too young and daft to have the measure of someone? Because I'm not… I know him better than you. I thought you liked him,' I bit into my roll and watched his expression closely.

'I do like him!' he sounded surprised. 'He seems like

a nice and polite young man, although if I'm honest, I think he is a little too old for you. Wait,' he put up a hand as I opened my mouth to argue. 'And I certainly don't think you're daft, not at all... *but,*' he sighed and seemed to brace himself. 'I know Liam very well, and I trust him. He seems very distressed by this.'

'So... basically you are saying you believe him and not me?'

'No, I'm saying I believe Liam and I believe that you believe Jaco.'

'Wow,' I stared at him. 'So, without actually just coming out with it, what you're *actually* saying is that you think Jaco is some drug-dealer and he's lying to me.'

'Roxy,' Howard implored. 'We are talking a few years ago now when Liam was into that lifestyle. Jaco may be scared of your reaction if he told you.'

'Don't try and sugar-coat it,' I said miserably, putting down my half-finished roll. 'Can you just take me home now, please?'

'Sure,' he nodded, his kind eyes full of sorrow.

I was tempted to go and spill my guts to Teddy when I got home, but instead I made a mug of tea and rang Jaco.

'Hello,' he said. 'Did it run over tonight?'

'No, I went and had a coffee with my stepdad.'

'I see, everything OK, sweetheart? You sound off.'

'Rough day, something horrid happened last night to Troy, you know, my manager? He was attacked outside work after leaving the gym.'

'Is he OK?'

'Yeah, I think so. Nothing permanent, anyway.'

'Poor chap,' he consoled. 'Not safe anywhere, are you?'

'No,' I suddenly wanted to get off the subject, so I asked about his day and then we chatted nonsense for ten minutes, before he said he had to go.

'Tomorrow night?' I asked.

'Oh yes,' he said. 'I'll ring you tomorrow. Love you, baby.'

'I love you too.'

After another terrible night's sleep which included me getting up at two and deciding to tidy up my shoes in my closet and sort out which may be suitable for the play, I felt drained and had terrible brain-fog as I got to work.

Albie, who had been off work the day before and had missed the drama, was full of speculation about Troy's attack... after sulking that nobody had texted to tell him.

'Somebody might have a grudge,' he mused as we stood around, making the most of the early morning quiet.

'Unlikely,' Spencer jumped up to sit on the counter.

'Why?' Albie shrugged his broad shoulders. 'We don't know him *that* well.'

'Well enough,' Spencer frowned. 'More likely a random mugging.'

'It wasn't a mugging though,' Kyle chipped in. 'Wallet, gym bag, phone, all still on him.'

'Maybe it was just a drunk or some nutter,' I went past them to make a drink, not wanting to keep dwelling on it. 'I'm just glad that he's OK.'

'Yeah,' Kyle said, his face thoughtful. 'I'll go out and get a card later.'

Kyle and I were going to go and see Troy at home after work – Spencer had plans with his girlfriend, and Albie gave swimming lessons on a Friday evening.

I wondered if I would feel better once I had seen him, already I felt a little less upset. I was still upset however, by my conversation with Howard and was refusing to think about it, obstinately pushing it away.

All in all, I couldn't wait until the weekend – I had Saturday off and only had to work two hours on Sunday. I was looking forward to seeing Jaco and forgetting all my worries and I was already planning on asking him if we could stay at his house for the weekend, thinking I would feel removed from it all away from home.

Another cheery note was that the summery weather had made a return, for the time being anyway, and I had packed my bikini to lay in Jaco's beautiful garden.

Jaco texted me late in the afternoon, saying he had been horrendously busy and apologised for not ringing – I asked if I could stay at his, to which he replied he would like nothing more.

Feeling suddenly filled with lust, I told him I would drive over later, and he sent me a load of x's.

Even after spending forty minutes that afternoon with the brattiest little boy I'd ever come across, rejecting every pair of trainers he tried on and complaining about everything to his poor harassed mother, didn't dent my unexpected good mood.

'Remind me never to have kids,' Kyle said after they had left. 'Come on, shall we escape now?'

'It's only half-four,' I said, stopping to check my watch as I tidied away trainers.

'It's hardly manic,' he watched our only customer being served by Albie. 'I'll pop back to do the alarm and lock up after we've been to see Troy.'

'Go on,' Albie said. 'We'll cope.'

'I'm not arguing with that,' I sped up with my tidying, then went to get my bag.

I followed Kyle's car to Troy's house on the new estate, nicknamed 'The Hills' as it is at the highest point of Fernberry, built next to a leisure centre.

Mila turned out to be a very petite blonde woman dressed in pink tracksuit bottoms and a Pineapple Studio vest top with a slightly acerbic manner, but nonetheless she welcomed us in, shooing away two Pugs that came snuffling towards us.

'Hi Kyle,' she nodded and looked at me.

'I'm Roxy,' I looked around with interest. 'Nice house.'

The hallway was all white woodwork and pale-green walls and the wooden floor was spotless. I slipped off my trainers without asking if I should and put them neatly next to a white dresser with a vase of yellow roses on top.

'Troy's just got out the shower,' she led us to the living room; I was glad I had taken my trainers off, the thick carpet was very pale. 'Would you like a drink or anything?'

'Just water, thank you,' I perched on the edge of the two-seater and Kyle muttered he'd like the same before sitting down too.

'Do you think she minds us coming?' I whispered.

'Dunno,' he looked uncomfortable. 'She said it was OK on the phone.'

The two pugs wandered in, one made a beeline for us, the other one trotted to the patio doors and disappeared into the garden.

'It's just tap, hope it's OK,' Mila returned with two glasses of water.

'Thanks,' I smiled up at her. 'Nice dogs.'

'Oh, yeah,' her expression softened slightly. 'That's Hector, the other one is Bertie.'

'Cute,' I watched her as she went back out. 'I'll just see if he needs a hand getting dressed, his ribs are sore.'

'OK,' I stroked Hector's head and made kissy noises at him. 'Hello, hello, you're a sweetie, aren't you?'

'Ugly fucking things,' Kyle said in a low voice.

'Aw, mean!' I slapped his leg, then watched in horror as some of his water sloshed on the floor. 'Oh, crap.'

'Bet you're glad it ain't coffee,' Kyle laughed and dabbed at it with a cushion.

'Kyle!' I giggled. 'Don't use that!'

Voices drifted in from the direction of the hall and we fell silent.

'Hey,' Troy came in and I clamped my hand over my mouth in shock.

His face was a mess. One eye was slightly closed and surrounded by a dark purple bruise, he had a cut on his temple and more bruising, and his bottom lip was split and sore looking. He walked to an armchair and sat down slowly, holding his ribs.

'Mate,' Kyle looked as horrified as I felt. 'What the fuck.'

'It looks worse than it is,' he smiled crookedly. I noticed that both his knees, visible in his shorts, were cut and bruised, the left one was noticeably swollen.

'Oh,' I whispered, my eyes filling with tears. 'You look terrible.'

'Thanks,' he chuckled.

'How are you feeling?'

'A bit sore, had a banging headache yesterday. All good now though,' Bertie came waddling in and sat on his feet. 'Hello mate,' he patted his back with some difficulty.

'Babe,' Mila said. 'I need to go and pick up something for dinner and get a few bits,' she gave us a nod and a smile. 'Nice to meet you.'

'You too,' I murmured.

'So, what the hell happened, man?' Kyle asked.

'Wish I knew,' Troy paused, then as the front door closed, he seemed to relax. 'I was walking towards my car one minute, the next I was waking up in hospital.'

'You didn't see anyone or hear *anything?*'

'Nope,' he winced as he sat back.

'You don't think it was anyone you know?'

'I bloody well hope not,' his eyes switched to me. 'Roxy, please stop looking at me like that. I'm fine, honest.'

'But you look so awful,' I smiled as I heard how I sounded. 'Sorry, I just wasn't expecting you to look like that.'

'Oh, here's a card from us lot,' Kyle handed him our card, full of little drawings and our get-well messages.

'Cheers,' he opened it and chuckled as he read it. 'That's ace, thanks.'

'How long are you off work for?' I asked.

'I'll be in on Monday, I reckon.'

'What?' I exclaimed. 'No, at least take next week off.'

'Why?' he raised his brow. 'I'll be much better in a couple of days. Got my painkillers.'

Kyle shook his head, 'You plank.'

'I'm bored!'

I let my gaze wander around the ultra-tidy room, thinking that Mila probably wasn't exactly a bundle of laughs.

'By the way, we're advertising for a new assistant if you know anyone. I've put it on *Indeed*. Kyle, can you stick a card in the window? I'll email the job description.'

'Sure, boss,' Kyle stood up. 'We better go. Good to see you, mate. Give us a shout if you need anything.'

'Will do,' Troy stood up too, groaning slightly as he straightened up.

'See you soon,' I gave him a very gentle and cautious kiss on his cheek. 'No more fighting, yeah?'

'I'll try not to,' he chuckled.

I said goodbye to Kyle and drove home to shower and change. Then checking my bag, I set off to Jaco's.

CHAPTER NINETEEN

I parked next to Jaco's BMW on his driveway and climbed out, smiling to his neighbour, a middle-aged woman in gardening gloves who was looking avidly over the low wall dividing the driveways.

'Afternoon,' she called.

'Hi,' I said as I got my bag from my backseat.

Jaco opened the front door and jogged over, barefoot and topless, then kissed me, 'Hello, baby.'

'Hello,' I wrapped my arms around him.

'Hey, Mrs L-B,' Jaco grinned over at his neighbour.

'Hello, Jack dear,' she said, all eyes.

'I don't bother correcting her,' he murmured as he led me into the cool of his hallway. Taking my bag from me and dropping it onto the floor, he kissed me again with more force.

'Hmm, nice welcome,' I said happily. 'How much have you missed me?'

'Oh, more than you'd believe,' he tugged my ponytail and gave me one of his wandering stares.

'Good,' I buried my face into his shoulder, heady with the feel of his warm skin and the smell of his aftershave, letting all my doubts of the last few days drift away; I just *knew* it was going to be a good weekend.

'Let's go and have a drink,' he pulled me towards the kitchen, walking backwards. 'I bought you some gin.'

'Lovely,' I hopped up onto a stool next to the island

and watched him as he made me a drink, then brought it over with a half-drunk bottle of beer.

'What do you want to eat later?' he asked. 'I dug out my Silence of the Lambs DVD.'

'You remembered!' I took a sip of my gin and lemonade. 'I have a gigantic craving for Peking duck.'

'Your wish is my command,' he grinned. 'I will go and pick it up later. The Chinese up the road do the best dumplings.'

'How was your day?' I asked, stroking his arm.

'Busy, chaotic and long. Yours?'

Just then my mobile rang; it was Dana.

'Answer it,' he stood up and dropped a kiss on my head before going to the fridge.

'Hey, you,' Dana said when I answered. 'I'm bored on the train and someone's got B.O. like onions.'

I laughed, 'Nice! I'm drinking gin.'

'Where are you, at Teddy's?'

'No, I'm at Jaco's for the weekend.'

'Lucky you, I'm going bowling with Tobias later and I don't wanna!'

'How come?' Jaco sat back down and started caressing my thigh.

'We're meeting boring Wayne and boring Jenny,' she made a noise of disgust.

'Awesome,' I sniggered - Tobias worked with Wayne, and Dana couldn't stand them. 'Just get drunk.'

'I reckon it's a must,' she giggled. 'So, when am I getting to meet him? Jaco? I hardly see you nowadays,' she didn't say it with any rancour, and I knew she wasn't hiding any, but I immediately felt guilty.

'Meal soon? Or something? Double date?'

'Count me in,' she said sounding pleased. 'And we need a night out with Ali and Freya, saw Ali the other night and she was nagging.'

'I'll text them.'

'Good girl.'

'I'm rubbish, I know,' I smiled at Jaco as he gave me an enquiring look. 'I've just been so busy with the play and everything.'

'Hey, girl, no need to explain yourself to me… as long as you're OK.'

'I am,' I assured her. 'Listen, come over to mine Sunday evening, mini catch up?'

'I'll be there. I'll let you go, enjoy your weekend.'

'You too.'

'Everything OK?' Jaco asked after I ended the call.

'Yeah,' I drank some gin, still guilt in the pit of my stomach.

'Good,' he kissed me. 'What would you like to do tomorrow?'

'Absolutely nothing,' I gave him a coy glance. 'I brought my bikini.'

'Ah, the weekend just got even better.'

'Unless you'd rather go out?'

'I'd much rather be *in,*' he let his hand wander up to the top of my thigh. 'I may need to put my head in the gallery first thing,' he said regretfully. 'You can either stay here or have a wander around the shops.'

'OK,' I didn't like to tell him I was skint, so shopping wasn't very likely.

'Anyway,' he removed his hand to pour more gin, 'we were interrupted… how was your day then?'

243

'Not bad,' I pulled a face. 'Nearly strangled a child…
but, hey, that's the joys of retail. Oh, and I went to see
Troy after work.'

'Oh?'

Straight away I could almost feel a drop in the
temperature, 'Yeah, me and Kyle popped in quickly,
took a card,' I said hurriedly.

'Right,' he nodded and screwed the lid on the
lemonade bottle then looked at me. 'And how is *Troy?*'

'Looks like he's been hit by a train, but he seems
OK. Doesn't remember much.'

'Well, he definitely pissed off someone,' he said in a
harsh voice.

I felt that awful fear that I'd felt before rising and
suddenly he seemed like a stranger, 'Maybe,' I
shrugged, deciding that arguing was not going to help.

'He married?'

'Yeah,' I said. 'Met her today.'

'Right,' he smiled thinly. 'Sweetheart, I'm gonna
jump in the shower, then I'll go and pick up some
dinner.'

'OK,' I said brightly.

'I'll take your bag up.'

'Thank you.'

As soon as he left the room, I let out a miserable
sigh.

*Why, Jaco? Why do you keep doing this? I love you
and you love me, so why do you get like this and spoil
things?*

I blinked away some tears and gulped more gin
before getting up to distract myself.

I went through to his living room and went outside

244

into the early evening sunshine. I kicked off my sandals and walked barefoot across the lawn. The grass had been cut and didn't feel particularly pleasant under my bare feet, rather dry and scratchy. I watched as a magpie swooped down from one of the tall trees at the bottom of the garden.

One for sorrow, I whispered, looking for another one. Glancing back at the house, I looked at the window that I by now knew was Jaco's bedroom.

I just couldn't work him out. I supposed another sort of girl might be flattered that her man was jealous, but not me. And it wasn't so much that he got jealous, it was because he denied it… but the most worrying thing was how he acted. He frightened me, and I just couldn't keep ignoring it.

I didn't want to spoil the weekend though… *he's spoilt it, not you,* a little voice told me… I had been looking forward to it so much – I needed to erase the hateful lies that Liam had told, forget how much Howard had upset me by siding with Liam and Shauna. I knew that *that* was not quite true, not lies *exactly*, and I knew that Howard loved me and would never hurt me, but I didn't want to be reasonable about it at that precise moment in time.

I had reached the bottom of the garden and stood for a moment, my eyes closed. I could hear at least two lawn mowers nearby, and I could hear children's playful yells somewhere to the left. I opened my eyes again and looked at the dappled light from the trees playing over my bare arms and stretched them out in front of me. Then feeling one of my urges, I turned and done a handstand, like I used to as a child.

'Woo, full marks,' Jaco called over from the patio. He was holding my drink and smiling broadly.

Embarrassed, I walked quickly over towards him, 'Thanks,' I smiled.

'Bendy little chick, aren't you?' he handed me my drink. Dressed in a plain white T-shirt and the shorts he'd been wearing earlier, his hair damp and tousled, he looked carefree and handsome, not tense and angry as he had earlier.

'I used to do gymnastics,' I told him.

'Nice,' he put his head on one side and looked at me with fondness. 'Come on, let's choose what we're eating, I'm starving.'

We ate outside - he'd bought so many dishes it was like a feast.

He was very talkative and seemed almost manic. I wondered if he realised how he'd been earlier and was trying to cover it up or compensate somehow.

He was also sneezing like anything, so I suggested we retreated indoors.

'Have you been taking your anti-histamines?'

'Yes, dear,' he laughed. 'I cut the grass earlier, it always sets me off.'

We sat on the sofa together, him chatting away and me zoning out slightly.

Eventually he squeezed my leg, 'Rox, are you OK?'

'Yeah,' I avoided his gaze.

'You sure, baby?'

'Yeah… actually, no,' I fidgeted. 'Can we talk?'

'Of course we can,' he sounded concerned but when I met his eyes, I thought he looked wary.

'OK,' I was finding it a lot harder than it should have been. 'I've been looking forward to this weekend, but… I kind of need to get this off my chest-' I trailed off, my thoughts all over the place.

'Go on,' he looked intently at me.

'Well, it's about earlier, when I mentioned Troy,' I swallowed hard. 'You seemed angry-'

'I wasn't angry!' he exclaimed laughingly.

'Well, you changed. Your mood changed… but it's not the first time,' I paused, trying to regulate my breathing.

'I thought we cleared this up the other weekend outside the pub,' he frowned.

'What about when you saw me with my ex?'

'Your ex?' his eyes narrowed slightly. 'What ex?'

'Outside my work,' I said, my voice trembling. 'You saw us and drove off, then came to my flat and-'

'You didn't say he was your ex.'

'Didn't I?'

'Your exact words were, *Just a guy I haven't seen for a while.*' You did not mention that he's an ex,' his curved mouth was suddenly thin and his eyes hard; it occurred to me fleetingly that he didn't look handsome in the slightest.

'I-I thought I did,' I was trying to maintain eye contact but could feel myself blinking rapidly. 'OK, sorry if I didn't… but the point is you got jealous, for no reason.'

'Maybe I *should* be getting jealous if you're hiding the fact that you're talking to an ex and covering it up.'

'What?' I said, shocked. 'No, Jaco… I wasn't covering anything up. Why would I? I love *you,* I want *you,* don't say things like that.'

'But why didn't you say who he was?' he persisted.

'I-I don't know,' I squeezed my eyes shut. 'Maybe because you were scaring me.'

'Oh, baby,' he threw his head back and closed his eyes, then looked at me with glinting eyes. 'I don't want to scare you… I'm sorry.'

'Well you did,' I said quietly. 'Like you did at the hotel. I don't like it, Jaco. I don't want to be treading on eggshells all the time.'

'You don't have to,' he said roughly. 'I'm not a monster, Roxy.'

'I don't think that.'

'Are you sure? Because I ain't coming off as boyfriend of the year right now.'

'It's just when you get like that,' I was torn between wanting to get up and leave and wanting to throw my arms around him.

'I love you,' he said softly. 'But maybe you don't love me like you say you do - not if you think so bad of me. I get accused of being a drug dealer, now of being some sort of jealousy-driven maniac.'

'I didn't accuse you of that,' I sat in stunned silence for a moment. 'I never thought for one minute you are or were a drug dealer.'

'Maybe you need some thinking time,' he got up swiftly and went outside and started stacking up the takeaway containers.

Just get up and leave, let him stew. Let him miss you.

'Jaco,' I walked up behind him and touched his back. 'I don't want to argue. I just needed to tell you how I felt.'

'Yeah,' he murmured, then turned around. 'I don't want to fall out... I'm sorry for whatever it is you think I've done.'

I'm not stupid... I knew that was a fairly manipulative comment, but I loved him so much that at that moment I just wanted to smooth it over.

'Do you want me to go home?' I asked in stronger voice.

'No,' he smiled a little sadly, his eyes full of affection again. 'I don't want that at all.'

'OK,' I looked behind him at the table. 'I'll help you tidy up.'

'Wanna watch your film?' he asked.

'Sure.'

We cuddled up as we normally did to watch the film, but I felt... I don't know what I felt.

Jaco seemed like his usual self, like we hadn't argued at all, but I kept going over it in my head.

I'd seen the film so many times, it didn't require much concentration on my part – I was ultra-aware of his breathing, every movement, his very presence, like my senses had been fine-tuned. Our argument seemed blurry, like it had afterwards at Johnny's party at the pub.

We didn't make love that night, he fell asleep so quickly, holding me. I was disconcerted that for the first time since we had been together that I didn't *want* to make love.

I suppose if I could have named an emotion that night it would have been lost. I felt so very lost.

The rest of the weekend would have been perfect if it wasn't for our argument hanging over me like shroud... and a troubling discovery that I will get to.

I was woken up with kisses and a mug of tea by a smiling Jaco, telling me he wasn't going to the gallery and he was all mine.

We made love and showered together, before cooking bacon sandwiches and sitting under the parasol on his patio to eat.

Jaco seemed relaxed and happy, keeping up a steady stream of conversation. If I occasionally zoned out or faltered in my quest to ignore things, he never said.

Going upstairs to put on my bikini and find a towel to lay on, Jaco said he was popping to the supermarket quickly to buy "goodies". He returned with champagne and more beers, a big bunch of flowers for me, a rack of ribs to barbecue later on and a load of junk food: chips, dips, biscuits and cakes.

'I'll burst out of my bikini,' I helped him unpack in the kitchen.

'Well, that just sounds like a really good thing.'

'Cheeky,' I murmured as I found room in the fridge for his beers.

'I like that,' he suddenly said.

'What?'

'You doing that, putting shopping away, making yourself at home. It feels right.'

I straightened up and looked at him from across the island, 'Huh?'

'I was just watching you doing that,' he waved an arm. 'Ah, ignore me. I was being soppy.'

'No,' I started to smile. 'I kind of like it.'

'God, I love you.'

'I love you too.'

After a lazy afternoon basking in the sun, I asked if I could go and shower and change before dinner.

'Of course you can, you don't have to ask,' Jaco said. 'I'll get the barbecue going.'

I went upstairs and stripped off my bikini, looking in his full-length mirror to see if I had caught the sun. Happily deciding that I had, I went and had a leisurely shower, thinking that I better moisturise myself well after being out in the sun for so long.

Returning to the bedroom, I rummaged in my bag for my body lotion, cursing as I dropped my deodorant and it rolled out of sight under the bed.

I crouched down and stuck my hand underneath, patting the carpet. Nudging the deodorant with the side of my hand, it rolled away further, so I tipped my head upside down to look. As I reached to pick it up, something else caught my eye, my first thought being that it was one of Jaco's ties.

I grabbed it and withdrew my hand, then felt like I had been punched in the gut. It was a blood-red choker. The very choker that Evie had been wearing when we had gone to the hotel with the repulsive Edward.

'What the-' I gasped and then stood up quickly. 'No,' I felt hot tears forming and sat down on the edge of the bed.

Think logically, don't go off at the deep end. It might not be what it seems...

Throwing my sundress over my head and not even

attempting underwear with my trembling hands, I charged downstairs holding the choker aloft, like it was likely to bite me.

'Jaco,' I said, louder than intended, 'what the hell is this doing in your room?'

'You what?' he looked up from his barbecue.

'This!' I thrust my arm towards him.

'What is it?' he frowned at it, then looked at me in bewilderment.

'Evie's choker,' I hissed. 'And don't even pretend it isn't, I remember it.'

'Ah, she's been looking for that,' his expression cleared for a second, then he frowned again, looking at me. 'What are you saying, Roxy? Are you thinking something... something?'

'Well, I would like to know why the fuck it's in your room!' I flung it on the table and glared at him.

'Where was it?' he asked, his eyes narrowed.

'Under your bed.'

'Right,' he raised an eyebrow at me before picking it up. 'And you're jumping to conclusions, I gather?'

'You've gathered correctly,' my heart was beating so terribly fast, I briefly wondered if it was possible to have a heart attack at my age. Then he started to laugh.

'Oh, Roxy,' he took a step towards me.

'Why are you laughing?' I stormed. 'Stop it!'

'Sorry, sweetheart,' he shook his head. 'But for someone who accuses me of being jealous.'

'W-what?' I stared at him in disbelief.

'Remember when I took Evie home? She took it off and threw it in the back of the car because it was annoying her – she said. I forgot it was there, I must have picked it up when I grabbed my jacket and paperwork.'

'How did it end up under your bed?' I asked, full of suspicion but starting to calm down.

'Baby, I'm not always this tidy, I have a mad clean up before you come over. More than likely I went straight up and chucked everything on my bed before showering,' he surveyed me for a second. 'OK, I shouldn't have laughed, I can see how it looks.'

'Yeah,' I continued to look at him, my mind working overtime.

'Look, she hasn't even been in my house,' he came and stood closer to me. 'Honestly, you can ask her. I wouldn't lie to you and I certainly wouldn't cheat on you.'

'No?' I bit my lip.

'No,' he said firmly. 'I love you, you crazy woman.'

'Oh, crap,' I sighed. 'I'm sorry, I j-just saw it and thought-'

'OK, don't finish that sentence. Can we call it quits now?' he reached down and stroked my cheek tenderly. 'I've been an idiot, you've been an idiot... do you love me?' I nodded. 'Well, I love you and you love me... that's all that's important.'

'Yeah,' despite myself, I was mesmerised by his beautiful eyes burning into mine and his soft and sexy voice.

'Come here,' he took me in his arms, then chuckled again. 'Sorry, but you are so cute when you're angry.'

After a few minutes he let me go and turned to turn off his barbecue, 'Sorry sweetheart, but I'm gonna have to take you to bed,' and with that he tugged the back of my hair and started to kiss me until I felt the last traces of mistrust leave me.

Much later, I lay on my side in Jaco's bed watching him sleep, wondering how I could ever have been contemplating that our relationship wasn't working.

So, he has faults… you're hardly perfect, Roxy. So what if he gets a little jealous? He's a passionate and fiery man… not like the gym boys you normally date. You're just not used to not calling all the shots. Jaco is older, wiser, he's intelligent. He's a real man… not a pretty boy who will do as he's told.

I badly wanted to wake him up, just to see those eyes looking at me, watch his expression as I turned him on.

Snuggling down and getting comfy I closed my eyes, but I knew sleep wasn't coming any time soon.

As we hadn't gotten around to eating, I began to feel hungry and a little sick. After another ten-minutes, my stomach was growling as I thought wistfully about the ribs that Jaco was going to cook.

It was no good… I got carefully out of bed, pulled on Jaco's T-shirt and went downstairs to the kitchen.

Swigging some orange juice out of the carton, I pulled some chili dip out of the fridge and then raided the cupboard for some kettle crisps and cake.

Feeling like a naughty child, I sat under a dim light above the island, stuffing my face and *thoroughly* enjoying it.

'Mmm, midnight feast?'

I nearly fell off my stool in fright as Jaco appeared in the doorway, completely naked and grinning.

'Sorry,' I said meekly, wiping my mouth. 'I was starving.'

'I thought I had a burglar,' he sauntered over. 'Although, if you were a burglar, I reckon I'd enjoy being burgled.'

'Wally,' I held out a cake. 'Want a bite?'

'Yeah, of you,' he swung my stool around and parted my legs. 'And you are *much* sweeter than any cake.'

'Corny,' I giggled, then gasped as he grabbed my hair.

'No, just horny.'

CHAPTER TWENTY

Something odd happened the next day. Well, maybe not exactly odd, just unexpected… in fact when I think about it, it wasn't *that* odd at all; it just seemed like it at the time… me in my blissful bubble of denial.

I had gone home after my shift at work in an excellent mood, my head full of Jaco.

I'd chucked all my weekend laundry in the washing machine, had a long soak in the bath and then opened a beer and curled up with *Rebecca*, the book Teddy had given me, and waited for Dana.

When Dana turned up, I don't know what it was – her expression, her tone… perhaps just seeing her… but I started to feel emotional. And then when she asked if I were OK, I burst into tears.

'What the… babe, whatever is wrong?'

We had settled ourselves on the sofa, a beer each and the usual array of junk food she always brought with her.

'Oh,' I was dismayed at how suddenly the tears had started and scared that clearly I was not OK, not one little bit. 'Sorry, shit,' I stared at her in despair, not even knowing what to say.

'Come on,' Dana put her arms around me and stroked my head until the first violent sobs subsided. 'Take your time, it's OK.'

And then it all came out. Jaco's reaction to seeing me

with Peter, the night at the hotel, what Shauna had said, *everything.*

'Holy crap,' Dana's expression was one of deep distress and alarm, 'what you got yourself into, girl?'

'I know it sounds, like, really bad,' I whispered, 'but he's not horrible… he's lovely, he is.'

'Look,' she said, with what I thought was caution, 'I haven't met him, I don't want to judge him, but… this isn't right, you feeling like this.'

'Am I going mad?' I started to wring my hands, an old nervous habit that I hadn't done for a long time. 'Love isn't supposed to be like this, is it? But I love him,' I felt my face crumpling again and the sobbing made a fresh return.

'Oh, Rox,' she sat and watched me. 'You need to sort this out, why did you bottle it all up?'

'I told T-Teddy about the n-night at the hotel,' I took a few shuddering breaths. 'B-but everything else… perhaps it's me? Like at the p-pub, Jaco said I was thinking things that aren't th-there.'

'Do *you* think that you're thinking things that aren't there?'

I looked into her big, dark eyes and felt like the bottom of my world had dropped out, 'No,' I said in a voice that didn't sound like mine. 'No, I don't.'

'Then you've got to do something about it,' she said gently. 'Because you're killing yourself. This ain't you, Roxy. I don't think you've cried over a bloke since Gavin Matthews kissed Hailey Cross at our leavers party at school.'

'I've never been in love,' I shrugged.

'No,' she fell silent again for a moment. 'What did

Teddy say, anyway?'

'Something about not letting love cloud my judgement,' I thought back. 'Oh, something like I shouldn't let anyone make me feel bad.'

'Teddy's got a point.'

'Yeah.'

'Can I ask you something?'

'Go on.'

'Please don't take this the wrong way,' she eyed me for a moment, 'but, if you took away the money, the nice cars, the house... all of that, would you still have fallen for him?'

'Yes!' I exclaimed, trying not to show I was rattled by her question – and I was. Extremely. 'I didn't know all of that when I first clamped eyes on him. Apart from the gallery of course...but even *that*, I didn't know he was a dealer, I thought it was just a regular gallery,' as I said the word *dealer*, my heart plummeted further.

'Right,' she picked up one of my scatter cushions and traced a long, purple nail around the picture of the Sausage dog on it. 'But that's just physical attraction, what about when you got to know him?'

'I thought he was funny and charming and clever,' I shrugged irritably. 'Why did you fall in love with Tobias? Why does anyone fall in love with anyone? You just do.'

'Yeah,' she smiled a little unhappily. 'Sure. Don't be mad, I want to help.'

'I know,' I sniffed and shoved a handful of Skittles in my mouth.

'Babe, you do need to sort this out with Shauna

258

though. Have you spoken to her?'

'No.'

'Howard?'

'No,' I felt my eyes welling up again. 'I don't know what to do. Nobody has bothered to ring me or text me.'

'Probably giving you some space,' she said wisely. 'And they both must be upset too.'

'Yeah,' I bit back a harsh retort, knowing it was unfair. 'My mum will find out soon enough, she's like the bloody FBI. I bet she's already guessed something is wrong.'

'So,' Dana looked at me steadily, 'do you think it's true?'

'That Jaco is some dodgy drug baron?' I forced a dry laugh. 'No. It's ridiculous. And he would have told me when I asked him. Liam was off his head back then, he's got it wrong,' but as I shook my head in derision, Shauna's voice filled my head... *they used to call him The Russian*...

'You OK? You look funny.'

'Thanks!' I tried to smile, but I suddenly felt sick. 'I'm just fed up of the whole thing.'

'Yeah,' Dana drank some beer and patted my leg. 'So... now what?'

'I dunno,' I heaved a sigh and ate some more Skittles. 'Stop over-thinking everything, stop worrying and wait until things settle down with Shauna... and I guess it's still early days with Jaco, so...'

'Well, whatever you decide, if you're upset, tell me! If you have a row, tell me!' she gave me a scented hug then looked at me sternly.

'I will, I will.'

'You better!'

The rain returned during the night and I woke up to grey skies and got drenched running to my car.

Troy was at work, looking as battered and bruised as he had on Friday.

'You'll scare the customers away,' I joked as I went to put my bag out the back.

'I couldn't spend another day at home being fussed over,' he followed me and switched the kettle on.

'I'll make the coffees,' I tried to shoo him away.

'Don't *you* start too,' he grumbled. 'I'll make you work late else.'

'Can't,' I smiled. 'Rehearsals tonight. And at least Mila cares! I bet she's not happy about you coming in.'

'She's happy about very little,' he pulled a face.

'Oh?'

'Hmm,' he smiled grimly. 'Actually… and I shouldn't say this… she's a little paranoid about you.'

'Me?' I paused in my spooning the coffee into the mugs.

'She says you're pretty,' he said.

'Oh! Well, that's nice, but surely she knows, like, I'm not about to steal you away,' I began to feel uncomfortable and continued to make the drinks.

'Hey,' Spencer came in, rubbing his damp hair. 'Three sugars, Rox. Any biscuits? I got up late.'

'In the tin,' I said.

'We're open in five,' Troy gave me a strange look and went back out, leaving me puzzled and feeling awkward.

I went to Teddy's flat for a cup of tea before rehearsals and I told him about my exchange with Troy.

'Ah, I wouldn't worry, babe,' he said reassuringly.

'But I don't want her thinking that!'

'Girls get jealous,' he was ironing a T-shirt topless; I thought grimly that Jaco would probably go nuts if he could see us.

'Jaco got a bit funny about Troy,' I confided. 'Makes me wonder if I'm missing something, I ain't the brightest.'

'Don't say that,' Teddy frowned at me before taking off his glasses and pulling on his T-shirt. 'You just see the best in people, there's nothing wrong with that. Troy probably does fancy you,' he said matter-of-factly. 'You *are* pretty. What's his wife like anyway?'

'Attractive, a bit chavvy, a lot moody.'

'Choody.'

'Yup,' I giggled. 'You do cheer me up.'

'Good,' he beamed, then started tidying his fair hair in his reflection in his glass cabinet where his collection of books and Star Wars Bobble Heads resided. 'I need a haircut,' he muttered.

'How was your weekend?' I asked.

'Alright,' he disappeared into the bathroom. 'Work… oh and I went out for a drink with Francesca.'

'Fun?'

'Yeah,' he said absently, coming back into the room. 'How was yours?'

'Ok,' I stood up. 'You ready?'

'Yup.'

It might have been my very vivid imagination, but I thought that Francesca seemed a little frosty towards both myself and Teddy. Also, Teddy seemed... sheepish almost.

Upon arriving at the theatre, Duncan announced that as we were rehearsing our final scenes tonight, dress rehearsals would commence on Thursday, and on Monday we would be having a photo-shoot for our posters and advertising.

That would include Violet and the main murder suspects on a backdrop of a Victorian mansion: myself, Crystal, Destiny, Bob, Finn, Lola and Nathan.

'I would like everyone here at least half an hour earlier, if possible,' Duncan said loudly as he scribbled in his notebook.

'Can I do my hair and make-up at home?' I asked. 'It's easier.'

'Sure, my dear,' Duncan waved an arm in my direction. 'What's required is in your costume list.'

'Cool,' I took out my script and had a quick scan. I had been dreading tonight's scenes as I had to confess my undying love to Finn and kiss him.

'You should have had garlic for dinner,' Teddy stood behind me with his chin on my shoulder, looking at my script.

'I'll swap places with you,' Francesca said as she walked past, giving us a cold smile.

'What's up with her?' I watched her progression down the steps and as she sat down on a front seat.

'Dunno,' Teddy removed his chin and busied himself cleaning his glasses.

'Hmm,' I watched him for a minute. 'Did you fall

262

out?'

'No!' he gave me a swift smile. 'Of course not.'

'Teddy, darling,' Crystal appeared. 'Coming for a drink later?'

'Maybe,' he took a tiny step away from her.

'It was my birthday yesterday, so you must,' she stroked his arm.

'You should have said,' I admonished her. 'Happy birthday.'

'Thank you,' she dragged her gaze away from Teddy. 'Ah, Jamie,' she grabbed him as he walked past, yawning. 'Pub later?'

'Oh,' he frowned. 'I shouldn't… the twins have been a nightmare.'

'Aw,' I said sympathetically. 'It doesn't last forever,' I momentarily thought of Emilie and suddenly felt low.

'So I'm told,' Jamie smiled weakly.

'Any new photos?'

'Yeah,' Jamie took his phone out of his back pocket and showed me a picture of them in matching blue sleepsuits in their cot.

'They are so cute,' I said. 'You are so lucky.'

'You wouldn't say that on four hours sleep a night,' he said, but smiled fondly.

Teddy slung an arm around me and bent a little to look at the photo, 'Sweet,' he grinned.

I glanced up and saw Francesca watching us with a bitter expression.

We had reached the final scene and I braced myself.

'Ladies and gentlemen,' Johnny said in a low voice, sweeping a gaze upon those of us gathered around, 'I now know who the murderer is.'

'Surely none of us,' I stood up from my seat and put my hands on my hips.

'Madam, please sit down,' Johnny cast me a kindly look. 'I understand that this is unbearable for you.'

I sat back down and bowed my head.

'Mr Graves,' he turned to look at Bob. 'Apologies sir, you have lost the love of your life.'

'And yet, been interrogated,' Bob sat up straight.

'As I had to,' Johnny said.

'Well,' Destiny stood up, 'my beloved sister has been murdered… murdered as she slept. I want an apology for all who loved her.'

'Oh, I apologise,' Johnny said. 'I extend my sincerest apologies to you all. Except to one person. The person that dares to stand here, proclaiming his mourning. Deceiving us all with his false claims of devotion and faithfulness. I am sorry Mr Graves, but the person that Miss Mabel had declared her love for and the person that feared her last will and testament would be deviated from… Mr Benedict Beckett!' Johnny pointed a finger at Finn.

'What?!' Bob, Teddy and I cried at the same time.

'I-I'm sorry Inspector?' Finn exclaimed.

Despite my dislike for Finn, I had to admire his perfectly mystified and distraught expression.

'Yes, Mr Beckett,' Johnny lowered his arm. 'And shall we enlighten the grieving, the *sincerely* grieving, why you committed this dastardly crime?'

'You are mistaken,' Finn wrung his hands.

'Am I?' Johnny took a few steps towards him. 'Let us examine the facts, Mr Beckett.

Would it be fair to say that you were Miss Mabel's confidante? Would it be fair to say that she shared her most personal thoughts and affairs?'

'She trusted me, yes,' Finn said in a louder voice. 'She was my friend as well as my employer.'

'So it seems,' Johnny paused. 'You were in her employment before Mr Graves became her husband-to-be, yes?'

'Yes,' Finn said stiffly.

'And would it be a surprise to you that Miss Mabel had left you a sizeable legacy in her will?'

'It would,' Finn widened his eyes.

'And would it be a surprise to you that Miss Mabel was in fact in love with you, Mr Beckett?'

'This is ridiculous,' Bob said in a shaking voice.

'I'm sorry, Mr Graves,' Johnny directed at Bob.

'It most certainly would,' Finn said with convincing indignance.

'I see,' Johnny turned towards the auditorium and walked slowly away from us, before directing to Derek, 'Exhibit A, please Constable Trowbridge.'

At this point, Derek was supposed to hand Johnny a large old-fashioned diary but improvised with his script.

'Where did you get that?' I gasped. 'Auntie had been looking for it, and jolly upset she was too.'

'Where indeed?' Johnny glared at Finn. 'Could you explain, please, how this was found under a loose floorboard in your room, Mr Beckett?'

'I cannot,' Finn stared at the paper in Johnny's hand.

'I won't disrespect the deceased,' Johnny said. 'But this contains Miss Mabel's most private thoughts, her most intimate daydreams, as well as conversations she had with Mr Beckett… including that she revealed that he would inherit a large portion of her estate. And if Miss Jones,' he nodded kindly at me, 'married, almost all of it.'

'I've been framed,' Finn blustered.

'Dear boy,' Teddy went and put his arms around Finn in a prolonged hug. 'I believe you.'

I had to work hard not to giggle, and I saw that Johnny started to smile.

'Gordon!' Francesca stamped her foot.

'Sorry!' I cried, leaping to my feet. I suddenly had a block on my lines; Teddy gave me a ghost of a wink and I took a deep breath. 'This is not true, it can't be!'

'Explain yourself,' Destiny demanded.

'Auntie, I'm sorry,' I gazed at her, then turned in a slow circle as everyone stared at me. 'But it can't be true, it just can't… because… *I'm* in love with him!'

'What?' everyone said in unison.

'Darling Benedict, I believe you,' I rushed towards Finn and flung my arms around his neck, before kissing him wildly until Destiny pulled me away.

'Handcuffs!' Johnny barked at Derek.

'Ooo, yes please,' Teddy said in a camp voice, again causing smiles.

'Benedict Beckett,' Johnny intoned. 'I am arresting you on the charge of the murder by poison and strangulation of Miss Mabel Nightingale.'

'No!' Teddy and I both yelled, clasping each other.

'Gordon!' Francesca stormed.

Finn glared around the room as Derek pretended to cuff him.

'Do you have anything to say?' Johnny said roughly.

'Yes!' said Finn in an angry voice. 'Alright… I confess, it was me. I killed the old dragon!'

'What?' I fell to my knees and Bob came and comforted me.

'I did it,' he said viciously. 'Years and years I put up with her touching me, waiting for some compensation from her disgusting advances.'

'No,' Bob covered his face with his hands, and I patted his shoulder.

'Then *you* came along,' Finn snarled at Bob. 'No doubt hoping the old crone would snuff it soon, and leave you all this,' he looked wildly around. 'Taking what's mine, *mine!*'

'You beast!' I cried.

'Take him away!' Johnny commanded.

'And curtain!' Duncan called, clapping his hands. 'Well done all of you.'

'Bravo,' a voice came from the very last row of seats. It was Jaco.

'Jaco?' I said in surprise as he stood up and made his way towards the stage.

'Hello, angel,' he came to the front of the stage and looked up. 'Sorry, I sneaked in, I didn't want to disturb you.'

I sat on the edge of the stage and slid off into his arms, 'How long have you been here?'

'Not long,' he kissed me and looked up again. 'Hello everyone, alright, Teddy?'

'Jac,' Teddy grinned briefly before he was engulfed in a hug from Crystal.

'You did wonderfully,' she said.

'Everyone is going for a drink,' I told him. 'Fancy it?'

'Sure.'

'I thought I wasn't seeing you until tomorrow,' I picked up my bag and rummaged for a hairband to tie my hair up.

'I know,' he stroked my bum. 'I just suddenly missed you.'

'Good,' I perched myself on his knee and kissed him. 'So you should. I'm a wonderful girlfriend.'

'Oh, you are,' he chuckled.

I felt the magic of his very presence working, but underneath I could feel the current of my doubts and fears pulling at me.

'You OK, sweetheart?'

'Yes,' I nodded. 'Give me five, and we can go.'

We all went to the pub, everyone euphorically discussing our last scene and that the real hard work would begin now.

Initially worried that Jaco would be bored of the talk about our production, I was pleased that he joined in, asking everyone questions.

'I was involved in a television production,' Duncan told him. 'So I know the ropes well.'

'Steven Spielberg eat your heart out,' Teddy muttered, making me giggle.

I watched Finn as he waffled on to his admirers about his performance and I pulled a face.

'You were awesome,' Jaco said, stroking my leg. 'Talented little lady, aren't you?'

'Who knew, eh?' I said lightly.

'I mean it!' he grinned. 'I can't wait until opening

night.'

'Are you staying tonight?' I lent my head on his shoulder, tiredness overcoming me.

'Can't baby, got to drive to London early.'

'OK,' I was secretly glad, I wanted a good night's sleep.

'Tomorrow I will wine and dine my clever girl.'

'Aw, you're so lucky,' Meadow said, who'd been sitting next to me and apparently eavesdropping.

'Ain't she just,' Francesca agreed, giving me an appraising look, then glancing at Teddy on the opposite side of the table.

I wondered again what was wrong between them but was too tired to try and work it out.

It was nearly eleven o'clock when we all went back to the theatre carpark.

Teddy went and started his engine while I said goodnight to Jaco before he drove home.

'I'm flipping knackered,' I closed my eyes as Teddy pulled out onto the road.

'Yeah, me too a bit,' he said.

I was about to interrogate him about Francesca when my mobile rang from my bag. Pulling it out, I felt my heart flutter as I saw Shauna's name.

'Hello?' I said cautiously.

'Rox, oh Roxy,' she said in a rush. 'I'm at the hospital,' she started to sob, and I sat up straight. 'It's Liam. He's… someone attacked him… oh please come, he's n-not… he's in a bad way.'

CHAPTER TWENTY-ONE

Teddy drove us to the hospital, all the while trying to reassure me.

As soon as he pulled into the emergency and accident car park, I jumped out, leaving him to park.

I found Shauna, Howard, my mum and Liam's mum, Julie, in the waiting room.

'What's happened? Where is he?' I went and hugged a tear-stained Shauna.

'Oh, he looks bad,' Shauna croaked. 'He was working l-late,' she glanced at Julie and Julie patted her leg, her own expression distraught, 'he was getting into his c-car and some guy, h-h-he jumped him and… oh,' she began to sob loudly.

'Oh my God,' I looked at the row of white faces.

'He was beaten nearly to death,' Julie, a dark-haired and attractive woman, said huskily. 'Luckily someone came out the building and they ran off.'

'Rox?' Teddy appeared behind me, then put an arm around me as he took in whatever expression I had on my face.

'Where's Emilie?' I asked.

'Emma next door came over,' Shauna said, then blew her nose.

'OK,' I went and sat next to my mum. 'Where is he, what's happening?'

'He's having a brain scan,' Howard said as Shauna and Julie both started to sob in earnest.

'Roxy,' Teddy knelt in front of me. 'I'll go honey, you stay with your family.'

'No!' I implored. 'Please stay.'

'OK,' he stood up. 'Anybody want a drink?'

'A tea, please,' my mum said, and Howard just nodded.

He went off towards the entrance, pulling change out of his pocket.

'When did this happen?' I asked my mum, who seemed the calmest despite her red eyes.

'About an hour ago,' she said in a low voice. 'The man who saw it drove him over, said he passed out in the car,' she gave a shaky sigh. 'I can't remember if anyone thanked him.'

'Jesus,' I stared at Shauna who was crying and seemed close to collapse. 'H-how bad is he?'

'Bad,' my mum shook her head despairingly. 'His face is awful.'

'I'll have to get his friend's car cleaned,' Julie said in a monotone voice. 'So much blood.'

'M-mum,' Shauna suddenly snapped her head up. 'Can you go to mine? If Emilie wakes up, she m-might be scared. And Emma can't stay long.'

'Oh, darling, I want to stay here,' my mum looked at Howard.

'P-please,' Shauna started to rip up the tissue clutched in her hands. 'I'll ring you... p-please?'

'Come on,' Howard muttered. 'Roxy? Are you staying?'

'Yes,' I avoided his gaze, but he reached over and patted my hand.

Teddy returned, balancing six plastic cups.

'Sorry Teddy, love,' my mum stood up. 'We're going.'

'It's OK,' he took my mum's seat and put the cups down on Howard's.

They hugged Shauna and Julie, then left, my mum telling me to ring as soon as there was any news.

It seemed like an eternity before the doctor came and spoke to Shauna.

The scan was thankfully clear. However, he had a severe injury to his right eye, his nose was broken, and his wrist had a fracture, possibly as he tried to defend himself. Apart from some deep cuts and bruises, he was OK.

Shauna took all of this in with a blank expression, thanked the doctor, then broke into heart-wrenching sobs.

'He's OK,' I put my arm around her, looking helplessly at Teddy.

'B-but what if he wasn't?' she shuddered. 'He could have been k-killed if nobody had turned up. Why? Why would someone do that? Who would what t-to hurt him?'

'I know, I know,' I let her cry, watching Julie as she took out her phone.

'Rox,' Teddy whispered and nudged me, indicating to two policemen walking in and approaching the reception desk.

I started to feel very sick and shaky, wishing that I hadn't drank so much wine at the pub.

Teddy and I left just after one in the morning, with me

apologising profusely for dragging Teddy into it.

'Don't be daft,' he reassured me.

I fell silent as we reached the dual carriageway, my exhausted brain trying to process the whole thing.

'You OK, chicken?' he asked.

'I was just thinking about Troy,' I murmured.

'Yeah?'

'It's almost the same thing,' I rubbed my eyes.

'Yeah, I suppose it is.'

'Nothing like this happens in Fernberry... it's so weird.'

'I guess.'

'Could be the same person.'

'Really?' Teddy sounded doubtful. 'Coincidence.'

'It's weird,' I repeated, not even sure what I was thinking.

'He's OK, just concentrate on that.'

'Yeah.'

'Honey, the police will find whoever done it.'

'They didn't find Troy's attacker.'

'But Troy was knocked out, all they had was a blurry CCTV image. This time there's a witness.'

'Yeah,' I looked at Teddy's profile for a minute. 'Hope they find him.'

All I could think at that moment, with the shame of disloyalty and a deep fear, was that I was glad that Jaco had been with me when the attack happened.

I laid awake until almost five o'clock in the morning, thinking about Liam, thinking about Troy... scared why my mind had turned to Jaco.

I knew that it couldn't be him, he'd been with me.

And the attack sounded so vicious, like Troy's had; I'd seen the evidence of that on his face… Jaco had his faults but he couldn't possibly be capable of such awful violence.

But… what are you thinking Roxy? Is it because Jaco is jealous of Troy and because Liam accused him of being a drug-dealer? They've both rattled him in different ways, is that the only connection? Because that's a giant leap in logic… it could just be a random maniac, Fernberry is a small town and it wouldn't be a huge coincidence that you know both the victims. Or separate attackers… that could be possible. And he was with you, he was at the pub with you.

When my alarm went off at seven, I texted Troy asking him to ring me, which he did straight away.

'Everything OK?' he sounded concerned.

'Please, can I come in late? I was at the hospital until late… my sister's husband was attacked-'

'What? Is he OK?'

'Yeah, well not great, but nothing life-threatening,' I swallowed hard and closed my eyes. 'Like, his eye is bad, I wasn't allowed to see him but she, I mean Shauna, said it looked b-bad… anyway, I've been awake most the night.'

'Take the day off,' he said gently. 'What happened?'

'He got jumped outside work, but someone came out and they ran off.'

'Jesus, is there something in the water?'

'I know, right?'

'Look, if you need anything or a couple of days off, let me know, yeah?'

'Thanks,' I said gratefully.

274

'No problem. Talk soon.'

I pulled the duvet over my head and surprisingly fell back to sleep almost straight away. I woke up just before ten-thirty and saw that I had a missed call from my mum and three from Teddy.

I went and made a mug of tea, texting Teddy while I waited for the kettle to boil to tell him I just had to ring my mum then I'd ring him.

'Darling,' my mum admonished me, 'why didn't you answer?'

'Sorry, I was asleep. How is he?'

'Shauna said he's in dreadful pain and shook up, of course. They are waiting to see what's happening with his eye, the something-ologist said hopefully it'll clear up with drops… oh it makes me squeamish just thinking about it.'

'Yeah,' I agreed, feeling slightly queasy. 'What about his wrist? And what did the police say? Have they spoken to his friend?'

'Slow down,' my mum said. 'His wrist is in plaster, that'll take a few weeks to heal. The police are speaking to Liam again today because he was too drowsy last night, but they said they are going to take a statement from his friend.'

'Right,' I didn't realise my hands were shaking until I sloshed tea on my bare legs. 'Is Shauna OK?'

'You know Shauna, brave face and all that.'

'She was in such a state last night,' I got up to wipe my legs with a tea towel, then started pacing.

'Ring her, she's at the hospital now.'

'Yeah. Yeah I will.'

We said our goodbyes and I continued to pace, my

275

head feeling heavy with worry.

Without thinking too much about it, I rang Shauna, knowing I would bottle out if I pondered on it too long.

'Roxy,' she answered, her voice husky. 'You alright?'

'Yes!' I started to cry and had to take a few deep breaths. 'How are you? How's Liam? I just spoke to mum.'

'I'm, you know… I'm OK. Liam's not so good. His face is a mess,' she sniffed and let out a shuddering sigh, 'so many cuts…Why?' she burst out. 'Who would do that to him? He's such a gentle giant, oh God,' she started to sob.

'I-I don't know,' I stopped my pacing and sat down again. 'Please don't cry, he's a big strong lump, he'll be fine. He will.'

'I spoke to Tommy, his friend,' she said croakily. 'He said the man was stocky looking, not very tall but big, you know, muscular. He was wearing a hoodie, he didn't see his face at all. Couldn't even tell how old he might be. He was so shocked, I don't think he took in much. He kept apologising.'

'Thank God he turned up when he did.'

'Yeah… he c-could have been killed,' she said thinly. 'He said he should have chased him, but Liam was on the g-ground, and bleeding-' she trailed off.

'Shit,' I murmured, unwelcome images in my head. 'He did the right thing.'

'Yeah,' she said in a clearer voice. 'He did. He's a nice bloke.'

'Do you want me to drive over? I'm off today.'

'Oh,' she sounded guarded and my heart dropped.

276

'Maybe not today. He's not up to it, not really.'

'OK,' I numbly wiped away a tear. 'Well, can I do anything? Do you need me to have Emilie?'

'No, no it's fine. Julie's got her now and Howard is picking her up later and taking her to mine to bath her and put her to bed. I'll go home tonight.'

'Tomorrow?' I asked, almost desperately. 'I can help tomorrow.'

'No, mum's taking the rest of the week off work to help.'

'I don't mind though, mum might need a break.'

'She's OK.'

'Shauna,' I scrunched my eyes shut. 'Is this about Jaco? Because I wouldn't like, leave her with him if you're worried.'

'What?' she said loudly. 'Do you think I give a shit about *that* right now?'

'No, I j-just... I've looked after her loads! I just want to help.'

'Nah,' she said harshly. 'You're just trying to get the focus of attention back on you, as usual!'

'Huh?' I suddenly felt cold all over. 'No! Why are you saying that?'

'You're trying to make it about you,' she raised her voice. 'Poor little Roxy, thinks I'm being mean because I won't let you play dollies for the day with my daughter... well actually, no, I don't want *him* near her.'

'Shauna,' I whispered in shock. 'Please don't be like this-'

'Look,' she said in a hollow voice, 'thanks for ringing, but I can't deal with your crap right now. My husband was nearly killed last night,' then she ended the call.

I sat in stunned disbelief for what seemed like forever, not knowing what the hell had just happened.

She's just upset, she's not thinking straight, I told myself, then broke into fresh tears, sobbing into my knees until I could hardly breathe.

Calming down slightly, I rang Teddy.

'Hi honey, how's the patient?'

'Oh,' I started crying again, unable to get any comprehensible words out.

'I'm coming home,' he said.

Teddy sat next to me on the sofa, stroking my back, his chin on the top of my head.

'I don't get it,' I stormed. 'Well... I do, but,' I buried my face in his chest – he felt so warm and reassuring, 'she was *so* horrible. Like she hates me.'

'She's upset and in shock,' he said soothingly. 'She'll be ringing and apologising, you just wait.'

'Am I that spoilt?' I drew my head back to look at him.

'No!' he smiled sadly. 'You are the most caring and kind person I know. She didn't mean it.'

'Teddy,' I took a deep breath. 'Jaco... could it be true? What Liam said?'

'I don't know,' he held my gaze but his eyes changed... they seemed to darken.

'If you know something... please?' I pleaded.

'Look,' he continued to look at me, 'I haven't been in touch with Jaco for a long time. He was no angel, I told you that. But dealing? I don't know, honey. If he said no and you trust him... then there's your answer.'

'OK,' I lowered my head back to his chest, not sure what to think anymore.

'Give it a few days then ring her.'

'Yeah.'

'Rox,' he said in a soft voice.

I looked back up at him, his turquoise eyes were troubled... then out of nowhere I had the irrational thought that he was going to kiss me, and I drew in a sharp breath.

'What?' I whispered.

'I wish you had told me what Shauna had said before. I hate you being sad.'

'I was embarrassed,' I shrugged under his arms. 'I'm... confused.'

'Yeah,' he nodded slowly. 'You must be.'

'Sorry to drag you out of work.'

'Don't be a doughnut, you're more important.'

'Go on, you can go,' I sat up and rubbed my eyes. 'I'm OK, I need to have a shower and sort myself out.'

'You sure?' he withdrew his arm and watched me closely. 'I don't mind, it's fine.'

'No, I mean yeah,' I nodded. 'Thank you, you are such a good friend,' I sat back again and kissed his cheek. 'I don't know what I'd do without you.'

'Aw, honey,' he gave a self-deprecating grin. 'Call me later, will you do that?'

'Yeah,' I fondly watched him as he pushed himself up and went to put his trainers back on. 'Thank you again.'

Jaco took me to a trendy little Tapas bar in Chembury

that evening. I told him about Liam on our way there, hating myself as I discreetly watched his reaction as he drove.

'Jesus, poor chap,' he glanced at me.

'Yeah,' I agreed. 'I can't imagine who would do that, he's such a nice man.'

'You need to be careful nowadays,' he pulled into a side street. 'Hope he's OK.'

'Yeah,' I murmured again.

Parking about halfway up the street, we walked quickly in the light drizzle towards the bar. Once inside, I shot off to the ladies' to repair my hair. My face looking back at me in the mirror was pale and tense.

We ordered a bottle of wine and our food; I wasn't remotely hungry.

After two or three sips of wine, I felt light-headed and drank some water instead.

'New dress?' Jaco asked, eyeing me appreciatively.

'Oh, no,' I fidgeted and tried to smile naturally. 'Been raiding my autumn clothes as apparently summer has buggered off.'

'You look lovely,' he took my hand and squeezed it. 'God, I'm starving.'

'Mmm.'

'Baby, are you OK?'

'Yes,' I said quickly. 'How was your day?'

'Better than yours, it seems,' he said gently. 'Not bad, up to my neck in paperwork.'

'Fun.'

'Ever so,' he grinned. 'Tomorrow we are hanging some paintings from a new artist, Donny Donahue, pretty sure that's a made-up name.'

'Any good?'

'Yeah, an eclectic mix, bloody weird some of them.'

I didn't even know what "eclectic" meant so I just nodded.

Our food arrived and he immediately began to eat, offering me a battered baby squid to which I recoiled.

'Tuck in sweetheart,' he nodded at our platter. 'Those olives are to die for.'

I ate slowly, forcing each mouthful of food down, feeling on the brink of tears and not even sure why.

'You're very quiet,' he observed, wiping his fingers on a napkin and taking a sip of wine, his eyes dark and watchful.

'Sorry,' I smiled in apology. 'Long night, and I'm worried about Liam.'

'Of course,' he said quietly. 'Maybe tonight wasn't a good idea.'

'No, it's nice to get out,' I dropped my eyes and picked up some bread, not really wanting to eat it but needing to do something with my hands.

'My poor baby,' his handsome face was so full of love and concern, my heart lifted slightly.

'I'm probably just tired.'

'Sure, things will seem better after a good night's sleep. What time did you get home?'

I suddenly realised that I had failed to tell him that Teddy had been with me, and my heart plummeted again. That didn't happen for no reason, and I knew it with a depressing certainty.

CHAPTER TWENTY-TWO

The rest of the week was a week of mixed fortunes.

After our date on Tuesday night, Jaco had took me home and told me to get some sleep, kissing me tenderly at the flats entrance. I was disturbed that I was relieved he wasn't spending the evening but that was compensated by the fact I could drop my pretence of all being fine.

Tripping over Jethro in the corridor and swearing loudly as I dropped my bag, Teddy had stuck his head out and we ended up drinking tea and eating a box of flapjacks from Lola on our seat in front of his balcony until way after midnight. As always, he cheered me up with his inane daftness and we talked about the play more than my troubles.

On Wednesday, Howard rang me in the morning.

'Hi,' I said cautiously.

'Hi,' he sounded equally as cautious. 'Liam's home, Shauna wanted me to let you know.'

'Right, thanks.'

'Roxy, she told me about your conversation. Are you OK?'

'She did?' I had been laying on my bed reading, having decided to take another day off. I immediately stood up and started pacing.

'She did. She feels bad.'

'Then why isn't she ringing me?' I said evenly, all the upset coming back, but also feeling angry.

'She's embarrassed, ashamed, maybe. She's going through a lot right now,' he paused. 'Are you OK? I'm worried about you.'

'Not really,' I admitted. 'It was rather uncalled for… I know she's stressed, but she was really horrible.'

'Yeah, it sounds like it. I'm having a hard time keeping all this from your mum,' he laughed dryly. 'She's beginning to sniff out clues of all not being well.'

'Yeah, I bet,' I couldn't help smiling.

'Hmm, well, let's try and heal this. Can we do that?'

'I don't know how,' I stopped at my window and stared miserably at the rain sodden car park. 'Maybe it's better if I lay low for a bit. Let her… let her sort herself out.'

'Sure. But sometimes the longer we leave these things, the harder it gets.'

'I know,' I muttered.

'Look, I need to get off,' he said. 'Come and see us soon, please, Roxy. Come over for tea. Give Jacob someone to annoy.'

'OK.'

I went back to work on Thursday, feeling a lot better and rested.

After talking to Howard, my mind eased a little and I felt hopeful that the rift could be mended. It wasn't in my nature to hold grudges and prolong an argument.

The thing that was troubling me the most was that it all came back to Jaco.

Is he really worth all of this? It was easy to think that when I was away from him, and I wasn't seeing him until Friday; he'd arranged for us to meet with Sadie and Eliza for dinner, but I knew once I was with him that his magic would steal over me and render me helpless.

Work was a nice distraction. Troy quietly asked how Liam was away from Albie and Kyle, then didn't bring him up again.

He was looking much better, the bruises more or less faded, although he was still hobbling somewhat.

I kept myself busy, spending the afternoon tidying the stock room with Albie and having a giggle – just what I needed… but yet again the thought of Jaco and if he could see me that he'd probably be angry, kept intruding in my thoughts.

I texted Dana; I needed some advice. She said she'd swing by the theatre to watch rehearsals and then we'd go for a quiet drink, or back to my flat.

Everybody, with the exception of two or three members, seemed hyped up that evening at rehearsals.

Duncan gave us a five-minute lecture beforehand, telling us that now we were in dress rehearsals, we needed to work harder than ever.

'He says the same thing every time,' Samantha grumbled in a low voice. 'We *do* know.'

Violet glanced up from a clipboard she was holding, 'Roxy dear, did you bring your shoes?'

'Yes,' I whispered, seeing Duncan giving her a dark look.

'- so my loves,' he continued, 'Violet will be helping with your costumes as always, but please know what you're doing, there's only one of her.'

'I can help the girls,' Finn said jokingly, making his fans giggle and Teddy mutter '*dick goblin,*' earning him a dirty look from Francesca.

There was more activity than normal as Tilly's "boys", the stagehands, were ready with the props. The only difference between our dress rehearsals and the real thing was that the scenery wasn't in place. I heard Pontus grumbling that Brad had changed his mind *again*, and that one day '*that poncey idiot*' would not have our scenery ready on time.

There were also the sound operators, two sisters called Karen and Nicky who had probably already been there a while setting up whatever it was that they had to get ready.

Those of us that were in the first scene trooped off to the changing rooms to get ready, Violet shrugging off her cardigan and unbuttoning her blouse as we walked backstage.

'I always get hot and flustered getting changed,' Lily-rose said in her soft voice, wriggling her leggings down.

'Least you get to stay in your maids costume,' I said.

My first costume was described in my list as "wide-legged trousers and high-necked short-sleeved blouse, flat shoes". The trousers were fine, a little long, but the blouse was cheap with a scratchy label on the neck and tight across my chest.

'Come on,' Violet shooed us out and proceeded us to the stage where there was a velvet sofa and an old-fashioned lamp next to it.

I settled myself on the right-hand side of the sofa, Violet perched herself on the left.

Lily-rose stood to one side and clasped her hands primly in front of her.

'OK children,' Duncan said. 'This'll be curtain up, off we go.'

Nearly two hours later I was both shattered and elated. Shattered because I had to summon every bit of concentration I had, elated because my scatty brain was behaving itself and I had been word-perfect.

I had been slightly distracted by Dana slinking in twenty minutes before we were due to finish, but I had managed to focus myself.

'You were super-duper,' Teddy hugged me when Duncan told us we were done for the evening.

'I wish I had a smaller role,' I shook my head.

'Hush,' he scolded me.

I was about to go and get changed when I glanced up and saw Francesca watching us, looking unhappy.

'Hey,' I lowered my voice. 'I know something's up, spill.'

'Urgh,' he started taking tiny steps backwards until I grabbed the front of his shirt.

'Please?' I blinked up at him.

'Pop over later,' he sighed. 'Nosy cow.'

'Yay.'

Me and Dana went to The Rose where I proceeded to fill her in on the latest developments.

'Jesus,' she surveyed me with her big, dark eyes. 'Drama, drama.'

'Right?' I knocked back some gin. 'Not good.'

'No,' she agreed.

'It's like when I'm with him I'm all… messy head. But when I'm not with him, I can see he's not good for me. But I love him… but… I don't know,' I threw my head back and groaned. 'I am *so* confused.'

'Yup.' Dana nodded.

She looked nothing short of amazing tonight, in tartan leggings and a loose red T-shirt, her hair clouding around her beautiful face in it's crazy afro. Next to her, I felt very pale and dreary. I experienced a stab of envy; she had a brilliant career, a man that adored her and she never seemed to doubt herself like I did.

'I feel like I need to, like, back off a bit,' I thought about it and shook my head. 'No, not back off, but *wean* myself off him.'

'Girl, cold turkey's better,' Dana frowned at me. 'End it,' she said bluntly.

'Oh no,' I felt my eyes fill with tears. 'I can't, it'll be too hard.'

'Rox,' she murmured, and put her cool hand on mine. 'I don't like seeing you like this.'

'I don't like *feeling* like this,' I watched morosely as a group of guys walked past, a couple of them eyeing us. 'It sucks. I wish I never met him.'

'One of life's lessons.'

'And what would that be?'

'No idea.'

I laughed weakly, then stood up, 'OK my round, then I gotta go and gossip with Teddy.'

I went to the bar and the girl serving nodded and smiled at me as she served someone else.

'Hello,' one of the guys appeared beside me.

'Hi,' I smiled automatically.

'I'm Charlie,' he said.

'Roxy,' I muttered.

'How are you?' he leant his head around slightly and I glanced at him. He wasn't bad looking, tall with fair hair in a standard short back and sides, dark with too much gel at the front. He had smiling dark eyes and nice straight teeth – I *always* notice teeth.

'Good, thanks,' I leant over the bar as the barmaid approached. 'Two gin and lemonades, one with ice, one without.'

'Can I get them?' Charlie asked.

'Oh, no thanks,' I willed the barmaid to hurry up. 'Me and my friend are leaving soon.'

'Pity,' he grinned boyishly, seemingly indifferent to the rejection.

I thought to myself that single me would have probably flirted with him a little, possibly going home with his phone number. I sighed, wondering if I really wanted to go back to that, whether it would just seem depressing and frivolous now that I had experienced love.

'See?' Dana grinned as I sat back down. 'Plenty more fish in the sea.'

'I think I would rather be single,' I sighed again.

'Little ray of sunshine, ain't ya?'

'I can't bounce from guy to guy forever, just in it for the fun.'

'Not forever babe, but you're twenty-two not thirty,' she gave an affected shudder. 'Might as well have fun until Mister Perfect comes along and ties you down.'

'Cheery thought,' I said sourly. 'I don't want perfect,

288

I want *normal*. Like, dependable but fun, without worrying and being on edge. And really good sex.'

'I wonder what Teddy's like in bed?' she mused, staring into space.

'Dana!' I nearly choked on my drink. 'Where on *earth* did that come from?'

She laughed throatily, 'No idea. He just seems like he'd make a good husband. Hard to tell if a guy's gonna be good in bed.'

At that precise moment, Charlie walked past our table and clearly overheard Dana's last comment. His eyebrows shot up, then he winked at me, making Dana laugh even more.

'You're a troublemaker,' I giggled.

'Sorry,' she smiled her wide and gorgeous smile at the table of Charlie and friends, then blew a kiss at them.

'Behave,' I scolded.

'Yeah, yeah,' she brought her attention back to me. 'OK, let's sort you out. What are you doing this weekend?'

'Out for dinner tomorrow with Jaco's sister and her mate... then I don't know.'

'Saturday night, me and you are going out. We don't even have to go out, we can get pissed at mine. First step.'

'Oh,' I started feeling my horrible, restless urge to pace. 'It's short notice, he won't be happy.'

'See?' she lowered her voice, staring intently at me. 'That isn't right, is it? Why won't he be happy? That's ridiculous.'

'God,' I stared back at her and felt a shiver pass over

me.

'We're gonna do this, together,' she said quietly. 'OK?'

'OK,' I was filled with an immense feeling of love for her and gratitude, but I couldn't verbalise it at all. I felt like I wanted to cry. 'Thank you.'

Glad of the distraction, I knocked on Teddy's door when I got home.

'Hello, you,' he said as he opened the door, looking resigned. 'Let's get this over and done with.'

'What's this?' I asked as I noticed his old-fashioned radio that was normally at his store on his worktop, the back off and screws and wires everywhere.

'Kaput, I'm fixing it,' he went to the fridge. 'Beer or tea?'

'Neither,' I went and flopped down in our seat. 'Gossip.'

'Bloody hell,' he grumbled. 'It's not really gossip.'

'I'll be the judge of that,' I patted the seat next to me and he reluctantly came over with his screwdriver in his hand then started twirling it.

'OK, in a nutshell,' he began slowly, 'she, that is Francesca, made... a pass at me.'

'No way!' I squealed and twisted around to face him squarely. 'And?'

'I, um, declined.'

'Declined?'

'Well, she kind of went to kiss me,' he squirmed slightly. 'And I told her that... I didn't like her that way... well, it may have come out wrong,' he shrugged helplessly. 'She got a little pissed off.'

'Oops,' I stared at him. 'What the hell did you say?'

'I d-don't really remember exactly,' he gave me a sidelong look, 'but she was kind of... persistent as to why, and I said, *really* kindly that it wasn't her, but she accused me of leading her on. I wasn't! Not intentionally I don't think... was I?'

'I can't really answer that,' I tried to keep a straight face, but I obviously wasn't doing a great job of it by his expression.

'This is exactly why I didn't want to tell you,' he folded his arms and stared straight ahead. 'It's not funny.'

'I'm sorry,' I put my head on his shoulder. 'No, it's not. Poor Francesca. She's probably just embarrassed, she'll recover.'

'Sure.'

'Unrequited love is hard.'

'Piss off.'

I saw he was trying not to grin, and I nudged him, 'Why don't you fancy her? She's so pretty.'

'She is,' he agreed. 'I just don't have the... the *feels*. It's either there or it's not.'

'Shame,' I sat up straight and stretched. 'I better go, I'm actually tired.'

'You smell of gin,' he poked my nose. 'Go on, bugger off.'

'Charming!'

After all the wet and miserable weather, I was happy to see when I woke up on Friday morning, that the sun was shining.

That alone made me feel more cheerful. My morning

at work was fun, I spent my lunch hour at the gym, and I was strangely looking forward to my evening out with Jaco.

I was, however, a little apprehensive about seeing Sadie as the last time I saw her I was throwing up in her garden, something I brought up when Jaco arrived at my flat.

'Silly you,' he laughed. 'Sadie's cool.'

As I had predicted, I felt the magic of him working on me by the mere presence of him.

As I finished getting ready, he lounged on my sofa, drinking a beer and chatting away, then complementing me as I emerged from my bedroom.

'You look gorgeous,' he gave me a slow up and down look that made my heart speed up. 'I'm so lucky,' he added happily.

We walked into town, hand in hand, chatting about nothing in particular. I started to wonder if my fears were groundless, as if I had turned him into some sort of monster with my tangled feelings.

Sadie and Eliza were already sat at the bar waiting for us when we arrived.

Sadie was as stunning as I remembered her, dressed in tiny red shorts and a black see-through blouse. She jumped off her stool when she spotted us, hugging me and punching Jaco lightly on the arm before kissing him.

Eliza greeted us shyly, putting her hand up in a small wave and self-consciously hitching the neckline of her top up. Jaco ruffled her hair and grinned.

'Our table's ready,' Sadie told us, draining her drink. 'What are you drinking, guys?' she looked at me, then frowned. 'You OK?'

'Actually,' I said hesitantly, 'I wanted to apologise. I'm still embarrassed about throwing up on your flowers.'

'Oh, my goodness,' she went into peals of laughter. 'We've all been there, right?'

'Right,' I laughed too. 'I'm a bit of a light-weight.'

'I blame my brother then,' Sadie ordered our drinks and we turned to go to our table.

'Roxy?' I looked over my shoulder and saw a dark-haired girl leaning across the bar, smiling at me.

'Lennie!' I exclaimed.

Jaco looked over enquiringly and I waved in the direction of the bar, 'I'll be over in a minute,' I told him.

Lennie and I had worked together the previous year at a coffee shop, The Busy Bean. We had both despised it, mainly because of our dreadful boss.

I had left before Lennie and we hadn't really kept in touch, but we had always got on. She was kind of *low-key*, I suppose you'd say, but she had a quirky sense of humour, albeit rather dark.

'How are you? New fella?' she craned her neck to watch Jaco's progression to our table.

'I'm really good,' I put my drink back down on the bar. 'How long you been working here?'

'Since last October,' she smiled a small smile. 'My fiancé owns it.'

'Oh!' I squealed. 'You're engaged! How lovely, show me your ring,' I examined her beautiful diamond ring and sighed. 'You are so lucky!'

We chatted for another five minutes, exchanged

mobile numbers, then I went to find the others.

'Who was that?' Jaco asked unsmilingly.

'I used to work with her,' I said, feeling suddenly wary by his tone. He kind of nodded and resumed his conversation with Sadie and Eliza, pointedly pushing a menu towards me.

I opened my menu, glancing up and catching Eliza watching me from across the table, 'I'm having potato skins,' she said.

'Oh, are we doing starters?'

'We have to,' Sadie said from next to Eliza. 'El's an eating machine.'

'Yup,' she agreed, shrugging.

'I might have the stuffed dates,' I murmured.

'That sounds like pudding,' Jaco said shortly, again his tone not one I liked.

Filled with puzzlement at his dark mood, I lowered my head again, feeling on the verge of tears.

'Mmm, me too,' Sadie said. 'They sound yummy.'

As Sadie and Eliza started arguing amicably over the wine menu, I leaned closer to Jaco, 'What's up?' I whispered.

'I just thought that was a bit rude,' he turned his head and looked at me.

'Huh?'

'They invite us out,' he said, his voice barely audible, 'and you bugger off and chat to your mate for ages.'

'I didn't *bugger off*,' I said as quietly as I could, 'it was a quick hello,' deciding that I wasn't going to display any weakness, I turned back resolutely and knocked back my drink, then smiled brightly across the table. 'Where did you go for your holiday?' I asked –

Jaco had mentioned they had got back a few days ago.

They started telling me about it and I nodded along, aware of Jaco's silent presence on my left.

We ordered our meals and wine, then Jaco excused himself and went to the gents'. I breathed out my tension without thinking and Sadie gave me an appraising look, a small frown creasing her forehead.

'You OK?' she asked casually, and I smiled and nodded.

We'd been chatting about tattoos and had moved onto to our jobs when Sadie also excused herself.

'So, why don't you like your boss?' I asked Eliza.

'Well,' she took a gulp of her drink, 'he's creepy. And he smells.'

I giggled, 'Of what?'

'B.O. and utter nerd,' she laughed, then snorted, which made me laugh even more.

'Why don't you leave?'

'Dunno,' she shrugged. 'Laziness, probably. I should, it's doing my head in.'

I looked over towards the bar and spotted Jaco and Sadie. They looked like they were arguing; most of Sadie was blocked by Jaco but I could see she had her hands on her hips and Jaco was gesturing with one arm. Eliza followed my gaze, then smiled awkwardly at me.

'I'm surprised I wasn't sacked to be honest,' she said.

'Oh?' I tried to re-focus.

'Yeah,' she laughed again. 'He took me for a drink after work and touched my leg.'

'No way,' I said, and she wrinkled her nose.

295

'Yeah. I'm not even sure it was… you know, *untoward,* but I flipped out,' she paused, looking above my head, then Jaco and Sadie came and took their seats. 'I'm just telling her about Richard groping me.'

'Ew,' Sadie said.

'What did you do?' I asked, giggling as she let out another laugh and snort.

'I started yelling at him,' she said. 'I kind of jumped up and told him he couldn't do that, and he started getting flustered. Half the fucking pub was looking at us,' she shook her head. 'Then I stormed out… felt like a right idiot five minutes later.'

I laughed, but more so because of her little snorts when *she* laughed.

To my surprise, Jaco chuckled too and put his arm along the back of my chair.

'You know what?' I said after a moment. 'We're advertising for staff. We've got a new part-timer starting next week, but we still need someone full-time.'

'Yeah?' she widened her blue-eyes and looked expectantly at me.

'Yeah,' I nodded, distracted by Jaco stroking my back. 'Give me your email address and I'll send the details.'

'That'd be brilliant,' she beamed.

The rest of the evening was strange. Jaco was talkative, almost manically so, and I wondered if he felt bad for being grumpy with me earlier.

Even when Lennie came over to say goodbye to me, he was courteous and chatty.

I thought that Sadie was giving us covert glances; I suspected that she had had words with Jaco when I had spotted them at the bar.

My suspicions were confirmed when we went to the ladies' with Eliza after our meal.

I told Eliza while Sadie was in her cubicle that Troy was rather sweet on me and that I'd put in a good word. Then I whispered, feeling disrespectful and not wanting Sadie to hear, that Jaco had a jealous streak so could she not repeat that.

I was still washing my hands when Sadie came out.

'You OK, lovely?' she said as she rinsed her hands.

'Yeah,' I looked at her in the mirror. 'I'm stuffed, the food is like, amazing in here.'

'Sure is,' she agreed. 'Can I just say something?'

'Oh!' I stared at her. 'Sure.'

'My brother,' she paused, then smiled her dazzling smile that was identical to Jaco's, 'don't take his little moods to heart.'

'Huh,' I looked down at the sink. 'You saw that.'

'Hm,' she passed me and stuck her hands under the drier. 'I mean, men as a whole are dickheads, right?'

'Yeah,' I giggled.

'You seem like a lovely girl,' she watched me as I dried my hands too. 'Just don't take any shit.'

'No,' I avoided eye contact as long as I could, rubbing my hands in the warm stream of air. When I looked up, she was still looking at me.

'It's been a great night,' she gave me a hug, then tugged my arm. 'Come on, don't want to miss last orders.'

CHAPTER TWENTY-THREE

We said our goodnights to Sadie and Eliza and walked back to my flat, arm in arm.

This is hard to admit because I don't want to be judged, *and my God, I was judging myself,* but I was ignoring Jaco's earlier sulks. After a few too many drinks, I was vaguely looking forward to some abandoned sex and being made to feel irresistible and splendid with Jaco's compliments and tender murmurings during our lovemaking.

As we walked around to the side of my building to the doors, Teddy pulled up and Jaco halted me.

'Hey, Teddy Boy,' he called as Teddy climbed out of his car.

'Hey,' Teddy shoved his keys in his pocket, clutching a Burger King bag.

'Lonely meal for one, buddy?' Jaco opened the doors as Teddy ambled over.

'A lonely meal for half a dozen,' Teddy smiled crookedly as he drew close. 'Alright Rox? I ain't eaten all day, gonna devour this and die in the bath.'

'Bad day?' I asked, thinking he looked pale and drawn.

'Nah, just busy,' he grinned.

Jaco let Teddy proceed him then we followed him up the stairs.

'Coming in for a nightcap?' Jaco said as we reached our respective doors.

'Thanks, but I've got a hot date with a burger,' Teddy opened his door. 'Laters.'

'Mister cheerful,' Jaco scoffed as I unlocked my door.

'He's OK,' I said lightly.

'Sure.'

I took off my shoes and went to brush my teeth, paranoid my breath stank after eating onions.

'Come here,' Jaco commanded from the sofa when I returned from the bathroom. 'I want a cuddle.'

I sank down next to him and closed my eyes as he wrapped me up in his arms.

'Did you have a nice time?' he asked.

'Yeah… they're funny.'

'Did you enjoy your dinner?'

'It was lovely.'

'Sure was,' he gave a contented sigh. 'What do you want to do tomorrow night?' he gently tugged the back of my hair.

Immediately I was on edge, 'Oh… Dana invited me over for a girl's night.'

'You didn't say,' his tone was mild, but I felt him tense up. 'That'll be nice.'

'You don't mind?' I said evenly, not daring to look at his face.

'Why would I mind?' he kissed the top of my head. 'We can see each other on Sunday. All day if you want, maybe go out for Sunday lunch? Or go shopping? Yeah, let's go shopping, I want to spoil you.'

Relief spread through me and I kissed his chest and snuggled closer, 'You don't have to spoil me.'

'I do. For being beautiful and perfect and for being mine.'

'Smooth-talker,' I looked up at him and he wrinkled his nose up playfully.

'Is it working?'

'Hmm, maybe.'

'I love you,' he murmured and kissed my forehead, then my nose, then very softly on my lips. 'Do you love me?'

'Yes.'

'*Moya milaya.*'

'Was that something dirty?'

'No, you little minx… although…'

'Wanna go to bed?' I stood up and held out my hand.

He stood up too and turned me around, pushing me towards the bedroom, his face buried in my neck, making me break out in goose bumps all over.

'Get undressed,' he growled as he started to strip off.

As we fell on the bed together, he started murmuring his usual endearments.

Then everything went wrong.

His usual passionate but gentle foreplay seemed rougher and drawn-out. His nibbles were hurting me. Not a lot, but enough to make me gasp.

'You like that, huh?' he hovered over me, his eyes glazed and hungry.

'Jaco-' I whispered, fearful again. He didn't look… *right.*

As he began to make love to me, I started to relax a little. Then suddenly a pain in my pelvis sprung up, making me try to sit up.

'Jaco… you're hurting me,' I said loudly, but he

carried on. 'Ow,' I felt tears filling my eyes.

'Baby, my angel,' he smiled down at me, but despite his words, there was nothing tender there.

'Jaco, please,' I croaked as another pain deep in my pelvis jolted me.

He suddenly became frenzied, then ten seconds later he climaxed.

I lay frozen beneath him.

Had I just been raped?

Looking back much later on, I thought that there were a whole bunch of things I should have said and done that night. Like our arguments before, my mind was strangely fuzzy about events.

I remember him rolling off of me, but I don't know how long after. I remember him telling me he loved me, but I don't know whether I replied. And I didn't cry. There were still tears of pain in my eyes, but I didn't cry.

He fell asleep on his side, his hand on my belly. His face that had looked like the devils a few moments ago looked once again handsome, relaxed and boyish in his sleep.

I got up and went to the kitchen, poured a glass of water and swallowed three paracetamols. As I walked back to my bedroom, I abruptly stopped and stared at my front door, thinking Teddy was only a few feet away. Never had I wanted to speak to someone more.

And then I was flooded with self-loathing and shame, leaving an acrid taste in my mouth.

I went to work the following morning, leaving Jaco

still fast asleep. I had stood watching him for a while, my mind torn.

Had I imagined it all? No, no, I knew I hadn't. Usually a light sleeper, I wondered why he wasn't even stirring. I tried to remember how much he had drank the night before.

I told Troy about Eliza, wondering why he was looking at me like he was.

'Sweetie, are you OK?' he asked as I paused.

'What?' I blinked at him. 'Yes! Hangover,' I forced a giggle. 'Anyway, she's super-sweet, I think she'll be great here. Plus, another girl would be *brilliant.'*

'Sure, yeah,' he grinned. 'Tell her to come in for an interview.'

'Thank you!' I clapped my hands.

Troy rolled his eyes, then left the staff room and I immediately burst into tears without any warning. I went into the toilet and rested my forehead on the cold mirror, taking deep breaths and clenching my fists until my nails were digging painfully into my palms.

'*Stop it, stop it. Stop. It.'* I whispered.

I looked at my pale reflection. I had violet shadows under my eyes and my nose was bright red. I stared and stared into my own eyes, feeling disconnected from the girl looking back at me.

'Coffee?' Spencer's voice came with a rap on the door.

'Please,' I called back, surprised how normal my voice sounded.

I took a few more deep breaths and walked briskly out, heading for my bag to powder my nose.

'New guy's starting today,' he said cheerfully. 'Ant.'

'Cool,' I untied my hair and re-did my bun. 'Hopefully he's not as annoying as the rest of you.'

'Ha ha,' Spencer said sarcastically.

Ant turned out to be a tremendously handsome and extremely tall black guy - a well-spoken mature student studying to be a physiotherapist. He would have been definite flirt material if I had been single and not a complete train wreck.

He was also *very* funny, not so much in the laddish, bantering way that the other guys were - more intelligent wit and funny anecdotes. And thankfully, it took the edge off of my fragile state and delayed the thought process I knew I had to go through at some point about the night before.

He wasn't flirtatious in the slightest, which I found weirdly attractive... although I hardly blamed him. I looked dreadful and I knew it.

Midway through the morning I went to make some drinks and take some more painkillers. My pelvis was still throbbing a little and my back was starting to ache from spending an hour on and off my knees measuring children's feet.

'Still suffering?' Troy asked as he followed me.

'Yeah,' I said vaguely.

'Here, let me,' he nudged me away from the kettle.

'Thanks.'

'You in tomorrow?' he squinted at the rota on the wall.

'No,' I got the milk out of the tiny fridge and put it next to the mugs. 'I hate doing Sundays.'

'Mila's away this weekend,' he said. 'I'm at a loose end, fancy doing something on Sunday?'

'Oh,' I said in surprise. 'Sorry, I've got a shopping date.'

'Shame,' he turned slightly and grinned.

Feeling desperately awkward, I watched as he stirred the drinks, then I grabbed two of them to take out.

'Roxy?' Ant's deep voice came from out front. 'Someone to see you.'

I walked out, carefully holding the mugs with Troy behind me. Jaco was standing to the side of the counter – his eyes flickered to Troy and his smile faltered slightly, then he turned it back on full beam.

'Sorry sweetheart, I didn't hear you leave this morning.'

'You were sparko,' I put the mugs down under the counter. My stomach was a tight knot and I felt nauseous.

'I just wanted to see you as you're abandoning me tonight,' he grinned. 'And to tell you to have a good time.'

'Thank you,' I hesitated then walked around the counter towards him. 'What are you doing today?'

'Popping in the gallery, grabbing some paperwork, then heading home,' he kissed my forehead. 'Netflix and a takeaway for me tonight, I'm knackered.'

I stared up into his face, my mind seeming to splinter into a million different directions. His beautiful dark-blue eyes were cheerful and affectionate. They wandered over my face and his curved mouth lifted slightly, then he gave a small sigh.

'I'll miss you, baby,' he kissed me lightly.

'Me too,' I whispered.

I didn't say a word to Dana. I simply couldn't bring myself to describe what had happened and see the horror on her face.

After work I had cried pitifully under the shower, great big awful sobs that tore at my throat and left my chest aching.

Then not even bothering to try and put make-up on, I threw on some pyjamas, packed a small bag and drove to Dana's two-bedroom terraced house.

'Babes,' she opened the door, dressed in her funky zebra-print leggings and a loose white T-shirt that showed off her flawless ebony skin to perfection. 'Get your sweet behind in, I've got nachos, I've got pizzas, I've got wine, and *all* the sweeties,' she closed the door with her foot. 'Kitchen,' she ordered.

Her usually immaculate kitchen was in slight chaos; paperwork was covering one worktop and the bin was over-flowing by the backdoor.

'Sorry, I was in the middle of tidying up,' she waved at the fridge. 'Get the wine out,' she lifted the bin bag out and tied the top. 'Tobias normally has a purge on Friday afternoon, but he's got man flu.'

'Is he in bed?'

'Nah, he's recovered enough to go down the pub with his brothers,' she said sardonically. 'Let me just go and put this out,' she disappeared into the hall and a moment later I heard the door open.

Opening the fridge, I was cheered up to see three bottles of wine sitting coolly in the wine rack. I picked up what looked like a bowl of dip and sniffed it.

'I wouldn't,' Dana said from behind me, 'that's my homemade face pack.'

Putting it back down, I grabbed a bottle and went to her cabinet where she kept her glasses.

'Are you alright?' she asked. I glanced up and she was frowning at me.

'Yeah,' I pulled what I hoped was a puzzled face.

'You're very quiet,' she continued to frown while attempting to open a new bag up to put in the bin.

'Oh, we were really busy at work,' I shrugged and then busied myself pouring the wine. 'We had a new guy starting today too, super-cute... reminds me of Laz Alonso, *so* yummy,' I spilt some wine and grabbed a tea-towel, then carried on, aware that I was rambling. 'I've been, like, knackered all day, we had quite a late-night last night. Oh yeah, and I'm trying to get Eliza a job at mine... she'll probably get it. She's really funny, her and Sadie had me in stitches. And guess what? I saw Lennie, do you remember her? From the coffee shop? Yeah, well she works at The Lounge Lizard now, her boyfriend owns it.'

'How was it last night?'

'Really nice,' I took a tiny sip of wine and shuddered. 'That's cold... yeah, had a good time. The food is amazing in there.'

'Good!' Dana smiled widely but I thought her eyes still looked kind of *watchful.* 'Was Jaco OK about tonight?'

'Yes, surprisingly!' I nodded.

'Good,' she eyed me for a second then smiled again. 'Come on, grab some plates, we'll splodge out in the living-room.'

After stuffing our faces and drinking too much wine,

Dana put on her Glee boxset and we were soon singing and screaming with laughter at each other and reminiscing about our school days.

Looking back, it was amazing that my mind that was so heavy with confusion and trauma managed to switch off from my troubles.

Tobias came home early, grumbling that he felt awful and couldn't even taste his beer. Giving us both a kiss, he blundered off to bed, telling us to try and be quiet.

'You're so lucky,' I said wistfully. 'He kind of reminds me of Liam,' I felt my chest tighten.

'Yeah, I s'pose,' Dana said looking at me thoughtfully. 'The big lummox.'

'It must be so nice to be so... *sure.*'

'Sometimes you've gotta kiss a lot of frogs to find your prince,' she said wisely. 'Remember Aaron King?'

'Eww,' I giggled and made a gagging noise – Aaron King had been Dana's boyfriend when we left school - what she had seen in him, I had no idea. He had been post-goth but still wore eyeliner and he had had really bad teeth.

'At least your frog is good-looking, even if he is slightly psychotic.'

'I wouldn't go *that* far,' I protested. 'He's just... I dunno. But not psychotic.'

'Nah, of course,' she picked up a wine bottle. 'Empty. We're all out!'

'Just as well,' I rubbed my eyes. 'I can see at least one and a half of you.'

'Shall I make some coffee?' she got unsteadily to her

feet. 'I'll go and get your duvet in a minute.'

I tucked my legs under me and opened Facebook on my phone, scrolling through without really taking much in. That is, until I saw a photo of a man that looked like Jaco – then I realised it *was* Jaco.

He was sitting at a bar, his head thrown back in laughter, and on his left with her hand on his arm was Evie.

Feeling ice-cold and suddenly very sick, I looked at the top of the post. Somebody called Timothy Olsson had tagged Jaco, Evie and somebody else called Oscar Mars at a bar in White City.

I wished I was stone-cold sober so I could process it logically. All I felt right then was sickening and painful white-hot pokers of jealousy and an erupting anger.

I stared and stared at Evie. Her dark hair was parted in the middle and hung in curls either side of her thin face. She was smiling and looking somewhere above the camera, her face in the light looked youthful and beautiful.

The picture cut off at her thighs, but I could see she was wearing a revealing and tight black dress. Despite her anorexic appearance, she looked vampish and sexy like a catwalk model.

'Rox?'

My head snapped up. Dana was back in the room holding two mugs and looking down at me in alarm.

Mutely, I held my phone out to her.

'What?' she put the mugs on the floor and took my phone. 'Who… oh it's Jaco… what's up?' she looked from my phone to me, clearly perplexed.

'He's done this on purpose,' I heard the tremble in

my voice and winced. 'He said he was staying home.'

'Who's that?' Dana asked. I knew she meant Evie.

'Evie,' I muttered. 'His star artist. She's... I don't like her. She makes me uneasy.'

'Evie Blackhouse,' she murmured to herself. 'Why is she with him?'

'They're kind of friends,' I said darkly. 'But... not. Like, she lives at his flat, temporarily.'

'Right,' she still looked puzzled. 'Why is she at his flat?'

'She wrote her car off. She's been working up there on her crappy paintings,' I hated myself for the malice in my voice. 'He said he has to keep her sweet.'

'Don't artists usually have an agent?'

'I – I don't know,' I stared at her.

'Yeah, they don't generally deal with the gallery or buyers, do they? They have an agent.'

'Well, he's hardly the Tate Modern,' I shrugged miserably. 'I really don't know.'

'Oh, Roxy,' she sank down next to me, putting my phone down. 'Don't be upset. So, he went out! Last minute plans... maybe?'

'Maybe,' I put my head on her shoulder. 'I just have this feeling, he's like, *punishing* me. And I have a bad feeling about Evie. She's so strange. And a coke head.'

'What?'

'When I first met her, at Jaco's flat, Teddy said she was coked up.'

'Rox,' she said slowly. 'You know what Shauna said... about Jaco being a dealer-'

'Shit,' I sat up straight, feeling horror filling me. 'Do you think... oh... no. Surely not.'

309

'Babes,' Dana tugged my arm until I looked at her. 'Whatever is going on with him, you know this ain't good, right?'

If only you knew what happened last night, I thought despairingly.

CHAPTER TWENTY-FOUR

Sleep-deprived and depressed, I returned home mid-morning, despite Dana's pleas to stay at hers.

I had lain awake until the early hours on her sofa under a duvet, alternating between crying and staring silently at the ceiling, full of bleakness.

I had slept between maybe three and eight-thirty when Dana had poked her head in and said my name.

I knew what I had to do, but I had no idea how to do it, what to say... and disgust filled me once more when I thought that I, deep down, didn't *want* to do it. It was like being in love with someone that had kidnapped me and abused me, that I was yearning for release from.

Without any enthusiasm, I showered and got dressed, wondering how to play it when Jaco came over to take me shopping.

It got to ten o'clock and I became twitchy and nervous about him ringing me. Then eleven o'clock came and went, and I started to wonder why he hadn't at least texted me.

By midday, I decided I was being ridiculous, so I rang *him*, but it went straight to voicemail.

He's playing games, he's punishing you, I kept thinking – but my predominant emotion was one of worry that something had happened to him.

I started to do some tidying and cleaning, wanting to distract myself, but my mind was firmly on Jaco and I kept checking my phone.

It was no good, I had to leave the flat. I thought idly about going to the gym, then decided to drive over to my mums'. If Shauna or Liam's car was there, I would come back home. If not, I would go and sit around there and kill a couple of hours.

As I was locking my door, Teddy was plodding up the corridor looking worse for wear, a bag slung over his shoulder.

'Hey,' I greeted him. 'Rough night?'

'I wish,' he grinned ruefully, stopping at his door. 'I've joined the gym. I'm dying.'

'Since when?' I followed him into his flat, noticing that his radio was still in bits all over his worktop. 'My gym?'

'Nah, Arena Fitness on the industrial estate,' he groaned as he dropped his bag on the sofa, before sitting down heavily beside it.

'How come?' I dragged his Star Wars beanbag away from the television and knelt on it.

'Decided that I was fed up of being unfit and baggy,' he threw his head back and groaned again. 'I'm starting to think unfit and baggy has its advantages.'

'You are not,' I said, feeling somewhat surprised. I had always thought he had rather a cute body. Not fat, not thin, everything as it should be.

'Perhaps I'm fed up of being single,' he opened an eye and looked at me. 'My weekends are getting progressively sadder.'

'Perhaps you're too fussy,' I scolded. 'Francesca was a *bad* choice to turn down.'

'Yeah,' he smiled mildly.

'Hmm,' I struggled to my feet again. 'Go and have a

hot shower and do some stretches.'

'Where are you off to?'

'My mums' for a bit. Don't forget it's photo-shoot tomorrow, we need to be there early.'

'If I don't die.'

'You won't die.'

'I might.'

I drove slowly up my mum's road, then relaxed when I saw just hers and Howard's cars in the driveway.

Just as I was opening my door, my phone rang. Seeing it was Jaco, I braced myself, my heart hammering.

'Baby,' he said. 'I am sorry, I had a killer night.'

'Oh?' I would sooner shave my head before confessing that I had seen that picture on Facebook.

'Are you mad?' he asked. 'I set my alarm and everything to ring you early.'

'No,' I said as merrily as I could. 'I had a late one myself.'

'An old mate came by,' he said. 'We ended up going to London, I got shit-faced,' he chuckled. 'Can't remember half of the evening.'

'Sounds fun.'

'Yeah... I ain't seen Timmy, my mate, for years,' he continued cheerfully. 'He swung by the flat, thinking I was still there. Evie rang and by the time I got there, they were flirting like a pair of teenagers,' he laughed. 'We ended up at some cocktail bar, me playing gooseberry all bloody night.'

I desperately wanted to ask who Oscar was, the other guy who had been tagged.

'Well, it doesn't matter.'

'It does,' he argued. 'I've thrown up twice this morning, can we take a rain check?'

'Sure.'

'You're mad, aren't you?'

'No!' I said, not sure what I was.

'Tomorrow night?'

'I've got rehearsals and the photoshoot,' I said, wondering if I was sounding short with him.
'Tuesday?'

'Tuesday's good,' he sounded relieved. 'I'll call later when I feel more human. I love you sweetheart.'

'I love you too.'

I stared unseeingly out of my windscreen, trying to take in what he had said and decide how I was feeling. I hated that whatever it was, there was relief about what he had said about Evie and his friend - there was still the horrible unease though. And I knew that I wasn't dealing with what had happened on Friday night. My mind seemed to be pushing it out every time it came to the surface. I also really wanted to cry again. Altogether, it was over-whelming me and I felt decidedly crappy.

I glanced up at my mums' house, not sure if I could face it, but not wanting to be on my own either.

Aside from my forlorn mood, I appreciated that it was a gorgeous day. The sun was bright and warm, and I noticed that some of the leaves on the trees that lined the street were starting to turn to their autumn colours.

I suddenly had a random memory of last autumn when Teddy was dog-sitting while his friend was on holiday.

It had been a crazy thing, a very pretty beagle called Bolan and we had taken him over to the park surrounding the boating lake and spent an afternoon running around and throwing sticks and generally having fun. Like two children we had started kicking leaves at each other while Bolan leapt about excitedly. I smiled sadly to myself... happiness seemed out of reach and foggy and I had a heavy thought of not knowing how I'd got here. I wished it would go away. I wished that I'd never laid eyes on Jaco.

It took a few seconds for me to realise that the car I had been idly watching drive towards me was Liam's, and I had a moment of panic.

'*Oh, shit*,' I muttered, unsure what I should do.

I slowly put my phone away in my bag and kept my eyes downcast while I tried to decide if I should just drive away.

I heard the rumble of Liam's voice and a car door slam and then the squeal of Emilie. Instinctively I looked up at my niece's voice, only to see Shauna approaching my car, her face expressionless.

I scrambled out of my car and awkwardly stood across from her.

'Hello,' she said, her voice low.

'Hi,' I tried to gauge her mood. 'Is it OK... OK if I come in? I'll only stay for like, half an hour.'

'Oh, Roxy,' she smiled tightly. 'Don't be daft. You don't need to ask me.'

'Right,' I looked towards Liam, who was battling with their baby bag and Emilie's walker, his wrist still in plaster and tape across his nose, clutching her on one hip.

'He's fine,' Shauna was watching me. 'And Emilie would love to see you.'

'Yeah?' I was longing to cuddle her and bury my face in her soft blonde hair. It felt like eternity since I had seen her.

'Yes. Come on,' she indicated stiffly with her head and walked away.

Full of nervousness, I followed her.

Liam had already disappeared inside, and I could hear my mum cooing at Emilie.

'Roxy!' she exclaimed when she spotted me shuffling in after Shauna.

'Hi,' I summoned a smile and glanced quickly at Liam; he kind of half-smiled and disappeared into the kitchen. I gazed after him feeling disturbed by his still bruised face and bloodshot eye.

'Are you here for dinner?' she brushed past Shauna and smoothed my hair back. 'You look tired. Have you been sleeping OK?' her eyes moved over my face, a small frown creasing her thin eyebrows. 'You haven't been over for ages.'

'I know, sorry. I've been *so* busy with the play and everything.'

'Of course,' she propelled me towards the kitchen. 'How's it going? How's that young man of yours?'

'Yeah, good, and good,' I muttered, thinking I had made a mistake in coming.

'Roxy, hello,' Howard appeared in the doorway. 'I thought I heard your voice.'

'Hello.'

He gave me a searching look then smiled kindly, 'When are the tickets on sale? I was talking about you

316

last night to my friend. His daughter is doing drama at school.'

'Next week, I think,' I sat on the edge of the kitchen bench away from Liam and Shauna. Emilie babbled at me and I wriggled my fingers at her – normally I would have just grabbed her, but I felt too unsure.

'Great,' he opened the oven door. 'You here for lunch? I'm cooking pork in cider.'

'Oh, I don't know-'

'Yes, she is,' my mum said fussily. 'You've lost all that weight you put on in the summer.'

I caught Shauna's eye and she covered a giggle, then I giggled too.

'Thanks!'

'Here,' Liam stood up and plonked Emilie on me. 'I forgot her pink pony, she'll be yelling for it soon.'

'Hello, my baby,' I felt tears prickling my eyes as I hugged her close, revelling in her fresh smell and softness.

'Ce-Ce,' she wrapped her chubby fingers in my hair.

'I've missed you,' I told her. 'I have… ooo but that hurts,' I blew gently in her face, trying to free my hair.

'Dee-do bang,' she smiled, showing her tiny teeth.

'Oh! What's that, now?'

'We have no idea,' Shauna slid up the bench and helped untangle her fingers from my hair. 'We have dee-do bang and romble… clever girl, aren't you?'

'Why don't you girls go and sit in the living room?' Howard said casually. 'I wanted to show Liam something in my greenhouse.'

'Subtle,' Shauna whispered, grabbing Emilie's bag.

We went and sat down, me on the floor with Emilie

and Shauna curled up in a chair.

'So,' she said a little flatly.

'So?' I raised my eyes to her, feeling sick inside.

'Are you OK? You don't look it,' she said in her usual direct way.

'No!' I burst out, then dropped my head.

'Go on,' she said a little gentler.

'How's Liam?'

'He's OK,' she said impatiently. 'Come on, Rox.'

'I've missed her,' I kissed Emilie's hand. 'And you guys.'

'And?'

'Jesus,' I picked at the carpet, not sure what to say.

'We don't have to do this,' Shauna said in a low voice. 'But I'm worried about you.'

'I'm fine.'

'No. No, you're not.'

'OK. No, I'm not.'

'Why?'

'Because... because I want to finish with Jaco,' I looked up at her and was comforted to see that her expression was one of love and concern. 'And I have no idea how to do it.'

'Why?'

'He's not good for me. But I love him.'

'Are you sure?'

'That I love him? Yes.'

'What's he done?'

'I-I... nothing,' I tried to dredge up something to say that summed it up, but my mind felt foggy.

'You're doing it again,' she muttered.

'What?'

'Just say it!'

'What?' I felt perplexed.

'Oh, Rox,' she bowed her head and I was shocked to see tears splashing on her clasped hands. 'I can't bear this.'

'What?' I sat Emilie on her bum and shuffled over towards Shauna, putting a hand on her leg.

'It's like this with dad. It's like this with the crash.'

'I'm like, totally lost here,' I suddenly felt horribly afraid and chilled. Removing my hand, I crossed my legs and wrapped my arms around me.

'You,' she said in a husky voice. 'Blocking things.'

'Blocking what?'

'I know you can't help it.'

'Seriously,' I felt annoyance rising up, 'you need to be more specific.'

'Ce-Ce,' Emilie toddled over and grabbed the front of my top.

'Hello, my angel,' I gathered her up. 'Shauna, either spit it out or stop it.'

'Something's happened,' Shauna wiped a sleeve across both eyes. 'And you need to deal with it, instead of doing this.'

'Doing what?' I almost shouted.

'Mumma,' Emilie reached her chubby arms up towards her.

'Come here, my good girl,' Shauna lifted her up and kissed her head.

'Well?'

'What do you remember about the crash?'

'Nothing!'

'Why do you want to finish with Jaco?'

'Oh my gosh,' I gazed at her for a second. 'OK, OK… if you must know, he gets jealous. He confuses me sometimes. I'm not happy. I love him, but I know that he's not… not totally straight and honest with me. Sometimes.'

'Has he hurt you?'

'Physically?' I asked, feeling shocked. 'No!'

'Are you sure?'

'Christ. Give me credit. No.'

'OK,' she closed her eyes. 'Roxy… what do you remember about the crash?'

'Nothing, like I said,' I stood up. 'I might just go… I don't want to get into an argument, I really don't.'

'Please,' she implored. 'Just think.'

'I was unconscious,' I stared down at her. 'I woke up in hospital and mum was crying. I asked her what had happened, and she told me I had been in an accident… then there was all the horrible recuperation. It was shit.'

'You weren't unconscious.'

'No disrespect,' I said, 'but yes, I was.'

'No,' she said, raising her voice slightly. 'You were screaming for mum when they cut you out, they had to sedate you.'

'No,' I argued. 'Mum told me; I was unconscious. I don't remember a thing.'

'Roxy-'

'No,' I shook my head. 'Can we just stop this.'

'OK,' she said in a defeated voice. 'Just promise me that he hasn't harmed you in any way.'

'No,' I looked at her squarely. 'He hasn't. If he had I would not be with him.'

'Good. OK… let's drop it.'

Not long after our fraught exchange, Jacob burst into the room and after greeting us with his usual insults, he started blowing raspberries at Emilie, making her giggle and squeal.

With the tension lifted, conversation soon became normal and Liam joined us, thankfully showing no animosity or awkwardness towards me.

However, I was confused and flustered. I badly wanted to ask my mum about the crash – I was *sure* that Shauna had got it wrong but couldn't understand why she had said what she had. It also reminded me of Howard calling me vulnerable, acting like I wasn't capable of using my own mind.

I am perfectly aware that my way of thinking is maybe… OK, I just call it scatty, but that isn't really fair to myself… *muddled* sometimes. But I don't know anything different to how I process things. I know that my ADHD causes my brain fog and my impulsiveness – but I also know there is no way I could completely erase something from my brain… surely not?

After lunch, I went home, telling everyone that I needed to read my lines – which I did – but in reality, I wanted to be alone.

CHAPTER TWENTY-FIVE

The photoshoot the following evening took a lot longer than expected. Chiefly because of Finn.

'Finn,' Pontus said in suppressed tones. 'I have the order of the shoot here,' he waved his clipboard. 'Let's just get on.'

'Look at his face,' Teddy muttered.

We were sitting on two of the rickety fold-up chairs, watching the photographer – a young guy in a baseball cap – adjust his lights in front of a white backdrop.

'My way makes sense,' Finn made a scoffing noise and disappeared backstage, no doubt to powder his very straight nose again.

'Darling, could you just stand there for two secs,' the photographer asked Meadow, indicating to the backdrop.

She obliged and stood there self-consciously in her maids costume as he took a couple of shots then went and moved a light again.

I watched as Derek came over, tugging on the front of his old-fashioned policeman's coat, 'I think I was measured wrong,' he grumbled sitting down with us. 'What's up with Finn?'

'Just being a prat, as usual,' I rolled my eyes.

'High-heels,' Violet trilled at me as she joined us.

I wriggled my bare toes, 'I know Vi, I'll put them on when he's ready,' I nodded at the photographer. 'They hurt my feet.'

'That dress is a treat,' she eyed me.

My dress was long and slinky in a dark gold; I felt very glamourous.

I also loved my hair, curled back and pinned up - with that and my shiny gold eyeshadow and bright red lips, I felt like I should be drinking champagne and dancing under a chandelier.

'You do look very pretty,' Teddy grinned at me.

'Thank you, but don't let Finn hear you, he'll get jealous.'

'He's a vain boy,' Violet tutted. 'Even if he is handsome.'

'And has the IQ of a crayon,' Teddy added cheerfully. 'It's painful listening to him - Pontus was nearly in tears earlier, trying to explain why the order of the shoot is what it is.'

'Sh, here he comes,' Derek muttered.

'Oh, is that my phone?' Teddy leapt up, patting his pockets.

'It's in the car,' I giggled.

'Shit,' he pulled out an imaginary phone. 'Hello? Hello?' he walked away holding his imaginary phone to his ear.

'Is he OK?' Finn gave him a bewildered look, then took his chair.

'He's fine,' I started leafing through my script, while Derek tried to cover a shout of laughter with a cough.

'I do love Teddy,' Violet smiled widely. 'Such an unpretentious and self-deprecating young man. Nice bum too.'

'Violet!' I kicked her ankle gently with my bare foot.

'So,' Finn folded his arms. 'Pontus is being a prick.'

'I'm sure he isn't, mate,' Derek said mildly.

Samantha and Francesca drifted over, both ogling at Finn.

Uncomfortable now in Francesca's presence, I pretended to be absorbed in my script.

'Cor, you don't half look nice, Rox,' Samantha said in a rare compliment. 'I bloody hate my dress,' she smoothed down her dark green dress disdainfully. She was playing Harriet, Jamie/James' wife, a bit of an old boot and a snob.

'Thanks,' I smiled up at her.

'Very nice,' Francesca agreed, but didn't smile. She looked pretty in a flowered blouse and black pencil skirt, her high heels making her lovely long legs go on forever.

I smiled anyway, feeling irritated that she was being frosty with me.

'You look very dashing, Finn,' Samantha simpered, making me cringe.

'Why, thank you,' he grinned boyishly, and Violet audibly snorted. 'Pontus is being a prick.'

'Oh no, how come?' Samantha took a seat and I decided to make my excuses and get up.

'OK, my dears,' Duncan clapped his hands. 'Whole cast shots first, then individuals, then our main suspects. Wander over.'

The whole cast shots and the individuals took nearly two hours, by which time I was restless and bored.

There was a slight break while the backdrop was changed for the main suspect shots and I went and sat on the edge of the stage and rubbed my feet.

'I hate high heels,' I moaned to nobody in particular.

'But they do compliment women's legs,' Jeremy said from behind me, making me inwardly shudder.

'Or men's,' Teddy sat next to me, quietly making his Psycho sound. 'Don't discriminate against your own gender.'

'Well, I really wouldn't know,' Jeremy said smoothly.

'You never dressed up in your mum's shoes?' Teddy nudged me.

'Stop it,' I whispered.

'No,' Jeremy sounded slightly outraged, throwing Teddy a dark stare as he walked off.

'You,' I poked his side, 'are a naughty bugger.'

'Ah, well,' he shrugged.

'Teddy?'

'Hm?'

'Francesca is making me really uncomfortable,' I lowered my voice. 'I don't get why she's off with me.'

'Probably because, you know, we are together a lot.'

'Sure… but she's *really* off.'

'Don't worry about it, honey,' he smiled at me. 'She is maybe embarrassed, like you said. And paranoid that I've told you.'

'With reason. You *did* tell me.'

'Well, yeah.'

'Perhaps I should talk to her?'

'No!' he looked at me in alarm. 'I don't think that'll help.'

'No, probably not,' I exhaled unhappily. 'I like Francesca, I don't like her being cross with me.'

Teddy chuckled, 'You are very sweet, aren't you?'

'Roxy!' Pontus yelled. 'Over here.'

I struggled up and re-arranged my dress, then winced as I squeezed my feet back into my shoes.

It took a while to arrange us for the shot, mainly because Finn wanted to be in the front but as the tallest, he had to stand at the back.

I was stuck at the far left in front of him in the end, being told to cross my arms and look "haughty".

Poor Lola had trouble looking "sinister", and Pontus started to get loud and bossy, making me secretly think that Finn had a point about him being a prick.

'Who's pissed on *his* chips?' Nathan muttered.

'His back is playing up,' Crystal said from the far end, pushing her breasts up in her low-cut dress. 'I offered him a massage.'

'Poor bloke,' Nathan whispered to me.

'Are we ready?' the photographer grinned and waved.

Twenty minutes later he declared we were done, and I slumped in relief; my back and pelvis were twinging after standing stiff and straight in my high heels. I kicked them off and rotated my hips.

'OK, my loves,' Duncan said loudly. 'You may escape, no time for rehearsals, but I want extra rehearsals on Wednesday.'

I didn't even bother groaning along with most of the cast. I hurried backstage to the dressing room to get out of my dress and into blessed leggings and my baggiest sweatshirt.

As I stood in my bra and knickers, Francesca came in. She stopped abruptly, then bowed her head as she picked up her bag from a chair.

'Hi,' I said awkwardly.

'Alright?' she turned and left again.

I got dressed quickly, feeling miserable about her being like she was.

I was just wiping off my make-up when Lola came in in tears, Destiny patting her back.

'Whatever's wrong?'

'Oh, Pontus being grumpy,' Destiny rolled her eyes at me.

'Aw, Lola, just ignore him,' I touched her arm.

'I know,' she sniffed.

'I can make a voodoo doll, you know,' Destiny said happily.

'I don't think that's necessary,' Lola said seriously, looking startled.

'The offer's there,' Destiny shrugged, 'Just going for a tinkle.'

'Roxy,' Lola said hesitantly, 'can I talk to you in private?'

'Sure.'

'Can we go for a drink or something?'

'Oh, yes, sure.'

After telling Teddy that I wouldn't need a lift home, Lola and I walked into town to a quiet wine bar.

It was virtually empty in there - just a middle-aged couple sat by the window and three women at the bar, all on their phones.

I sat in an alcove and whipped out my compact mirror as Lola went to get us two orange juices. I felt really scruffy and my face was pink and shiny from wiping off my make-up.

I watched Lola at the bar, thinking she looked rather pretty tonight in a mustard coloured corduroy pinafore, her fair hair in a loose ponytail. I was dead curious as to what she wanted to talk about, we weren't really friends as such – I certainly didn't feel like I knew her well enough to be her confidante.

'There we go,' she put my drink down in front of me and sat opposite me looking unsure of herself.

'Thanks. So… what's up?' I asked gently.

'Well,' she chewed her lip, 'Pontus *did* upset me, but I only said that to Destiny because… because I didn't want to tell her the real reason.'

'OK,' I smiled in what I hoped was an encouraging smile.

'It's… it's Derek,' she burst out, then went bright red.

'Derek upset you?' I asked in surprise.

'No,' she fiddled with her glass, not looking at me. 'I-I like him.'

'Ooo,' I clapped my hands gleefully, then stopped as I remembered she was far from happy. 'So… why the tears?'

'I was going to ask him out,' she squirmed slightly. 'It's my birthday next Saturday, and I was plucking up the courage to ask him to the cinema.'

'Right.'

'We text each other sometimes,' she glanced up, her blushes increasing, 'just chatting about the play and stuff, mostly. I kind of thought he liked me back.'

'Sounds like he does.'

'No… he likes Francesca.'

I was about to say that Francesca was *way* out of his

league, but then realised how that sounded, 'Why do you think that?'

'He looks at her.'

'Oh, Lola,' I smiled to myself. 'She's pretty, that's all. *I* look at her! It's natural. I bet they have zero in common though, and I bet he likes you back.'

'It's OK for you,' she said miserably. 'You're pretty. You're confident and popular.'

'Don't be silly,' I frowned. 'I'm not especially confident and certainly not popular! And as for pretty, well, what's pretty to some isn't to others.'

She stared thoughtfully at me, then smiled sadly, 'But how do I know if he thinks I'm pretty or l-likes me back?'

'Ask him?'

'Oh, no,' she said looking horrified.

'Ask him *ever so* casually about the cinema, like, as friends. Then see what happens.'

'I guess I could do that,' she nodded. 'I might text it though, in case I go red.'

'Good idea. And you can word it perfectly instead of babbling… I babble a lot. Texting is much easier. Ooo, do it now!' I said a little louder, making her jump. 'Gimme your phone, I'll do it, don't worry I won't send it!'

Warily, she handed me her phone.

Hey, I typed in, *I was meant to ask tonight but Roxy wanted to go for a quick drink, do you fancy the cinema on Saturday week?*

'There,' I handed it back to her.

'Oh wow,' she beamed. 'Perfect. Except not the "hey" - I'm not a "hey" person.'

'See? Super casual, no big deal at all.'

She looked intently at her phone for a moment, then sent the text, 'Too late now!'

'Yay,' I wriggled in my seat.

'What if he says no?'

'He won't,' I said bracingly, thinking I better be right.

'He might,' she said, then jumped as she got a text alert. 'I can't,' she thrust her phone back at me.

'*Hi*', I read out, '*I'd really like that. Yeah I wondered where you'd gone to tonight, I looked for you. Speak to you Wednesday.*'

'Thank you,' she breathed, snatching her phone back to read it. 'Thank you so much.'

I only had a ten-minute walk home, but the tree-lined street up to my flat was not one I liked walking alone and in the dark.

It was well lit-up, but the trees made eerie patterns on the road at night and the shadows of the parked cars looked huge and sinister.

All the houses were set back from the street with long driveways and most of them had tall hedges – the "posh road" my mum always called it. There was a short-cut that brought you out near the carpark that my flat overlooked, but it involved walking down a dark alleyway and past an old abandoned building that used to be an army cadet's club that was very creepy.

Ever cautious, I took off my sweatshirt, put my bag over my shoulder and put my sweatshirt back on over it so I looked like I had a potbelly.

'What *are* you doing?' Lola watched me with a

bemused expression.

'I'd die if someone took my bag,' I giggled.

'Fair enough,' she gave me a shy hug. 'Thanks again, Roxy. I feel silly now.'

'You're welcome,' I hugged her back. 'See you on Wednesday.'

I watched her hurry over to the taxi rank across the road before I headed off home.

I walked briskly past the brightly lit convenience store on the corner, crossed the road to where the local juniors' school was, and turned into the road where my flat was.

I passed a man walking his dog, and across the road there was a couple strolling in the same direction as me, which made me feel slightly safer. Slowing my pace so I was more or less walking parallel to them, I turned my mind to the evenings events. I smiled to myself thinking about Lola and Derek. I supposed they'd make a rather sweet couple.

I heard a car approaching from behind; it passed me then stopped a few metres away. Suddenly wary, I considered crossing to the wrong side of the road so at least the couple were nearby.

Just as I thought that, they turned into a garden. I was in close proximity to the short-cut and slowed down even more, feeling torn between the two routes.

Stop it, I told myself. The driver was probably just on his/her phone or something.

Speeding up again, I carried on with my head held high, but I felt my heart pounding slightly.

As I drew level with the car, I walked as close to hedges and driveways as possible, thinking wryly that if an axe-wielding maniac jumped out of the car, I could scoot up somebody's driveway.

I was maybe two houses away when I heard the car approaching and I felt a real thrill of fear, but secondary to that I felt ridiculous with the thought of breaking into a run. So instead I stopped, turning slightly so I was standing on the edge of a driveway and looked at the car.

It stopped and a man leant over, the passenger window opening.

'Roxy?'

I froze and tried to make out his face, my fear decreasing somewhat, recognising the voice vaguely.

'I thought it was you… it's Billy.'

'Oh, for crying out loud,' I muttered. 'Hello,' I walked over. 'You scared me.'

He chuckled, 'Need a lift?'

I looked down into his swarthy face, suddenly puzzled as to why he was driving up my road late at night, 'Uh, I'm practically home, but sure. Thanks.'

I opened the door and he moved a laptop case, reaching around and putting it on the backseat, 'Sorry if I scared you,' he pulled away, 'I just realised how dodgy I must have looked. I just didn't want to yell out to a random woman and scare her.'

'Instead of just stopping in the middle of the road and scaring me?'

'Yeah,' he chuckled again. 'You been at rehearsals? Jaco mentioned it.'

'Yeah,' I delved under my sweatshirt to rummage in my bag for my keys. 'We had a photoshoot for the publicity and the tickets and stuff. How come you're around here?'

'I have a friend on Crestwell Drive. I was picking up my laptop from him.'

'Right,' at least that explained why I'd run into him a couple of times in the summer.

He swung into the carpark and drove nearby to the doors, 'There we go, love. Sorry again for startling you.'

'No worries, thanks for the lift.'

Back in my flat, I ran a bath and took my painkillers before throwing myself on the sofa to rub my sore feet.

'*Wally*,' I whispered to myself, thinking about my earlier scare. Fernberry was a safe little town, but it didn't hurt to be careful. Then, like a traitor, my mind turned to Troy and Liam's attacks. The man or men who had done that had never been caught, and unlikely to be now.

Inevitably, Jaco drifted into my thoughts and I stood up, not wanting to sit and dwell and get depressed again.

Snuggled up in bed, despite yawning my head off, I didn't feel tired enough to go sleep, so I had a scroll through Instagram, then Facebook. Feeling like doing a bit of detective work, having resisted the urge since seeing the photo of Jaco and Evie, I tapped on Oscar's name to take me to his profile.

He was a nice-looking blonde man and his profile picture was of him sitting on a wall with a beach behind him, topless and wearing Bermuda shorts. My eyes drifted down to his information, then I sat bolt upright, my throat constricting painfully.

It read, *in a relationship with Timmy Olsson.*

CHAPTER TWENTY-SIX

My morning started badly. After hardly sleeping at all, I woke up late for work then my car refused to start.

'*Fuck, fuck, fuck,*' I almost sobbed.

'Roxy?' Teddy knocked on my window, nearly sending me into orbit.

'My car won't start,' I opened the door. 'It's dead.'

'OK, honey,' he looked at me with concern. 'I think you have a flat battery. You might have left your lights on?'

'I don't bloody know,' I climbed out and then promptly dropped my handbag.

'I'll jumpstart you, it's no biggie.'

'I am *so* late for work,' I grumbled. 'Oh, bugger!' I cursed as I realised that I had broken a nail. Then like a complete idiot, I burst into tears.

'Sh, sh, sh,' Teddy put his arms around me and rubbed my back. 'Come on now, what's all this?'

'Sorry,' I croaked. 'I'm tired and crabby.'

'Ring work, and I'll sort your car,' he held me at arm's length until I looked at him, then he went cross-eyed, making me laugh weakly. 'That's better.'

Work was very quiet, giving me plenty of thinking time.

I had lain awake the night before, tossing and turning, unable to come to a conclusion that I liked. In plain black and white, Jaco had lied. He had quite clearly made out that he was playing gooseberry all evening while his friend and Evie flirted to mislead me in some way. He must be guilty of something or he wouldn't have gone to those lengths.

I was really sick at heart, and I was *really* angry, but I felt that this was more fuel to end what was becoming a toxic relationship.

Troy came and told me that Eliza was coming in on Wednesday for an interview but hinted that she'd probably get the job anyway. I felt a *tiny* bit guilty for using his soft spot for me but told myself that she had been in retail for a while and was as good as anyone else for the job.

I began to worry though that maybe she was too connected to Jaco for my liking – especially if, *when* we split up. As I mulled it over, it occurred to me that I very much got the impression that Eliza didn't like him… I couldn't really decide why I thought that. But she was Sadie's best friend and I hoped that it wouldn't make a difference.

Jaco rang me late in the morning, making my stomach clench in anger and nervousness.

'Sweetheart, you're going to hate me,' he began.

'Is that so?' I said calmly.

'I can't make it tonight.'

I felt a very bizarre mixture of relief and rage, 'How come?'

'I'm in London, I can't see me getting away until late… I'm really snowed under. Can we wait until the weekend? Friday?'

'Yeah, sure.'

'Oh, you're annoyed, I can tell. I'm so sorry baby, I

can try for tomorrow?'

'I've got extra rehearsals,' I summoned all my acting skills to change my voice to casual cheerfulness. 'I'm not annoyed! I know you get busy, it's fine!'

'You sure?'

'Yes, sure.'

'OK, I'll call you later or tomorrow. I love you.'

'Me too.'

I immediately rang Teddy.

'Hey crabby,' he answered.

'Sod off,' I giggled. 'I'm OK now. I was actually inviting you out for dinner tonight as a thank you, but if you're going to give me lip, I might change my mind.'

'I withdraw the crabby. Yes please… but please let it be my treat.'

'No, I insist.'

'We can argue about it later. Or fight… arm wrestle?'

'Stop it,' I shook my head. 'You're such a dork.'

'Crabby and Dork, we should fight crime.'

'See you later.'

We went to an Indian restaurant in town and decided after arguing to go Dutch.

I ordered a prawn curry to which Teddy made a gagging noise to and a bottle of wine to share. Teddy ordered his usual lamb madras.

'You should branch out,' I told him as we munched on the free popadoms and chutney.

'Why?' he grinned.

'Just should.'

'What was with Lola last night?'

I filled him in, making him promise to keep quiet.

'Fair play. They'd make a good couple.'

'You said he had a face like a potato smiley,' I reminded him.

'And frozen potato products don't deserve love?'

'Pack it in,' I laughed despite myself. 'You are so rotten.'

'Sorry, he's a nice bloke. And she's a sweetheart. Hope they get it on.'

'What about you?'

'What about me what?'

'You've been single forever.'

'So?'

'You are so cute, you should be snapped up.'

'I don't want be cute,' he grumbled. 'I want to be a rugged hunk,' he puffed out his chest. 'And I will be when I go back to the gym.'

'Haven't you been since Sunday?'

'Yes. I went Monday.'

'And?'

'I really pulled my calf,' he pulled a face. 'I'm in recovery.'

'Aww, poor baby,' I reached over and squeezed his cheek gently.

'Geroff, you patronising cow.'

'Sorry, did I hurt you?'

'I'm going home in a minute.'

I giggled and he joined in.

'I'm sorry. I don't want to hurt your feelings too.'

'Piss off, you horrid small woman.'

I laughed and looked up to see if our food was

coming. Catching the eye of a smiling woman on the next table, I smiled back.

'Sorry dear,' she looked us both over. 'You two *are* making me laugh. Such a sweet couple, you remind me of my daughter and her fiancé, always giggling. It's lovely.'

'Oh, no, we're not-' I pointed at Teddy then myself.

'Oh!' she gasped. 'Sorry, how embarrassing. I assumed!'

'It's OK,' Teddy assured her. 'Common mistake… I'm her carer,' he added in a whisper.

'Teddy!' I screamed with laughter. 'Sorry, ignore him, he thinks he's funny,' the woman smiled blandly and went back to her meal. 'You idiot,' I hissed.

'Sorry,' he grinned, not looking sorry at all.

Later that evening I knew I had to keep my brain busy so not to obsess on anything Jaco-related. Friday nights *incident* kept drifting in and out though, but it seemed like… weeks ago. I wasn't even clear anymore about what had happened, which made me wonder about what Shauna had said. And that was *really* bothering me. It made me feel… broken. Like I was wired up wrong.

To combat all the negative thoughts, I absorbed myself in my script, sitting at my dressing table and reading my lines in the mirror. I wanted to be word perfect and perform well, leaving no room for criticism.

Opening night wasn't far off at all and I was wracked with nerves. It seemed like such a huge part now, and so many people I knew were coming to watch it.

It was gone midnight by the time I had decided to call it a night, and I at least felt tired enough to sleep for once.

Eliza came in for her interview looking nervous. Troy didn't even ask her too many questions, they went and chatted in the staff room and she came out grinning.

'You'll get it,' I said in a low voice, following her to the door.

'I hope so,' she smiled politely at Albie who was giving her the eye. 'Richard clearly had garlic last night and has been breathing all over me,' she pulled a disgusted face. 'He really is foul.'

'Lovely,' I giggled.

Soon as she was gone, I belted back to the staff room in search of Troy.

'Hello, you,' he greeted me.

'Well?'

'Nice girl,' he said casually, then laughed. 'Yes, I'll email her tomorrow!'

'You are the best,' I threw my arms around him.

'Yeah, yeah. Go and do some work.'

At rehearsals that evening, I was glad to see that Lola was full of smiles. I also thought that Derek looked more cheerful than usual and less unattractive in jeans and a polo shirt, rather than his customary short-sleeved shirt buttoned up to his throat.

'They should name their first child after me,' I said to Teddy as we fondly watched them chatting together.

'Well, it probably would have happened anyway.'

'Hush, I want to feel useful.'

340

'Teddy, my darling,' Crystal approached, as usual her breasts seeming to have a life of their own. 'We have a scene; Duncan wants us to get a move on.'

'Great,' Teddy muttered.

I went and sat in the front row to watch them.

'Hello,' Violet settled herself next to me.

'Hello.'

'You haven't got any scenes tonight, have you?'

'Probably won't get that far tonight,' I yawned behind my hand. 'Just as well, I'm knackered.'

We watched as Teddy and Francesca strolled onto stage, miming conversation. Crystal was sat with Bob on the couch, empty glasses in their hands.

'Duncan wants to know if you can put some posters up in your shop,' Violet offered me a sweet from a paper bag. 'They'll all be ready tomorrow.'

'That was quick, when do the tickets go on sale?'

'Friday, I do believe.'

We carried on watching the stage in silence, both chuckling in the right places at Teddy's little one-liners.

'Steals every scene,' she said affectionately.

I noticed that even Francesca had to fight to keep a straight face a few times.

Finn strode on, handsome in his butlers' uniform, carrying a wine bottle on a tray.

'Knob,' Violet whispered, making me burst out laughing. Finn frowned in our direction, looking irritable.

'You kill me, Vi,' I sunk a little lower in my seat while she looked completely unabashed.

'Who wants some gossip?' Destiny joined us and sat

on the other side of Violet.

'I feel like I should say no, but I won't,' Violet popped another sweet in her mouth.

'Guess who had a one-night stand last night?'

'Who?' me and Violet said in unison.

'No, you're supposed to guess!'

'I dunno,' I looked at Violet who shrugged. 'Jeremy and Duncan.'

'Don't be silly,' Destiny looked cross as me and Violet giggled. 'Finn and Francesca!'

'No!' I stared at her. 'Really? Ew. Poor Francesca.'

'Fancies him though, doesn't she?' Violet scoffed.

'I thought she fancied Teddy,' I said without thinking, then clapped my hand over my mouth in horror.

'What?' Violet twisted around to look at me. 'Really?'

'Oh,' I stammered. 'I-I was joking.'

'No, you're not. She does,' Destiny gave me a sly look. 'Of course, Teddy isn't interested.'

'I don't know why, she's jolly attractive,' Violet settled back in her seat. 'Anyway, let's not gossip anymore, it's not kind.'

'Fair enough,' Destiny sat back too, smiling to herself.

Duncan called for a break and Destiny got up humming quietly and wandered off.

'So,' Violet faced me again. 'What was that about Teddy and Francesca?'

'Nothing.'

'Oh, come on, I'm not an old gossip like The Happy Hippy.'

342

'I know,' I considered her for a second. 'But it's not my gossip and I shouldn't have said that.'

'I see,' she offered me another sweet and I shook my head.

'OK, OK,' I looked around to see who was nearby, then moved my head closer to hers. 'Francesca made a pass at him and he rejected her. Now she's pissed off at him *and* me... no idea why... Teddy's very embarrassed about it. *Please* don't say anything.'

'No, of course I won't, dear,' she patted my arm. 'But I bet I know why she's pissed off at you too.'

'Because she thinks Teddy told me... which he did, obviously.'

'No, because he has his sights set on you, silly.'

'He does *not*,' I rolled my eyes. 'Why can't a boy and a girl be friends without people thinking there's more to it?'

'Well, yes, people do think like that,' she said slowly. 'But, it's quite apparent, isn't it? Bless his heart.'

'No,' I shook my head. 'Really, really not.'

'Oh, Roxy,' she smiled and patted my arm again.

'What?' I said, feeling incensed. 'I'm not an idiot. We spend enough time together.'

'I'm not saying you're an idiot.'

'Look,' I lowered my voice, 'Jaco,' I swallowed painfully saying his name, 'has known him longer than me, and he said he's a bit of a player... in which case he would have made a pass at me by now.'

'Teddy?' she laughed. 'I don't think so.'

'Well, Jaco knows him from old.'

'Uh huh.'

'What?'

'Tell me,' she looked at me thoughtfully. 'Is your Jaco the jealous type?'

'Er, a bit,' I hedged.

'I thought as much… darling, men are more perceptive to other men's intentions.'

'Sorry?'

'Battle of the dicks.'

'*What?*'

'I think your Jaco may be painting Teddy's character black for his own benefit.'

'What? I don't understand,' I stared at her. 'They're old friends.'

'So? Dicks have no loyalty.'

'Oh my God,' I giggled. 'Sorry Vi, but you're talking rubbish.'

'Maybe,' she smiled serenely. 'I'll just say this – don't go thinking bad of Teddy by what someone else says. They might have their own agenda.'

'I don't think bad of him! He's my friend.'

'And a very good friend he is too.'

CHAPTER TWENTY-SEVEN

By Friday I felt like my brain was fried. I rang Dana for a gossip before rehearsals on Thursday and she very much supported what Violet had said, confusing me further.

Twice on our drive to the theatre, Teddy asked if I were OK, making me paranoid that I was being odd with him. I supposed I was kind of analysing his behaviour towards me.

I was also dreading seeing Jaco on Friday evening. I had no idea how to play it. Dana seemed afraid for me, telling me to just end it on the phone. Her reaction made me all the more anxious – but I simply couldn't end it that way. Whatever Jaco might be, it seemed a callous way to do it.

I was trying to sort things out in my head, catalogue his crimes – but I knew, I just *knew* what his responses were likely to be. I knew he would talk me around, cast his spell over me.

He had said he would pick me up and take me out for dinner. This had pros and cons.

I thought to myself that I would feel safer talking to him in a restaurant and that the worst he could do was storm out. The fact I was even thinking that way gave me comfort that I was doing the right thing.

I was uneasy however, that we would be in his car and I may end up stranded somewhere. I tried but failed to come up with a reason why I should drive or even meet him there. I voiced this dilemma to Dana, and she said she would come and rescue me if needed.

So Friday evening, full of apprehension and heartbreak, I waited at my window for Jaco to arrive, wondering what the hell the next few hours were going to bring. And as it happened, even the worst scenarios in my head were nowhere near as bad as it turned out.

My resolve started to dissipate before we even got to the restaurant. He greeted me as I climbed into his car, deliberately dressed down in black trousers and a very non-revealing blouse tucked in... his face lit up though as he looked me over and he leant over to kiss me, making my stomach flutter in longing.

'You smell wonderful,' he nuzzled my neck. 'I've missed you so much, sweetheart. You look gorgeous.'

'Thank you,' I smiled and gazed into his sexy dark eyes, feeling like my head was filling with cotton wool.

No, Roxy. Don't weaken.

'Are you hungry?'

'Yes,' I lied.

'Good. I've booked a table at The Blue Canteen-' I inwardly groaned; it was not far from his house, '-they do amazing shellfish there. I'm going to spoil you tonight. I've been neglecting you.'

'Don't be silly,' I demurred.

'You deserve it.'

The Blue Canteen was a modern and expensive restaurant with a coastal theme and an extensive menu. I'd only been there once with an ex-boyfriend, something that I didn't mention to Jaco.

As soon as we were seated, he ordered champagne cocktails and their famous sharing seafood platter starter, then sat back and smiled at me. I found it very hard to act naturally; my face felt frozen and my shoulders tense.

He looked exceptionally handsome – or maybe it was a case of absence making the heart grow fonder – in an olive-green shirt that turned his eyes almost a teal colour.

As he started to chat about his week, full of enthusiasm and charm, my mind literally started to go blank and I began to panic about what I wanted to say.

If I was acting strangely, he either didn't notice or ignored the fact. By the time our main courses were brought to us, he was asking about what I wanted to do that weekend.

I can't do it, I thought in panic. *It's too hard, I can't even think straight...*

'Eat up,' he stroked my arm. 'I wish I had what you've got now, it looks nice.'

'It is,' I put a forkful of my rock lobster in my mouth and tried to look like I was enjoying it, when in all honesty I felt like throwing up.

'Bet you're dying to put ketchup on it,' he laughed softly. 'I've bought you some biscuits to dip in your tea when we get back to mine.'

'Thank you,' I felt my eyes burning as I stared in dismay at all the food on my plate.

'I put nice clean covers on the bed too,' he continued, oblivious to my distress. 'I know you like that.'

'I do,' I murmured, my panic now so vast that I wanted to bolt the restaurant.

'I can't wait to get you home.'

I followed him into his house in almost a dream-like trance, my heart in my throat and my legs weak.

I had two choices: act like nothing was wrong and allow him to take me to bed or just come out with it. Tell him it wasn't working.

'Make yourself comfy, angel,' he pushed me towards the living room and disappeared into the kitchen.

I considered just simply running out the front door and ringing Dana, but I numbly walked into the living room and sunk into his sofa where we had made love so many times.

I stared unseeingly at the bookcase in front of me, feeling an awful primeval fight or flight sensation.

'Your cuppa, my baby,' Jaco came in with two mugs on a tray and a plate of biscuits. He placed it carefully on the coffee table, then turned to look at me. 'What's wrong?'

'Huh?'

'You're crying.'

In confusion I touched my face, disturbed to feel tears.

'Roxy?'

'Jaco,' I whispered. 'I don't feel well, can you take me home?'

'What's wrong?' he came and sat next to me, his expression one of worry.

'I-I just don't feel good.'

'OK,' he lightly felt my forehead. 'Just go and snuggle up in my bed, I'll bring your tea up.'

'No!' I said loudly, standing up and stepping away

348

from him. 'I want to go home.'

'This is…weird. What is up with you? Why are you looking at me like that?'

'I just want to go,' I almost shouted.

'OK, OK,' he frowned. 'Something is very wrong here. I'll take you home, sure. But only when you tell me what's wrong with you.'

'I can't,' I burst out, then started to cry in earnest.

He stood up and tried to put his arms around me, but I backed off, hating myself for losing control.

'What the hell have I done?' he said angrily. 'Look, you've gone from perfectly fine, to *this*… tell me what is wrong, and tell me now.'

I stared at him, my vision going in and out of focus, 'Sorry, sorry,' I said hoarsely. 'I just really want to go.'

'No,' he said bluntly. 'Tell me what the hell is wrong, Roxy.'

'OK,' I tried to calm myself and gather my thoughts. 'I need to say something.'

'Go on,' he said darkly.

'I-I want to know…. why you l-lied about your friend and Evie.'

'What?'

'Last Saturday,' I started to tremble. 'You said him and her were f-flirting-'

'Yes,' he said in an exasperated voice. 'Oh my God, is this about me going out?'

'No,' I shook my head. 'You lied… I looked on Facebook… the t-two guys, they are a couple. So, you lied.'

'Are you being serious right now?' he curled his lip. 'You've been checking up on me? Really? You… I guess it's OK for you to be friends with men, but the minute I'm anywhere near a woman, you do this?'

'No!' I felt a spark of anger and tried to cling on to it. 'I was being nosy. That's what I saw.'

'OK,' he crossed his arms in an exaggerated gesture. 'I lied. You want to know why?'

'Why?'

'Because I knew you'd get jealous. I know you have a ridiculous problem with Evie. I couldn't be bothered with your hysterics, so I lied. I apologise.'

'What?' I gasped. 'Why are you even saying that?'

'When you found her choker?' he raised an eyebrow.

'And what was I supposed to think?' I raised my voice, furious at how he was twisting things.

'Er, trust me?' he spat. 'Not jump to conclusions? Act like an adult? For fuck's sake Roxy, don't I treat you good enough? Don't I take you to nice places, be attentive enough?'

'I never said that!' I yelled. 'Stop it! It's you that gets jealous and sulks and carries on... stop making out you're perfect.'

'Why are you shouting?' he lowered his voice. 'Stop acting like a child. Jesus Christ... are you sure you shouldn't be on medication for *that?*'

I gasped and gazed at him in disgust, 'I can't even believe you said that.'

'Well,' he laughed nastily, 'something isn't right up there,' he prodded the side of my head. 'Have you heard yourself?'

'Why are you being so vile?' I took another step back. 'Just because I questioned you?'

'Questioned me?' he suddenly grabbed my wrist,

making me wince. 'I love you, you stupid woman! And you're making me out to be a bad guy.'

'Let go,' I wrenched away, trying to hide how scared I was right then. 'What about last Friday?'

'What?' he suddenly looked shifty.

'You hurt me,' I hissed. 'I asked you to stop but you didn't,' suddenly a sob caught in my throat and I lowered my head.

'And what crap are you making up now?' he said mildly.

'You know *what*,' I turned away and strode toward the hall.

'I'm sorry, but I really don't,' he caught up with me and pulled me around.

'We were having sex,' I whispered, refusing to meet his eyes. 'And I told you that you were hurting m-me. I told you to stop.'

'No, you didn't,' he said incredulously. 'What the fuck? What are you saying?'

'You hurt me,' I shrugged him off.

'And I thought you liked it rough, *Roxy,*' he said contemptuously.

I looked up at him in complete horror and disbelief, 'I'm going home.'

'Fine,' he let his arms drop to his sides and his expression went from one of fury to completely blank.

I reached the door and grabbed my bag, my hands shaking uncontrollably.

'Wait,' he suddenly said. 'I'll drive you.'

'No,' I opened the door and nearly fell down the step. 'I'll call someone.'

'Don't be daft,' he followed me. 'Look, stop a

351

minute… OK, we both need time-out here. Let's be adults. I'll drive you.'

'I-I… OK,' I said, every part of my being telling me not to accept.

'This is ridiculous,' he muttered as he went back indoors. A second later he reappeared with his keys and after looking at me coldly as I stood rooted to the spot, he opened the passenger door, sarcastically sweeping his arm towards it. 'In you get.'

I climbed in and clutched my bag to me.

'Get some sleep,' he said calmly, 'sort yourself out and then we'll talk. Just think about what you've accused me of.'

'OK,' I whispered.

I was as mad as hell with myself. I couldn't believe how badly I had handled it. I was also in shock at the way he had turned. I looked sideways at him as he pulled out of his driveway – a lock of his dark hair had fallen over his forehead and his jaw was tense. He looked dark and dangerous and I had a premonition of dread.

As he silently drove through Chembury, I noticed with unease that he was driving carelessly and seemed to be braking at the last moment.

When we reached the dual-carriage way, he put his foot down and I began to feel real panic.

'Jaco, slow down a little, please,' I asked quietly.

He turned his head and eyed me, before speeding up even more.

The acid taste of fear was strong in my mouth and my heart was racing frantically as I realised my mistake, 'Jaco,' I pleaded, 'you know I'm n-not a good passenger, please don't, just because you're angry.'

'I ain't angry, sweetheart,' he said flatly. Then he put on a burst of speed as he passed a car in front of us who beeped their horn.

'Jaco,' I closed my eyes and tried not to cry. 'Please.'

Ignoring me, he turned the radio up so it was horribly loud and carried on driving fast and recklessly.

I was shaking all over, waiting for the terrible impact of a crash, waiting to hear a squeal of tyres or his shout of a warning. With irony, my pelvis and hip started to throb on one side, and I pushed my hands deep into my abdomen, keeping my eyes squeezed shut. I was so scared I felt like I was going to wet myself and clamped my legs together.

As he left the dual carriageway and turned on the roundabout, I opened my eyes and looked at him again. He was staring fixedly ahead, a small smile on his lips.

You're enjoying this, you bastard.

A sob escaped me as he drove through town with the same careless aggression, he was braking so hard that I could feel where the seatbelt had dug into my shoulder and chest.

As he sped up the final road to my flat, I held my breath, *nearly there, it's OK, you're nearly home.*

As soon as he stopped in the carpark, I undid my seatbelt and almost fell from the car, sobbing hysterically. I'd barely slammed the door when he drove off with a shriek of tyres.

'Roxy?'

I spun around towards the voice; Teddy was by the doors, a black tied up bin bag in his hand. He took one look at me, dropped it and ran over to me, where I

353

practically collapsed in his arms.

'What's happened? You're shaking… what's wrong? Are you hurt? Has someone hurt you?'

'Teddy,' I sobbed into his chest, feeling my legs buckle.

'Shit,' he held me tight. 'Come on, let's get you inside,' he kept an arm around me and led me inside, then sat me down on the bottom steps, crouching down in front of me and holding both my hands. 'You're frightening me,' I glanced up and could see how pale he looked through my tears, his eyes large and scared looking.

'We h-h-had a row,' I shuddered. 'H-he d-drove me home, a-a-and…' I couldn't get anything else out and started to cry almost silently, my head bowed.

'Jaco?' he squeezed my hands and I nodded. 'Did he hurt you?' I shook my head. 'OK, OK… let's go upstairs honey, you're cold.'

He took my hand and we walked upstairs. His door was semi-open, he pushed it and led me to his sofa.

'I'm going to get you a drink,' he disappeared out of my blurred vision, then returned, putting a glass in my hand. I took a sip and coughed as brandy hit my throat.

'Thank you,' I took a few deep breaths.

'There,' Teddy handed me a tissue and I blew my nose. 'Now, what happened?'

'H-he knows about the accident,' I stared at my knees. 'He knows I g-get anxious. And b-because he was mad at m-m-me, he drove too fast, like, he really scared me,' I felt my face crumple again and I took a few more deep breaths. 'I asked him to s-slow down and he just ignored me.'

354

'Bastard,' Teddy almost snarled and I looked at him in surprise – he looked simply livid… something I'd never seen before.

'Right?' I said weakly.

'Oh Rox,' he came and sat next to me and put his arm around me. 'You do know this makes him the biggest twat ever, don't you? What a shitty, shitty thing to do.'

'I know.'

'What did you row about?'

'I was going to finish with him,' I sighed shakily. 'I never got that far. He lied about s-something… oh, just something stupid… then h-he twisted everything and… oh, it doesn't matter…' I trailed off.

'You don't have to tell me,' he dropped a kiss on my head, and we sat in silence for a few minutes.

'He asked if I should be on meds,' I tapped my head, 'you know, for that.'

'What?' he turned to look at me, his face angry once more.

'Teddy… am I… am I weird? Am I… not right? I feel like I'm just… crap.'

'Oh, honey, no, no, no,' he frowned. 'You are sweet and you are funny and you are kind… you're perfect as you are.'

'Perfect,' I repeated. 'No. Nobody is perfect.'

'Well, you are to me,' he chuckled. 'You are perfect as *Roxy*, and I'd hate you to be anything else.'

'Thank you,' I giggled feebly. 'He just made me feel… *wrong*. But it was nothing I haven't asked myself… like, I need fixing.'

'No. And no again.'

355

'I don't know what I'd do without you,' I said huskily.

'Ditto.'

'I need a pee,' I struggled up and went to his bathroom. I washed my face and gazed at my bloodshot, swollen eyes and pink cheeks in revulsion. I looked hideous.

When I came back out, Teddy was making two mugs of tea.

'I actually look like I've had a crash,' I muttered.

'Don't say that,' he grimaced.

I sat back down and drew my knees up to my chin, 'Well, I guess it *is* over at least. Nice dramatic ending.'

'Yeah,' he put our teas on the floor and sat cross-legged in front of me. 'How are you feeling?'

'I dunno… angry. Hurt, sad, pretty much the shittiest I've ever felt.'

'You've stopped shaking at least.'

'I feel really sick.'

'That's shock,' he said gently. 'You're calming down though.'

'What if we had crashed?' I shuddered. 'Why would he risk killing us both just because he was angry?'

Teddy shrugged and handed me my mug.

'I just can't believe him… he says he loves me and then does that. You don't do that to someone you love, do you? No matter how angry you are at them?'

'No,' he said solemnly.

'Then… it's all been a lie,' I closed my eyes against the fresh onslaught of tears. 'He never loved me at all.'

CHAPTER TWENTY-EIGHT

On Saturday evening, after an unbelievably awful day at work, Teddy knocked while I was waiting for Dana to come over to mop me up.

'No arguing, I know you won't eat,' he held aloft a takeaway bag from the Chinese in town. 'All your favourites – shredded duck, yucky prawn toast, sweet and sour pork, rice *and* noodles-'

'I won't eat all that,' I shook my head as he walked past me and dumped it on the worktop in my kitchen.

'You won't have to,' he said, 'I'm starving and so is Dana. She's bringing wine.'

'And how do you know she's coming over?' I said, completely nonplussed.

'She texted me,' he started getting out plates. 'She's worried about you.'

'So, you're chatting behind my back, eh?' I hid a smile.

'Of course.'

Dana arrived, armed with wine and chocolate. She swept me into a tight, perfumed hug then kissed Teddy on the cheek.

'Babes,' she looked at me closely, 'how are you feeling?'

'Been better,' I said, thinking that was a huge understatement. 'But, can we please not talk about him tonight?'

'Absolutely,' she nodded. 'Whatever you feel like

doing.'

I'd filled her in on my lunch break, sitting behind the gym, crying on my phone. After muttering darkly about what she'd like to do to Jaco, she sounded upset for me and said she would be over in the evening.

She opened the wine and told me to sit, then her and Teddy arranged the various cartons of food on my coffee table. As I watched them chatting and laughing, I felt drab and pathetic. She looked dazzling as always in tight red jeans and a vast black fluffy jumper, a gold bandana in her hair. I sat in my old grey jogging bottoms and a grey hoodie that I'd pinched from an ex-boyfriend, my face looking like I was recovering from a terrible illness.

Surprisingly, I managed to eat more than I thought I could. I was enormously touched by Teddy and Dana's gesture; they barely knew each other really. Teddy soon had her roaring with laughter as they gossiped away like two old friends.

I knew I was being quieter than normal, and I knew I was drifting in and out of the conversation and zoning out. But they acted like everything was normal and I was so grateful for that.

'We were going to be the next big girl band, weren't we?' she giggled as Teddy cleared away our plates.

'Oh God,' I covered my face with my hands.

'Do you remember, we used to make videos of us dancing?'

'Thank goodness I didn't have Facebook,' I said with feeling.

'Oh, I was all about Myspace,' Teddy interjected as he returned from the kitchen.

358

'You're old,' I teased.

'Watch it,' he waved a fist at me. 'I had dreams too, you know... I wrote a song once.'

'Did you?' I sat up straighter.

'Yeah,' he grinned crookedly. 'While all my friends were out losing their virginity, I was learning to play the guitar and writing Travis-esque shit.'

'Wanna join our band?' Dana asked laughingly.

'Sure,' he gave a thumbs up before taking the last of the left-over food out.

'I love him,' Dana whispered. 'How can you not fancy him?'

I looked at her in astonishment, 'It's Teddy, innit?'

'He's *so* adorable... and funny.'

'Yeah,' I agreed.

'Oh, girl,' she elbowed me, 'you're crazy.'

I watched her in bewilderment as she got up and after shaking her head at me, joined Teddy in the kitchen.

'So, who's Travisesque?' I heard her ask.

'Travis... esque,' he answered. 'As in, like Travis. You know, Travis? The band?'

'Nah, mate. *What* year were you born?'

The next few days were hard. I seemed to be either obsessing about Jaco and what had happened or having complete brain fog and not seeming to have any cognitive thoughts at all. And that wasn't very good as far as rehearsals were concerned.

On Monday's rehearsals, I messed up everything and ended up in tears.

'Roxy?' Duncan approached me as I stood alone backstage, trying to pull myself together. 'Is there something bothering you?'

'I'm fed up with bloody Finn tutting all the time,' I stormed.

'Uh huh,' he scratched his head. 'OK, but please try and concentrate.'

'Yup,' I said a little more calmly. 'Sorry, Duncan. Just an off day.'

'Okey dokey,' he looked uncomfortable as he walked off.

Five minutes later, I was back on stage with Teddy, Francesca, Bob and Finn.

'Mr Graves,' I said to Bob, already knowing that I didn't know the next line. 'I-I…'

'-*shall look in my diary,*' Teddy whispered.

'Oh, stop bloody well spoon feeding her,' Finn said loudly.

I felt tears sting my eyes as I glanced at Francesca, who smirked slightly.

'Sorry,' I tried to clear my head. 'I shall look in my diary, but I'm almost certain that we were alone that day.'

'Thank you, my dear,' Bob rose from the sofa and crossed the stage, stopping and bowing his head. 'It won't bring back my Mabel though.'

After a pause, Teddy whispered, '*Roxy,*' – it was clearly my line.

'Sorry,' I closed my eyes, trying to ignore Finn's exaggerated sigh.

'This is pointless,' Finn said bluntly. 'I told you, Duncan, she should have been given a smaller role.'

'Now, now,' Duncan called.

'Leave off,' Teddy said angrily. 'She's having a bad

time at the moment, you floppy haired sandwich.'

Despite my upset, I burst out laughing.

'He has a point, though,' Francesca shrugged and gave me a pointed look.

'Really?' I hissed, surprising myself with a rare flare-up of temper. 'Stop taking it out on me because you got turned down.'

'What?' Finn glared from me to her.

'Roxy,' Teddy groaned.

'Sorry, but I'm fed up of it,' I crossed my arms.

Francesca had gone rather pink as she stared fixedly above my head, refusing to look at Finn.

Bob sidled away from us and looked pleadingly at Duncan.

'Can you explain that, please?' Finn demanded.

'OK, children, let's take five,' Duncan said loudly.

I noticed that everyone was looking avidly at us. Lily-Rose and Samantha were whispering madly, and Stuart was openly laughing.

'You wally,' Teddy dragged me away by the elbow.

'Sorry, I'm sorry,' I muttered. 'Please don't be mad at me.'

He looked gravely at me for a second, then smiled, 'How can I stay mad at you?' he chuckled. 'But I *really* wish that you hadn't said that.'

'Sorry.'

'Well, OK,' he exhaled. 'But... eek.'

'Yeah,' I glanced over at Finn and Francesca, and saw that they were clearly having a very quiet argument.

'So, they're a *thing* now, I take it?' he followed my gaze. 'I thought it was just a bunk up.'

'How do you know about that?'

'Destiny, of course.'

'Of course.'

'She could do better.'

'You had your chance,' I mocked. 'Regretting it?'

'Nope,' he shook his head. 'But Finn's a plank.'

'Yep.'

The rest of rehearsals were sketchy to say the least, and the atmosphere was thick with tension.

I decided, without telling Teddy, that I was going to apologise to Francesca.

When my part was done, I went to the dressing room. Lola was in there on her own, brushing her hair in the mirror.

'Hi,' she smiled shyly. 'Are you OK, Roxy?'

'Yeah,' I wriggled out of my dress and she averted her eyes. 'How was the cinema?'

'Oh, it was lovely,' she blushed. 'We're going out for dinner on Friday.'

'Are you? How nice,' I said wistfully.

'Yes, we're going to Cambridge,' she bit her lip. 'Like a proper date.'

'Go you,' I grinned.

'What happened earlier?' she lowered her voice.

'Oh, nothing really, just Finn being Finn.'

'Yeah,' she nodded. 'You seemed upset.'

'I'm OK, rough weekend,' I shrugged. 'Me and Jaco... we split up.'

'No!' she looked genuinely dismayed. 'I went to Teddy's shop at lunchtime, he didn't say anything.'

'Well, not really his news,' I scraped my hair up and

peered in the mirror – my dark circles were terrible and I had a spot coming up on my chin.

I heard voices approaching and looked around. Meadow and Crystal came in and both gave me a curious look.

'Alright?' I said breezily.

'See you later, Roxy,' Lola picked up her rucksack and left.

I went out to the corridor thinking I would accost Francesca there, away from ears. Less than a minute later she appeared, talking to Lily-Rose.

'Francesca,' I said loudly. 'Can I have a word in private?'

'Uh, OK,' she stopped in her tracks and looked suspicious.

I walked a little way down the corridor to where it was dim and she followed, seeming to be reluctant.

'OK,' I said briskly. 'I'm sorry for what I said, it was out of order and I hope I didn't cause any trouble.'

'OK,' she nodded. 'Thank you.'

'And... I don't know why you've been off with me, but if I've upset you, sorry.'

'You haven't,' she said in a monotone voice.

'Great,' I said. 'OK. See you later,' I went to walk away but she suddenly put her hands up. 'What?'

'Look,' she blinked rapidly a few times. 'No, look, *I'm* sorry. I've been a bit of a cow... haven't I?' when I didn't answer, she smiled thinly. 'So, obviously Teddy said something... OK, I was just jealous. That's all.'

'Jealous of what?'

'Well, of you,' she sighed. 'I just really liked Teddy... I thought he liked me. A bit wrong, wasn't I?'

'He didn't give me a blow by blow account,' I said hastily. 'And I dragged it out of him because I noticed you were being... off.'

'He's a nice guy.'

'Yeah, he is.'

'I'll sort it out... I'll apologise to him. I was just embarrassed.'

'OK.'

She nodded, almost to herself and went towards the dressing room, her posture kind of hunched.

Feeling *slightly* better, I went back through to the stage and jogged up the auditorium, where Teddy was waiting for me just inside the doors.

'Ready?'

'Yup.'

On Wednesday, the texts started. I had been in a world of misery, crying randomly, missing Jaco *horribly*, questioning possibly just about every decision I had ever made, feeling stupid, feeling used... but feeling like I was coping by the skin of my teeth. Just.

I had been on my lunch break, eating an apple on my own in the staff room. Hearing my text alert go off, I thought it was either Dana or Teddy asking how I was. When I saw Jaco's name, I had to go and spit out my mouthful of apple in the bin, my mouth suddenly dry and my stomach clenched in a painful knot.

When I opened the text, it was one word: *Sorry.*

It was amazing how just one word sent me spiralling into terror and trauma. Just seeing his name alone made me feel on the edge of a panic attack.

I switched my phone off and went and sat in the

toilet, shaking and fighting back tears of distress and anger.

When I eventually switched my phone back on later in the afternoon, I had two texts and a missed call from Teddy and three texts from Dana demanding if I were OK.

Just before five o'clock, Teddy came in, looking both worried and annoyed.

'Answer your texts,' he reproached.

'Sorry,' I looked over at Troy, who was messing around with some new stock, some fluorescent wristbands.

'Go on,' he said. 'Go home.'

I went and fetched my bag and jacket.

'You OK?' Teddy asked as we walked out together.

'Hold on,' I rummaged in my bag for my phone. 'Look,' I opened the text and showed him.

'Right,' he murmured. 'You going to answer?'

'No,' I shoved my phone back. 'He can go screw himself.'

'Oh, honey.'

'It would have been more sincere on Friday night or Saturday. Four days later is just an afterthought.'

'Sure, but he might actually *be* sorry,' he put his hands up. 'I'm not defending him, not at all. He's a twat. But if he *is* sorry, accept it. You'll feel better.'

'What?' I shook my head. 'No. He can just be sorry on his own. Why are you being nice?'

'Because I *am* nice,' he said mildly. 'I'm just saying don't hold onto grudges. Let it go… staying mad will just eat you up.'

'I kind of want to stay mad, I want to hate him.'

365

'Indifference is much better.'

'Yeah, I suppose.'

'Wanna grab a pizza and read lines?'

'Sure.'

An hour later we were at either ends of my sofa with our respective pizza boxes while we read lines, Teddy reading from the script, as he was reading other people's lines for me.

'Word perfect,' he announced after we read a particularly long dialogue between me and Johnny, who was playing the inspector.

'Hope I don't get stage fright,' I fretted.

'You've been fine up until your wobble yesterday, sweetie. You'll be fine.'

My text alert went off, and my stomach clenched as I saw Jaco's name.

I'm missing you Roxy, are you ready to talk?

'Is he for real?' I showed it to Teddy.

'Talk about what?' he grimaced.

'Hold on, you told me to forgive him,' I said, perplexed.

'Yeah, accept the apology, move on… but talk? Be careful, honey. Please.'

'Yeah,' I put my phone down again. 'I don't want to talk to him, what's the point? It's over.'

'Does he know it's over?'

'Well… I assume so.'

'But you didn't actually get around to dumping him, did you?'

'Crap!' I stared at him with rising horror. 'So, he might think we are still together? After what he did?'

'He might.'

'OK, OK.' I picked up my phone again.

'What are you doing?'

'Texting him,' I said grimly.

I typed in, *I accept your apology, but please leave me alone. It's over.* Then I sent it before I chickened out.

'To the point,' Teddy read it. 'How do you feel?'

'Awesome,' I answered sarcastically.

Surprisingly I slept well that evening. Waking up, I saw that Jaco had sent several texts in the early hours. The first one said, *It's not over,* which I found rather sinister. Followed by, *Sorry, I'm drunk. We need to talk, I love you so much.* Then, *I can't believe what I said and did. Please don't hate me. I love you so much darling.*

An hour after that he told me he loved me, a few minutes after that he said sorry again.

'Great,' I said loudly.

It was hard to concentrate at work that morning, I kept expecting Jaco to burst in at any moment.

As if sensing my preoccupied mood, Troy stuck me in the stock room, giving me his sweatshirt as it was cold in there. I turned up the radio, quite happy to be all on my own.

Mid-afternoon, Ant joined me, and we spent a pleasant hour discussing books; it turned out that he was a fan of the classics too.

On my drive home it suddenly occurred to me that I was actually relaxed – not fretting about Jaco's little moods, that he was a drug dealer, a thug… even though my heart was aching, I wasn't worrying. I grabbed that thought and held onto it tightly. It might have been a small crumb of comfort, but it was *something.*

As I walked up the corridor to my flat though, I spied something outside my door, and I felt my mood slip a notch.

It was a huge bouquet of flowers. The card attached to it had a heart drawn on it with the word 'sorry' in the middle.

'Oh, for crying out loud,' I almost shouted. Marching back down the corridor and down the steps, I went outside to the bins.

'Hey,' Teddy was climbing out of his car.

'Hey,' I replied sourly, pushing down on the flowers.

'Oh,' he peered over my shoulder.

'He texted me like a million times in the middle of the night.'

'Really? That's not good.'

'Well, four or five,' I closed the bin forcibly. 'He needs to leave me alone.'

'Are you hungry?'

'Not really.'

'Want to have a bite at mine before rehearsals?'

'OK,' I relented. 'Sorry, I don't mean to be grumpy with you.'

'I don't mind being a Roxy punch-bag,' he followed me to the doors. 'You're only diddy.'

'Watch it,' I laughed.

Excusing myself to go and get changed, I had a quick shower and put on the only clean pair of jeans I could find and a T-shirt.

Ok… you're going to the dogs. This weekend you're

368

going to do laundry and housework.

Teddy was stirring mince and onions when I let myself in, 'I'm cooking burritos,' he told me.

'Cool.'

'OK, stand here and stir, I need a shower. Don't burn it,' he poured in some sauce and turned the heat down.

'Funny,' I stuck my tongue out and took his place at the stove.

He re-appeared five-minutes later in shorts and his black T-shirt with 'i like cheese' on the front.

'See, I haven't set fire to anything.'

'Good girl.'

Rehearsals went well, better than the last fiasco anyway. Duncan was becoming very serious, telling us we had only six weeks until opening night, and we must work harder than ever.

'I hate how he has a complete personality change before opening night,' Crystal grumbled.

I didn't comment; I could see why he got uptight.

As the evening wore on, I noticed that Francesca was acting less hostile. She also was giving Finn a wide berth.

'Short-lived, wasn't it?' Destiny caught me watching Finn giving Francesca covert looks.

'Seems so,' I said vaguely.

'You know why?' she lowered her voice.

'Because he's a dick head?'

'Ha,' she shook her head. 'No, but yeah he is.'

'Why, then?' I hated gossip but I couldn't help being curious.

'He's terrible in bed,' she grinned wickedly. 'A two-second wonder.'

'Figures,' I scoffed. 'Most good-looking men are.'

'I wouldn't know,' she said dreamily. 'My Robin isn't a looker, but my goodness he's a tantric lover.'

'Great,' I truly hoped that my face didn't reflect my slight disgust. I was also glad that Teddy wasn't nearby; he would have loved that.

Leaving the theatre, everyone was in good spirits and laughing. It was very often that way on a Thursday, compared to the beginning of the week. I was giggling at something Teddy had said to Nathan, when I looked up and saw Jaco leaning against his car watching us.

The laughter died on my lips and I stopped in my tracks, making Teddy and Nathan both turn and look at me. Teddy followed my gaze and then came and put his hand on my arm.

'You don't have to talk to him,' he said seriously.

'Hi, Jaco,' Meadow called out and he waved.

'Fuck,' I felt like my feet were rooted to the ground.

'What's up?' Nathan asked.

'We split up, and not too nicely.'

'Oh,' Nathan looked over at him. 'Want me to hang around?'

'It's OK, mate,' Teddy was watching me closely. 'I'll take her home.'

'Can we get in the car,' I put my head down and walked quickly to Teddy's car.

'Rox!' Jaco called.

I climbed in and felt panicky as Teddy walked around to the driver's side. I had no idea what the hell I thought Jaco could possibly do with so many people milling about, but my logical side wasn't exactly on the surface right then.

'It's OK,' Teddy reassured me.

I glanced around and saw Jaco approaching the car, 'Shit.'

'He won't do anything,' Teddy started the engine.

'Hold on,' I suddenly burst out. I didn't want to involve Teddy. I didn't want Jaco to think Teddy was standing in the way of him speaking to me. I wasn't really frightened, but I was frightened *why* I didn't want to put Teddy in Jaco's bad books. People in his bad books seemed to end up getting hurt.

'Roxy?' Teddy was watching me.

'I'll speak to him,' I said levelly. 'Just stay here. Please.'

I was expecting Teddy to argue, but he simply killed the engine and nodded, 'I won't go anywhere.'

I got out of the car, fully preparing myself for some sneering comment about me and Teddy being cosy, or me walking out of the theatre with two men.

'Well?' I walked up to him and stopped, putting my hands on my hips.

He looked pale and shadowed under his eyes, his hair slightly dishevelled... I thought it was too artfully so.

'I just wanted to talk to you,' he said quietly. 'I get you're mad, I do. Roxy,' his voice broke a little and I had to fight to keep emotion off of my face, 'I'm so sorry. I did a *horrible* thing.'

'Yeah you did,' I said coldly. 'Really horrible. But I accepted your apology.'

'Yeah,' he smiled sadly. 'You did. But baby, you are still angry... I don't want to leave it like this.'

'Well… I'm not sure I can help you with that one.'

'Don't you love me?'

'No.'

'Liar,' he gazed soulfully at me. 'But OK, too soon,' he turned and walked back to his car, leaving me to stare after him.

'What happened?' Teddy asked as soon as I got back in his car.

'You know what?' I turned my head to look at him. 'I have absolutely no idea.'

CHAPTER TWENTY-NINE

I had Saturday off, and spent the entire day cleaning, doing my laundry and organising my wardrobe. Then I drove to the supermarket and had a *proper* shop, stocking up on everything.

By late afternoon I felt very accomplished, *but…* Jaco rung me four times before I switched my phone off, and it was hanging over me like a little black cloud that kept drizzling on me every now and then to remind me it was there.

I had my door propped open as nobody ever used the fire exit at my end of the corridor as it only led to a dirt path that ended up in weeds in front of a sub-station.

Teddy stuck his head in just after five o'clock, and after complementing me for my hard work and saying how tidy my flat was, he left his door open too so we could randomly talk to each other, as we often did. It made me feel cosy and safe, almost like having a flat mate.

I kept looking at my phone and feeling tempted to turn it on… after losing the momentum with my tasks, I gave in and wandered into Teddy's flat, where he was laying on his sofa playing Rocket League on his Xbox.

'Hey,' I dragged his beanbag across the floor so I wouldn't be in his way and sunk down in it.

'Alright, Mrs Mop?' he greeted me. 'Jobs all done?'

'Kind of,' I watched his game for a minute. 'I want to ask you something.'

'One minute,' he swore under his breath and then whooped. 'Ha, you loser!'

'Boys!' I rolled my eyes and waited patiently for him to be done.

'OK, shoot,' he said eventually.

'You going out tonight?'

'Is that what you wanted to ask me?' he raised his eyebrows.

'No.'

'I might pop out for a quick one,' he sat up and stretched. 'What's up?'

'I can't switch my phone on,' I waved it at him.

'Oh, honey, it's the little button on the side.'

'Funny,' I glared at him. 'No, because of Jaco.'

'Is he hassling you?'

'He keeps ringing me.'

'Block him?'

'I thought of that, but what will he do then?'

'Get bored eventually, hopefully.'

'Hmm,' I got up and opened up his cupboard in search of snacks. 'Can I ask you something?'

'Of course.'

'When you and he hung out, was he like, stalker-ish or…persistent with girls?'

'Sweet, that was a long time ago. But, no. He was always laid-back and kind of… plenty more fish in the sea attitude.'

'Right,' I pondered on this. 'I'm thinking maybe I should just hear him out properly, instead of being stroppy and clear the air. On the phone, of course.'

'Are you ready to do that?'

'Dunno. I just want him to leave me alone.'

'Well… sure. That might help,' he looked doubtful.

'You have no junk food,' I declared slamming the cupboard. 'Can't you just tell me what to do? I'm rubbish.'

'I'm afraid not,' he shrugged his shoulders. 'It's your call, honey.'

'That's not the answer I wanted.'

'You have a lot of faith in my love-life advice, when in fact I have no love-life and also in fact, I'm not good with advice.'

'Well, Dana's out for the evening.'

'Well, gosh darn, I feel special now.'

'Sorry,' I giggled and went and gave him a hug. 'I didn't mean it like that.'

'Keep your hands to yourself,' he wriggled out of my hug. 'Look,' he said, his expression turning serious, 'you need to do whatever feels right for you. As long as you're safe.'

'OK,' I nodded slowly, not wanting to argue that I had no idea what felt right.

Back in my flat, I made some toast and sat and admired how nice and clean everything looked.

Teddy had gone to the pub and I felt inexplicably lost and a little vulnerable. I double-locked my door before I went to run my bath, I even locked my balcony doors – not that I expected anyone to climb up… but I felt safer.

As I lay in the bath, I thought it over and wondered if it was because of the flowers. I didn't think Jaco had delivered them, he more than likely had sent Billy. But the fact that *someone* had left them bothered me.

Normally when I had a soak, I had my music on loud, but I didn't feel comfortable enough, I was listening out for every sound.

Once I was in my pyjamas, I switched my phone on, and waited for any notifications to come through.

Two more calls from Jaco, and a text from Freya.

I took three painkillers and decided to get into bed and at least be comfortable, even if I was too uptight to sleep.

I started pondering over my conversation with Teddy. I could see that he thought talking to Jaco wasn't a good idea, but the more I thought about it, the more it made sense to me.

I went back and forth in my head, then came to a decision.

'Hello?' Jaco answered quickly and I almost ended the call.

'Hello.'

'It's really late. Are you OK?'

'I'm fine... listen,' I was trying to modulate my voice, but I sounded shaky, 'I just want to clear the air. And I want you to stop ringing me.'

'OK, OK,' he sounded emotional. 'Sorry... I'm just struggling... I know it's my fault, I do, but I want to say so much to you. And I'm missing you so badly, Roxy.'

I irritably wiped away a solitary tear on my cheek and exhaled, 'Then maybe we both need closure.'

'Then... it *is* over? We can't... sort this out?'

'No.'

'Why, baby? You know we're good together. And I know you love me as much as I love you.'

'There's just too much stuff,' my voice finally betrayed me and broke. 'I-I can't deal with it all.'

'Then talk. Talk to me, tell me.'

'What you did, driving that way, *knowing* how I am, that was evil, Jaco.'

'I know, I'm so sorry, I hate myself. It would never, ever happen again.'

'It's not just that.'

'Go on, tell me everything. Please.'

'You get jealous and you scare me,' I said abruptly. 'You're too controlling, I'm sick of you sulking. I can't get what Liam said out of my head… I'm scared it was something to do with you when he got hurt. Ditto my boss… I don't trust you. I think you have something to do with Evie's drug habit. You and her make me uncomfortable. And the other Friday,' I swallowed hard, 'I *did* ask you to stop, I did. You hurt me.'

'Sweetheart,' he sounded muffled, then he sniffed. 'It's all wrong… you've got me so wrong.'

Oh no, is he crying? Please don't cry Jaco… be mad. Get nasty…

'Well, I can't be wrong about everything.'

'OK,' he cleared his throat, 'I get jealous. I know it's ridiculous, but baby, you are so beautiful. I've never been jealous before, not once. I don't know how to stop… I'm scared of losing you.'

'You're scared of losing me, so you frighten me and sulk. Right.'

'I know, I know… as for Liam… sweetheart, he is mistaken. I don't know how to prove it. And it hurts me that you don't believe me.'

'What about when he was attacked?'

'You know it wasn't me, we were together! But I wouldn't hurt him, or anyone else... I wouldn't.'

'I-I don't know-'

'Baby, please listen… and as for Evie, well, it's no secret what she shoves up her nose. It's nothing to do with me. All artists are the bloody same.'

'But what about when you… when you didn't stop.'

'Oh sweetheart,' his voice cracked, and I felt more tears spilling over. 'I get so… so carried away with you. You are so sexy, so wonderful… I'm sorry if you did, I didn't hear you, I didn't know,' he gave a small sob and stopped for a second. 'You're my angel. I didn't know. If I heard you say stop, I would have stopped.'

'Would you?' I choked back my tears and closed my eyes.

'Yes. Yes… please think it all over. Please give me another chance. I love you, I want to *marry* you, I want you forever.'

'Jaco,' I whispered, not knowing what to think.

'Do you love me?'

'Yes,' I murmured.

'Will you think it over? I'll give you all the time you need. I won't ring, I won't text. Just please say you'll think it over.'

'I don't know,' I said, my thoughts all over the place… I knew he was weakening my defences though.

'Please, just think it over. It won't hurt.'

'OK.'

Confused didn't even come close to how I felt for the next few days.

I kept going back and forth on my belief in what Jaco had said. He had sounded so sincere and cut-up. Had I just built him up to be a monster, listening to everyone else? With that in mind, I didn't tell anyone about our conversation; I needed to make this decision on my own.

But it was hard... so hard. There just seemed to be so much stacked against him. Once again, I hated myself for not trusting my own judgement.

A week passed, and I was no closer to making a decision. I threw myself into rehearsals, spent a lot of time at the gym and from the outside I probably seemed to be picking myself up and getting on with things.

Eliza started her first week at work and it was indeed refreshing to have another girl in the store, even though she seemed more blokey than most blokes.

It amazed me for someone so lithe-looking, that she ate constantly; never had our fridge been so well stocked up, and she shuddered at the talk of exercise.

She was funny too, and always messing around with the guys and swearing like a sailor. I kept wondering if she knew about Jaco and I. I didn't think he saw *that* much of Sadie, as close as they seemed – Eliza never mentioned him, so I just kept our conversations neutral.

She confided in me that her friend Tom had gone back to Ireland and that she was missing him, and in a moment of madness I nearly spilt my guts about Jaco... I reeled it in though. I would have liked to confide in someone I barely knew, but she was a little too connected for me to be entirely comfortable.

Saturday evening arrived with no plans, and I knew that I had to give Jaco some indication as to where things stood. As good as his word, he had not rung or texted me.

Teddy asked if I fancied a takeaway and a drink and I jumped at the chance – anything for a distraction.

'Why are you not out tonight?' I asked as I shared out some pilau rice onto two plates.

'Knackered.'

'Going out is over-rated.'

'Well, you keep reminding me that I'm old.'

We ate our food and drank beer and half-watched whatever was on television, but my mind kept wandering towards Jaco.

'Hey,' Teddy said eventually. 'You're a little out, you OK chicken?'

'Eh,' I shrugged.

'Want to talk?'

'I dunno,' I considered him for a moment, not sure that I wanted to see a negative reaction from him.

'If you're not up for company, I can bugger off home,' he said good-naturedly.

'I rang Jaco,' I blurted out.

'Ah, OK,' he didn't seem especially fazed. 'When did you do that?'

'Last week when I left yours.'

'Oh! You kept that quiet.'

'I know,' I muttered. 'Just been… thinking.'

'Honey, don't bottle things up. You should have told me. I hate you being upset.'

'No, no… it's not that,' I swigged some beer and suddenly wished I hadn't said anything.

'OK, well as long as you're OK.'

'Yeah, I am. Sort of… I'm just confused. You know, he said some stuff and I don't know now-' I trailed off as Teddy's expression darkened a little.

'Fancy a cuppa?' he said suddenly. 'I'll clear up.'

'Oh, sure, thanks, but I'll clear up,' I followed him to the kitchen. 'What's up?'

'Roxy,' he said slowly. 'Are you thinking of going back to him?' he filled the kettle, keeping his back to me.

'I-I don't know… he just explained some things, and-'

'Roxy, no,' he turned around, his face oddly closed. 'You seriously can't be thinking about it, not after what he did.'

'Yeah, I know,' I wrapped my arms around myself, 'it sounds bad, but… it's hard. I might be wrong about him.'

'Are you for real?' he shook his head disbelievingly. 'It's none of my business, but I can't just sit back and let you do something stupid.'

'Thanks for the faith in me,' I said, feeling my face colour.

'I-I need to go,' he said, then to my amazement he simply dropped the teaspoon he was holding and walked out.

Temporarily stunned, I stood staring after him before absently picking up the spoon and walking across to his flat.

'Teddy?' I knocked on the door.

'It's open,' came back his muffled reply.

He was bent over the worktop, his broken radio in front of him, some wire cutters in his hand.

'What the hell was that?' I demanded.

'Nothing,' he muttered.

I realised that I was still holding the spoon and stepped closer to put it on the side.

'That's not my spoon,' he said distantly.

'I know,' I cocked my head, trying to see his expression as he clipped some wires. 'What's wrong?'

When he didn't answer, I started to feel annoyed… OK, I knew he clearly didn't approve of my decision to ring Jaco, and he was probably worried for me, but this seemed absurd.

'Are-are you OK?'

'No!' he suddenly straightened up and glared at me. 'Because I'm fixing *this*,' he waved a hand over his radio, 'like this is the *real* fucking problem,' he turned and yanked up his kitchen bin and swept the radio into it viciously. 'And I can't fucking say what I want to say.'

'What?' I took a few steps back, 'Teddy, I'm sorry but I-'

'Roxy,' he said in a calmer voice. 'I'm *imploring* you, don't go back to Jaco.'

'I never said I was,' I was rattled but also very upset, Teddy had never been even vaguely angry with me. 'But I can make my own decisions.'

'Well, that would be a really bad one. Please, Roxy… just… don't.'

'This is not easy for me, you know,' I said, folding my arms.

'No?' he smiled bleakly and looked down for a second. 'Do you know what else isn't easy?' he raised his voice again, his normally cheerful turquoise eyes dark and pained. 'Watching you *hurting,* seeing you getting sucked in by that bastard, and I can't do a damn thing about it.'

'Why are you so mad at me?' I stormed, thinking it would be better to just leave; my precarious state wasn't needing another drama, and definitely not with the person that had been my rock.

'Why? *Why?*' he walked towards me until we were only a foot apart. 'Because I love you. There, I said it. *I. Love. You.* I've loved you since the moment you walked into my bookstore. I love you more than that shallow bastard could possibly love anyone. I would never hurt you like he has... but I've just had to sit back and pretend I don't, because,' he suddenly shouted, '*I can't lose you. Now I've fucking lost you!*'

There was a ringing silence as I stood, shell-shocked and trembling, and he stood there breathing hard and looking distraught and furious in equal measures.

'W-why... why have you never... what are you...' I stared at him, feeling completely stunned, 'you n-never said-'

'You know why?' he said hoarsely. 'Because... *look at you, Rox,*' he looked anguished. 'You are so out of my league, and I've known it from day one. Look at the gym guys you've been with... I might love you but I'm not an idiot.'

'Teddy!' I was genuinely shocked that he *even* thought that. 'That's ridiculous.'

In one swift movement, he stepped forward, took my

face in his hands and started to kiss me. I kissed him back, overcome with a sudden rush of *rightness,* of safeness and a growing desire... then I panicked.

'No,' I broke free and put my hands in front of me. 'What the hell are you doing?'

'You kissed me back,' he said, looking mortified.

'You're my friend,' I started to cry, not even sure why I was. 'We can't... why did you do that?' suddenly I was angry. 'Jaco was right,' I said, hating myself even as I said it. 'He said you were a player!'

'What the fuck?' he laughed without any mirth, then looked at me with a hint of disdain. 'He said that, did he?' he turned and walked away then turned back, his eyes full of hurt. 'A player? You believe that? Are you *that* gullible? Yeah, I was a *huge* player.'

'Well, you just did that,' I said weakly.

'After *months* of ignoring the fact that I love you so much, I want to kiss you every minute of every day,' he spat. 'Roxy, I was the weird indie kid that tagged along... for fuck's sake,' he laughed shortly again. 'That's almost funny.'

'So he lied.'

'He lied,' he ran his hands through his hair. 'But like you would even notice... like you even noticed me, protecting you, listening to you, being your friend. You notice so very little it's frightening,' his voice started to rise again. 'You, in your own little world of everything being lovely and fluffy-'

'That's unfair, and you know it!' I yelled.

'Yeah?' he yelled back. 'You don't even notice when your boyfriend is coked up to his eyeballs.'

'Like when?' I felt the blood leave my face.

384

'Like every time I've fucking seen him with you!'

I clamped my hand over my mouth as a sob tried to escape me, 'If you were my friend,' I said in a small voice, lowering my hand. 'Why didn't you tell me? Why didn't you warn me?'

'Why? Because you are so blinded by him, I knew I would lose you. He'd feed you some bullshit and we'd be done. That's why.'

'I'm going,' I felt all the fight leave me.

'Roxy,' he came over and gently grabbed my arm. 'Shit, look… I'm sorry. I should have just… got on with it.'

'Doesn't matter, 'I said numbly. 'I-I need to go,' I blindly reached for the door and yanked it open.

'Roxy?'

'No,' I nearly fell out into the corridor and pushed my door hard before he could say anything else.

Without even getting undressed, I climbed into bed and pulled he duvet over me, before finally letting go and sobbing like the world was about to end.

When I woke up the next morning, my pillow covered in mascara, it took a few seconds for everything to come flooding back.

I rushed to my window and saw that Teddy's car wasn't there. I went and started clearing up the remnants of our takeaway, not knowing what else to do. I didn't even have any tears left in me – just a painful and empty feeling of numb misery.

Teddy, my dear friend… I didn't know… I'm sorry. Please don't hate me…

I'm not sure how I felt about the fact that my misery

was coming from losing my friend and not Jaco. In fact, Jaco seemed like a distant memory right then.

I had a shower and then went and sat next to my balcony doors, watching the flow of traffic and praying that Teddy would come home from wherever he was, and I could try and smooth things over. How I would do that, I didn't know, but I knew that I had to. I simply couldn't lose him.

After an hour of sitting in some sort of stupor, I got up and started to pace. I needed to talk to someone. Not Dana – as much as I loved her, I knew she would be *too* anti-Jaco. I needed some very impartial advice.

Suddenly Violet popped into my head. I dickered for a bit, then rang her.

'I need some advice,' I said. 'I'm in a mess.'

'Come on over,' she said straight away. 'I'll text you my address.'

Violet's house in the village of Barkenwell wasn't what I expected – not that I was exactly sure what I was expecting.

It was on the edge of the village with a field next to it, sitting in a very tidy garden. As I pulled up next to her little Gold Kia, I noticed a lot of security cameras.

She answered the door, her grey hair in its usual bun, wearing lilac leggings that showed how skinny her legs were, and a floaty white blouse.

'Come in, my dear,' she greeted me. 'It's nearly lunchtime, we can have a G and T.'

I followed her down her duck-egg blue painted hallway, charmed to see a large framed photo of the cast on a table, then giggled when I saw she had stuck two googly eyes on Finn's face.

Her kitchen was kind of cottage-y but painted a bright red with black and white tiles.

'Sit your bum,' she said and went and fetched two glasses and a bottle of gin.

I talked, probably for about twenty minutes, telling her *everything.* She listened intently without saying a single word.

'Well,' she said finally. 'That's a tale and a half.'

'Right?' I closed my eyes, feeling exhausted.

'You know I won't pussy-foot or bullshit you.'

'Go on.'

'Jaco is clearly bad news.'

'He doesn't come across well, eh?' I smiled sadly.

'No. Not at all. And I don't like to judge someone that I don't know, my darling. But,' she took both my hands in her slender, liver-spotted ones, 'cut your losses.'

'Yeah,' I felt my throat constrict.

'And as for dear Teddy,' she squeezed my hands. 'What's wrong with you?'

'What?'

'Look at him. *Think* about it... he's everything.'

'He's my friend,' I exclaimed. 'I love him, I do. As a friend.'

'Have you tried to look at him differently? Have you ever wondered?'

'No.'

'How was the kiss?'

'Violet!'

'It's a valid question. Close your eyes and think about it.'

387

'OK,' I complied and thought hard. 'It was...
unexpected... it was... nice. He's a good kisser, I
guess.'

'How did you feel?'

'Safe. I felt... like it could have gone, you know,
further, if it wasn't Teddy.'

'Well, that's unfair.'

'Huh?'

'Not wanting it to go further because it was Teddy.
You know, he's not just your friend. He's a man too.'

I opened my eyes and stared at her.

'Go and think about it. Take your time, of course.
But *think*. He's like any other man. He has feelings and
desires and everything else.'

'Yeah,' I whispered, suddenly feeling ashamed. 'Oh
God, I'm just *horrible*, aren't I? Horrible and selfish.'

'No, not all. You're lovely and sweet. Just... a little
naïve.'

'I'm so confused.'

'Listen. Go and see your Jaco, get your closure by all
means. But whatever you decide to do, be kind to
Teddy. He's a beautiful human being, and if you don't
want him, set him free. He deserves some happiness, if
not with you then with somebody that will love him.'

I left Violet's house feeling *marginally* better. Still
confused, but not as distressed as I had been, and it had
been a relief to get it all out.

On a whim on my way home I decided to drive to
Jaco's house, catch him unguarded. If he wasn't home,
I would just go straight home and wait for Teddy.
With that decided, I swung around and drove towards

Chembury.

CHAPTER THIRTY

Only Jaco's BMW was on his driveway. With relief, I sped away, thinking it was a stupid idea anyway. I wasn't in a fit state for any sort of emotive conversation.

As I drove through town, I slowed as I approached the road where his gallery was.

Just go home. Go home and have your thinking time and try and relax. You're not in a good place.

I drove slowly down the road, berating myself for not just doing the sensible thing.

His Porsche was parked down the side of the building. I crawled along, having an internal argument with myself.

I parked in front of a white van and took some deep breaths. I hadn't seen him for two weeks now, I had absolutely no idea how I would feel when I saw him. After ten-minutes, I got out and walked towards the gallery with weak legs.

As I pushed my way in, a young woman with vibrant red hair looked up from the desk.

'Hi,' I said breathlessly. 'Is Jaco about?'

'He was,' she smiled. 'Have you an appointment?'

'Oh, no,' I suddenly wished I was dressed more smartly, instead of ripped jeans and an over-sized shirt - maybe she thought I was an artist. 'Just an off-chance. I thought I saw his car.'

'In that case he might be upstairs.'

'Thanks,' I backed out the doors, not sure what to do.
Go home.

I walked around to the back of the building past his car and looked up the flight of steps.

Go home.

I slowly climbed the steps, having an awful premonition of him snorting cocaine with Evie off the coffee table, surrounded by her painting paraphernalia.

Seriously you idiot, just go home.

As I reached the door, I could hear loud music – American Girl. I thought of the scene in The Silence of the Lambs, when the senator's daughter is driving along, unknowing of her dreadful fate, singing at the top of her voice to it. It didn't seem like a good omen. I entered the hallway; the music was coming from the living room at the end of the hall.

I walked past the bedroom, a shaky breath escaping me as I saw the unmade, empty bed.

I wanted to call out Jaco's name, but I didn't have a voice… my breathing was erratic, and my chest ached.

The music really was so deafeningly loud, I was certain Evie was alone and painting. I edged towards the living room, my brain racing to come up with a viable excuse if she was in there.

I was greeted by the sight of Evie's bare white back, her vertebrae visible as she straddled Jaco on the sofa. His head was thrown back with an ecstatic expression on his face that I knew only too well.

I froze in the doorway, the shock keeping me rooted to the spot. As he brought his head forward, his eyes glazed, he spotted me. His expression went from euphoria to horror in a split second.

I felt like I was moving in slow-motion, but I must have turned fast, as I practically fell over my feet as I bolted for the still open front door.

By the time I reached the bottom, the music had been killed and I thought I heard his voice.

I didn't stop running until I reached my car, practically throwing myself in and starting the engine with shaking hands.

As I turned haphazardly to drive away, he ran out from the side of the gallery in shorts and a T-shirt, looking frantically around.

I put my foot down, dimly aware that an awful whimper was coming from me. I knew he was going to follow me, and I knew that his Porsche went a lot faster than my little car.

You dirty, lying piece of shit… I knew I had to slow down as I could hardly see through my tears, but I was terrified. How I got home without killing myself, I have no idea.

I wasn't even sure if I locked my car properly, I had one thing on my mind and that was reaching the safety of my flat.

I locked and bolted my door, then lurched into the bathroom and threw up and up until I was dry heaving and sobbing, the taste of blood in my throat.

How could you? After all the begging and pleading? Have you been screwing her the whole time? Do I mean that little to you?

I heard the screech of his tyres before I even got to the window. I closed my blind and huddled up on the sofa, clutching my phone.

It seemed as if only seconds had passed when he

started hammering on my door.

'Roxy!' he yelled.

'*Fuck off and die,*' I muttered to myself.

'I know you're in there… please open the door,' he banged loudly.

Then there was a new voice, 'Mate, turn it in will ya?' I recognised it as Pete's, Teddy's neighbour with the cat.

'Roxy!'

'I said, pack it in.'

'Fuck off.'

'Roxy, are you alright in there?'

'I seriously suggest you go back in, my friend,' Jaco sounded furious and I started to worry.

'Make me,' Pete said, equally as aggressively.

I got up and marched to the door. After bracing myself, I opened it and stepped into the hall, frightened that Jaco would just charge into my flat. About two seconds too late, I realised I had just locked myself out with my phone inside.

'Roxy,' Jaco was pale and dishevelled, now dressed in jeans.

'*Don't* touch me,' I hissed. 'Pete,' I said without taking my eyes off of Jaco, 'I'm fine, it's fine. Go indoors please, I need to talk to this… *person.*'

'Rox,' Jaco ran both hands through his hair.

'Well I'll be right in there,' Pete narrowed his eyes at Jaco's back as he backed into his flat and shut the door.

'Roxy,' Jaco began, 'please listen… it's not what you're thinking-'

'So, you weren't fucking her?' I spat viciously. 'Because that is what I'm thinking. By the fact she was

393

on top of you naked and your dick was in her.'

'Sweetheart,' he shifted from foot to foot in high agitation. 'I know, I know, I'm sorry, but let me explain... please?'

'No!' I yelled, wiping both my eyes. 'No more, Jaco... no more! Leave me alone! I don't love you, I don't want your filthy hands anywhere near me, just go!'

We both turned as someone came up the corridor.

'What's going on?' Teddy stopped a few feet away. He looked worse than Jaco did, his fair hair was untidy and he looked like he hadn't slept at all.

'Nothing,' Jaco looked irritable.

'Jaco's just leaving,' I glared at him.

'I heard shouting,' Teddy stepped closer to me. 'Are you OK, Roxy?'

'I will be when *he* goes,' I threw Jaco the filthiest look I could manage.

'Ted, mate, can you just leave us alone a minute?' Jaco said through clenched teeth.

'Roxy?' Teddy asked in a low voice.

'Jaco, if you don't go *right now*, I will call the police,' I turned to Teddy. 'He's leaving, it's fine.'

Teddy didn't budge, instead he stared coldly at Jaco.

'You're being ridiculous,' Jaco gave me a beseeching look. 'Just let me explain, please?'

'No!' I said firmly, thinking that it would have been so much better if I could storm back in and slam the door instead of just standing there. 'Just fuck off and finish off with her,' I felt satisfaction as he flinched slightly. 'If you're not gone in five seconds, I'm calling the police.'

'OK, OK,' he held up his hands. 'I'll let you calm down,' he gave me another hurt look and walked away, his head down.

'Well you'll be waiting a long time!' I shouted after him, then as he disappeared around the corner, I burst into tears.

'Hey,' Teddy awkwardly put his arms around me.

'Sorry, I'm sorry,' I gasped.

'Can I do anything?'

'No… yes, I need my spare key, I'm locked out.'

'OK, honey,' he withdrew and went inside. I hesitated, then followed him.

'I caught him screwing Evie,' I blurted out.

'What?' he spun around, his face shocked. 'Oh, Rox.'

'Yeah,' I looked down, the night before jumping into my head. 'But, I'm OK. I think.'

'Are you sure?'

'Well… it was a shock, you know, seeing them,' I shivered. 'But I guess it was a good thing, right? Now I know.'

'I guess.'

'And… last night-' I began.

'No,' he handed me my key. 'Let's just forget about it. I shouldn't have told you. And I shouldn't have shouted.'

'OK,' I simply couldn't meet his eyes, it was too painful.

'Are you sure you're OK?'

'No but yeah,' I smiled fleetingly.

'OK. As long as you are. I'm here if you need me.'

'Thank you.'

'OK. Rehearsals tomorrow?'

I was being dismissed.

'Yeah… my turn to drive.'

'Yeah.'

Two weeks went by.

I hated myself. I hated everything that was happening to me. Everything had changed, everything felt wrong.

Teddy seemed the same on the outside, but there were awkward undercurrents – our friendship was not the same. And I was grieving. Grieving for the "old" Teddy and Roxy. It was horrible.

I made my peace with Shauna at least. Leaving Emilie with Liam, I took her out for a meal and filled her in, the evening culminating in tears and apologies. I also spoke to Howard, who was saddened by my story. My mum showed disappointment that Jaco and I were over. She remained clueless to everything that had happened, and I wanted it to remain that way.

Work brought me no joy either. I wondered if I were acting differently, but it seemed to me that Eliza had stolen the show… yeah, that sounds unfair, but where I had been the only girl and enjoyed the attention and banter, I felt like she had taken my place.

She was also in love… Tom had returned from Ireland and they had become an item. I was happy for her, but it just reminded me that I was alone and lonely. And loneliness was not something I had ever felt, not really. It was pretty awful.

Jaco never contacted me after that Sunday afternoon. I was surprised but relieved. I felt like I had no fight left inside of me, not one drop. The whole of the summer now seemed like a distant memory and I tried not to re-live it. I was no longer sad about him, but I missed being happy.

To me, life had become a rather pointless task. Not even the pending opening night done much to lift me. Everything was just... flat.

I hated feeling emotionless, I hated feeling empty... then one evening Evie paid me a visit.

I was halfway through painting my toenails when there was a knock at my door. I instantly went on red-alert – it was nearly nine o'clock on a Wednesday evening, I never had random visitors that late, apart from Teddy.

I limped to the door with cotton wool between my toes, opening it an inch. When I realised it was Evie standing there, I let out a gasp.

'Hello,' she said politely, her hands clasped in front of her and her face impassive.

'*Really*?' I said loudly.

'Sorry,' she shrugged. 'I would have rung but I couldn't get your number. Can I come in?'

'What the hell do you want?' I asked, nausea rising up.

'I would just like to talk to you,' she said evenly. 'We can do it here, I don't mind.'

'Jesus,' I stared at her, then opened the door wider. 'OK, but I don't think anything you have to say will interest me,' I walked away, my heart picking up tempo as I heard her close the door behind her.

I sat on the end of the sofa and watched her as she wandered in. She was dressed all in black - black tights under a black mini skirt, with a black high-necked jumper. Even her nails were painted black. Her dark curls were brushed back emphasising her thin face. She hesitated, her strange amber eyes wandering around the room, then she sat down on the other end of the sofa.

'Well?'

'How are you?'

'Super. What do you want?'

'You're being nicer than I would be,' she blinked at me. 'OK… I want to apologise.'

'Sure,' I had a sudden image of her pale back as she rode Jaco and I shuddered.

'I really do,' she put her head on one side. 'You know, you are way too good for *him.* I thought that when I met you. I saw him honing in.'

'Well, thank you, but I know that now,' I angrily started to pull the cotton wool out from between my toes. 'He's all yours.'

'He was having you followed, you know,' she said suddenly.

'What?' I sat up straight.

'Yeah,' she shook her head slightly. 'Billy has got a mouth like a tunnel.'

'Who was following me?'

'Billy, of course,' she frowned. 'I didn't approve. I said to them that it was wrong.'

'Christ,' I whispered. 'This is like a conspiracy.'

'Jaco was very pissed off that Billy told me… I kinda hoped you'd realise.'

'No,' I swallowed hard, feeling sick to my stomach. 'Why would I even think that? Who even does that?'

'Jaco,' she said simply.

'Shit,' I stared at her. 'Why are you telling me?'

'Because he's a shit,' she said frankly. 'I know you've been texting him... I hate that you're still hooked. He won't change... I've known Jaco a *long* time.'

'What?' I gasped. 'I haven't texted him!'

'Right.'

'I haven't,' I said, fury filling me. 'What has he said?'

'That you want him back.'

'Bastard,' I whispered. 'I don't ever want to see him again... he can die for all I care.'

'I thought that might be a possibility,' she stood up. 'I'm sorry to come here. I just wanted to make sure you're OK.'

'Why the hell do you care?' I scoffed.

'I don't mind if you hate me,' she said seriously. 'I don't care what you think of me. But I did you a wrong... I owe you.'

'Thanks... I guess.'

A million thoughts were in my head as our eyes met... had her and Jaco been at it the whole time? The image of her choker under his bed swam before my eyes and I almost opened my mouth to ask her.

I wanted to ask her about the attacks on Troy and Liam and I wanted to ask her if it were true that Jaco was a dealer... as I struggled to push the urge down, she broke eye contact and bowed her head.

'I'm going to go,' she got up and walked towards the door. 'I *am* sorry. Please take care.'

I watched her leave, rooted to my seat. She turned and smiled wanly before closing the door.

I accepted there and then that I had never known the

real Jaco at all. And it wasn't a very nice feeling.

CHAPTER THIRTY-ONE

Opening night…

In a weird way, I thought I would have been more nervous if all had been right in my life. I *was* nervous, but not as much as I normally was before a performance.

I had been focussing almost entirely on the play, practising lines alone, going through my script and getting into my role as Milly.

I had desperately wanted to go and ask Teddy for help, to get absorbed in our cosy little line reading sessions that we usually did together but knowing with a cold certainty that it was now a thing of the past.

The tickets had been sold out for opening night, which was both encouraging and scary.

A lot of local businesses had been advertising our show for a free space on our programme, which Duncan kept reminding us – we must make our performance memorable.

I arrived at the theatre alone and sat for a while in my car trying to calm my nerves. I saw that Teddy's car was already there and felt desolate. Normally we would have gone together.

The dressing room was full of activity and thick with a nervous energy. I spied my costumes hung up on the rail with 'Roxy' on the stickers, and butterflies started up in my stomach.

The classical music playing in the auditorium drifted

through the building, adding to my nerves. I began to get ready for my first scene with shaking hands, re-applying my lipstick and going through my lines in my head.

'Darling,' Violet appeared behind me in the mirror. 'Do you need any help?'

'Unless you have wine, no,' I joked.

'Violet, Roxy, Lily-Rose,' Pontus bellowed from the corridor.

I took one last look at my reflection and rose, aware that the general chatter had died down. I walked out down the corridor behind the slender figure of Lily-Rose and to the stage. I took my place to one side of the sofa and tried to still my trembling. The music became quieter and there was a hush. The curtain rose and the lights brightened. Unseeingly I stared ahead, knowing that my mum, Howard, Shauna, Liam, Dana and Tobias were in the front row. With a feeling of unreality, I adjusted my pose to Milly's… the show had begun.

My nerves had disappeared as I realised that we were putting on a top performance. Teddy was simply hilarious in his camp role as Gordon, Francesca brilliant as the disgruntled wife. I began to revel in the role of Milly, spoilt and melodramatic, feeling proud of myself as I heard a few laughs at my lines.

In the intermission, I grabbed a bottle of water and took some painkillers, then went to sit on my own in a quiet corner in the corridor on an upturned bucket. Now my nerves had faded I just needed to clear my mind and let my body relax.

'Hey,' Teddy appeared, looking dapper in his suit with his hair combed back.

'Hey.'

'I was meant to give you this before, seems pointless now,' he handed me a small envelope.

I looked up at him before opening the envelope. Inside was a card with a black cat on the front and 'Good Luck' written on its collar. Inside the card he had written '*Good luck Roxy for tonight. You'll always be my super star.*' He had signed his name in his bold writing, with three kisses underneath. Inexplicably, my eyes filled with tears.

'Doesn't seem like you needed it really,' he said. 'You are doing wonderfully.'

'Thank you,' I looked back up and tried to smile. 'I didn't get you anything.'

'Ah, buy me a burger later,' he grinned widely but his eyes were sad.

'Double cheese and bacon with onions?'

'That's the one.'

We gazed at each other; I wondered what he was thinking and if he was wondering what I was thinking.

'Teddy-' I begun, then smiled down at the card. 'Thanks. And you're doing great too. Stealing all the laughs as per.'

'Thanks,' he looked like he was going to say something else, then he touched the top of my head gently. 'Better go and touch up my make-up,' he pulled a face. 'I'm sweating under those lights.'

'Yeah, me too.'

I watched him as he ambled back towards the men's dressing room and felt a hitch in my chest as it hit me… it finally hit me…

'*Teddy what the hell have I done?*' I whispered to myself.

It was our final scene and I had gone onto automatic pilot. I wanted to cry and I wanted to just run away.

Johnny as the inspector had just confronted Finn with Miss Mabel's diary.

'-this contains Miss Mabel's most private thoughts, her most intimate daydreams,' he waved a red leather-bound diary. 'And also her conversations that she had with Mr Beckett. Including that she revealed to him that he would inherit a large portion of her estate. And if Miss Jones married, almost all of it.'

'I've been framed!' Finn declared and somebody booed in the audience.

'Dear boy,' Teddy shook his fist in the direction of the booing and there was a ripple of laughter. 'I believe you,' he said adoringly as he hugged a poker-straight Finn to more titters.

'Gordon!' Francesca stamped her foot and looked furiously around.

'Sorry,' I jumped up from my seat and clutched myself dramatically. 'This is not true! It can't be!'

'Explain yourself,' Destiny also stood up.

'Auntie, I'm so sorry,' I turned in a circle and everyone looked at me. 'It can't be true, it just can't be… because,' I looked at Finn, then my eyes flickered to Teddy, '*I'm* in love with him!'

Everybody said 'What?' and gasped and the audience rumbled with laughter.

I stared up at Finn for a fraction too long and he

frowned, imperceptibly nodding as if to say, *'your line,'* but I turned to Teddy.

'Not him,' I glanced back at Finn, then up at Teddy. *'Him!'*

'What the fuck are you doing?' Finn hissed.

Teddy looked stunned and utterly bewildered as I gazed up at him. I was aware of a ripple of confusion going around the stage.

'Darling Gordon,' I cried loudly, 'I love you!' then I flung my arms around him and kissed him hard.

'What *is* she doing?' I heard Destiny whisper, and there were murmurings from the wings.

We broke apart and Teddy stared at me, then shrugged and carried on kissing me to hesitant laughter from the auditorium.

Next, Destiny was supposed to pull me away from Finn – who I should have been kissing – clearly trying to repair the damage, she tugged at my arm.

'Bugger off,' Teddy growled, then scooping me up, he carried me off stage to rounds of applause, past curious faces and into the corridor.

'Handcuffs!' I heard Johnny say as Teddy carried me to the storage room. He put me back on my feet and held me at arm's length.

'Hello,' I said meekly.

'You're going to be in trouble,' Teddy said solemnly.

'Oops.'

'Oops indeed. So… what just happened?'

'Yeah, that,' I looked down at my feet. 'I, um, love you. And I kissed you. And I ruined the play.'

'You love me?'

'And kissed you and-'

405

'-ruined the play, yes.'

'Hm.'

'Roxy, look at me.'

I raised my eyes and saw that he was smiling his big, happy smile that I hadn't seen in all its glory for weeks.

'You love me? Really?'

'Yes, yes I do.'

'Oh, this is just swell then, because I love you too!'

I giggled then jumped as there came the sound of cheering and applause.

'Play's finished,' he said pointlessly.

'Should we go and do the bow thing?' I wondered.

'We should really,' he said.

'Do you think Duncan is going to kill me?'

'Oh, most likely.'

'Perhaps I'll stay here.'

'No, come on,' he sighed. 'We need to repair some damage.'

I edged out behind Teddy, suddenly the enormity of my crime descending on me.

Everybody was lining up on stage, ready for the curtain to come back up for our bows. Johnny spotted me first and burst into a roar of laughter.

'Well,' he said. 'Had to think on my feet there.'

'You fucking idiot,' Finn stormed.

'Oh, piss off, you meatloaf,' Teddy pulled me to the edge of the line.

Duncan was on the other end; he leaned forward, gave me a cold look and then stared straight ahead.

'Uh oh,' I whispered.

'You diva,' Violet patted my bum before wriggling

in next to me. 'I haven't laughed so much since my ex-boyfriend died.'

'Vi!' I giggled, then composed myself as the curtain came up.

The audience cheered and clapped their appreciation - if they knew that things had gone rather wrong, I didn't know. I thought they were possibly left slightly confused at least.

As the final curtain went down, everyone seemed to converge on me, with varying degrees of anger, amusement or just plain bafflement.

'I'm sorry, I'm sorry,' I kept muttering, baulking as I saw Duncan storming towards me.

'You two,' he glared at me and Teddy. 'A word, now!' he stalked off and we followed him, heads down like two naughty children.

He led us to the kitchen and shut the door behind us.

'Duncan, I am so sorry,' I said quickly. 'It's not Teddy's fault, its entirely mine. I'm sorry, I'll leave.'

'Leave?' he snapped. 'We have six more shows.'

'I'll do them, and then I'll leave,' I flinched as he almost snarled, his usually kind face furious.

'Too right you will,' he shouted. 'All our hard work, ruined!'

'Oh, stop it,' Teddy cut in. 'The audience didn't know.'

'They must have thought I was drunk when I wrote it!' Duncan was so red in the face, I started to worry he was going to pass out.

'Sorry,' I muttered again.

'Come on,' Teddy grabbed my hand. 'Sorry, Dunc, but I have rather more pressing matters.'

He pulled me out the door, 'Grab your stuff, we need to talk.'

I fought my way into the dressing room, trying to ignore the questions pouring over my head.

'It's lovely, I love it,' Violet looked almost tearful.

I hugged her, then shouted, 'See you tomorrow!' before going out the back entrance and looking around for Teddy.

'Hey,' he was waiting by his car. 'Get in.'

I climbed in and turned my body around to face him. He still had traces of eyeliner under his eyes.

'Are you sure?' he asked quietly.

'I'm sure... really sure. I've been blind and stupid – I can't believe *how* stupid. You've been, like, right here all the time,' my voice broke slightly. 'Teddy, I love you and I want to be with you so badly. I've missed you so much.'

'Wow. OK,' he leaned over and kissed me. 'This is... amazing. And a very dramatic way to do it.'

'Well, you know us actresses,' I said lightly, and he chuckled.

'So... are we a thing?'

'We can be a thing,' I tried to hug him, but I hit my elbow on the steering wheel.

'Can we go home?' he placed a hand on my cheek, his face suddenly serious.

'Are you OK?'

'Oh yeah, sure,' he nodded. 'I just really need to do some things to you.'

I screamed with laughter, 'This isn't going to be the most serious and grown-up relationship in the world, is it?'

'Probably not,' he pushed up his glasses with a forefinger and shrugged. 'It's going to be fun though, right?'

'Right,' I put a hand on his leg, and he caught his breath. 'Come on then, you. Let's go and do some things to each other.'

'Now you're talking.'

Acknowledgements

I would like to thank the following people for their kindness, their help and advice…

Angela Herbert, AC Smith and Jen Cameron. I asked some tricky questions and I'm eternally grateful for your help.

Josh Clarke, Daniella Brady and Dr Hayes.

Huge thanks to Harriet Connell, Tim Orchard, Nik Plumley, Kelly Millar, Bernie Massey, Gail Varley, Kirsty Bressington, Cher Cooke, Ian Fairgrieve, Rachel Holliday, Shauni Reed, Katie Clinton, Amy Farmer and Laura Preston. I brought your characters to life, but you sowed the seeds for me. It was a lot of fun.

And finally, thanks to my husband Paul for his support in a career that doesn't really make me easy to live with sometimes, and his technology knowhow that saves me from many tantrums. Many. I love you ♥

Printed in Great Britain
by Amazon